THE LONE WOLF

"Come on," Wulff said after a while. "You can talk now. Tell me."

Díaz lay there. It would be interesting to study the psychology of a man who had reached absolute hopelessness, Wulff thought, but he did not have the time for that now. "Names and addresses," he said, "or I'll kick you again, and this time I won't go low."

Díaz began to talk. He told Wulff what he wanted to know, with admirable specifics. Wulff listened without comment. It was highly interesting. He would not have imagined, having gone this far in, that there was this much of a new echelon left. It just went to show you that enterprise was endless.

"All right," Wulff said when the man was finished. "Thank you very much." He leveled the gun at Díaz and shot him in the head three times. Then he put the gun away and went out of the room and started immediately upon his final mission.

"The Lone Wolf series takes the reader on a guided tour of the modern Circles of Hell."

—George Kelley

THE LONE WOLF #13: THE KILLING RUN

THE LONE WOLF #14: PHILADELPHIA BLOWUP

by Barry N. Malzberg

Stark House Press • Eureka California

THE KILLING RUN / PHILADELPHIA BLOWUP

Published by Stark House Press
1315 H Street
Eureka, CA 95501, USA
griffinskye3@sbcglobal.net
www.starkhousepress.com

ISBN: 978-1-951473-97-6

Text design by Mark Shepard, shepgraphics.com
Cover design by Jeff Vorzimmer, ¡caliente!design, Austin, Texas

First Stark House Press Edition: January 2023

Some Notes on the Lone Wolf

By Barry N. Malzberg

Don Pendleton's Executioner series started as a one-shot idea at Pinnacle Books in 1969. By 1972 George Ernsberger, my editor at Berkley, called it "the phenomenon of the age." Eventually Pendleton wrote 70 of the books himself and the series continues today ghosted by other writers. Mack Bolan's continuing *War Against the Mafia* (the working title of that first book) had sold wildly from the outset and less than three years later, when Pendleton and Scott Meredith had threatened to take the series from a grim and obdurate Pinnacle, New American Library had offered $250,000 for the next four books in the series. Pendleton stayed at Pinnacle—the publisher faced a lawsuit for misappropriated royalties and essentially had to match the NAL offer to hold on—but the level established by the properties could not fail to have inflamed every mass market paperback publisher in New York.

A few imitative series had been launched by Pinnacle itself—most notably The Butcher whose premise and protagonist were a close if even more sadomasochistic version of Pendleton's Mack Bolan. It was Bolan who had gone out alone to avenge his family incinerated in a Mafia war while Bolan was fighting Commies in Southeast Asia. Dell Books launched The Inquisitor, a series of books on the redemptive odyssey of Simon Quinn (by a then-unknown William Martin Smith, who under a somewhat different name was to become famous in the next decade), Pocket Books and Avon began series the provenance of which is at the moment unrecollected and Ernsberger at Berkley, under some pressure from his publisher, Stephen Conlan, was ready to start his own series.

What he needed in January 1973 was someone who could produce 10 books within less than a year and although my credentials as a Pendleton-imitator were certainly questionable (they were in fact nonexistent), there was no question but that Ernsberger had found one of the few writers close at hand who clearly could produce at that frenetic level. In 1972 I had written nine novels, in 1971 a dozen, in 1970 fourteen; ten books that quickly were not an overwhelming assignment. What he wanted was a series about a law enforcement guy, say maybe an ex-New York City cop, thrown off the force for one or another perceived disgrace, who would declare war upon the drug trade. The cop could be a military veteran with (like Bolan) a good command of ordnance; it wouldn't hurt if he had a black sidekick either still on or just off the force so that they could get some *Defiant Ones* byplay going in those pre-Eddie Murphy days, and the violence was to be hyped up to Executioner level as the protagonist, after an initial festive in New York, took his mission throughout the States and maybe overseas. Ten novels, $27,500 total advance with (it is this which caught my total attention) 25% of it payable upon signature of the contract. Only a brief outline would be necessary and the tenth book was due to be delivered on or before 10/1/73.

I had never read a Pendleton novel in my life.

Hey, no problem; $6750 for a five-page outline at a time when I perceived my nascent career to be in a recession-induced collapse cleaved away scruple and, for that matter, terror. I read Executioner #7, which struck me as pretty bad, mechanical, and lifeless (like most debased category fiction it depended upon the automatic responses upon the reader, did not create characters and an ambiance of its own), wrote the usual promise-them-a-partridge-in-a-pear-tree outline, signed the contracts and began the series on 1/16/73. The third of the novels was delivered on 2/14/73.

Incontestably I could have delivered the entire series by May (the early plan was for Berkley to bring out the first three novels at once, then publish one a month thereafter) but George Ernsberger asked me to stop after *Boston Avenger* and wait for further word. There was a problem, it seemed. In the first place, I had given my protagonist, Wulff Conlan, a name uncomfortably close to that of the publisher whose name at the time I had not even known, and in the second place Conlan's victims, unlike Mack Bolan's, were real people with real viewpoints who seemed to undergo real pain when they were killed which was quite frequently. Would this kind of stuff—real pain as opposed to cartoon death that is to say—go in the mass market? Berkley dithered about this while I sulked, wrote a novelization (never published) of Lindsay Anderson's *O Lucky Man!* for Warner Books, and waited around to accept an award for a science fiction novel, which award caused me much difficulty, you bet, in the years to come. (See the letter column of the 2/74 *Analog* for any further information you want on this.)

Eventually, Ernsberger called—during dinnertime, in fact, on 3/16/73—to say that I could go ahead with the series and would I please change the name of the protagonist? Grumbling, fearing that I might never get back to the center of those novels, I started again and in fact did deliver the tenth book on 10/1/73 after all. (The first three were published in that month.) As is so often the case with imitative series, sales steadily declined from volume #1 which did get close to 70,000) but held above unprofitability through all of those ten, and I was allowed two sequels in 1974 and then two more in conclusion (at a cut advance). I insisted upon killing off Wulff in #14 against the argument of Ernsberger's assistant, Dale Copps, who reminded me of Professor Moriarty.

I signed off on #14: *Philadelphia Blowup* in 1/75. That means that I am now at a greater distance from these novels than many readers of this anthology are from their birthdates ... and for that reason my opinion of the series is not necessarily any more valid than would be the opinion of Erika Cornell on her essays in ballet class in the mid-seventies.

The purpose and development of these novels would, in any case, be clear to anyone, even the author. It is evident to me now as it was then that Mack Bolan was insane and Pendleton's novels were a rationalization of vigilantism; it was my intent, then, to show what the real (as opposed to the mass market) enactment of madness and vigilantism might be if death were perceived as something beyond catharsis or an escape route for the bad guys. As the series went on and on and as I became more secure with the voicing and with my apparent ability to circumvent surface and not get fired, Wulff became crazier and crazier. By #13 he was driving crosscountry and killing anyone on suspicion of drug dealing; by #14: *Philadelphia Blowup*, he was staggering from bar to bar in the City of Brotherly Love and killing everyone because they obviously had to be drug dealers. Finally gunned down for the public safety by his one-time black sidekick, Wulff died far less bloodily than many of his victims while managing a bequest of about $50,000 to his overweight creator. The novels sold overseas intermittently—Denmark stayed around through all 14; the other Scandinavian countries bailed out earlier; the gentle Germans found it all too bloody and sadistic and after editing down the first 10 novels quit on an open-ended contract, paid off and shut it down. I haven't seen anything financially from these since 1979 but entries in various mystery reference sources and the invitation to discuss the series in this anthology suggest that it might have found a particle of an audience. (My real pride in this series, beyond its ambition and sheer, perverse looniness is that I was able to run it through the entirety of its original contract and manage four sequels as well; no Executioner imitator other than those published by Pinnacle went past four or five volumes.) The vicious Rockefeller drug laws ("drug dealers get life imprisonment") were being debated and eventually rammed through the New York State legislature at the time I was writing through the midpoint of the series. It was a propinquity of event which led to some of the more profoundly angry passages in these novels and imputed a certain timelessness as well. (The laws were horseshit and we are still living with their existence and terrible consequence.) Calling a crazy a crazy, no matter how anguished may have been the aspect of the series which was the most admired but for me the work lives in the pure rage of some of the epigraphic statements, notably Kenyatta's. Writing these brought me close to some apprehension of how Malcolm, how H. Rap Brown, how the Soledad Brothers might have felt and how right they were: The Lone Wolf was my own raised fist to a purity and a past already obliterated as they were written, rolled over by the tanks and battery of Bolan's ordnance. (Operating under Bolan's pseudonym: "U.S. Government.") Bolan killed to kill: I think Wulff killed to be free. It all works out the same, of course.

THE LONE WOLF #13: THE KILLING RUN
by Barry N. Malzberg

Writing as Mike Barry

I thought it was right, Congressman. Here you have
something terribly dangerous, something that was
destroying our young people, the introduction of hard drugs
into their lifestyle . . . we needed the stiffest possible law to
get these dealers off the streets and into jail . . . .
>—Nelson A. Rockefeller, at confirmation hearings

There are no laws; there are only men. Men make the laws;
men break them. So it has to be done hard and fast and
simple. If you want them off the streets, you kill them off
the streets, that's all.
>—Burton Wulff

PROLOGUE

The slender Mexican whose name was Díaz leaned over Wulff near the pool and said, "We shall meet at eight o'clock, then."

"Fine," Wulff said. He closed his eyes against Díaz, against the dazzling sun. "It's all arranged."

"In my room."

"If you wish."

"It was agreed," Díaz said. Wulff could smell the faint odors lofting from the man's mouth, but he could not, at least for the moment, see him, which was a relief. Díaz was five-feet-seven and ninety pounds, but his face was that of a very old man with deep scars laced into it from some knife or knives, which, Wulff supposed, had not been forgotten. "Are you saying that it is no longer agreed?"

"Whatever you say," Wulff said.

"You will have your . . . cache at that time."

"Yes."

"My partners and I would be extremely distressed if your cache was not with you," Díaz said. "This represents a rather substantial investment on our part, you realize."

"I realize that," Wulff said.

"It is only in pursuit of assurances of your own earnestness that we make this request," the Mexican said. "If it were not necessary . . ."

"That's enough," Wulff said, and opened his eyes, stretched on the deck chair, and stood quickly in a single vaulting motion that carried him past Díaz and toward the pool. A few tourists spread out against the sun, breathing slowly through their mouths, looked at him without energy. "We've made the arrangements that had to be made," Wulff said. "There is nothing further to say."

"As you please," Díaz said. He made a gesture toward Wulff—a mysterious gesture which might have been placating but then again could have had an aspect of menace in it, impossible to tell, impossible to figure out the man—and adjusting his coat, left the area of the pool. He was the only one in the vicinity who had any top clothing on at all. Which might have differentiated him, Wulff thought, if anyone had been around to keep a watch on things. On the other hand, no one was looking. The tourists closed their eyes again, opened their mouths wider, passed into sleep. Wulff watched them meditatively, watched Díaz walk through the large swinging doors which led to poolside, and then impulsively jumped into the pool, swam two full laps, a hundred and twenty feet, quickly, came out on the ladder, and toweled himself off. The sun was intense, but that was not the reason that he began to sweat again even before he had completely rubbed himself dry. No, it had something to do with the arrangements that had been made with Díaz. To meet him later in his hotel room. To bring to the meeting a pound of pure junk that he had picked up from a friend. To use that pound as earnest goods to procure from Díaz at least a hundred times that much. To take it from Díaz. To kill Díaz, of course, and any other of his associates whom he might have chosen to bring along. A busy evening's work, but hardly routine, even in terms of what his life had been.

He shook his head, thinking of it. It was going to be absolutely necessary to kill the man, of course. The meeting could have no conclusion otherwise, because if he failed to kill Díaz, then surely Díaz would kill him. Still, there came a time when no matter what your capacity for murder, you had to reel back a little bit, feel a shade of repugnance—unless, of course, you were a criminal lunatic. That was one thing which Wulff was not. He was not a lunatic. He was a perfectly reasonable man who had dedicated himself months ago to the elimination of the international drug trade, in the course of which a good deal of damage had been done to people at all levels of this segmented but highly organized industry. But that did not make him crazy. It did not even mean that he looked forward to his confrontation with Díaz tonight. At every step of the way there had been regret not untinged with hopelessness—the job, after all, was so large, the outcome so murky. If you killed the present proprietors, you were only doing their ambitious successors a favor. Still, you had to go ahead. He shook his head again and went to the deck chair, picked up his clothing, and headed toward the doors on the way to his room. At all costs you had to move on. To stay in place was to go back; to go back was to die yourself. Very quickly and painfully.

A man and a woman came out of the swinging doors as Wulff walked through. The woman was tall and beautiful, a quick brunette with perceptive eyes and full breasts, but it was the man, after an instant, who caught his attention, a short, older man only up to the brunette's shoulders, leaning against her, looking upward as he said something in a low, intense voice. They kept on walking. After a moment the man looked back at him and the brunette too, but when they saw that he was standing there staring at them, their gazes dropped, and they turned, went away quickly.

Wulff stood there for another moment and then went back through the lobby and up to his room, feeling thoughtful and pressured.

I

Wulff had taken several pounds of pure heroin out of the house of the man whom he had killed, and then had come some seventy miles north to this resort hotel in the mountains far from Mexico City. The junk was in a bag that he had then filled to the top with fifty thousand dollars in crumpled hundreds, which had also been part of his victim's cache, and on top of that Wulff had put two .45 pistols which had been on his victim's body. If there was one thing that could be said about the late Montez, it was that he had not only lived well, he had arranged his life so that the good things were always on hand. For immediate exit or otherwise.

Montez ran drugs out of an estate in Mexico City, and Wulff had killed him. He had also killed Montez's henchmen and mistress, and before making his getaway in one of Montez's spare limousines, he had dynamited the house and watched it burn. So disposing of Montez had been in many ways Wulff's most satisfactory strike to date; he had killed high figures in the network in every pocket of the United States and in several foreign countries, he had run his oldest and strongest enemy, Calabrese, to ground in Miami Beach, but he had never until then faced down a man as he had faced down Montez, turned the situation around on an enemy, and killed him not only in terror but humiliation. But he had done it and killed the others and had gotten out of it cleanly with only Montez's goodies to keep him company, and then Wulff had decided, not unreasonably, that he needed a rest, deserved a real rest for the first time—being in jail in New York City not counting at all—and he had driven to this elegant resort hotel, ditched the car a few miles away, checked in with his one loaded valise, and gotten himself a suite. His appearance at the time he had checked in had not, perhaps, been outstanding, but this was the kind of hotel in which anyone's appearance and background were satisfactory if the front end was taken care of. Thanks to Montez's cache, Wulff had the front end well taken care of.

So he had checked into a suite thinking of R&R to which he was richly entitled. If anyone was. He had covered eleven cities in a little more than three months since he had decided in his night of fury to bring an end to the international drug trade. First and foremost it had been New York, then San Francisco, back east to Boston, and then out to Las Vegas; into Havana and back north again toward Chicago, hitting and killing, driving and seeking the blow, the force, the combination of kills which would once and for all end hard drugs in America; and it had been difficult, oh, it had been very difficult indeed, with first the organization and then virtually the entire law-enforcement network of the country coming down upon him. But Wulff had done it. From the cold, frightened men he had killed in their estates in the East, to the beach on which he had left a girl he might have loved, he had gotten the job done. Only at the end of it, coming back to New York for the second time, had he found his resolve ebbing, and then only for a little while. They had put him in jail in New York. But he had gotten out, too; an assassination attempt had gone wrong, Wulff had sprung the courtroom, and then, with renewed fire, he had bent his will toward the mission. He could see the enemy beginning to fall back now. So it had been Detroit and then Phoenix, and finally his strange capture and flight to Mexico City, where he had come face to face with Montez, who might have inherited it all, had talked him down, and had won. Montez was dead.

All of them were dead. His ambition was not; the fact that a lot of the top men had been eliminated did not, Wulff well knew, have anything to do with the ending of the drug traffic itself; all that it was going to do was open up vacancies. As long as the supply held up—and if there was one thing his years on the NYPD narc squad had taught him, it was that the supply would always hold up, that there was too much money in it for it to ever be shut off—there would be men to run it. But for the moment he had run out of possibilities. Calabrese dead on that plane to Chicago, Montez shot once in the head in the mansion the color of flame. He would have to start from the beginning.

It was that realization, that he would have to pick up new leads, new contacts, as much as any need for R&R itself, which had sent him to the resort hotel. The resort hotel was seventy miles due north of Mexico City, near its own airport; it was fifteen stories high to the wind and the sun; it catered to a kind of clientele who could have no possible interest in coming to a place like this unless it was either to get very far away or to do business with one another. Either way, it looked promising. He could use a few days of rest too. In any event it had looked like a reasonable place to go to start picking up the trail of the network again, and there was no doubt in his mind that there would be no end to his quest until he was dead. He could not give up now. He had gone this far, he had hurt the organization that much, he had brought the system toppling to collapse; here, at the precise moment that he was closing in, he could not give up. Even though there were probably ten thousand people of one sort or another gunning for him. Very few of them knew his face, however. Certainly no one at the hotel.

And things had gone well. Things had worked out almost as if there had been some set of controlling factors, as if, as he had always suspected anyway, his mission was being overseen by some divine forces which understood its strength and importance. He had not even had to go fishing for further contacts; indeed, it had been Díaz who had come to him, Díaz, the slender Mexican who less than a day after Wulff had checked into the hotel had approached him in the bar, offering to sell Wulff a hundred pounds of heroin.

Of course, it had not been quite that simple; nothing ever was, and Díaz was not, by a long shot, that stupid. You did not approach strange Americans and offer to traffic in drugs without having at least minimum assurances that you were not walking into a bust, or worse yet, someone who would simply take it from you with a gun. No, there had to be some investigation, some negotiation, but then again, Díaz prided himself on his ability to intuitively size up prospective contacts, and a strange American traveling alone and with little luggage in a place like this was automatically promising. It became even more promising when Díaz, after having initiated a conversation in the bar, asked Wulff what he was looking for and Wulff had told him he was looking for some shit to take north with him. He had his own cache, Wulff had said, a cache from his traditional sources of supply, but it had worked out, this time, to less than he had hoped for, and rather than leave Mexico empty-handed he was keeping his eye open for the possibility of picking up something additional. Díaz had said that that was very interesting, because it just so happened that he might have exactly what Wulff was looking for. Of course, you could not be sure of matters like this; he might have the wrong idea of what Wulff was seeking. What *did* Wulff want, anyway? Falling into conversation in the dim and elegant recesses of the bar had been easy, easier still on the drinks that Díaz kept on ordering round after round, and Wulff felt himself succumbing, after an hour's conversation with the man, to the enormous apprehension of good luck. Just when his quest had seemed to be dead-ended—by success, but that was as ruinous as failure if it put him out of business—Díaz was here to inaugurate exciting new chances. Díaz was obviously no minor figure, not if he had the amount of junk on hand which he seemed to be promising. It was then, in the bar, that Díaz had brought up the even more complicated issue of the bicentennial.

According to Díaz, Philadelphia in 1976 was going to be some kind of focal point for the biggest influx of drugs into the United States in the last fifty years, at least since the great drug wars in Chicago in the mid-twenties, before the organization had found Prohibition to be a far safer and livelier investment. Because of certain shifts and realignments in the power structure, Díaz said grimly, because of rumors that some maniac was going around deliberately killing off important heads of various sectors, there had been and was continuing an intense power struggle at the second echelon of the organization, and much of it had to do with the distribution of the massive influx that would be coming into Philadelphia. According to Díaz, the shipments in would come from various and disparate sources, but they were going to go out in a body; some central figure was going to take control of all the pipelines and turn them to his advantage. It might even be Díaz himself, although that of course was nearly a year in the future; you could not be sure. You could not these days be sure of anything even a month in the future. *Madre de Dios*, Díaz said, and ordered another round of drinks.

Why the man had found it necessary to talk so freely, and exactly what he made of Wulff was hard to figure. It did not matter anyway, not in the long run. What mattered was that Díaz had indicated willingness to put some heroin into Wulff's hands, quite a bit of heroin if Wulff were interested. He assumed that Wulff would be, that there was no other reason why an American would be in this hotel by himself at this time of the year, let alone willing to fall into conversation with a poor Mexican like himself.

They had arranged the meeting for eight that evening. Díaz had offered to sell Wulff as much as he wanted, within reason, of course. The only demand Díaz had, and which he hoped Wulff would understand, was that Wulff bring his own cache to the meeting. Just to prove, of course, that he was earnest about this, not someone who was merely trying to lead Díaz into a trap. You could not be too careful about these things, Díaz had warned; most Americans who came to this hotel north of Mexico City were in the same business that he was, but you could not get away from the possibility that there were enforcement personnel also, although this was unlikely. Still, fair was fair.

That was all right with Wulff. He found himself on the rim of an idea anyway. Ideas had never been his long suit—from the beginning it had not been an idea that had led him on, but a certainty, the certainty that if he did not take his mission seriously, no one would—but here was something. Díaz's cache was part of it, and another part was the running of drugs into Philadelphia, the bicentennial city. It was interesting that America would celebrate its official two hundredth birthday with the largest single influx of junk in history into the old capital city, but when you thought about it, it made perfect sense, was completely rational.

Someone else would be there, Wulff decided.

So he put a few samples together from Carlin's stock and prepared to meet Díaz in his room. He put a .45 into his pocket as well, although he was quite sure that if Díaz were as intelligent as he guessed the man to be, that was going to be the first thing that they would look for. Still, you did the best you could, you took reasonable preparations, and from then on in you just played it by instinct.

Wulff got ready for the meeting. It was very much on top of his mind. He didn't need the reminder by the swimming pool at all.

II

Felipe Díaz was playing it by ear too. The first thing that he was improvising was of course his name, which was not Díaz at all, but something else—something more Hispanic, a name that might well be found unpronounceable by the stupid but dangerous American with whom he was dealing. But his improvisation went far beyond his name or even the little shifts of identity with which he teased the American, drew him in; what it came down to was a profound conviction—he could not really give the source for this, he was just sure of it—that the American was someone very important, that he was not who he said he was, that he was either a powerful law-enforcement officer of some kind or a really major dealer. Either way, of course, it amounted to the same thing. What mattered was that bringing him in was going to be a coup for Díaz.

He could use a coup. His luck had been lousy for a long time; sometimes recently he had given in to the feeling that he was truly doomed. Of course, he had a small amount of power left, he had people who would free-lance for him, and he had a cache of heroin, small but nonetheless pure, which he had been moving around with him over recent months; a cache which in certain circumstances might be leveraged to his benefit, but the problem was that he was dipping into it himself; more and more; against all the principles with which he had originally entered this business, he was beginning to dabble with the stuff himself, and that was something that a dealer simply could not do. An eyedropper here, a little bit of a snort there . . . He had not, thank God, taken to the needle yet.

Still, at the rate things were going, why should he not? Somewhere in his future lay his own habit; at certain times he could grasp it, sense it, as he might intimate his own depth or the presence of a long-ago woman in his bed. Up north there was a crazy American who had gone crazy, was going around the country shooting all of the leadership and destroying the existing distribution channels; he was even killing down to the second and third levels, so that it was impossible within any brief period of time to reconstruct supply and the mechanics of the organization, and even from this distance, from the remove of what was little more than a free-lancer's position, Díaz had felt the shocks; not only was the American screwing up his business, but Operation Intercept two years ago, the government of the United States cutting off free flow through the border, had made things exquisitely difficult for him; he was still recovering from that. Of course, Operation Intercept had been largely a fraud; it had been little more than the government cutting off one source of supply so that the other could have freer channels, be better manipulated—South America's loss, in short, was Turkey's gain. It was the kind of vicissitude you had to put up with in almost any business; Díaz understood that, but Intercept had been infuriating and had marked the beginning, right there, of what had been the turnaround in his career; no longer a simple matter of garnering supply and finding a few men to work on a piece basis, but rather the whole thing—negotiations, manipulations, politicking, hard risks. Intercept had made things much more difficult for him, although it had made a number of other people whom he knew rich.

But that was behind him now. His troubles of the last two years, he knew, were behind him, if only he could bring this off properly. From the moment he had met the American, had begun to talk with him, had started to put the outlines of the deal together, he could see that there was a way out which had been offered him. This American knew drugs, and he was carrying them. Taking him over, taking his supply, was promising enough, but even more promising than that was the prospect of where it might lead him. The information that the American might be able to give him was potentially fascinating; it could lead, for all he knew, back to new, rich, completely untapped sources of supply that would give Díaz an edge for all time. Maybe this was all fantasizing; all right, he had a tendency, maybe, to imagine more of a situation than the situation might actually produce, but at least you had to start with an element of hope. "Be hopeful," he said to the short, bitter man whom he had hired to guard him in the room that night, to disarm the American, and to help him take control of the situation. "You must be hopeful."

"Whatever you say," the short, bitter man said, and helped himself to another drink from the bottle on Díaz's nightstand. Díaz looked at the man, at the tight walls of his room, and watched the tremor as the short man lifted the glass to his lips; he was not fully in control of himself. If anything, the short man was a weak bodyguard; he had energy and the proper amount of menace, but at some deep level coordination and force had been lost. Still, you had to do the best you could with what was in hand; Díaz was armed too. "I am very hopeful."

"We must do this quickly and cleanly," Díaz said.

"I expect so."

"Do you think that you can do that?"

The short man shrugged. "I will do whatever you say."

"I have reason to believe that this man has access to large amounts of drugs," Díaz said. "I do not think that this is any small operation here; I think that it can lead rather to some very important things. If you cooperate, if you do well, you can be part of them."

The short man said nothing, looked at the floor. After a long time he took another sip of his drink and put it down on the nightstand with a crash, the tumbler clattering. "I think I'd like to get some rest now," he said.

"You can rest here."

"I could go down to my room—"

"No," Díaz said. "I would feel much better about the matter if you would stay here. You can rest on the bed."

The short man looked up at him, a single, glinting stare, and then went to the bathroom, leaving the door open. He stood there urinating, only his arm and shadow protruding against the door ledge, and after a long time there was a surge of water, and the man came back, leaned against the wall, leaned there without motion, staring at Díaz. "You seem pretty nervous," he said.

"Not really."

"Who is this American, anyway?"

"A man of no significance. A man who simply has some items which I may be able to use. Which *we* might be able to use."

"What are they? Shit?"

Díaz said, "Yes, that is what they are."

"Then why didn't you say so?" the short man said. "You could have saved us both a hell of a lot of trouble if you had said that in the first place. For shit I wait," he said, and coughed, little sprinkles of moisture coming from behind his hand. "For shit I definitely wait." He gave out a single groan of laughter and went inside his pocket and took out a .38-caliber pistol, looked at it with interest. "All the time in the world," he said.

Something about this new aspect of the bodyguard made Díaz tremble, and abruptly his bowels felt weak. He stood and went to the bathroom and closed the door, sat with his pants down around his ankles for a long time, but nothing came, his bowels subsided, and he knew then what he had come into the bathroom for. He stared for some time at the closed medicine cabinet, trying to put down the urge, and finally he could not; he stood, his pants still bunched around his ankles, and shuffled toward the cabinet, opened it, carefully took out the bottle with the stopper and from another part of the cabinet a delicate eyedropper.

Slowly, slowly he unfurled the bottle.

III

At exactly eight-thirty Wulff walked into the hotel room on the eighth floor where Díaz had directed him, and as soon as he had passed the open door, found it slammed behind him abruptly, he felt the situation shift around him, then went into a lower, cooler perspective, the action slowing up, as it often did when he found himself suddenly at danger pitch. A short man, back to the door, was covering him with a pistol, looking at him out of curiously disinterested eyes; at the other side of the room, Díaz, also with a pistol, was smoking a cigarette and looking at him almost with amusement. High, thin vapors were in the room, cutting underneath the smoke; they might have been perfume, but Wulff had smelled it before; it could only be the dense odors of marijuana. Then he saw that the odors were coming from Díaz and the cigarette he was holding, and that the more common odor of smoke was coming from the short man, who was very calmly lighting an ordinary cigarette one-handed now, his pistol at Wulff's belly.

"Too much," Wulff said unnecessarily, "too much."

"Quite to the point," Díaz said. "Frisk him down."

The short man came close to him, cigarette between his lips, his hands extended for frisking, and passed them up and down the levels of Wulff's body. He paused somewhere in the area of the hip, his eyes giving a little gleam of pleasure. "Right here," he said.

"Disarm him," Díaz said.

Wulff said, "I wouldn't do that."

"You wouldn't do it?" the short man said. "Do you mean that I need permission?" The cigarette bobbed in his lips; he took it out, looked at it without interest. "You can give me permission, then."

Wulff shook his head, held his ground, and said, "I came here to make a deal, not for this."

"Then you should have no objection to being disarmed," Díaz said. "After all, coming here with a pistol is hardly an example of good faith, is it?"

"Covering me with guns when I walk in doesn't show faith either."

"Don't give me your evaluations of faith," Díaz said. "This is a faithless profession, a faithless world. One must protect oneself as one is able. I am trying to defend my interests."

Wulff looked at the man in the distance, little trick shadows of light playing in and around his face, giving him a moody and sensual aspect, which was not, certainly, what Díaz was intending. Then he looked down at the shorter man, who had curled himself now into a half-crouch, his eyes alert but questioning, something tentative in his gesture. He seemed to be awaiting further instructions. But as the two of them swung their glances back to Díaz, *he* seemed to be awaiting instructions also, almost as if there were some unseen party in the room from whom all of them were taking orders. Wulff could feel that sense of presence too, and he knew exactly what it was; it was hard to put your finger on exactly, unless you were as sensitive to the issue as he had become. The other force in the room was the drugs themselves. They played their music, whispered their message, created their own necessity. "No," Wulff said.

Díaz shrugged and said delicately, as if with enormous pain, "I am afraid, then, that we are going to have to be forcible."

"Everybody's forcible," Wulff said. "Everybody's willing to use force, everyone talks of death, but no one knows what it really is. You ought to understand what you're talking about anyway—that's the least that could be asked." And he put an elbow suddenly into the short man's face, hitting it dead center, the nose, as if eager to yield, pulping under the point of the thrust. The short man screamed once, unwillingly, and staggered away, and Wulff fell on top of him, reaching for his gun.

A shot hit above his head; he could feel the little flakes of plaster falling, but it was almost peripheral to his purposes. A missed shot meant nothing; you were either dead or you drove straight through it. The second bullet, from across the room, came even closer, driving a path only a few inches above him, but by that time Wulff was wrestling and clawing with the short man toward certainty, his fingers falling around the cold and deadly surfaces of the gun, and then he had it free, had yanked it up and high above the grasp of the man underneath him, and in the same motion he kneed the man hard in his stomach, feeling the groan of deflation, the air coming past him in a sour explosion, and he kicked the man away, rising.

Díaz was in the same position that Wulff had seen him last, crouched a little, perhaps, the gun extended, trying then to get off another shot, but Wulff knew that he was not going to make it, could see and sense the hesitation in the man even before he had started his own plunge across the room. The fact was that if Díaz was going to kill him, he would have done so already; he had had two shots in open territory, and a third as Wulff had come free with the gun, but the third had not even been taken, and that could only mean that there was at some level in Díaz the absence of the willingness to kill. Of itself that meant nothing; it made Díaz neither a better man nor worse, it was merely a character trait, or like another part of the physiognomy, but one thing it sure as hell did indicate: Díaz was in the wrong business. You had no business messing with guns or men who had guns unless you were perfectly willing to use them. He came in low in a hurtling dive under Díaz's extended gun hand, rolled against the man's knee, and toppled him. He could feel the surprisingly thick weight of Díaz tumbling down and around, and then the two of them were rolling in opposite directions. Somewhere in the distance the short man was groaning.

Wulff got a shot off in that direction reflexively, half-turning as he came out of the roll, putting the shot in the direction from which he had heard the groan, and the short man screamed. It was less than twenty feet, a reasonable shot, and hard to miss under even these circumstances, but the scream was surprising anyway, shocking in the little cramped space of the room, and he quivered, felt the need to put out the scream as quickly as possible, not to let it take its normal course, and so he put another shot into the short man, this one slightly lower, penetrating his neck and causing a small crown of blood to leap out at the flowered and open space. The short man warbled once in a deep, suffering tenor, as if he were experimenting with some difficult line of song, and then put his hands to his neck and fell to the floor, kicked once, froglike, and lay there spewing blood, the line of that blood a trail to lead back to the head. Wulff turned from him and looked at Díaz, who had stumbled to a crouch at the far corner of the room, the gun flapping in his hand, shaking there uselessly. A broken wrist, obviously. Wulff smiled at that; there was something appropriate about a broken wrist in the gun hand, if only because it made real all of the weakness that he had already sensed in Díaz, the inability to shoot already there with the wrist whole, and he went over, quite deliberately now, feeling quite at peace, quite at ease, and kicked the gun out of the man's hand. It went spinning across the room. He looked at Díaz then, the uneven damp blotches coming out on the spaces of his cheeks, the internalized glare of the eyes, and said, "That was stupid."

Díaz said nothing. He looked up at Wulff, a delicate, almost poetic kind of pain oozing through the spaces of his cheeks. The pain was exquisite; Díaz looked transcendent. Sweat came out of him more furiously, and with it, the odor that Wulff had smelled upon coming into the room intensified. "It doesn't help, does it?" Wulff said.

Díaz blinked.

"The pot," Wulff said. "Anyone could have told you that. It doesn't act as a mask for feeling at all. Anything that happens to you is just going to be felt more deeply. That goes for pain too."

He brought down his gun, still holding it around the butt, and pressed it carefully against Díaz's wrist, putting pressure on the point of the break. The man yelped once, like a dog, and then tears mingled with the sweat.

"All right," Wulff said, relaxing the pressure slightly. "All right, now. Tell me what's going on. Tell me what you had in mind."

Díaz shook his head. Wulff put the gun down a little harder, working it into the break now, kneading it. Díaz screamed and fell back, lay on the floor gasping, looking up at him. "All right," he said, "all right, then."

"I'm listening," Wulff said.

"I can't talk."

"Oh yes you can," Wulff said, and took up the gun and leveled it at Díaz with his hand on the trigger, and let the man consider that for a while. "I think you can make it. What are you doing? I want to know what you had in mind."

Groaning, retching, but getting the words out distinctly and at length, Díaz told him.

IV

Wulff's career had been interesting long before he had gotten into the business of single-handedly trying to blow the international drug trade out of the water. He had started off in the NYPD as a foot cop, and when things had broken open in Vietnam, he had enlisted in the Army, probably the only cop in New York who had done so. It was a voluntary decision; he was draft-exempt by nature of his profession, but he was interested in the war and compelled by something that when he was much younger he might have called a sense of duty; in any case, he wanted to see what the hell was going on there. He found out, spending two years in Saigon and out in the field in combat artillery, and by the time he came back it was with one overwhelming conviction: in Vietnam he had seen the future, and he wanted no part of it.

He also got his first taste of the international drug trade, although he didn't think of it as that at the time. He was concentrating upon a smaller perspective, that of Vietnam itself, and it seemed to Wulff that the so-called battle for the independence of the republic of South Vietnam was nothing of the sort; it was, in fact, merely a drug war under ideological baggage. The stakes were high, and a number of interests were fighting for their piece of the action. Who these interests were was a little bit on the clouded side, but there appeared to be at least three or four factions, of whom the American command was only one, and the least successful. In any case, the drugs coalesced in Saigon. Shit moved through the area like water through the pipelines of a major city, and it became increasingly clear to Wulff that more than anything else the war was being fought to determine who moved how much shit and in what direction. And the streets of Saigon had shown the effects of the drug war; he had seen there a vision of how America, faced by uncontrolled distribution, would itself look in ten years: the bombed-out crevices and faces of the city blending in his mind toward a kind of inseparability, so that the faces and the city were one, and all of them were being broken over and over again under the jabs and torment of the needle.

He had come out of Saigon, then, a fairly disillusioned man, and a bitter one, but he was also at that point at least realistic. If the international drug trade was one of the key factors in the world today, and if it was killing people by the millions, he at least accepted the fact that he could hardly do anything about it. It would be best to live a reasonable civilian life, maybe to try to move up in the department, become a detective, just get as far away from the streets as possible. Meet a nice girl and get a house in Maspeth. Unfortunately, the NYPD had seen fit to put Wulff on the narcotics squad.

Now, the NYPD had not done this to be malicious or even humorous; they had done it because in those days, the late sixties, when Wulff came back, narco was, next to vice, considered the softest and most enjoyable detail the department had to offer, and they gave it to him as a present, a guilt offering for the services he had rendered in Vietnam on behalf of the department. Vice would have been the ultimate plum for personnel, of course, but vice was simply too tightly controlled; no outsider could get onto that softest and most rewarding of details. But narco had been almost as good; there was plenty of graft and easy assignments, and now and then, under political or journalistic pressure, a routine sweep where the informants would be busted and sent back quietly on the streets fifteen days later or until the next exposé. Narco and the informants worked together, and things went along pretty smoothly; it was certainly a tight and commodious operation, and it did serve an important function, which was to assist and promote the flow of drugs through New York City, so everyone was happy.

Unfortunately, Wulff took it seriously—that is, he took the idea of being a narco seriously; he entered upon the squad with the idea that the job was to eliminate or at least harass the drug dealers rather than to keep them going. He could not be blamed for taking it seriously; he had the advantage of having seen in Saigon exactly what happened when the drug trade took over the essential administration of human affairs. But taking it seriously did him no good at all; it merely stoked his rage without there seeming to be any outlet. All of narco was predicated upon graft and getting along in good times and the busting of informants in bad to give the appearance of control. Of course, the informants, once the good times came again, had to be paid off for their services, which led to more graft and getting along, which meant merely that the operation was cyclical; but then, Wulff discovered that this applied to most of human affairs and should not, perhaps, be taken personally.

Still, he might have gotten along. He met a good woman and became engaged to her; they negotiated a down payment on a house and planned a wedding, and because Marie Calvante was beautiful and loved him, Wulff felt that he might be able to exist in a world in which narco seemed to be the median of human affairs. But things from that point of resolution had deteriorated so quickly that, looking back, Wulff was unable to pinpoint exactly that time at which it had all been destroyed.

Had it been when he had busted the informant for possession? Well, maybe, maybe: the man had been laughing at him, defying him, taunting Wulff with his invulnerability, just grinning and glinting at him in that bar, and Wulff could not bear it anymore; he had taken the informant right in with his cache. But that in itself hadn't been the turning point; a bust was a bust, after all. All right, then, was it when the lieutenant at the booking precinct had taken the informant away and had left Wulff in a small trap of a room almost as ugly as interrogation, and led Wulff to realize in two hours of pacing that the precinct was not on his side? Well, that too, but he should have seen it from the moment that he had brought the informant in. Okay, then, how about the lieutenant finally coming in and telling Wulff that it had been a false bust, there was no cache at all, an innocent man had been arrested without evidence, and what the fuck did those narcos think they were, anyway. Wulff could get into plenty of trouble for that kind of thing, and the lieutenant was damned well going to take it up the line.

Oh, that had been pretty bad, all right, and the informant laughing his way past him and out of the precinct. But it was not crucial, because it was hardly as if Wulff had been unaware before of corruption. Of course, precinct was closer to certain aspects of the situation than narco; of course, precinct would protect them. That hadn't been the pinpoint either, then; he had merely learned again what he had already known—that you did not lose your temper working narco.

Okay, then, how about being yanked off narco by an angry superior and sent back on beat duty, riding sidesaddle in a car driven by a rookie? Well, that had been the beginning edge of the real killing rage; it was one thing to encounter corruption—life itself was corrupt, after all, and everyone over the age of thirteen knew that—but it was another to find the knife end of that corruption turned against you, to realize that the full force of the institutions for which he worked could be brought to bear upon him for simply having taken those institutions too seriously. Still, he might have gotten by that one too. He had pretty well determined to get out of the department; only Marie urged him to hold on, at least until they got married and got the mortgage and moved into the house; after that, with all of that in his pocket he could throw everything back at them and go off for himself. But only for a few months, she urged him, only for a little while, try to hold on.

So he tried to hold on. Even the demotion might not have broken him. But what finally put him over the edge was picking up a blind homicide report on the radio of the patrol car, and his first night on duty at that, going over to a single-room-occupancy rooming house in the West Nineties, and finding out that the body the squealer was talking about, the young girl who had OD'd out, either accidentally or deliberately induced, had turned out to be his own. Marie. Marie Calvante. His fiancée. She was the one who had been lying on the fifth floor of that wretched tenement in a cold and empty room, and as he looked at her— the dull, fishlike stare of the dead, the glaze of her open eyes as her mortality had passed from her—something within Wulff had broken. It was at that time—and not a moment before—that he had made his pact against the international drug trade. He would destroy them. He would kill every single one. He would kill the men who had killed his woman, and there was nothing that they could do against him, nothing that could be held that would buy him off the quest, except a bullet, because from the moment that he had seen her, he had passed over the line. He had died, all but the functioning part of him. There was nothing more that the murderers could do.

As it turned out, it had not been the dealers who had killed his girl, after all. One by one, as he chased and killed them from New York to Vegas to Mexico and Miami, they had sworn that they had nothing to do with that murder, that they knew nothing, and it had turned out that they were telling (for perhaps the only time in their lives) the absolute truth. The murderer of Marie Calvante had turned out to be none other than his old friend, the lieutenant in the precinct where he had tried to book the informant for drug possession. The lieutenant had been tied in tight with certain interests who might find the bust embarrassing, and in his enthusiasm to please—he was very well paid—the lieutenant had not only destroyed Wulff's case and evidence, but had arranged things that he thought would break Wulff's spirit as well. It had been a very unfortunate decision, of course, and the lieutenant had died for it, but dead or alive, the lieutenant had affected not only Wulff's life but

about three hundred others through his gesture of overzealousness.
There were a great number of people dead because Wulff had come to
the decision that the drug trade and he could no longer coexist, and none
of them had to be in that condition: almost all of them could have been
alive if the lieutenant had not gone out of his way to please imagined
superiors. Wulff at this moment could have been a married man living
in a split-level with a pregnant wife and a bright future somewhere in
a department of police science. It all went to show you. Instead, he was
somewhere north of Mexico in a room with a dead man and a dying one,
drugs all over the place, zeroing in on target.

It just went to show you, all right.

He got a lot of information out of Díaz. Once the man started to talk,
he was inexhaustible; that was the way so many of them were, once they
got into pain, became vulnerable. It was as if the urge to talk, to express
themselves, to let everything be known, so long bottled within them
because of the necessity for absolute cunning and control, once released,
proved stronger than any impulse for retention. Wulff had found this
again and again: the toughest and most brutal of bosses became almost
chatty when he was facing death, when he was feeling pain; what it
meant was that at the root most human beings were the same, had the
same needs and responses; and although they could be shut off by
conscious will, these needs would sooner or later, given the chance to
balance, reassert themselves. The most controlled and dangerous
became the most vulnerable and communicative under stress, as if they
were seeking, indeed welcomed, the opportunity to give up small parts
of themselves, just as the most cowardly in normal circumstances
would, under stress, surprisingly often turn out to be among the most
courageous. It all came down to a matter of balancing action, Wulff
supposed.

In any event, Díaz had plenty to say, and he gasped it out in little
bursts until interrupted by pain or the need for another drink of water,
which Wulff would bring him from the bathroom. The short man in the
corner, having died some time before, was unavailable for duties of this
sort, but Wulff did not mind: it made him feel useful. According to Díaz,
a good quantity of drugs and potential successors to the old organizers
were planning to descend upon Philadelphia, the bicentennial city,
sometime late in the year or early in 1976, for the purpose of a general
realignment and restructuring of the network. There was some irony

in that they had chosen the bicentennial city at the anniversary of America to set up this kind of meeting, but if Díaz was aware of it, it did not come through in his little whimpers and gasps; it was simply a matter of setting an important meeting at a logical place at a logical time. And then too, there was going to be a lot flowing through Philadelphia in 1976, not only many tourists, but important federal personnel, all of whom might be expected to have an interest in the new arrangements.

It was for these purposes that Díaz had set up the meeting with Wulff, allegedly to buy some drugs, in truth to kill him and take his own cache. There was nothing personal to this, Díaz wanted Wulff to know; he had no quarrel with Wulff at all. It was just a matter of building up his own influence and position within the emerging line of the network-to-be. As crude as it might sound, the new positioning that would come out of Philadelphia would be at least partially the outcome of the size of each cache. The man who brought the largest amount of drugs into the city (although he would not be stupid enough to take them to any meetings, of course; he would cache them somewhere else for secret manipulations and viewings) had a good chance of coming out near the top of the organization, and Díaz was as anxious to be in that position as anyone. Not because he was naturally ambitious, Díaz pointed out weakly, but because lack of any ambition in his business would almost certainly result in elimination. There could be no halfway measures; if a man was sincerely committed to rising in the profession, he had to be willing to do anything to implement that rise. Otherwise he would find his career very quickly aborted. There were a lot of corpses resting in various areas of the continental shelf, and in the Atlantic and Pacific oceans, who had only wanted to be decent businessmen and make their way without hurting anyone.

Wulff heard him out. It really took only fifteen or twenty minutes, all told; a man in great pain tends to talk in a kind of shorthand, particularly if he is trying to be communicative after many years of being the reverse. But just at the point when he seemed to have reached the end of what he had to say, Díaz lurched into a new position and began to tell Wulff about his itinerary.

He was planning a trip through the United States, it turned out, beginning just as soon as the planned business in Mexico had been concluded. Meeting Wulff in the bar and going for his cache had caused a slight delay, but in any case, it could not be put off any more than by the end of the week. At that time Díaz would leave the hotel, cross the border into Texas, and begin to make his long, slow way north, with stops scheduled at Shreveport, Mobile, and Raleigh, finally ending in

Philadelphia in three or four months, depending upon what kind of connections he would make at the various cities and exactly how much complication there would be.

At every city along the way Díaz was to pick up a load of junk from a specified source.

It was a matter, the man explained, of being a negotiator, of putting together a position which would be representative of many other subsidiary interests. What he would be picking up from each of his steps would enable him, Díaz said, to go into Philadelphia in very strong bargaining position, a position, hopefully, which would be superior to anyone else's. He might well emerge from the series of conferences and arrangements there as the most important figure. You never could tell. In any event, it was certainly worth the risk.

It was only at that that Wulff balked. Up until then what Díaz had been saying seemed credible; a little bizarre, perhaps, but then, almost everything having to do with the international drug trade was bizarre, but the business about converging on Philly, all of the second-rank elements in the country trying to carve up the territory for the next two hundred years, sounded right. At the first Continental Congress they had settled up the country for two hundred years of slavery; why not set it up for two hundred years of drugs at this one? That was acceptable. What wasn't acceptable was the image of Díaz hopping from town to town in the southernmost part of the country trying to pick up a larger cache, working in earnest if subterranean negotiations. That somehow did not figure at all.

"You were going to kill these people," he said.

Díaz, weakened from pain and conversation, was still able to summon some energy as he looked up at him. "No," he said.

"You were going on a killing quest. You were going to murder your contacts in these towns so that you could show up in Philly with a lot of credit. You're a murderer, Díaz."

The man bit his lip, said nothing. He cast a haunted look toward the corner where the corpse of the short man lay. Deep in his eyes was burning a kind of reminiscent hope, as if he thought that the short man would come off the floor roaring and change the balance of power. "No way," Wulff said. "He's dead."

Díaz said nothing this time. His left hand was splayed over his smashed wrist. "Are you going to get me help?" he said quietly, almost reasonably.

"For a broken wrist? You'll make it."

"I am in great pain."

"Give me your list," Wulff said.

"What? What's that?"

"The people you were going to see. The sources that you were going to meet, Díaz. You must have it written down somewhere, or at least in your head. Tell me who they are."

Díaz said, "I can't understand you."

"Yes you can. You understand me perfectly."

"There is no list," Díaz said. "Nothing is put in writing. Do you think that I would be that foolish? Do you think that any of us are so foolish?"

"Yes," Wulff said.

"Leave me alone," Díaz said. The outburst of confession had left him white and drained, even beyond pain, as if for the first time he had become aware of what he had said. "I have told you everything; there is nothing more to say."

"The list."

"My shame is entire," Díaz said. "There is no more shame than what you have brought upon me. I appeal to you now to leave me alone."

"All right," Wulff said, and crouched next to the man. "If there's no list, suppose you tell me."

"What is this now?"

"Tell me the people you were going to see. Their names and addresses."

Díaz said, "I cannot do that."

"Oh yes you can."

"I don't care anymore," Díaz said. "Whatever you do to me must be done. I cannot give you that information."

Wulff had been through that before. It was not the first shattered form beside whom he had crouched, it was not the first man who had come through the first haze of pain to find resistance. In Díaz's business there were worse things than dying or being in pain; there were the consequences of truth. Still, you had to go ahead. You had to educate them in the differences, that was all. You had to present them with alternatives worse than confession.

Wulff took his pistol and pointed it at the man. He held it almost casually, his finger easy on the trigger, just beyond range of a desperate grab for the gun. "If you don't tell me, I'm going to kill you."

"What does it matter? What does this information have to do with you, why do you want it?"

"I'm going to have a party," Wulff said. "A whole series of parties. I'm going to invite myself over to see some people, and we're going to have some fun."

"I cannot do that," Díaz said, looking at the gun, his eyes pinned on it. "I just cannot."

"Have you ever died?"

The man said nothing. His face was shattered, yet the separate parts of it seemed to be seeking realignment. "No," he said after a time, "I have not."

"You're going to die," Wulff said. "'My death is in your hands,' you can say. You can see your own death happen to you, in full consciousness, in full control. That's something that very few men can have, you know. Most people are unconscious when they die; they've been sick for a while anyway. But you'll have it in the best of health, Díaz, and that puts you in a special category. They'll want to know all about it down in hell."

"Listen," Díaz said, "This is ridiculous. There is no reason for us to be enemies; surely we can cooperate. What you have against me is only a matter of speaking, a question of possession. You may have everything that I have; I give that to you fully. All that I ask is that you respect—"

"Drugs are death," Wulff said. "Drugs are shit that goes into the body and destroys the mind and probably the soul. You're a murderer, Díaz, you and all of the others, the cunning men who were too smart for the law and too smart for all of the procedures, the men who were going to turn the country around by giving it death for your own profit. You're as much of a murderer as if you had taken the gun in your hand and killed people by the thousands, but you never even had the guts to look at your wreckage, were never even willing to face them down and do it on your own hook, and that makes you even worse. There must be a very special place for men like you, Díaz, the men who walled themselves off, lived in the high places, lived by the sea and in the mountains with space around you, and all of the time it was shit and death which had put you there. How does that make you feel now? You're going to die. You're wrong about us being in the same business, but in a way, you see, you're right; we're both in the death business, both dealing it, and now I'm going to give you yours."

Díaz said nothing, did not move, and then in a single spasmodic gesture his hand came out for the gun. It was a well-timed grab. Wulff could admire it—the tension and the control and the way in which Díaz had shielded his intention until the last moment, all necessity masked until he had sprung—but the man was hurt and in fear; he could not coordinate to the best of his ability, and the single spasming reach went far wide, threw him off balance. Díaz fell back on the floor. Coming out of his crouch, Wulff methodically kicked him near but not exactly in the solar plexus; a blow there had to be controlled, or it was killing. He did not want to kill Díaz just yet. The man let out a low scream, and then he simply lay there, arms rolling out above his head, legs spread, in an attitude of submission and despair. Eyes closed, he seemed to be waiting for the perfect blow that would lead him toward ascension.

Wulff looked down at him and said, "All right. Names, dates. Addresses."

Díaz said nothing, breathing in shallow little gasps. Tremors moved up and down the length of his body. Blood from the short man, still moving in thick ribbons, trickled near Wulff's feet. Distractedly he rubbed a little of it into the polished linoleum surface of the floor. Almost instantly the linoleum began to fade. Cheap. Cheap goods. There was absolutely no quality control at any level anymore.

"Come on," Wulff said after a while. "You can talk now. Tell me."

Díaz lay there. It would be interesting to study the psychology of a man who had reached absolute hopelessness, Wulff thought, who had moved from control to its utter loss within a period of half an hour, but he did not have the time for that now. Besides, he had seen all of that before. "Names and addresses," he said, "or I'll kick you again, and this time I won't go low."

Squinting, thrashing, rolling on the floor, Díaz began to talk. He told Wulff what he wanted to know, with admirable specifics, and he did not stop at any private confidences about the personalities involved. Wulff listened without comment. It was highly interesting. He would not have imagined, having gone this far in, that there was this much of a new echelon left. It just went to show you that enterprise was endless.

"All right," Wulff said when the man was finished. "Thank you very much." He leveled the gun at Díaz and shot him in the head three times, very fast, making the blood jump, the skull slam against the wall. Then he put the gun away and went out of the room and started immediately upon his final mission.

VI

David Williams, the twenty-five-year-old black patrolman who had been the rookie in the squad car the night that Wulff had discovered Marie Calvante, who had first shared, then joined Wulff's mission against the organization, who had been almost knifed to death near a methadone center on Lenox Avenue, had almost been killed by Wulff in Los Angeles before an attack had caused them to rejoin forces against the bigger enemy; David Williams, who had given it all up at the age of twenty-four to come back to his pregnant wife and small house in St. Albans, feeling like a burned-out case, who now wanted only a little bit of the peace that life had denied him; Williams, who had been part of the squad of special cops who had been put together to trap Wulff in New York, and then, after apprehension, had watched him escape from the courtroom; David Williams, who had had at least fifteen years of very complicated experience jammed into something less than seven months, sat across a desk in the office of the assistant commissioner and said for the third time that week to the third person, the third level of hierarchy, that he had no idea where Wulff was.

"We're not saying that you're in contact with him anymore," the assistant commissioner said. "We believe that there's a complete break there. Still, we had hoped you might have some ideas. Maybe you had gotten a call or a letter from him."

"This man doesn't write letters," Williams said, "and he would call only if he wanted something. He doesn't want anything more from me. I mean, he may want a lot more from me, but he knows that that's finished. He's an honorable man. He knows that if he called on me I'd probably want to help him but I'd have to break the law to do it, and I'm not going to do that." He almost said "do that again," caught himself. The commissioner's office was pretty sure, but without a grain of hard proof, that it had been Williams who had been working side by side with Wulff during the Los Angeles shootout; that during the month when Williams had mysteriously jumped the department, his home, and the East Coast, he had been participating on the hard end of Wulff's mission, but they had never been able to make the tie; the only people who could tie Williams directly to Wulff were dead, and Williams wanted to keep it that way. He would just as soon stay with the NYPD now. He had functioned at all levels of the system in his life, first hating it, then surrendering to it, then becoming joyfully part, then turning on it with Wulff in an attempt to bring it down by outreaching, but now, at the end of it, with a deep knife scar in his belly and a world's worth of pain in memory, he wanted nothing but to stay out, stay under, stay away for the rest of his life. That included giving Wulff any kind of help, or for that matter, participating in bringing him down. He did not care anymore. It was something that a lot of men took forty years or more to learn, but Williams had accepted it at the deepest level at barely a quarter of a century: nothing mattered but to survive. You hung on, you got as much life as you could, death would take you soon enough, and it would be permanent; in the meantime, you did what you could to stave death off. Hero or martyr, poltroon or tyrant, death was all the same to you. It did not matter. So you held on. "I'm sorry," Williams said after a long pause, all of this going through him while the commissioner sat tolerantly but impatiently on the other side of the desk, tapping with his knuckles and rubbing a small area to a high shine. "If I could help you, I would, but there's no contact."

"This man is dangerous. He's damned dangerous. We shouldn't have let him get away," the commissioner said. "Goddamnit, that was a royal fuckup! How we could have let this man get out of a crowded courtroom is beyond me. It was the stupidest goddamned thing I've seen in twenty-six years of police work." He looked sullenly at the polished spot and worked then to obliterate it. "Of course, I didn't see it," he said. "I wasn't there."

"May I be excused, commissioner?" Williams said.

The commissioner stared at him. "I don't think you understand why you were called in here. You were deeply involved with this man."

"I know that. But I'm not anymore."

"Your involvement with him was greater than that of any other person in his life."

"I doubt that very much, commissioner," Williams said levelly.

"I'm not talking about his personal life. I mean when he started to get involved in this business. For Christ's sake!" the man said, and pushed back his chair and stood. "This man is a murderer. He's killed over five hundred people, and he's still at large. There are indications that he's been in Detroit and somehow got down to Phoenix or somewhere near there in the Southwest. I don't know what the hell he's done in Phoenix yet; we won't get the reports on that for a while, but he seems to have bombed out an assembly plant in Detroit because it might have contained drugs. Where does it end, goddamnit?"

"I don't know, commissioner."

"This has got to come to a finish. This man is our responsibility, don't you see that? In a certain sense, all of this can be said to be on our heads. We had him on our payroll, we wind up with him in custody, and then we lose him, he disappears somewhere into the Midwest, and the next thing we hear, he's blowing up factories . . . . What does the man want?"

"I think he wants to blow up the drug trade, commissioner."

"Well, that's just fine," the commissioner said, "but he wants to blow up the world with it."

"Maybe if he had been allowed to do his job within the system, he wouldn't have come to this point. Maybe it's your fault for that too. Maybe it was the system that killed him and sent him outside of it."

The commissioner turned, his face old and parched in the gray half-light that was cast through the stones from the courtyard. "Whose side are you on, patrolman?" he said.

"Are you saying I'm on his? I'm not on his. I'm on mine. But you've got to see it his way, too. He lost his girl, commissioner. He lost someone he loved. She was murdered. One of our men murdered her."

"I'm not sure about that. I've heard it around, but there's no proof, absolutely no proof at all, and we'll never get any now. Even if that's true, one rotten cop—"

"It isn't a matter of a rotten cop. The system is rotten, and it makes almost everybody turn out that way."

"All right, Williams," the assistant commissioner said after a pause, "this isn't getting us anywhere."

"But it couldn't. It couldn't get us anywhere, because you don't even know what you want. You just want to find someone to blame for your own predicament, for what you call your own fuckup. This whole thing is stuck on the NYPD, and you know it. I don't mean his escape, I mean what started Wulff off in the first place. It was built right into the system," Williams said, "and he was forced to it step by step until he went over the edge and there was no one to haul him back. I'm not going to take it, commissioner. I don't have to take it. It isn't me who sent him out there, it's you and what you represent, and you know it. You're going to have to look for your own goddamned causes," Williams said, and he stood then. He had not known until that moment about the extent of his rage, but there it was, building and stoking within him, forming little drops of perspiration that he could feel moving like animals up and down the ridges of his back. "And you're going to have to live with this in whatever place you live, because goddamnit, if there isn't an honest cop in this whole damned department, the couple of hundred that you might have left, who aren't cheering him on, who don't want to see him go on and on until he blows up everything and proves what every one of these cops knows in his heart anyway. That one man operating single-handedly can do a job that a thousand honest men within the system can't. The system isn't for them, it's for the criminal, it's for the shit-purveyors," Williams said, and turned and walked out of the office, leaving the commissioner standing there, the little astonished bulb of his face blinking and receding in his memory. Jesus, Williams thought as he went down the grimy receding corridor, little shaking waves of rage seeming to carry him, disconnected, from the floor, Jesus Christ, that wasn't bright at all, was it, was it really, now? I had no business doing that. I'm in enough goddamned trouble in this PD anyway, and now I'm called on the carpet by the assistant commissioner and wind up attacking *him*.

That wasn't bright at all. I'm not going to get anywhere with that kind of shit, I'm going to blow myself right out of the nice little house and the nice little career and salary plan at exactly the time that I've decided that this is the only way that I can stay sane. And yet, as clerks and cops and citizens drifted by him, as he went quickly through the ripped and dirtied halls of the municipal building toward the outside, Williams could not keep from himself the knowledge that he was smiling, nor conceal the realization that there was a bounce and drive in his step that had not been there for a very long time.

Since he had come into Los Angeles, as a matter of fact.

VII

Cohen lived by a freeway on the outskirts of Shreveport in a large, high house and thought about drugs all the time. He was not in the business in a big way, but soon all of that would change. For the time being he worked as the sales manager of the largest Chevrolet dealership in the New South—or at least that was the way it was billed in the *Times-Picayune* when the owners got fancy and went into a full regional campaign—and he spent almost all of the time not actually involved in work in planning how, with the top echelons staggering or dead, he would move into a position of power within the business within the next couple of months.

Cohen did not have everything that he needed yet, but he was getting there. He had contacts and sources and a small amount of credit, which he was building slowly month by month into the possibility of a really large pipeline. More significantly, he had made contact in recent months with a strange Mexican named Díaz, who represented himself as having access to a mother lode of the purest stripe, for which he needed a few chosen American distributors. Cohen had a good reputation on the inside; Díaz had heard that he came highly recommended, and it was agreed that Díaz would be coming into Shreveport within the next weeks to work out the details of an agreement, which, although it was still nebulous, struck Cohen as being among the most promising he had ever heard of. It might make him, along with a few others, one of the truly important figures in the business as it began to shake down into new form. It might even put him at the absolute top, all depending. In any event, Cohen could wait. A long time ago, when he had first gotten into the business on the very fringes, he had been a restless and impatient young man, but he had long since learned the virtues of taking the long view. If there was any way to survive in the business, it was in not being greedy. Cohen was prepared to wait.

His patience had well-served him already. The mass murderer who went under the guise of the Lone Wolf had swept through the country a few months before, toppling figures at the highest level of the network, and Cohen had had a long and impressive lesson in the power of being obscure. If he had pushed hard, if he had willed himself into a precipitate rise in the organization, he might have been at a high level of notoriety; might even have been a Calabrese, who he understood was the shadow figure behind the manipulations in the Southern district. But he had not; he had settled for pushing and arranging strictly as a sideline, and so it had been Calabrese who had died in the Miami massacre, and not William Cohen. It was not worth being a Calabrese if you were going to come to an end like that: that was the thing that had occurred to Cohen as soon as he had heard the news. No one needed power and wealth if you were going to end on a beach with bullets in your head, water lapping into your ears. Comfort; comfort and survival were enough. Also, Cohen had a habit that was more important to him than power; he sometimes thought that the reason he had drifted into distribution to begin with was that it was the easiest, least humiliating way of keeping himself supplied.

The habit was at about a hundred dollars retail a day, which was a hell of a habit, Cohen realized, except that he wasn't paying retail, he was going wholesale or a little bit under that, and it had no effect on him other than to make him feel good. He sure as hell wasn't addicted, not if being off the drugs had no physical effect upon him. He could quit anytime he wanted. It was just that he felt so much *better* when he was on the stuff, that was all. His normal, pleasant personality reasserted itself; he was the same optimistic, hopeful man that he had been at twenty-three when he had started off in the agency as a salesman fresh from college, rather than the rather nervous, unhappy thirty-four-year-old he had been fifteen years ago when he had had his first contact with smack at a party. It was true that his old drive was there only in flashes and that it was harder and harder to take the dealership seriously, but that was as much a consequence of getting older as of supporting a mild heroin habit. Besides that, without heroin, getting older would have made him even more bitter.

He lived in a house by a freeway in which there had once been a wife and children, but, thank God, they had not been there for several years: the divorce had been amicable and without scandal, but they were gone, and good riddance to them. In San Francisco, now living with her parents. They could stay there for the rest of his life; he didn't even care if he never saw the kids again. No custody battles for Cohen. Now he had a mistress, or at least a semimistress, who worked as a hairdresser and came to see him two or three nights a week and stayed until the morning with him and otherwise stayed out of his life. Every time she left the house he would give her seventy-five or a hundred dollars for a gift. What the hell? That didn't make her a whore; it was just a gift freely offered, not for services rendered, a means of showing his affection for her, and June's taking the gift didn't make her a whore in her eyes either; they had long since established that she was not at all embarrassed by the money. In fact, the idea of giving her money after every visit had been hers in the first place, not his; she said that she knew it would be easier for both of them if he gave her a gift every time he wanted to rather than feel an overwhelming sense of obligation to buy her something really incredibly expensive for birthdays or Christmas. And he was just the sort of generous man who would want to give her a gift every time that she was there; both of them knew that. So it had been a very satisfactory arrangement. Everyone down at the dealership knew June; he took her often enough to the parties and conventions and end-of-the-year special deals for the top salesmen, and no one thought any less of him or her because they were together. It had been a completely friendly divorce, and since it everything had been peaceful and happy. And June knew nothing about his habit at all, or at least she had never mentioned it; she would have to know something, maybe, going to the bathroom at night, when he would leave all the paraphernalia around, but she never said a word, and sure as hell Cohen didn't bring it up. If she had, he would have told her everything she wanted to know, except for the fact that he was dealing in it, of course. If she got into the area of dealing, she would have to go.

On this Thursday night in late November Cohen had just injected one cc of dynamite shit, feeling the kind rush move in little blotches into all of the crevices of his body, feeling the old gratitude and warmth for what had been given him, when he heard the doorbell ring. That in itself was not surprising; the doorbell rang quite often, and June herself would have to ring to get in, since he had never given her a key to his place. Cohen felt that he had a right to protect his privacy; give her a key and soon she would move into other areas of his life. But the way the bell sounded was unusual. It hit in two sharp bursts, and then, with only a little break, whoever was there pressed it in and left it—one burning, continuous peal, which resounded through the house. Cohen was in the bathroom, bent over the sink, taking the full rush of the jolt, and was able to come away from it only in little stages, limping and hobbling toward the door. Whoever was at the door certainly had no manners, he thought vaguely, but then again, manners had nothing to do with the situation; all that mattered was helping yourself along, getting a little edge. The same kind of edge that the drugs gave him was probably provided by the doorbell for the visitor. What the fuck? Cohen staggered merrily through the living room and down the small hall that led toward the door, thinking about all the peculiar ways that people managed to get out of life what they needed and ignored the rest. Like

June and her gifts, like himself and the dealership, with only enough drug action on the fringes to keep a hand in, to mostly guarantee his own supply. That was the primary reason he had gotten into it, come to think of it. He always had his best thoughts in the first damp, clinging rush of the shit; it seemed at these moments as if he had utter insight into every aspect of his life. Of course, the wonderful thoughts and insights would go away, sure as shit, and he would be back where he had been before, but he could always take another jolt, always climb up the mountain again. Climb every mountain, Cohen thought, ford every stream. He lurched to the door and opened it.

A man with a gun was standing in the open space in front of him.

Cohen stood there and looked at the man. He could not believe it. He simply could not believe it. On the other hand, the drugs were a little disorienting, and he was, perhaps, imagining all of this. In Shreveport, Louisiana, no one was coming to his door at night with a gun. This kind of thing would happen in Baton Rouge, and of course it was very common anywhere north of here, but Shreveport was a peaceful town. Cohen had lived a controlled existence. He backed away from the door, moving slowly, on legs that felt insubstantial, away from the door.

The man with the gun came in.

He moved in short, determined strides, the gun leveled at Cohen, and now, in the improvement of light as he came into his house, Cohen could see that he had not imagined it at all, that this first flash had, in fact, been perfectly true, and that this was no joke, this was something real that he was living through. A stranger had come into his house with a gun, and now, even through the dark haze of the drugs, Cohen felt a lurch of inadequacy that moved toward terror. He had his own gun, of course, would be a fool not to have it, but it was buried under a pile of underwear in the second drawer of his bureau and had not, as a matter of fact, been checked for more than a year. He could not remember the last time he had looked at it. For all he knew, it wasn't even loaded, would malfunction. Helpless, he thought, backing through the hall and into the living room, absolutely helpless, and it wasn't fair; he was coming down now, he had taken a good rush of fine smack, and there was no reason why it had to be wasted, absolutely wasted because of an intruder. This turned his fear at least momentarily toward anger, which was strengthening. "What do you want?" he said. "I'm going to call the police."

The man pointed the gun at Cohen and fired. The bullet went by his right ear, no more than by a few inches, impacted into a wall behind, and Cohen felt his legs go on him, felt himself, as if in a dream, pitch toward the floor, hit it face-first, collapse, and run into the floor like water, his body breaking, spreading out. The man was crouched over him, his hand enormous, grasping him by the collar. "You son-of-a-bitch," the man said, "did you think I was playing games?"

Cohen, looking up into the face, tried to say something, but could not. His throat gathered on him. He hawked, choked deep back in his throat, and began to gag. The man twisted his collar more tightly. "You're on shit," the man said with disgust. "You son-of-a-bitch, you've just taken a dose." Cohen felt the man's hand move across his face; there was a clatter deep in the back of his skull. He fell into the floor, gasping. I'm going to die, he thought, I'm going to die, and I'm not even fifty years old. It had never occurred to him that he could lose his life. He had avoided a violent existence for precisely that reason; other men might get killed messing on the fringes of the drug trade, but not him. *Not him*. It was just not that important to him. He felt the hand around his collar again, and the man had yanked him upright. "You stupid son-of-a-bitch," the man said, "you're going to talk whether you like it or not. You're not going to get out of this so cheaply. You're going to *talk*." And he hit him again. Cohen felt channels open and then close in his mind, and he pitched forward against the enormous bulk of the intruder, moving through a long, dark passage, a clinging, wet cunt of oblivion.

VIII

Wulff had had a lively time crossing the border. Up until that time it had been a piece of cake, a stolen car from the Díaz estate winging him free and clear, not a trace of harassment, and driving the long miles toward El Paso, he had coaxed himself into the illusion that the true danger was over. He had been out of the country for weeks; it had really been months, except for Detroit, since he had conducted a large-scale campaign, and it was sensible to believe that, filled with their own problems, the organization and law enforcement alike had forgotten about him, gone on to other matters. There were, after all, so many other problems with which they had to deal; even a Wulff could be only a temporary diversion from their basic mission, which was to promote the distribution and sale of junk. But as he had come up to the border at El Paso it had been with the sudden and astonishing feeling that the wedge of containment was dropping on top of him. There had been a long, long line of cars backed up at the checkpoint, nearly a two-hour wait until he had squeezed the Díaz Oldsmobile up to the guards, and the first thing that they had asked was for him to get out of the car so that they could do a thorough check. That had given Wulff a little thrill of tension, all right. He was not worried about junk being found in the car, there was none, but what he had was the Díaz cache on his person, rammed up and down his legs and thighs, strapped in tightly against his body in tight leather bands, almost ten pounds of good if not entirely pure heroin, and the danger of personal search had to be considered. There was also the possibility that they would have his picture and description at the border; NYPD at any rate must have been laying for him some time now, and one thing balanced against another, it had been with a distinctly uncomfortable feeling that Wulff had gotten out of the car and moved into the small pen area where tourists were held while their cars were checked. His options if they actually decided to search or stop him were quite narrow. He could either submit, in which case he would almost certainly be in a federal prison within an hour, or he could resist, which would probably render him dead, or at least completely outside the law. All in all, there seemed nothing to do except to wait it out and hope for the best.

As it turned out, he had had reasonable luck. The Oldsmobile was clear, and personal search was not in the agents' mind, at least at that time. They had taken a cursory ID check, which was easy, because Wulff in the past ten months had picked up enough false ID's to float an entire platoon of enemy infiltrators, and they had done a superficial check of his pockets as he had gotten back into the car, but had not gone beyond that. Obviously they were very nervous but feeling their way. It had only been on the way over the border, then well past it, that it had occurred to Wulff that he might not have been in as much trouble as he had feared while in temporary detention; for all he knew, enforcement might have been very sympathetic. He was, after all, a one-man Operation Intercept. Still, it was a nervous procedure, and the Díaz kill had left a series of ugly sensations; there was nothing wrong with killing, it was absolutely necessary, it had to be done, and he had long since accepted the necessity, but this kill had been one of the most painful so far; his tolerance level was ebbing, that was for sure. One thing that he did not think he quite had the stomach to do, at least at the time that he had crossed the border, was to come into confrontation again. There was no saying what he would have done if the border guards had come to him after a little while, solemn expressions on their sad, bleak faces, and had said, "Excuse me, Señor, we must detain you to ask further questions." Would he have gone for the gun in his right pocket, attempted a shooting-and-escape, or rather would he have gone quietly, wearily even, submitting to the pressure of their hands and voices with a sense that underneath all of the struggle, the thing that he had really wanted from the start, what had driven him, was the urge to submit? Had it been weakness, exhaustion, the desire for that submission that had really been the key from the beginning?

Well, there was no way of knowing that; it was not a question, thankfully, with which he would have to deal. At least, not at the Mexican border. The guards had done nothing of the sort; they had checked him through, the drugs had jogged unpleasantly but with authority against his thigh as they had nodded at him and sent him on his way. Operation Intercept be damned; it was all bullshit, everyone knew that. Even when it had been supposed to be in full swing, it had never been more than hit-or-miss. Wulff knew that. In any case, he was out of Mexico now, and he put the Oldsmobile into the long task of the miles, hundreds adding up on the odometer in a dreaming, half-connected state, stopping only for gas, only once pulling over to sleep, and there in a wretched motel in which he had been able to spend only three hours, the sound of dogs shrieking into the darkness knifing into his sleep and sending him on his way. There would not be any more sleep for a long time now. Whatever he had needed he had caught up on in the hotel, but that was behind him, and with it another period of his life.

He headed toward Shreveport. Shreveport would be his first stop. Díaz in his last gasping monologue had laid it all out to him: the names, the places. Cohen in Shreveport, Nolk in Mobile, and Sperber in Raleigh. Three dealers, three exchanges in the South before the long flat drive into Philadelphia. It had been Díaz's plan—he had, dying, confessed it all—to meet with them one by one on the pretext of putting together their forces and pooling the supplies they had on hand and to kill them, moving on toward the bicentennial city then, with not only the supplies of these three but with a reputation that would stand him in good stead when it came to showdown. It was a risky business, Díaz admitted, but the stakes made the risk worth it, and the four he had set up appointments with were for various reasons at an acceptable level of challenge; they were among the weakest of those who had enough standing in the network to matter at all. Cohen was first, not only geographically but because of all of them, Díaz had said, Cohen was the weakest; he was less of a dealer than a junkie, in fact, the only reason he had gotten into dealing at all was probably to grant himself an assured supply.

So Wulff had picked up the trail. Coming into Shreveport had been like coming into any of the hundred American cities that he had seen or passed in the months of his odyssey; once again he had been overwhelmed by the flattening of America, the gathering of all its cities into one, so that not only difference but any sense of partition had been obliterated. Now it was truly one country, all of it united by highways, loops, cloverleafs, abandoned downtown districts, hamburger stands, and the flat, blank surfaces of the screens of drive-ins coming up hard against the broken horizon; through that corpse where all cells had become one flowed the deadly silvery milk of heroin, which had first killed and was now embalming the corpse in clear frozen strips of hard poison, which yet glinted like something beautiful in the darkness. The vision of what drugs had done to his country was beautiful to Wulff only in the way that total disaster, utter corruption could be, but he did not think of this as slowly he pulled the folds of the tent which was Shreveport aside, looking for the place in which Cohen lived. When he found the man, he was going to kill him.

No question about that. He was, in fact, going to kill them all; he had passed now over any line which separated intention from execution. The Carlin kill in Mexico City had been the start of it, absolute ruthlessness, but the Díaz kill had launched him all the way: now and for the first time Wulff found that he was taking an almost physical pleasure, great chunks of open sensation, from the act of murder. In the beginning it had been revenge; later on, past the first clean, mass kills and long-distance snipings, it had been business, but now it had launched itself into a third stage, and he could see that killing could become an end in itself. It was something that it was possible to enjoy on its own terms, like alcohol or sex, needing no rationalization past the necessity and the feeling it evoked upon discharge.

Of course, he was killing scum; that made it much easier for him and meant that he did not have to deal with the more complicated issues of exactly what it meant to be a man who enjoyed killing. As long as it served the right function, that was sufficient. Still, he had a lot of time on the way to Shreveport to think this over, to decide what he was becoming and whether he liked it, and what it came down to, he guessed, was that if you appointed yourself on a mission of revenge against the worst elements imaginable in the realization that anything you did to them was deserved . . . well, if you became that, then a little bit of them would have to rub off on you, too. You could fight them only by using their methods, in other words, but so much of these men *was* the method that they had adopted. There were risks. You had to face that. There was the possibility that you could become something like them. But essentially Wulff wanted to believe that there was a difference, that there was a whole level which separated him and them. If that level were ever obliterated, it would be time to get out.

But in the meantime he could enjoy the killing. Hell, it was one of the few bonuses that his job afforded. He might as well take pleasure out of it; it wouldn't make much difference either way, and it would keep him functioning.

In Shreveport, by the freeway, in the lair to which he had tracked the man named Cohen, Wulff came in fast, backing the man up the long mouth of the hallway, then found himself in the bright, aseptic spaces of the living room, Cohen backing into a wall, his eyes the largest part of his face, glaring, glaring. He was a short man in his late forties, a little overweight, maybe a hundred and seventy pounds spread over five and a half feet, his breath coming out in uneven little gasps, his hands shaking as he held them in front of his face. Obviously he had just taken a dose; the rush had stained his cheekbones as if a faucet had sprayed blood against dark glass. He backed against the wall until he could go no further, holding his hands poised, tried to say something, failed, tried again. His voice came out in a thin, wailing scream. How could a man like this even be on Díaz's list as a possible rival? Wulff wondered. But then again, he had gotten to know Díaz pretty well before he had killed him; this was exactly the kind of customer that the man would pick up. Weakness. Díaz loved it; fastened upon it. And in the new cast of the network, with the top echelons gone, scum like this of course would now represent the top. Discouraging, Wulff thought, and gun extended, came on the man.

"Don't," Cohen said, "don't kill me." Drool came down his chin in uneven little spatters. "I didn't do anything. I tell you, I didn't do anything to you."

Wulff put a shot into the wall above Cohen's head. The idea had been to shake him up, to convince him with that one shot that he was in serious trouble and he had better talk, but Wulff had not intended the shot to come as close as it did; it just barely missed the man, and Cohen's face broke into something past fear, absolutely past sensation of any kind, and onto it came a loose, hanging kind of smile. He must have thought he was dead. "Shit," Cohen said, "shit."

"Where's the stuff?"

"Where's what stuff?" Cohen said. He turned the smile full on Wulff, a full, curious, beaming smile with much attention on it but little comprehension. His eyes were crazed. "Man, I don't know what you're talking about," Cohen said. "You shot and killed me, remember? I'm dead now. But you can't follow me into the afterlife. That isn't fucking fair at all."

"Listen, Cohen . . ."

"No," Cohen said with a slow, awful reasonableness. "Fair is fair. You come into my house, you back me up, you scare the shit out of me, and then you start shooting, and finally you kill me, and that's the end of it, you understand? I'm out of it now."

"I want—"

"You can't do a fucking thing to me," Cohen said. "You've killed me, and I've died, and I'm not here anymore. You absolutely cannot push a man past a certain point." He came down against the wall in a slow, clinging drop, his feet extended, back sliding down with a squeaking noise, and fell onto the floor with an astonished expression as his rear collided. "I'm not dead," he said. "Shit, I'm not dead."

"Where's the stuff?"

"If I were dead, I wouldn't *be* here still," Cohen said meditatively. "If there's some kind of an afterlife, it stands to reason that it wouldn't be exactly like what we've got here. Doesn't that sound reasonable? Because there would be no point to it at all, unless it was different." He nodded, flicked a little sweat away from the edge of his nose. "So the afterlife would be different, and if there was no such thing as an afterlife, well, then, I would be in oblivion, wouldn't I? Instead of being right here. So you didn't kill me. That was just a wrong guess, a poor matter of opinion." He looked up at Wulff with an assumed expression of benignity then. "All right," he said, "what do you want of me?"

"I'm doing Díaz's business."

"That would figure. That sure as hell would fall into place. Someone ought to do the son-of-a-bitch's business. He sure as hell couldn't have done it himself."

"Where's your cache?"

Cohen looked up at him. "I don't know what you're talking about."

"You've got some drugs here. A hell of a lot, at least, according to Díaz, but I'll take what I can. Where are they?"

Cohen said, "You've got this all wrong."

"I don't have anything wrong."

"I don't have any fucking cache. I have a little private supply, that's all. When I need some more, I know where I can score. But I don't have anything in the house. In this town? No way." His eyes seemed suddenly laughing and relieved. "Hell, is *that* what you came here for? Is that what Díaz expected? The bastard was even stupider than I thought."

"I want the stuff."

"I hope you killed him," Cohen said seriously. "I really hope that you did that; a guy so stupid doesn't deserve to live. Really? He really thought I had smack in the house? That's the goddamnedest thing you ever heard. Hey, you mind if I stand up now? It's pretty tough to be in a position like this, and as you can see, we've got no quarrel at all. Nothing's wrong here, mister, you're looking for something that doesn't exist." Cohen rolled over easily on his palms and knees, arched his back, came to a standing position, slapping dust from a pants leg. "It's just too goddamned much," he said. "It's the stupidest thing I ever heard of in my life, but at least it's all settled now, you see, there's nothing here for you at all, so maybe you'll just get the hell out of my house."

Wulff sighed and hefted the gun, turned the business end around, put it deep in his palm, checked to make sure that it was on safety, and in one motion whipped it out in front of him, struck Cohen hard. The blow hit the man's left cheekbone, and Wulff could hear the crack and splinter of bone even before Cohen's shriek, but the shriek, high and piercing, had even more terror in it than the sound the man had made when the bullet had hit the wall. It was a satisfying sound, but Wulff was not interested in satisfaction right now; his rage had shifted to its older, more comfortable level. He kicked out, caught Cohen's ankles behind his feet, and the man landed in a tumbling screaming heap at his feet, spread out all over the rug, holding onto the left side of his face and whimpering. Wulff stood over him, legs spread slightly, and showed the man the gun.

"Stop it," he said. "Stop crying."

Cohen looked up at him. His face was small and helpless. "It wasn't much," he said. "It was only a little."

"But it was something."

"Yes, it was. Yes, it was something."

"It's more than you would have admitted to unless I had broken your cheek. You could have told me that," Wulff said almost gently. "You would have saved us both a lot of trouble."

"I'm entitled," Cohen said. "I worked hard. It wasn't very much. It was the only fucking thing I had. You think anything else meant anything to me? It was all bullshit. But I worked, I worked hard to build up a little edge. You can't take everything from me."

"Where is it?"

Cohen said, "It's in a safe-deposit box."

"What?"

"It's in a fucking safe-deposit box downtown." His hand worked around in his back pocket, quivering, took out a ring of keys, thumbed one. "That's it," he said, "that's the key right there. I think you broke something inside. I think that I'm bleeding in the brain."

"You'll live."

"No. Really. You broke the cheekbone, but you might have gone into the brain tissue."

"You don't shut up, do you?" Wulff said. "Now, what the fuck am I supposed to do? I can't get in there on my own."

"I'll go down tomorrow and pick it up and bring it back to you. You can wait right outside the bank."

"I don't intend to be here tomorrow."

"Then there isn't anything that I can do. I can't do it tonight, and you sure as hell can't break into a safe-deposit box."

The man's resilience was extraordinary, Wulff thought. Cohen's house had been broken into, he had been fired at, beaten up, sustained a broken cheekbone, and screamed with irretrievable pain, and yet here, after all of it, he was still defiant. Credible, Wulff thought, because it could only be sustained, this defiance, in terms of a craziness that he was beginning to understand. It was the same craziness that drove Wulff—a refusal to admit the reality of circumstances, an inability to come to terms with the fact that they were beaten. Call it obsession, call it what you will, these little dealers and pushers and the big ones too were set apart. So was Wulff. Perhaps that was what held them together when all was done. "Give me the keys," he said.

Cohen gave him a wondering, phased-out stare. "I told you, they won't do any good."

"Give them to me."

Cohen extended the ring. Wulff took it, put it in his pocket, and then leveled the gun.

"You're not going to kill me, are you?" the man said.

"I think I'd better," Wulff said.

"You can't kill me. I've cooperated with you in every regard, I've given you everything you wanted."

"But you haven't given me your life," Wulff said. "I've got to have that too, because as long as you live, you see, right up to the minute of your death, you're still a murderer. You're still dangerous."

"Now, wait a minute," Cohen said, "now, just wait a minute here . . ." Wulff pointed the gun at Cohen's head and pulled the trigger in one convulsive motion. The bullet came forward, tore off the left side of Cohen's skull, and blew it against the wall; from the open spot that had been created, blood charged in a muddy explosion, a series of spurts like semen moving out unevenly. The corpse rolled over onto the floor, kicked once in an absent way, and lay there in that peculiar and knowledgeable way of all the dead everywhere, seeming simultaneously to embrace all knowledge and to reject it, as if that knowledge, of what it was like on the other side of passage, was no longer worth passing on to the desperate and trivial living.

Wulff looked at the body with disgust and then put his gun away and went over and kicked it once in the ribs, feeling the dull give, the amorphous crackle of the useless bone. Then he went to the door and down the hallway almost absently, fingering the safe-deposit key and trying to plan his next move.

Shit. And shit again.

IX

Marie Calvante had said to him, "I'll do anything. I'll do anything that you want to do. If you want to quit the department, you can do it, I don't care, we'll get married whenever you want. In the meantime, I'll live with you. I won't stop you from doing anything that you feel you have to. But don't you think that it's better to stay in? You can't fix anything from the outside, because once you're out, you lose control of it, but inside, inside you can work for change. You can work to better things. Don't you think so?"

And he had said, "I don't know. I just don't know. You can't change them from the inside, because they turn you into the enemy, don't you see that, Marie? You've got to become one of them just to survive, that's the way they have it rigged. Once you're on narco, you don't last unless you play their game, and if you go off narco to complain, they take care of you in other ways. They'll put you on a nowhere beat in Brownsville until you're fifty years old, that's what the hell they'll do." She had been a very pretty girl, oh my, had she been pretty; there had been something heartbreaking as well to her aspect, the nature of her sensuality had been such that it seemed likely to shatter at any time, shatter into something gentle and weeping, or had that only been the way that he had felt when he had looked at her? Well, he would never know now, that was for sure. "I don't know," he had said again, "I don't want to stay, but I don't want to do anything to hurt us, either. I need this job, we need it for a little while." And she had said, "Anything that hurts you hurts the two of us," and that had almost broken him, hearing her put it that way, but it had broken him into something stronger rather than the reverse. A reassembly plant of the soul—that was what she had called him once, thinking of her own background, but it had not been true; it had gone the other way. She had put all the pieces of him together: the Vietnam pieces, the narco pieces, all of the things that shrieked and squeaked in the night.

Well, that had been a long time ago. That had sure been a hell of a long time ago, a different stage of existence for Wulff, although the time could be really measured only in months since he had taken the steps two at a time in that miserable SRO building to find her dead. OD'd out alone and in the middle of a bare room. That just went to show you where you would get, going around busting informants and taking narco seriously. It would have been a good lesson for him if he had taken it on that level, resolved to shape up and from that time onward follow the dictates of the department under the rules and regulations of the career and salary plan. Of course, it had not gone that way at all; seeing Marie dead in that room had sparked him to a hell of a lot of killing; a lot of people had come to regret the death of Marie Calvante, but still, sometimes, he wished that he could go back to the way it was when she had told him that even if he stayed with the department, if he played it as rotten and corrupt as the rest of them, she would still love him, it would make no difference at all. Maybe it would not.

Maybe it would not at all, but she was indisputably dead, and since then nothing had been quite the same, notably the careers of a couple of hundred top-echelon drug dealers. Still, now and then Wulff would find himself thinking, without any conscious control or understanding, of the way it might have been if none of this had ever happened. He would be living in a house with his wife, Marie, right? He would still be a part of the narco squad, absolutely. He would be keeping his mouth shut and doing what narco required, and not making any waves at all— well, maybe. Maybe, again, not. Perhaps he would have turned himself to working from the inside, subverting narco instead of carrying it forward. It was the kind of angle that anyone who knew his way around the squad could have worked out; it would have meant turning down all graft, turning all supplies of drugs confiscated over to the property clerk, going after the to-line street dealers without letting the informants take the heat. Well, again, maybe not. He wouldn't have lasted more than a month on narco carrying on that way; busting an informant had gotten him thrown off in a day, but how long could he have gone the other?

No, there was no point in thinking about it. There was no reason to carry it on through; what had happened had happened to him, all right, and the only comfort that he could find might be in understanding that it would have worked out this way in any case. Maybe Marie had to die anyway. Maybe it was ordained that she would die and fate had thus contrived her death in a way that would have the maximum effect upon Wulff and the maximum effect upon the evil people toward whose destruction he was bent. Maybe. Maybe you could see it that way.

All that he knew was this—that he had turned toward her in the dense spaces of the car when all of the talking was done, and just before they had gone out of there, he had held her, held her against him, and said, "I don't want anything to hurt you, that's all. Whatever happens, I don't want you to be hurt by any of this," and she had come against him, against him in the night, the slight, beating moths of her hands against his cheekbones, and had said, "Don't you understand that you can never hurt me, never, no matter what you do?" And it was that that he would have to live with always, not the way she had kissed him then, or later how she had come against him in that small and final enclosure that they had made of their connection in the close and gripping theater of his bed.

✕

Heading the car east, pushing toward Mobile, Wulff had a blazing moment of total insight: they would mass together to get him. Probably at Atlanta, but not beyond Philadelphia, they would be in wait for him, and this time there would be no reprieve, this time they would be there by the hundreds, all of them massed in a final pact of desperation, and he would not have a chance. It was obvious; they could not allow this to continue. News of what had happened to Cohen would have gotten around; they would have picked it up, and from that they would have assimilated the one message that they could not bear—that Wulff was back in action, that he had somehow swung clear of all the traps that Mexico and the international organization had set to trap him, and that now, extremely angry, he was out after them again, his anger, if possible, intensified by the fact that there was an element of personal revenge.

And they would not be able to stand for it. This last news, coming at a point when they had reason to believe that Wulff was out of action or dead at last, would be sufficient to drive them together for the first time in a pact to preserve their mutual interests. These vermin tore at one another, they simply refused to cooperate, and it was this, really, that was the only reason Wulff had managed to get as far against them as he had: they had as much stake in the bad luck of one another as enforcement did, and so Wulff had been able to go at them without at least a unified counterattack. The memos they were passing one another through intelligence, the verbal agreements they had made to try to kill him, the supposed thousands of messengers or button men who were alert at all times to find and kill him for bounty—that had been so much bullshit. Calabrese loved what Wulff had been doing just as long as it did not affect him; it was just that much less potential rivalry. Carlin could not have hoped to rise to the top levels without Wulff working for him, and so on. No, their fracture had been his strength, but now, Wulff thought, it could not possibly continue that way, because at last they would see through the fact of Cohen's murder that the situation was desperate if they did not mass together; but if they did so, it was no-lose. Surely they would see that. Surely they would know that he was working alone, that he had long since exhausted all possibilities of assistance, that he was now officially an escapee from the New York City prison system, among everything else, and that he had blown the last chance that he might have had of assistance from law-enforcement personnel. They would never protect an outright felon; they had to protect their own asses too. No, if they gave it a little careful and patient thought, no more than a couple of minutes apiece, a few phone conferences, a little bit of give and take in their informal councils, they would see that alone he was quite dangerous, that he might be able to do to them what he had done to Cohen; but if they worked together now, he was helpless. He had absolutely no chance against them once they got together, and after everything that they had been through, they certainly would. Probably from the fact that he had hit Cohen they had a good idea of where he had come from and what his information would be and where he would be going next. They had to know that by now, all right. And they would be waiting.

So why, he thought, hustling Cohen's Toronado through the fast, dense Southern night, why was he going on? Why was he pushing toward Mobile when death was almost certainly waiting for him, death by the hundreds? Well, there were many interesting reasons for that; he would have to consider them sometime. In the meantime, he was going to go on, add speed if possible, hasten the moment of his rendezvous with Mobile so that it would all come to a point quickly. He guessed that he needed confrontation; what he might be in pursuit of now was not so much victory as an ending, fast and conclusive, to his mission. He would rather, toward that ending, take them on by the hundreds than one by one. It was almost empty on the flat span of the Interstate tonight; he had not passed a car, nor a car him, for several miles. Locked into the utter isolation of the Toronado, Wulff felt himself succumbing to the illusion, which he had had before, that he was the only person in the world, that the world contained no motivations, no possibilities other than his own, that indeed these men whom he had been fighting and killing from coast to coast could in themselves be constructions out of his own imagination, projections from his own necessity, and that were he to pull the Toronado over to the side of the road, cut the engine, clamber out of the car, and say to the night, "This is enough now, I have reached the end, no more, no more of it," everything would dissolve, all would be as it had once been, and he would awaken probably to find himself on the floor of some Harlem bar, stiffed out on a dose that had been slipped to him, his senses reeling, stomach sickened, as the informant leaned over him and Wulff realized that all of this had been a dream of alternative. Well, if he had it to do over again, he might not bust the informant.

Maybe. And then again, maybe not. When you came right down to it, there was an air of inevitability to his entire mission. That air was filled with the odor of outrage. It had started in Vietnam, merely solidified when he had come back to narco. If one thing had not set him off, another might. He might have married Marie and done it anyway. And in a sense, that would have been worse. Look at what had happened to Williams, who had come out of a house in St. Albans to do war. A car on his left moved over fast, cutting him off, and Wulff felt himself bouncing on the shoulder of the Interstate even before realization had caught up with reflex. It was reflex that gathered him over the wheel, contracted into something tight and cold and in command as he yanked the Toronado over the sudden ruts and incisions of the difficult ground, forcing it to a stop; it was reflex, too, which made him aware of the other car, a stain to his near vision as it rebounded from its one clanging contact against him and then rolled clear, ten to twenty yards in front of him, coming into the shoulder at an easier angle than Wulff had.

The Toronado under control, he started to make a run for the Interstate again. It was the only thing that he could do, acting reflexively or not; he could only hope that the other car had been surprised by his failure to go off the road; but even as he put down the accelerator, began to yank the car toward the hard panel of road to his left, lights within the other car flickered, the dome-light switch being jabbed as someone came out of the right door, diving, then blackness again, and Wulff felt the shot hit his right-front tire.

That meant that they were very serious, although he should have known that already; anyone who would come along at seventy-five miles an hour to try to blow you off the road had to have more than a mind for risk; there had to be a little desperation there as well. Arrogance, after all, could take you only so far. In the echo of the gunshot there was a much louder, denser sound, that would be his right-front tire going, giving out in a single explosion, and then the car was coming back onto the shoulder then, even less controlled now, skidding and lunging for the weeds beyond and he pumped the brake, killing his lights in the same motion, brought the car back into control, and let it roll right off the shoulder and into the difficult little thickets of grass, as, in the same motion, the car still moving a little, he got his pistol and dived for the floorboard, lay there.

Around him now he could hear shouting, tearing noises, and then the sound of another gunshot, this one coming from the rear-quarter panel behind the driver's door. They were confused; that was obvious; they had not expected him to come off the road a second time, much less in a slide that would take him immediately out of their angle of vision. That might mark them for nonprofessionals, but then again, it might only be that they had miscalculated in a way that was apt to happen to anyone. There was more running and shouting, two voices now, and then another gunshot, this one imploding the windshield above him, little glistening spangles of glass sifting downward, and then he could hear one of the voices shouting, "There he is, I've got him!" and the footsteps came closer.

Now, that was really stupid, Wulff thought, exposing a position like that. It meant that they probably were amateurs, after all; no one who knew his business would want to reveal a position like that. It was very quiet above them on the road; the two cars lay in a shallow recession a foot or two below the level of asphalt, and there was no indication of cars in any direction. It must have been early morning by then. Amateurs though they were, they had at least shown enough professionalism to plan their attack so that it would play out without interference. "Here he is!" the same voice shouted again, and Wulff waited for the gunshot, but there was none; instead, he heard footsteps coming nearer, and then a dull sound as something struck the metal.

The man had run into his door. That was really stupid, Wulff thought; in fact, the whole thing was a fiasco, if you wanted to look at it objectively. The only thing was that the assailants seemed to take themselves damned seriously, a lot more seriously than Wulff did, and the third gunshot that came into the door at very close range was disturbing; it ripped through the backing before depositing the bullet, now a dispirited little pellet only a foot or so from Wulff. "He's got to be in here!" he heard the voice say. "He can't have gotten away; I *know* that he's in there." But the voice did not sound very confident.

Someone else was shouting. The other man out in the weeds was screaming, calling the near one a damned fool or something like that, calling him an asshole and telling him to get the hell out of the way before he got himself shot. That sounded to Wulff like reasonable advice, and when the near voice shouted back that he wasn't going to leave, that he was going to stay right here, stay right here by the car and *shoot* the son-of-a-bitch out, he felt a strange and reasonable calm descend upon him. If he could simply stay here curled up, the pistol in his hand, the two of them out there would settle the issue themselves. They would kill each other, that was what the hell they would do, and thus go away quietly, so that Wulff could pick up the pieces at his leisure. The only trouble was that the passenger compartment of the Toronado was beginning to fill with the scent of gas; he must have stripped the tank, rolling as he came off the Interstate. The suspension on these cars was really terrible, disgraceful in view of the fact that this and the

Eldorado, which was on the same body shell, were being sold as ten-thousand-dollar alternatives to the European Grand Tourismo. A Jensen Intercepter wouldn't even have gone off the road here; it would have accelerated its way out of it.

But that was of no matter now. What was of concern was that the compartment was reeking and stinking of gas, and if Wulff could smell it, then the two clowns outside could smell it too, and that would lead them—would have to leave them—to one of two assumptions. Either they could wait patiently while Wulff slowly asphyxiated in the compartment, which of course he would not do, so what they could do was simply wait him out, until he came stumbling and gasping into the air; or they could decide to hasten matters along a little, help the course of nature, so to speak: they could strike a match. With loose gas running around and out of all the ends of the Toronado, the only thing that they would have to make sure of was not to be too close to the car when the match struck. Judging from the kind of luck that they had been having so far, this was not too likely; they would probably be in the center of the explosion; but it was hardly going to be of much satisfaction to Wulff that all of them would go up together. It did not seem as if this would do him any good at all.

Already he could hear them squealing with excitement. They were trying to moderate their voices, apparently had decided that Wulff could hear them and it would be worth their while to conceal their intentions from him. Exactly what their intentions were was not hard to figure. They must have smelled the gas by now. They were giggling.

Well, Wulff thought, there was nothing to be done. There was no way around it. He had always known that he would come to a difficult and painful end, but in terms of how far he had gone, how he had struggled, and what he had accomplished, it did not seem right that he should end by being crushed, humiliated, and incinerated in a wrecked fat man's sports car while two idiot free-lancers probably joined him in the pyre. There would have to be another, less dramatic, but more dignified way to go. He sighed and wedged the pistol tightly into his hand and reached up to the switch that controlled the power door locks, carefully flipped it across. The locks popped up with a stale *click*. Charge up one to General Motors engineering, anyway.

The fools had not heard him. They were still whispering outside, probably making coin matches to decide who threw the match while the other ran. They were deep in consultation at the moment that Wulff rolled out of the car, feeling the dank and poisonous mud of the interstate valley embrace him, tear free of him with a sucking noise as he wrenched his way to his feet, and then, pistol extended, began to fire.

The trigger came comfortably against his finger; as shaky as his new footing seemed to be on the mud, he felt calm and absolutely in control. The recoil of the pistol, in fact, seemed to put him ever more firmly on his feet, taking him into stanchion.

He heard a scream on the first shot, and there was a brief flare, light arcing against the sky as if a match had been dropped, and then from behind the screamer there was a deeper, groaning gasp and the sound of answering fire. He had put down the near man, the man who had surveyed the car instantly, which figured; of the two, he was the more clownish and incompetent, the one about whom they would say that he had been ambushed in a situation where no other man could possibly have been taken by surprise. It would make a hell of an epitaph, Wulff thought, and heard the giggling sound of the man drowning into the mud, trying dreamily now, Wulff could imagine, to separate the clods of earth from his mouth, trying to imagine what had happened to him, and then the roar of fire came from somewhat in back of the downed man, the first shot splattering what was left of the Toronado's windshield, the second coming into the mud only a few feet in front of him, and the second man, the man firing, was screaming now, unconscious or uncaring of his new and exposed position. "You dirty bastard," he was screaming, "you rotten son-of-a-bitch, you can't do this to me," and Wulff could appreciate the sense of what he was saying. From the man's point of view, Wulff was fucking him up pure and simple; he was not being an easy target in a blind alley, was not submitting in the terrified and graceful way that routine targets did, but had come out unpleasantly capable of fighting himself, and that made things difficult: complex assignments were not for men like these, they were used to handling only the simple ones; whoever manipulated them was careful not to put them beyond their depth. "Stupid bastard," the man said again, and fired awkwardly. In the uneven flash Wulff could see him as if brought to exhibition in some grotesque museum of twentieth-century minor American crime; there he was, a short, slightly deformed man, both hands on the pistol, hunched over it, his face tight with concentration, seeming to be in the act of fighting the pistol down, the gun rising in his hands. "Son-of-a-bitch," the man said, and fired again.

The bullet went so wide of Wulff that it was impossible to judge what the man had in mind, exactly where he had placed his target. It was almost impossible to miss by such a wide margin, but there was no time to consider that; housewives were able to kill their husbands at a range of three hundred yards, first shot, sometimes; and even a man like this was capable of getting off a killing shot. Wulff leveled his own .45 and shot the gun out of the man's hand so easily, so crisply, that the man could only look in astonishment as the gun detached itself, landed somewhere in a pile of mud downrange. He looked at Wulff, a slow, stupid expression on his face. "Oh, no," he said.

Wulff held the gun on him, looked at the other, who was lying on his stomach near the car, the fumes of gas ever thicker and fuller, like flowers in the air, and said, "I think we'd better get out of here. That car is going to blow up."

"Shoot me, I don't care."

"I said, I think we'd better get out of here."

"I don't give a fuck," the man said loudly. "You're going to shoot me, fucking shoot me here. I know that you're going to do it, so do it now and get it over with. I tried and I failed, and now I have to die." He raised his hands, the fingers fluttering, hands dangling like leaves from his wrists. "Isn't that the way you operate? You shoot to kill as soon as you win?"

"I really think we'd better get out of here," Wulff said pleasantly. "There's a big car leaking gas over here, and it's going to blow up sooner or later, no two ways about it. Why should we get incinerated? We can get out of here and discuss this like gentlemen."

"I'll never talk," the man said. "I'll never reveal a thing. You might as well kill me now. No matter what you do, you'll get nothing out of me."

"Oh, shit," Wulff said, and resisted an impulse to shoot the man on the spot. It would be satisfying and would end the problem, but then again, he knew that he had no business doing it until, at least, he found out who had sent him. If they were on his trail again, if they had the net big and complex enough to pick him up on an Interstate in the early morning, then it meant that they were certainly closing in again and tighter all of the time. "Just get moving."

"You killed Gerry," the man said.

"I'm going to kill you too if you don't move," Wulff said, and moved the gun in his palm; the man shrugged, let out a deep sigh, and turned, trudged his way from the car toward his own. It was a bare Fairlane, black and pockmarked with what seemed to be scars from old gun battles. The man walked to the driver's side and stood there patiently, leaning on the half-open door, his head bowed, his attitude patient. Wulff came across to the other side of the car. "Get in," he said, "get in and drive. I'll keep you covered."

"Shoot me now. Shoot me now and drive out yourself, why don't you?" The man's voice suddenly wavered. "I mean, what the fuck, if you're going to die, you might as well *die*, right? Don't string me along, mister. I'm ready to stand up to it if you do it now. If you do it now, I can die like a man, but if you carry it on—"

"Oh, shut up," Wulff said, afflicted with a sudden weariness, not only for these men but for their codes, the necessity they had to die *brave*; the scum seemed obsessed by this, but then again, there was another kind of scum which he had dealt with that wanted nothing more than to die *scared*—all of those who had sniveled and wept at the sight of the gun—and they had to be considered too. You had to figure all kinds into the equation; the basic point was that dying was more than most men could put up with sensibly. Living was enough trouble. "Get the hell into the car and let me cover you and start driving. You want that thing to blow up while we're here?"

He thought momentarily of the cache of drugs that he had back in the Toronado, just the excess of what he had gotten out of Mexico, that which couldn't be taken out comfortably on his person. It was the only thing worth going back for; the only firearms were on his person, and there was nothing in the suitcase in the trunk worth thinking about, except for the drugs. He wavered for one moment standing at the car, thinking of the few grams that he was going to lose, twenty-five grand in street value anyway, if he could make a proper estimate. But then again, he wasn't going to take them on the street; the cache had value only as a means of bringing him into contact with others; he would have to let it go, then. He would have to let everything go.

He made a gesture with the gun. The man at the other side shrugged, made a pleading gesture with his hands, and then, as if all force had been drained from him, shook his head and ducked inside. Wulff came down into the passenger seat, held the gun on the man with low-key professionalism, and cocked it.

Desperately fighting with the ignition, the man got the Fairlane into gear and drove it raggedly away. They were not even half a mile down the road when the Toronado blew up.

XI

At four in the morning the man in Mobile got a hysterical phone call on the private line that fed into the receiver by his bed. It was the only way that anyone could get to him at that hour; even his wife was sealed off in the separate bedroom down the other corridor. The phone could not be avoided; he had to be there to pick up the only kind of messages that would flow through it. "Hello," he said in the darkness, looking for his cigarettes.

"Hello," a voice said. "Is this you? Is this you, Mr. Nolk?"

"Who else would it be?" the man in Mobile said. His patting hand located the crushed pack of Pall Malls, he pulled one out and got the lighter and lit it one-handed, the receiver of the phone perfectly jeweled and symmetrical in the quick flare of light. Pleasing. But the caller was not pleasing. "You know who it is. Now, what do you want?" He paused, waited for the man to say something, then shook his head and inhaled. "Did you get him?" he said.

"He let me go," the voice said. It sounded shaky. "He could have killed me, he had me right there, and he let me go. I thought I was going to die."

"You fool," Nolk said, "are you trying to say that you found him, you had him and he *captured* you?"

"It was a strange situation. I can't begin to describe to you what it was like; his Toronado blew up."

"You stupid bastard," Nolk said. He almost never cursed, had a thing about it, would not permit any foul language to be used in his house or in front of a woman, but there it was now. Better to let it out, he guessed, than to keep it bottled up; that was how you lived to fifty-eight in the best of health, not by bottling things up, by letting them come out. "What do I care about his Toronado? What are you talking about? How could you find him and let him get away?"

"He could have killed me, do you understand?" the voice said. It was now completely out of control, whimpering and gibbering, moving up and down the scale of contact. Nolk could feel little waves of revulsion as he listened to the man, waves that he knew would turn into nausea. "But he didn't. He let me go. He said that I could deliver a message to you."

"What message?"

"He said to tell you that he's coming. He's coming to kill you."

Nolk said nothing at all. He held the cigarette flat in his fingertips, letting it dangle against the floor, blanking his mind, concentrating on perfect control, and then he said, "Well, that's no news at all, is it? That doesn't mean a thing; we know that he's coming to kill me. The point is that people like you were hired to make sure that that event would be even more unlikely than it already appears. You seem to have fucked up very badly."

"We couldn't have done anything! He had us off the road before we even had a chance. Strauss is dead."

"I wish you were," Nolk said. "I'll take care of that job sooner or later."

"Now, look. That isn't right. That isn't right to say that, Mr. Nolk. We did the best we could, we really did. It wasn't our fault that we got into this. The guy's a killer, he's a combat operator, everybody knows that he's good. Hey, we had a real good shot at him, that's more than most people can say, we got him ditched off the road and in real trouble. And he's got nothing now except one pistol; all of his stuff was in the car when it blew up. So we did the job, you understand? We did everything that we could have."

"And he left a message that he was going to come and kill me. That's how you did your job."

There was an empty space on the wire, and then the voice said thinly, "Listen, it didn't work out, all right? But we gave it the best shot we could. Anyway, that's all bullshit. You know that he's coming, and you'll meet him with enough goddamned firepower to destroy a regiment. So what the hell is the sweat?"

"The sweat is that you screwed it up," Nolk said. "You're an idiot. Both of you are idiots. I'm glad that Strauss is dead, and I wish that he had done the same job on you. If he's as goddamned efficient as everyone says he is, you'd think that he could have taken care of that one little detail. Where did all this happen?"

"I don't know. Maybe a hundred, hundred and fifty miles east of Shreveport, you know? Plenty of time, anyway. He's a good distance from there."

"What's he traveling in?"

Once again there was a long singing space on the wire. "Well, he's got a black Fairlane, pretty beat up, with Jersey license plates. Not too good a car . . . ."

"He got your car, didn't he?"

"Well, all right, yes. But I got out of it with my ass, anyway. Listen," the voice said, "You think it's so goddamned easy, you're so tough lying in bed there giving orders and telling me that I'm an asshole and Strauss who is dead is an idiot, you really think that that's so goddamned easy, *you* take this guy on. He's a fucking killer, can't you understand that? He's a murderer."

"You're a fool," Nolk said to the voice. "Both of you are fools. One of you is dead because of it, and the other one deserves to be."

"You don't understand."

"You'd better not let me see you," Nolk said. "You have any sense at all, you will make yourself difficult for me to find because if I do, I'm going to take care of the job that Wulff should have done. You bastard."

The voice made astonished, revolted gibbering sounds. But Nolk was already without interest; first his attention and then the receiver itself had been withdrawn, placed on its pedestal. Closing off the voice was like tying off one abscess, only to open a tunnel into a deeper wound; he found, lying on the bed, that he was shuddering. Little movements of revulsion worked their way up and down the panels of his body, and

Nolk found that he was cold, fifty-eight years old and heaving in the spaces of his bed like a child, an infant who had tossed off the covers in the middle of the night and had now somehow lost control of himself. He pushed the covers back suddenly, and in a convulsive motion stood, his feet on the floor establishing a connection that felt curiously insubstantial, disconnected. Wavering, he felt for his slippers, put them on, and then went for the door of the bedroom. I am getting old, he thought. It was the first time that he had thought this in a very long time. I am getting very old, I become cold in the middle of the night, I look for comfort, something in the network of night to hold against me. He went out the door and through the corridor. He opened the first door on his right, peered in, saw the sleeping form of his wife against the pillow. Looking at her in sleep was shocking; he had not seen her this way for a very long time—it must have been eight or nine years since the new house and the separate bedrooms—but seeing her that way reminded him of how it had been in much different times. Oh, he guessed that he had to go back almost thirty years to get that image properly fixed, but there it was: the way she had looked huddled in the bed of their hotel room on the first morning when he had come back from the bathroom to see her there in the spattering of sun, stricken by the light and yet framed by it as slowly, slowly she had turned then, held her arms to him, and he had moved toward and then upon her.

She moved now too, sensitive to him as she had always been in some part which he could not touch, which he must not have known about, and the two images must have meshed then: recollection, in which in a profound abyss of connection he moved upon her again and again, and the present, in which slowly he came toward her, driven by emotions that he had not had in many years. As the fires in recollection battered and tore at one another, rising and falling in the light, so in the present, in the harsh, guttering bulb of the nightlight, did he come upon her, and now, as then, she turned and held him; he felt her gathering him in, a sudden hardness in her touch as she brought him against her, and he felt her move toward him, damp. He can't reach me, he thought as he worked within her grasp, he can't touch me, he can't get near, I will have a hundred men around this house and all of them trained and all of them ready to kill. To kill for me. I cannot be touched. But she could touch him, he felt himself beginning to grow within her, struggling to pull himself free from his clothing, not able to do so, settling into her with sighs and groans, and oh my God she was slack, she was loose down there; he had never realized until now, driven by need, how far gone she was; he had maintained in his mind some image of sufficiency which must have again and again circumvented realization so that time and again in these years of the separate bedrooms, when he had plunged into her he had been fucking not the woman she had become but the woman she had been; but now he saw, he was in the bed with *her*, not some recovered image, not some dream, but Jennifer herself, and heaving and bucking against her, her cries filling the air, he knew that they were cries not of the young girl he had married, the girl in the hotel room in the sun, but rather he was fucking the groaning and submissive fifty-three-year-old woman grunting beneath him, whose breasts slid like water to her sides, as insubstantial as the blood that ran within him, and his orgasm was diminished, feeble, coming out of him in little weak sprays.

That was, in a way, the worst of it—the fact that he was able to climax. If he had been impotent with her, seeing this new aspect, if he had turned in revulsion, unable to function, it would have at least made some statement on himself and how far he had come from the imposed fantasies which had enabled him to fuck her all these recent years; but he could not; reflex was stronger than recognition, habit leaped higher than disgust, and at the end, moving within her, Nolk felt not only emission but a kind of lust, actual lust, which made him reach farther into her, his prick a claw, the flow of his semen little nails to catch her more deeply, and it was his revulsion which must have peaked the orgasm, made it even more intense so that in reacting against it he found himself moved more strongly by her, so that he came in a long, thrashing, bleating series of movements that banged her against the bed and made her groan with pain, all of her soft against him, a feeling of waste. Fucking offal, he thought, I am fucking offal; and that part was all right, but not the perverse and rising excitement that, even in the aftermath of orgasm, tricked him over into his second and more violent coming, and he lay on top of her as those spasms passed from him, looking at himself in a kind of interior astonishment: he would not have imagined that he had this kind of thing within him. He would not have really thought that he was this kind of person.

Slowly Nolk separated himself from his wife, slowly he pivoted to an elbow, rolled, brought up his legs to guard against strain of the lower back, and looked then at the ceiling, dimpled and full above him. His wife lay there, his juices and hers running from her, an overturned urn, now leaking parts of the evening's wreckage. He knew that he should talk to her, but he simply could not think of anything to say. What he really wanted to do, of course, was to get back to his own bedroom and lock the door and lie on his bed planning the retaliatory campaign. He would have to have a hundred men around the house. That was correct. He would not take on Wulff with less than a hundred, and a hundred and fifty would be better if you could raise that number in this area on short notice, but he doubted it. Settle for a hundred, then. He would have to begin calling around at once; he would have to be on the phone for hours, starting immediately, because there was not that much time in which to make arrangements, and there was no saying how near Wulff had already come to Mobile. He would have to do that. But somehow he could not force himself off the bed, not before he tried to talk to her, although he had no idea what to say. He simply did not have the slightest idea of what to say.

Neither did she, apparently. She lay there running her palm over the sheets in slow, skilled, expert motions of arousal, as if the sheet were he and she was trying to move him once again. He stopped the hand, put his palm over it. She looked at him. "It's no good, is it?" she said.

"It was all right."

"You don't have to say anything. You don't have to lie. I know when it's no good, for God's sake."

"All right, Jennifer," he said. "All right."

"Go on, tell me it was no good. I can take it."

"I don't want to tell you anything."

"Yes you do. You're dying to tell me. I can see how badly you want to. Well, go ahead and do it. Do it now and get it over with."

It was hopeless. It was all of that; he was married to a fifty-three-year-old woman who (how could he have forgotten this?) was not only aging but querulous, not only unsatisfactory but raised to a pitch of awareness about her weakness which was to make it doubly unbearable. "All right," he said, and sat up in the bed. "All right."

"You come into my room in the middle of the night, you have sex without saying a word, and now you just want to walk out? No," she said, "no, it won't work out at all. You could at least say something. You could tell me how it stunk."

"Oh, my God."

"Don't just sit there. Say something. Let it all out of you. I can take it. I can take almost anything now."

"Oh God, Jennifer," Nolk said, and stood, swaying uncomfortably on the uneven surfaces of the floor. "Will you leave me alone?"

"That's ridiculous. That's the most damned ridiculous thing I ever heard. You start all of this off and tell me to leave *you* alone."

"I shouldn't have gotten into it," he said.

"Don't start with your foul mouth. You can tell me anything you want, but you don't have to get into dirt. I don't have to listen to that."

"I don't mean what you think I mean," Nolk said. "It wasn't that at all."
And he was almost ready to get into it then: I never meant to get into

distribution, is what he would have said. That wasn't what I wanted, but it was too easy an opportunity to pass up, I couldn't let something like that go, no one would have. I would have been a fool to pass it up, and when things started to shake down here, when it looked like I had a shot at the top, I was really committed, but now I see I shouldn't have done it, and it's too late. Oh my, is it too late. To her he only said, "Good night, Jennifer,"' and went toward the door of the bedroom.

"Come on," she said behind him, "say it."

He stopped at the door, turned. "I said it," he said, "I said it all," and he knew that this was absolutely the truth, that in all of the motions of his body, in all of the moans and gutturals in his throat, he had said it to her in a way that was absolutely and purifyingly clear, which had resonance in a way that he could never give with words. It was too late. Everything was too late. All that he could do now was to stand and fight. The stakes were, at least, absolute; he could see now that if he succeeded, it would be in a way that would entirely change his life.

I should have gotten a mistress, I should have fucked around more, Nolk thought as he went back to his room, closed the door. I would have been far better off spreading it around instead of getting hammered into this, but it's far too late for that now, it's far too late for any of that. It comes down to smack. He bolted the door and shut off the light, and there in the darkness at five in the morning began the phone calls to build the force that he would use to withstand the challenge of the enemy and thus catapult himself to the absolute head of all manipulations and distribution for the important Southern district.

XII

Wulff called him at about four in the morning on a Thursday. Williams had figured that the call was only a matter of time, that sooner or later it was going to come in, and he only hoped that he would be able to handle it the right way. It was no surprise at all. It did not wake his wife, because he had taken to sleeping in the living room in recent weeks, the phone right by the head of the couch. Things had not been the same between them since he had come home, and he guessed they would not be again. In line with that, it had seemed only good common sense to sleep separately until things cooled down. But then again, you never knew. Maybe they would get back together again. "I figured you'd call," he said to Wulff when the man had said hello. "I just was wondering when it would be. Where are you?"

"I'm in the South," Wulff said.

"How far south?"

"Not as far as I once was. I came out of Mexico. Now I'm heading toward Mobile."

"That's a tough-ass area," Williams said, "that Mobile is a real motherfucker. I do not think that my father would miss Mobile at all if he were still alive, which he is not, because Mobile, among other places, left scars on him."

"Want to come down here and get back at Mobile?"

"Oh, shit," Williams said, "I had that bit in Los Angeles."

"I thought Los Angeles worked out pretty well."

"It almost killed me," Williams said. "I knew after Los Angeles that I wasn't cut out for this kind of life."

"No one's asking you to be cut out for it. You can lend a hand, though. You can free-lance a bit."

"Wulff," Williams said, and then paused, got the receiver the other way so that the cord was now wrapped around his neck, not in a smothering grasp, just little tentacles to take him deeper into the conversation, sheltering and nestling his voice, "Wulff, I think you ought to pitch it in. You ought to come back."

"Not for a little while."

"They're serious, Wulff. They're goddamned serious. They're pressing me to the wall. The bureau is in on this."

"That's nothing new."

"You're an escapee, Wulff. That puts you in a different category. You go on killing people, it's on their heads now. They had you in custody."

"I'm doing the right kind of killing. You want to join me?"

"I can't do it," Williams said. "I thought that all over. I went through that back in L. A. You understand, Wulff, I get into that again, and there's no end to it. I'll never get out of it alive."

"Afraid?"

"And other things."

"It's a hell of a lot of fun," Wulff said. "You'd be surprised; I'm starting to enjoy it for its own sake now."

"I don't ever want to enjoy it, Wulff."

"You don't have to enjoy it to do it. You can get the enjoyment just from knowing that it's an important job and that it's being well done."

Williams drew his knees up carefully to his chest, felt the even beat of his heart under his wrist. "I can't," he said. "I just can't do it, Wulff."

"Well, I'm not surprised. It figured."

"It's better if we cut this short, Wulff. You start to press me, and I'll have to say something to them. I swear to you I don't want to do it, but I'm abiding a fugitive on a federal rap, and that's serious. I can't get into that."

"You really want out, don't you?"

"Back in L.A. That was the time. That was the time when I got out, Wulff."

There was a little pause on the other end. Wulff might have lit another cigarette, Williams thought, but then again, he had a more vivid mental picture, the man bent over the receiver, his features resolved to a fine point of concentration, the tired eyes suddenly luminescent as the next idea occurred to him. He was always thinking, that was the point. Wulff was always functioning; you thought that he was somewhere, and he turned out to be steps ahead. It was a remarkable thing, but then again, in his business it was inevitable. "All right," Wulff said, "it was just an idea. I didn't figure that it would come to anything, but I thought I had to ask. I need some ordnance, Williams."

"Shit," Williams said automatically, "oh, shit."

"I know you don't like to be asked. But there's nowhere else to turn right now. I'm a little out of my normal territory and kind of out of options. I had some stuff in a car, but it blew up on the Interstate."

"Still blowing up cars on the Interstate, Wulff?"

"Don't be funny, Williams, I'm goddamned serious here. I need some ordnance. I'm heading into Mobile, but I have a feeling that I'm going to be walking into some pretty heavy fire, and I can't manage it on the lightweight arms I've got. I've just got a couple of pistols. I'm going to need some grenades and full clips. We can work out a drop point; if you ship them air mail—"

"No, Wulff," Williams said.

"What? What's that?"

"I'm not going to do it. I'm not going to ship you any stuff. In the first place, I don't have any more damned sources; I'm on office patrol."

"Bullshit. You have contacts. I met some of your contacts."

"They're all gone. While you were blowing up Harlem, Wulff, you took care of some pretty brisk sources. And in the second place, whether I could find some stuff or not, I'm out. I'm out of the game. I'm about seven or eight towns behind, Wulff. I'm pulling out of this."

"That's the way you want to play it?"

"I have no choice. That's the way it has to be."

"Gone back into the system, eh? You've made the full round trip in a little over eight months. That's a pretty damned fast cycle, rookie."

"I'm not a rookie anymore. That's for fucking sure," Williams said. "I'm no rookie."

"You're talking like one. Back to St. Albans, hey, rookie? Back to the split-level."

"It's not a split-level."

"Bullshit, rookie."

"Listen," Williams said. He drew the receiver closer, closed his eyes against the mental picture of Wulff now stirring within the telephone booth (or was he calling from some diner, was that faint sound of music he heard the jukebox drifting and pounding through the thin panels of the open phone? Some truckers' diner in Mississippi, that's what he would imagine it to be, the *feel* of it was somehow drifting through the wire, or was he once again overreacting?), his fingers twitching on the cord, looking toward the parking lot outside where his latest dangerous, fast car would be. "Listen to me, Wulff. It's bullshit, all right. That's what I want to tell you. It's all crap. You can't fight them. You can't go on this way."

"Don't tell me—"

"But you *can't*," Williams said. "Goddamnit, we know what the hell's going on here, don't we? Every fucking cop on the beat knows what you used to know and won't admit anymore—that if you clean it out at one level, you've just got a vacuum, and they'll move in at the next level. You'll just get another bunch of names; the system goes on."

"Does it? Does it really?"

"Traffic is the same," Williams said harshly. "I'm a little closer to the goddamned New York statistics than you are, Wulff, I know what's going on at street level here. There's the same amount of shit as before. It gets through, don't you understand? It always gets through."

"Are you going to ship me some ordnance?"

"No," Williams said, "because it doesn't make any fucking difference. There's twice as much traffic since the new drug laws were put in, there's twice as much since you started killing, Wulff. All it means is that the game has become more dangerous and the stakes are higher. It isn't a picker's game anymore, it's scared the weaker people off, so those who are ready to come in and play can do so for greater reward. Nothing you do is going to make any difference at all. Can't you understand that?"

"You're a coward, rookie."

"You're fucking right I'm a coward. I'm watching my own ass, that's what I'm doing. It doesn't mean a bit of difference whether I live or die to the world; it's going to be the same shit no matter what happens to me, so I'd just better stay alive and hang in the game for the people that matter. I'm not playing anymore, Wulff. This is the end. It ended in Los Angeles, and I'm not going to go back to it."

There was a long pause at the other end. Williams could hear the drifting sounds of the juke, could hear clattering and smashing in the background, imagined Wulff huddled there against the panels, the phone clutched very close to him. It would not be hard to move from this mental image to a kind of pity; he could feel pity for Wulff if he pushed it just a little bit further, saw the man as essentially helpless and defeated at a level where defeat left him no rationalizations whatsoever, where, having been in the game up until the end, he could only understand that to play was to be battered, but he would not make that connection. He would not feel sorry for Wulff if he could help it at all, because that too would lead nowhere. It would at worst force pity, and if pity came, he would feel the need to make it up to Wulff somehow, and he did not want to do that. He could not. "All right," Wulff said finally, "all right, if that's the way it has to be."

"Come back," Williams said. "Give yourself up. I don't think that they would make it too hard on you. You've done a hell of a lot of good work, a valuable service. I don't even know if they'd want to hold you, if they'd have the heart for a full prosecution. You could cop to something smaller and be out in no time. You'd make bail right away. I guarantee that; I'd help you make bail."

"Never. I'm never coming back."

"It won't get any easier."

"Nothing gets any easier. But you don't think I'm going to turn myself over to them, do you? You don't think that after all I've been through I'm going to go into a cell."

"You can't change the world, Wulff."

"You're a coward, rookie."

"Somewhere along the way you've got to give up. This is my way; I just don't want to see anybody hurt anymore. I can't do any more hurting. And it won't make any difference."

"You're a fool," Wulff said. "Goddamn you, you're a fool," and the music came over, and then he paused again and said, "Maybe you're not a fool."

"No way."

"But I'm not coming back. I'm never going to come back, don't you understand that? I've got to play it out until the end."

"If you have to."

"I really wish you'd work with me, though. I'm going in there naked, rookie. I need some submachine guns and some grenades. The grenades would help more, I guess, if you could send a few."

"No," Williams said, "it's all over, Wulff. It's all over," he said, and the line at the other end went dead, and for a while he lay there with the phone on his chest looking at the dark and swollen aspect of the ceiling as it seemed to curve down upon him and finally take him, phone still disconnected, to deep and murky sleep.

XIII

Nolk had done everything that he thought he could. Within reason. He had covered the grounds with five men on patrol, stationed another two at the end of the one-way street on which he lived, the only way in which a car could turn in; he had three of them in the house at all times, two of them downstairs, one of them up to serve as a person force. That made ten altogether, which wasn't the one hundred that he had dreamed about, the twenty-five that he had reasonably anticipated as being a protection force, but after he had started calling around, he began to see how ridiculous that was. Twenty-five men to defend a single household against one crazy man! It was ridiculous. Furthermore, it was exactly the kind of ridiculous thing that could get around; certain people might get the idea that Nolk was afraid of Wulff, pathologically afraid, that was. That would not be good. His own situation was pretty good, bound to get better all the time with so many of his potential competition out of the way, but word that he needed twenty-five men to defend himself would not have been helpful. It was better to just settle for the ten and keep a stiff front. They were expensive enough; it would be tough enough in the aftermath to get ten to keep their mouths shut, let alone two and a half times that number. Fuck it. He would ride with what he had, that was all. Besides, what could Wulff do to him? What could anyone do to him, really? He was sealed in. Tight and behind the barriers, he had the situation under control.

Jennifer didn't like it, of course. But then, Jennifer did not like anything at all; less and less did she seem to be able to get along with any of the facets of Nolk's life, and after worrying about it for a while, he no longer gave a damn. He was the only man of all the men he had known who had made, until very late on, a serious attempt to bring his wife along with him and make her a part of all his life, who had not even done much screwing around on her. But all of that was over; that last scene in her bedroom the night that he had gotten the call on Wulff had just about done it. She could go fuck herself, Nolk thought. These men were in here for her own protection, and if she didn't like it, then she could bloody well pick up and get out, which, as far as he was concerned, would be a break for both of them. Once this situation was resolved, once he had Wulff out of the way and had the meeting in Philadelphia taken care of, he was going to make real changes in the rest of his life. Fifty-eight was not too late to change, to make a new start and have another way at solving the problem, which was what he regarded life itself as, just one goddamned problem. But soluble. He did not have to put up with her anymore.

So he had the house outfitted and the men stationed and Jennifer pretty much under control, or at least out of the way now, and it was just a matter of waiting. He did not think that he would have to wait too long. Wulff would make his move quickly or not at all; that had been the man's characteristic from the beginning, and now, as the pressure increased, as the evidences of alert became greater, he would become even more anxious to strike before forces could be gathered; there was the likelihood that Wulff would do something really desperate, and when it happened here, when it turned out that Nolk was the man to dispose of him . . . well, that would increase his prestige accordingly. It would send him to Philadelphia a few months hence with the equivalent of a full house. They might think in the North that the Southern people were a bunch of meatballs and shit-kickers, good only to run moonshine and kick niggers around the plantation, but they would learn differently when Nolk became the man to do the job that they had been unable to do. Wulff had pretty well decimated the North; the South was still there, wasn't it?

Nolk entertained himself waiting for Wulff by bullshitting with the guards and for kicks watching them beat the shit out of Harris, the man who had gone on detail with Strauss and had made the frantic call of alert. Why Harris had turned up at Nolk's door the next morning stammering and confused was beyond Nolk; it didn't seem to make any sense to him, but then again, you never could tell with this hired help. Sometimes in their stupidity they did dependent childlike things like turning to the man who had hired them to get them out of a tough spot. Actually Harris would not have been in a tough spot at all: Strauss was dead, and Nolk would have been willing to write off the whole thing as a bad investment, that was all. But Harris showing up, still babbling apologies and offering to help out when Wulff attacked, because Harris thought it was his responsibility to do so—that was too much. Too much by far. Nolk tossed him in the basement, and every time he got bored, went downstairs with one of the house men and stood off in a corner while the man beat Harris up a little. Harris whimpered and pleaded, bleeding from many new and old places while he was worked over, and begged Nolk to give him just one more chance, one chance to prove his loyalty, and Nolk laughed and threw in a couple of kicks himself, even though he did not like, as a rule, to get physically involved. That was what you hired people for. Then he would go upstairs with the house man, leaving Harris whimpering down there, and pace around a bit, waiting for Wulff to come. Now and then they would dump some bread and water downstairs so that Harris could keep going. Actually it was quite tense and boring waiting for Wulff to strike, without any real means of controlling the time of his coming, and if it had not been for Harris downstairs to beat up for laughs, it might have been a tough vigil. So Nolk was not ungrateful. In the long run, maybe Harris had done them all a favor by showing up, kept them from getting too nervous. Nolk had Jennifer segregated in one of the bedrooms far away from the screams, so that she couldn't hear a thing.

It was Jennifer, however, who was making things difficult. She finally got hold of him after he had made another phone call in the bedroom, checking various sources, trying to find out if Wulff had been picked up anywhere in transit (he had not), and said, "I don't know what's going on here, but I don't like it. Why are all these men in the house?"

"That's my business, Jennifer," he said, trying to push past her, get downstairs again, where the action was. "You let me worry about that, and you take care of your own business."

"Why are you staying home, and why are all these men here? What's going on?"

"Please," he said, "don't ask me questions. If you want to leave the house for a few days, maybe that would be the best thing. You could go to Atlanta—"

"No," she said. She stood against him, blocking passage in the hallway, and he looked at her, the differences in their height minimized by the heels she was wearing and by the bright flush spreading across her cheeks, which seemed to have brought her to a level of attention that lifted her further. "You're not going to walk away from this. You're going to tell me what's going on."

Nolk stared at her. She was aging. He had an aging, ugly, tired wife. Furthermore, it was ridiculous. How could something like this be? Who else in the distribution business had a wife who insisted upon participating in his life, had a wife with whom he had to negotiate almost everything that he did? It was unheard of; if the word got around to what degree he was involved with the woman, how close she was to his situation, he would be laughed or assassinated out of the business. It would be even more devastating than Wulff. The thing was, of course, that he should have had a cover occupation like everyone else in the business, a little firm or at least a payroll somewhere where he could go during the days and collect a false salary to keep the taxes at bay. To say nothing of keeping away from his wife. But instead, starting from the time ten years ago when he had fallen into it, he had decided to play it straight, give it his full time, work out of the house, do his negotiations over the phone, and so on. That was stupid. It was even more stupid to think that Jennifer knew nothing of what was going on, even though he had tried to keep as quiet about it as possible. But she would have to know something. Anyone would, granted the situation. Definitely he should have had an outside job of some kind; for one thing, it would have made adultery a hell of a lot easier. As it was, he had to scramble for it, he had to invent appointments and urgent business across town and lie his way out of the house, and the way it worked out, if he could get clear for a couple of hours it was unusual. The separate bedrooms might have been a help, he could have sneaked out during the nights, but he was so damned tired when he went to sleep anyway that it was simply too much of an effort to get up. "Look here," he said to her now, shaking his head and feeling the old despair, "this is serious business here. Please stay out of the way. You can't get involved in this."

"I won't be pushed away. You've got men all over the house, and you won't tell me anything that's going on."

"Look," Nolk said, taking her by the shoulders, her skin like crumpled paper under his fingers, her body seemingly translucent. He could have peered through her toward the light. "I don't know if you know this or not, Jennifer, but maybe it's time that you did know. You see, for a good many years I've been dealing in drugs, not taking them, you understand, not trying to hook anyone either, just in the distribution part of it for the market that's already established, and I seem to have gotten into a complicated situation."

"I knew that," she said. "I knew what you've been doing. Do you think I'm stupid?"

"So if you knew what I was doing, Jennifer," Nolk said reasonably, "then why are you objecting to it now? This is all part of the business, don't you understand? Now and then you get into problems, complications, and there's a little bit of that now, other interests, you understand, that may want the share of the business that I've carefully built up, without having any right to do it. I've put my *life* into this, you understand, don't you, Jennifer? I've got a good piece of myself wrapped up in this, and so do you, because it's provided a good living—"

"I don't care about that," she said. "I don't care what your business is, don't you think that I knew that years ago? Anyone could tell that. And I never said anything against it, because if it was something that you wanted to do, well, then you were entitled."

Downstairs two of the guards were shouting at each other. Apparently one had stumbled over the other while coming into the living room, and the second was in a rage, not only because he had been inadvertently kicked but because the living room was his territory and he took it as an infringement. Nolk let the shouts go on, feeling little shudders of passage through his body. It really was a ridiculous situation, he had to admit that. In certain ways Jennifer had a point. It was not a normal suburban weekday morning. "You son-of-a-bitch!" one of the guards said, and there was the sound of a slap. "They'll settle it," Nolk said quickly, taking his wife's wrist. "Just let them work it out between the two of them; it doesn't have to concern us at all."

"It can't go on this way," she said. "I was willing to put up with it because, after all, it was your life, you were doing what you wanted to do, and I wouldn't stand in your way. But when you start bringing men into the house, when they start to carry on in here, when even the house isn't mine . . ."

"Oh, come on, Jennifer," Nolk said, "come on, be reasonable."

She stamped her foot. He could not believe it; it was a literary expression, but he had never in actuality seen a woman stamp her foot, even the helpless, dim little girls he had bedded, when he had left them in the late evening telling them that it was impossible for him to stay any longer, and no, he could not make arrangements to see them again. "Don't you tell *me* to be reasonable," she said. "This is your business, your disgusting choices, and it was *you* who brought all these people into the house. I didn't mind as long as you kept to yourself, but this is *my* house, too. Remember, I signed the mortgage, I was the one who got the down payment up. I tell you, I don't have to stand for this!"

Nolk looked at her and thought of murder. He had never murdered anyone in his life, at least face to face; assigned jobs and things like letting the guards kick the shit out of Harris were different, of course. He really was not responsible for things like this. But looking at his wife, it occurred to him that he could indeed kill her, that, pushed to the edge of patience, he could strangle her in his own hallway and entertain no other feeling than a hope that he could get away with it. "Get out of my way," he said, and moved her wrist up, pushed her across, and tried to move past her. Downstairs, to the guards, to the basement and Harris, anywhere. But away from her. "Get out of my way," he said again.

"You can't do it," she said. "You can't just walk away from your problems, you've got to face them. I want to talk to you, I'm going to talk to you, and you can't avoid it." And she came against him like a net, grappling with him, her arms swinging. She was drawing him in, he could not stand it, she was bringing him in closer and closer, and he could not drag free, and fury seized him, he wrenched away furiously and said, "Goddamnit," and brought his hand, slow and awful, upon her, her eyes turning solemn, but just at that first satisfying moment when he would have struck her, and everything therefore would have changed, there was a sound of rustling downstairs, and then a dull explosion, and the screaming and chanting of the guards broke the more interior and deadly chant of his own consciousness telling him to kill her, as he broke and ran down the stairs and toward the man who would kill him.

XIV

Wulff had had a difficult trip, but now he was at the end of it, and he simply would have to take his chances. Williams' turning him down had not been unexpected by any means, but he had had, after all, to have a try; his dedication was complete, and if you were dedicated to a mission, you worked every alternative. Williams had refused, as Wulff had suspected that he would, and that had left him in a hell of a spot; a beat-up Fairlane and a couple of battered pistols were not exactly the equipment that you would want to take into Armageddon. Still, he had struggled with worse and had gotten through. Letting the man named Harris go might have been a bad move, but Wulff had recoiled, finally, at the sight that he had had into the joy that he was beginning to take in murder, and in that spirit he wanted to let at least one sure victim go. It wouldn't make any difference in his battle; Harris was a pitiable basket case, hired muscle without muscle, but it might give Wulff credit on some abstract balance sheet somewhere, and he had a suspicion that the way things were going, he could use all the credit that he could get. Wulff did not exactly believe in the concept of an afterlife, but he did not reject it either; it seemed to fall into a perilous kind of half-possibility, like really good sex or an absolutely unblemished, angry, incorruptible narcotics squad in a major American city, and granted that it was best to make some kind of preparations, give himself a little credit just in case it should turn out that what he had rejected all along turned out to be true, and there he was dragged up before judgment and called a murderer, crazy too, because he had been trying to come to terms with the international drug trade. Harris had been slobberingly grateful. He had crawled out of the car like a bent, broken little animal, almost licking at the mud of the Interstate on which Wulff had let him go, and as he had raised his eyes, wide and damp, caught in the flickers and reflections from the Fairlane's dome light, he had said with awesome simplicity, "You wouldn't put me through all of this to kill me, now, would you? I mean, you're not just doing this to torture me and you're going to shoot me just as soon as I think that I've been freed." No, Wulff had said, he was not going to do anything like that; he understood that Harris probably did work for men who would operate in such a fashion, take pleasure, as a matter of fact, in that torment, but he, Wulff, was on the level. Then, in a flare of disgust he had tugged the door closed and left Harris there, his last image of the man being of supplication, the form crouched in the roadway.

Shit. It was all shit; in certain ways he had become as corrupt and despicable as the men he was fighting. Still, you became your enemy in Christian crusade; that was Western religion for you, and your only salvation was the mission itself as purifying. So he would not worry about that anymore, and if Harris carried back word to Nolk about what he had done, so much the better: scare the shit out of Nolk. That was all. Harris had told him plenty about that man on the way; Wulff thought that he understood the situation pretty well. Nolk was a key. He was not *the* key, the ultimate enemy, in the sense that the old man Calabrese had been, but he was good enough; scoring off him would be scoring something. He was on top of the new rank that was coming like scum to the surface in the removal of the old.

Wulff needed some weaponry, though. He got it by knocking down a sporting-goods store in suburban Mobile no more than two hours before he made his attack on Nolk. The sporting-goods store was in a huge shopping center, and it was easy for Wulff to pull his car right up in front of it, leave the doors open, the engine running, set his pistol, and walk right into the empty store, where he saw the old owner bent over the counter showing a single customer the open stock of a rifle. "Big son-of-a-bitch," the owner was saying. "It'll knock the ass off an elephant at a hundred yards, I'll tell you that." He adjusted his glasses, which were slipping down on his fat shining face, then looked up at Wulff as if he could not believe the presence of the pistol. "Yes sir," he said.

"I want about five rifles," Wulff said, "and I could use a steel trap big enough to hold a bear, although it's not a bear I'm looking for, and a couple of hand grenades." He gestured with the pistol. "Fast," he said.

The customer, a man in his twenties wearing a stocking cap in eighty-degree weather and apparently none the worse for it, made a gulping sound and fell to his knees in front of the counter. "Oh, my God," he said, "you're not going to shoot me, are you? I just can't stand it, you can't come in and do this to me." Hunched against himself in what seemed to be a sudden wind, he wrapped his arms around his neck. "It isn't fair," he said, "it just isn't fucking fair."

The proprietor, however, seemed to have a striking calm, or then again, it may only have been the sheen of sweat which made a brief mask on his face, which gave him a solemn but controlled acceptance. "Hey, now," the proprietor said, "this here mall is patrolled by twenty-four-hour security guards, you can't just come in and do something like this. They got the cable tv, they got a coaxial connection right into the police chief's office."

"Don't fuck with him, Maury," the customer said on the floor. "He's a killer, can't you see it marked up all over his face? He's as ready to shoot us dead as to ask nicely, Maury. Give him what the hell he wants, Maury."

"Now, you look here, Fred," the proprietor said, leaning down, fixing Fred with a steely eye, "this is my store, you just let me handle it the way I find necessary. You see, you can't get away with it," he said to Wulff gently, "not with this here fucking security patrol and with all the protective mirrors and devices we have here. Now, if you have any sense, young man, you'll just leave quietly."

"No," Wulff said, and gestured with the pistol, then shrugged and put a shot into the ceiling, the sound of fracture in the plastic of the overhang making the three of them jump, "I don't have time to listen to your reactions," he said, "I just need what I asked for. The five rifles and the steel trap. I guess you wouldn't have the grenades, though," he said almost wistfully.

"Oh, my God, Maury," the customer said, and seemed, if possible, to grip himself even more tightly, "he's a criminal maniac. He's going to kill us all."

"The security system," the owner said. His calm was really amazing under the circumstances, but then again, he might merely have been stupid. That was the more logical explanation—that the full significance of the situation had not permeated and never would. "A shot like that is going to set off security in the mall. There ought to be ten people in here in just a few minutes. That's all right, though," he said, as Wulff lifted the pistol again, "I'll get you your stuff. I mean, it doesn't matter to me, everything's insured. If you think that you can get it and get away before they come in, that suits me."

"Maury, you know that security doesn't mean a shit here," Fred said from the floor. "Don't tell him about security; you're liable to get him mad. I don't want to die; all I came in here for was a little instruction. Let him clean out the whole store, Maury; what's a store to a life? Don't be a stubborn fool."

But Maury had already turned, was heading toward the storeroom. Wulff covered him carefully with the pistol. "That's all right," Maury said at the small door that opened into the back, "I won't do anything. I'm just going to come back with your stuff."

"No good," Wulff said. "I'll have to go in there with you."

"What about me?" Fred said hopefully. "Does that mean that I can leave now? I won't say a word. I'll just go right to my car and drive out of here. I swear to God I don't care what you do. I wish you *luck* holding up the place. It doesn't matter to me."

"He can't let you out, Fred," Maury said, "he's going to have to tie you up or something. I think that's the only way this is going to work."

"Oh, for Christ's sake," Wulff said. It was certainly one of the clumsiest robberies that had ever been pulled off, he thought; there was no grace to it at all. Also, despite what Fred had said about security, there was the chance that they would be efficient and show up, although Wulff's limited experience with shopping-mall private cops had been that they were even less efficient than the old night watchmen at government installations, who were otherwise the bottom of the barrel. "Just go in there and get me some rifles and grenades. Forget the trap. I'll stay with him. You try anything," he said to the owner, "and I'll have to shoot him, that's all."

"Now, listen here," Fred said, "I don't want to get involved. I just came in here to—"

"It's all right," the owner said. "It's up to you. It's your business; I'm not going to try anything at all," and then he went through the door and into the rear of the store. Wulff looked down at Fred, who stared at him sullenly, massaging his shin. He seemed, in Maury's absence, now to be utterly embarrassed. "Security really is shit in this place," he said. "No one's going to bother you."

"All right."

"They had a rape in a bakery here last week. Some fifty-three-year-old woman. That'll show you what kind of shit-kickers we got around here. The guy must have been with her fifteen, twenty minutes, with the buzzers going and everything. No one came. They won't bother you."

"Hope not."

"Far as I'm concerned, if you can get away with anything, it suits me. Everything comes out of the insurance anyway. The mall will have to carry it."

"That's their problem."

"You need the rifles and flak for anything in particular, or you just kind of like them?" Fred said.

"I'm fond of them. I'm very fond of rifles and grenades. I'm trying to build up a collection."

"Well," Fred said, "well, that's a good thing. I guess. Building up a collection, I mean." He rubbed his shin again meditatively, and a silence passed between them. There seemed little more to say. Looking through the bleak surfaces of the glass, Wulff could see no bodies, only cars moving, drifting around like confused insects in the open lanes of the parking lot. No one seemed to be on foot, no one was in the vicinity of the sporting-goods store, which, Wulff noticed for the first time, was named Maury's, the name in fine running script fore and aft. He stood there with the pistol balanced in his hand, feeling awkward and wondering if he had made the right decision in allowing Maury to go into the back room by himself. He could, of course, have another telephone in there and be using it to summon the police at just this moment. The threat to kill Fred, Wulff suspected, did not hold much water with Maury. He was not exactly holding the owner's wife and children. But then again, it was the best that he could do. He was doing the best that he could under the circumstances; it was all that could be asked of a man. Considering the circumstances under which he had to work, he did not think that he was open to criticism Not really, anyway. What the hell.

Maury came back, rifles strewn over his body, one dangling on a strap from his neck, two jammed under his arms, another in the fold of his waist as he sidled out, bent over. In his hand he had a large, dirty gray box in which something jiggled. "I could find only four in good order," he said, staggering to the corner and letting the rifles drop, putting the box between them. "And they're hunting rifles. They're really only good for that, but they're the best that I can do under the circumstances. I got the grenades, though," he said, shaking the box. "They're pretty old Army-issue stuff, but I think they work. You know, we're probably the only sporting-goods store in the whole state of Alabama that would even carry them."

"Maury, don't fuck with him," Fred said. "Don't tell him about the fucking state of Alabama, just give him the stuff and let him go. That's what you want, isn't it?" He staggered to his feet, apparently cramped from his position of retreat, slapped dust from his pants. "I mean, you don't want him to exhibit the fucking rifles, do you? He doesn't have to prove that the grenades work one by one. You're pulling a robbery here. You just want to take the stuff and go, right?"

"Fred . . ." Maury said.

"I mean, I'm just out of patience, Maury. There's a guy in here with a gun trying to pull a robbery here, threatening us with a firearm, willing to kill, and all you can do is talk about how you're the only fucking sporting-goods store in the state of Alabama that might be able to give him some grenades. Now, that just don't make no sense, Maury. You ought to give him the stuff and let him go. I don't think he wants conversation anyway; I think that he just wants to pull the robbery and get out of here. Ain't I right, mister?"

"You have a point, Fred."

"Maury, why don't you and I just give this man here a helping hand with these goods. We can put them in his car for him and just send him on his way. It's the Ford right out there, isn't it?" Fred said, and pointed.

"That's the one."

"Well, come on," Fred said. "What are we waiting for? It's all arranged, isn't it? We're going to give him a hand and get these goods into his car, and he'll take off. Don't worry about us looking at the license plate or anything like that. I mean, we don't give a damn, friend, it's all covered by insurance anyway, isn't that right, Maury?"

"Damned straight," Maury said, "except for those grenades. Nobody knows I've got grenades here. That would come as some little surprise to a lot of people if they realized what I had stored up in that back room. Those little beauties are uninsurable."

"See what I mean?" Fred said, gesturing at Wulff. His eyes were heaving and twitching within his face, as if manipulated by inner strings, but his voice and manner were firm, firmer at any rate than Wulff had seen them so far. He was probably a pretty good man on his own terms, Wulff thought; the fact that he was a little bit of a coward was something that would show up under only unusual circumstances, and ninety-five percent of the men like Fred in this world could get through without even realizing themselves what they were, because the world would never put them in a situation like this. "Here's a man really putting out for you."

"All right," Wulff said. He supposed that the situation had its aspects of humor; at least, if you looked at it in a certain way you could see that it might be amusing. There was an absurdity to this which he might have investigated if he had the time, but right now, only putting together some ordnance and making the attack on Nolk mattered. "Sure, you can help me get it out to the car."

"You see, Maury?" Fred said, as if he had won a bet, "you see what I mean, you see what I'm saying now?" and went to the counter, gathered up all four rifles in a staggering lift and tottered toward the door. The older man took the box of grenades, giving the counter a few swipes, as if to clean the part where the dust from the box had settled, and followed him, and Wulff brought up the rear, holding the pistol on them. He had the suspicion, however, that he would not need it at all.

And he did not. At the Fairlane, Fred and Maury waited politely, almost deferentially, while he put in the keys and popped the trunk, then inserted the rifles and grenades quickly, with the deftness of stevedores, and stood quietly while Wulff wrestled down the lid and then looked quickly over the flat parking lot, at the line of shops like thin lights on a panel behind him. There was a little car movement in the distance, but otherwise there was no one else around at ten in the morning. "I don't think that this place has much of a future," Wulff said.

"I'll agree with you there," Maury said. "It's dropping dead."

"But it's a nice place," Fred said. "They got a lot of nice shops, don't they, Maury? Nice people working here. They just don't do no good promotion."

"Nice people? Not nice people, they're just a bunch of thieves," Maury said. "They've been milking us blind, going for every cent that they could in rent and improvements; otherwise we don't give a damn. We're trying to get some kind of an association together," he said, "but everybody's afraid, really. That's the trouble, you know, everybody's scared. They don't want to band together to help themselves, so you can't get anywhere."

"Well," Wulff said, "why don't you get back in the shop, then? I'm afraid I'm going to have to tie you up or something; I don't want you calling the police before I have a chance to get out of here."

"Oh, we wouldn't do no such thing," Fred said, "believe me, we wouldn't think of it, would we, Maury?"

"Sure not."

"We'll just go back there and sit and chat for maybe twenty minutes, twenty-five minutes, until you have a good head start. Matter of fact," Fred said a little wildly, "we'll go in there and talk for an *hour* if you want. I mean, everything's insured, right, Maury? What do we give a fuck about it anyway. Let the damned companies worry about it, let the mall itself—"

"Except the grenades," Maury said. "You can't ignore the grenades. I couldn't get insurance on those, because no one's supposed to know that I had them, and possession is probably illegal. But what the hell, there was a good market for those grenades. I could have gotten a hundred, maybe a hundred and fifty apiece for them if I had a chance to sell them. Not that I'm mad about this," he said hastily, looking up at Wulff, spreading his palms. "I mean, it's all in the line of business, right? Win some, lose some. I shouldn't complain."

"Yeah," Wulff said, "you shouldn't complain," and made a gesture with the pistol, and willingly they shuffled back ahead of him into the store and then under the fluorescence turned toward him expectantly, their eyes questioning. "All right," he said, looking at them, "all right, then. The hell with it. I'm going to go."

"That's damned nice of you," Fred said, "and you're not making a mistake, let me get that clear to you, because—"

"Don't call anyone," Wulff said, and backed out of the store. "Give me half an hour. If you break your word, you know that I'm going to find you somehow. You know you'll pay for this. If I don't get you, friends of mine will."

"Sure," Maury said, "sure, I understand."

"Yeah," Wulff said, and went back into the car and drove away from there straight into the area of Mobile where Nolk lived. Harris had given him some specific instructions, and he had little trouble in finding the house, which, like the houses of almost all the men with whom he had dealt, was expensive and nicely insulated. One thing you could say about these men was that they lived well.

He wasn't too worried, somehow, about Maury or Fred putting in a call to the police. Perhaps he was looking at matters in too wry or optimistic a way, but there was a feeling of collaboration with the two, almost as if they secretly admired and felt themselves to be on the side of a man who would so willingly take on the system and its assumptions. No man who sold weapons for a living and had a secret cache of grenades could identify with the police. Then too, the insurance *would* cover the theft, and Wulff had the feeling that whatever happened, Maury would make out considerably better from the insurance than he would have by painfully, piece by piece, trying to sell off his inventory.

The block on which Nolk lived was being patrolled by guards. Wulff could see that, could see the two men casually standing near the trees at the turn-in point, and knew right away from the way that they were handling themselves, a certain counterpoint in their movements and sense of connection between the two, that they were definitely on patrol and that the patrol had everything to do with Wulff. You could pick up those signals if you had had any kind of reconnaissance experience in combat; Wulff had had plenty of that in Vietnam, but more important, he had spent the last several months coming close in on men who had urgent reasons not to want to see him.

The first thing to do was to take a pass, handle the situation the way the bullfighter handles a dangerous bull, with cape and grace and evasion. He drove the Fairlane unobtrusively past the two men at right angles to the street which they were covering, hoping that they did not have a specific description of the car, or that if they did, they were not paying close attention. On long patrol, lapses of attention were inevitable, and any commander had to take them into account, for the enemy, for his own troops. Wulff drove the car down half a mile of empty street quietly, just letting it coast, moving by the curb at slow idle, playing with the brake. It was a Saturday morning in what was already a quiet neighborhood. No one was around. A little later on there might be a few children, but in a neighborhood like this, the children were indoors or in their own backyards, and the adults and teen-agers took automobiles everywhere. Two men on an empty street stood out. That was one of the advantages or disadvantages of suburban living: street reconnaissance could hardly be undertaken subtly.

It was a nice neighborhood on the northern outskirts of a relatively cosmopolitan Southern town. The houses, most of them ranch or split-level, got their space by spreading across the property, not arching above it, as was common almost everywhere except in the Northwest, where land had a different valuation. The houses, Wulff estimated, were in the forty-to-fifty-thousand-dollar range, expensive for Mobile, but then again, hardly palatial. They were not estates. It was just a nice area for nice people who worked hard at nice jobs and wanted to give their children nice lives. If there were suicides, cancer, miscarriages, and death here, they would occur offstage in the quiet areas of the inner city, the hospitals and funeral homes, which were left to deal with the refuse of the suburban life when the refuse came home.

But right now it was just a nice, quiet suburb. All of Wulff's quarry seemed to live in nice places. It was those whom they serviced, those at the bottom of the line, who lived in alleyways or bombed-out SRO flats in the central cities; it was the customers who shot the shit who lived there, but the dealers and distributors, the quiet, semipolished men who had created and serviced the habit, all lived very nicely, thank you. In Boston they lived by the Charles, in San Francisco by the Bay, in New York by the Sound; here by the Gulf of Mexico. And, here too, almost every house had its swimming pool.

Wulff could almost enjoy the pastoral serenity of the same Mobile morning that must have entranced Grant's troops before they began their final sweep, just sitting and contemplating the way in which these new Americans had come to rest in a way that, on a smaller scale, was little more than a reconstruction of the old. Instead of plantation lawns, instead of slaves humming, instead of a rigid caste system, a nice inner city to stuff the majority of the blacks into, while the few who were able to get out of the inner city could be put into an equally nice but different suburb. America always came back to itself, that was for sure; the country was a wheel, that was all; it was not progress, but mere turning. Oh, Wulff could have thought about it for quite a while, including the complicated and interesting role that junk had come to play on the wheel when it seemed for a few perilous years in the early fifties that the lower classes just might do something really mindless and angry and attempt to pull down the system. That wouldn't have worked at all, and that was when the shit had really begun to pour into the inner cities. However, he had other business to do, which was to plan out an attack upon Nolk's house.

Nothing mattered but killing the man, of course. He had had quite enough of negotiations, quite enough of impassioned discussions with the likes of Díaz. After a while, sitting there with the car parked in neutral, left foot on the brake, right foot idling the motor, which had a severe miss anywhere above two thousand rpm, Wulff shrugged and reached behind him, plucked one of the rifles from the back seat, and put it beside him, then reached across the front to the gray box that Maury had yielded so reluctantly. He pried off the lid lovingly, looked at the little black turds of grenades nestled against one another, twelve of them squat and mysterious in the box, and then worked his hand in, took one out, hefted it carefully.

It felt all right. A live grenade had a certain cast and heft to it, which this one possessed; he could feel the fragments within sifting and settling. He looked at the pin, dead center, and the pin looked all right too, well oiled and slick, no rust on it; they were good product, all right. Maury had done himself proud, from whatever source. The only question was whether they would work, and that was something that he could find out only in performance. There could be no test runs in this quiet and sleeping neighborhood. It would lead to difficulties he was not prepared to face.

Wulff smiled finally and laid the object in his lap. He loved grenades. Every man had a weakness, it was said, and in his new person, his post-Marie Calvante persona, that was, this must be his. From where he was sitting, the grenade was the most efficient, deadly, workable instrument of war available. It was also the most satisfying. There was a lot of pain from a grenade. The fragmentation was apt to cause blindness, the shrapnel could cut a body open.

Still smiling, Wulff turned the car around and drove back to the street on which Nolk lived. At the street entrance he cut sharp left and came past the two men, tires screaming, pistol cocked, moving one-handed. He was twenty yards past them before they could react, and by that time he was beside the house, had stopped the car, and had both hands free.

Wulff yanked the car into neutral, picked up the grenade, stepped out of the car quickly, coming around low to use the hood as cover, and in one easy pitch threw the grenade at the house, aiming high for a rooftop punch. It came down, and at that moment the first shots came, and Wulff used the pistol to return fire and put down one of the men at once, and while the other halted at once, thinking about this, the grenade fired and the house started to blow up, and Wulff, diving beneath the left side of the car, was able to have a perfect view of all of it in almost complete safety.

The second man, however, standing, had no such opportunity, and soon fell from Wulff's line of sight.

XV

Nevertheless, hating himself but feeling that he had to do it—but not able to explain the reasons for feeling that way either—Williams went the next day to the assistant commissioner's office without an appointment on his free time, waited through the chain of command until the inspector had allowed him in, then, without any introduction, told him everything he knew about Wulff, which was, of course, not much. But he told about the phone call, the request for ordnance, and the fact that Wulff was near Mobile.

The assistant commissioner had the same question too. "Why are you telling me all this?" he said.

"I'm cooperating with the law. Why are you asking me why I'm obeying the law, commissioner?"

"It isn't that. Of course the law should be obeyed. But yesterday you said you knew nothing, and now you're prepared to put all this information on the line."

"The call just came in since we spoke, commissioner."

"I understand that too. But still . . ."

"It's puzzling? You don't know why I'd turn him in? You think I think he's a hero, that I shouldn't squeal on a hero?"

"He's not a hero. He's a maniac. We settled that. Anybody who thinks this man is heroic is crazy. He's more dangerous than the people he says he's fighting."

"I know that."

"But it's still hard to believe. It's hard to believe that he just happened to call."

"He would call me, commissioner. I'm the only man that he could call. He's got no one else now."

"All right," the man said, "all right. I accept that. He's in Mobile, then."

"He says he is. He was heading in that direction, anyway. Of course, he might have been interrupted."

"We ought to be reading about that pretty soon if it's true," the commissioner said with a little smile. "I'm sure that he'll make his presence known."

"Aren't you going to call in federal strike?"

"I'll handle this as I see fit," the commissioner said. "I want to thank you for the information, of course."

"You're telling me to get out, right? I told you what I had to tell you; now I should just get on my way."

"Patrolman, you're a little out of line. You know I appreciate your cooperation; in fact, your cooperation has been deemed essential, but—"

"My ass is in a sling," Williams said, standing. "It's been in a sling for eight months now, but it's practically hanging out."

"Now, I don't know what you're talking about."

"I think you know exactly what I'm talking about."

"I don't take to this kindly. I said you're out of line, and I'll repeat it. Now, I'm ready to thank you for your cooperation and to ask you to keep us posted should any other calls come in, and I think we should control ourselves, patrolman."

"Wulff was right," Williams said, "he was right. I thought he was wrong, and then I thought he was right, and then I've been thinking he was wrong again, but now I know. Now I know what's going on. It's the only way."

"Don't counsel felonies, patrolman."

"I'm not counseling anything," Williams said, and went to the door. "I'm at the bottom of the ladder. What the hell influence does a cop have? I don't have to counsel felonies," he said, "the law does," and the door opened and he went through it, and all the way down the gray line of offices past the gray people in the hallway performing in their gray fashion in the bright and terrible tasks of the city, he thought: general delivery Mobile, general ordnance Mobile, oh, shit, if he calls again, if he gives me one more chance, I'll do it . . . and am I ever, ever going to be out of this?

XVI

After the first blast there was a secondary explosion that made the house shudder, and then up and down the block glass began to blow out in the other dwellings. Wulff, crouched behind the Fairlane, watched it dispassionately, knowing that in just a few seconds now doors would start to open, the screaming would begin, the phone calls to the police would be made if phones were still in operation; but he had time, he had just the necessary little bit of margin that he needed, and in that small bubble of time he watched the house with unusual intentness, waiting to see who would come out. If no one did, he was going to go in there, but it was worth waiting, to judge what kind of shape the people within might be in at this time.

A man with black all over his body, clothing ripped, came staggering out of the door, his hands flailing, his mouth an O for a scream that Wulff could not hear. Wulff aimed the pistol and dropped him with a clean shot in the solar plexus, then held his position and waited. A second man came the way of the first, looking just as disheveled but with the presence of mind to be holding a gun. He was shouting, shrieking, looking frantically around him, and Wulff stood for an instant, just so the man could see what had happened to him, and then pulled the trigger, and this man too was dead. Wulff crouched down again, waiting, and a third man came out, his eyes flicking right and left, searching the street for the guards. Wulff shot him in the neck in a clean, pumping shot that dropped him on top of the body of the second. That was excellent.

He did not know which one was Nolk, of course, but it was reasonable to assume that he had just killed three bodyguards. Nolk would not come out of that house first; to the contrary, he would, if conscious, have ordered the others out first, and only then, after having seen what had happened to them, would he come out. That was merely business; it was the way any businessman would act. Still, Wulff was a little surprised to see a woman come staggering out of the house next, a woman in her fifties who was obviously in distress, and yet, unlike the men, showed no signs of dishevelment; she was probably Nolk's wife. At least, that was as good a guess as any. Wulff kept the pistol trained, and then, after a moment, he lowered it slightly. He could not shoot a woman, at least without absolute provocation. She might have everything to do with Nolk's business, she might for all he knew have been the originator of all schemes, but you had to draw a line somewhere. Otherwise you were nothing but an indiscriminate murderer, he thought. He held the pistol steady, at his side. The woman leaned weakly against the side of the house and began to retch.

He should be going, Wulff knew. It was impossible to stay here much longer; a hundred calls must have come into the police by now, and it would be a matter of moments or less until they were swarming all over. He had a better than reasonable chance to escape now, but only if he did it immediately, and yet, tight against the Fairlane, he found that he could not move. Not yet. He wanted to see Nolk.

A man appeared at the door of the house, a stout man in his late fifties, who like the woman, did not appear disheveled, merely confused. That would have to be him, Wulff thought. It would have to be Nolk and his wife who had come out of the house last. Not near the front, not near the site of the explosion, they had been protected from physical injury, and yet, from the man's appearance, he had been as shaken as if he had been hurt. These people were good at insulating themselves, they were not nearly so adequate in putting up with what they routinely subjected their employees and victims to. Wulff looked at the stumbling, shaken man who stood in the doorway and smiled. The first sound of sirens, wavering, came at him.

Easy, he thought; it was almost too easy to shoot the man where he stood. There had to be another way, one which would pay ample penalty for what this man had done to thousands of others. Death, quick death, was the easy way out; Nolk would go scuttling down the trap of his mortality, and then he would be out, clean at the other end, never to be touched again. It was not fair at all; it should not be this way; there would hopefully be developed by science sometime a means by which the dead could be resuscitated to full awareness and pain only so that they could be killed again over and over, each time more horribly, and this would be a treatment reserved only for the worst of criminals; but until that time, you had to settle for the clean death, the quick one, and leave it to other forces to extract true vengeance. You had to sustain belief in religion or an afterlife only in the hope that people like Nolk would get theirs in full measure. He stood so that the man could see him then. He wanted to be seen.

"Here I am, Nolk," Wulff called to him. "Look at me, you son-of-a-bitch. Look at me."

In the doorway the man twitched his head feebly, looked at him. The woman, four yards downrange, still against the house, bracing herself now with her arms, looked at him too. "No," she said. Her voice carried very distinctly. It was remarkable how well her voice carried against the background of the sirens. "Don't do it."

"Look at me, Nolk," Wulff said again, "look at me," and the man twitched his gaze downward, was looking at the concrete. He does not want that moment of contact, Wulff thought; he thinks that if he does not recognize me, if he turns away and denies, that I won't kill him, and this made him giggle slightly, because Nolk of all people had no business working through implied codes. "It's me," Wulff said to him, "it's me, Burt Wulff, that's who it is," and pointed the gun at the man and shot him in the head.

The thing that was Nolk, already dead, came down into the doorway and then lay there openmouthed. The woman was screaming in a high, thin, contained way. Wulff looked at her and then put his pistol away and opened the door of the Fairlane.

But she had stood away from the house now, was impossibly moving toward him. She was a woman in her fifties who had been destroyed a long time ago, with whose destruction the events of the morning had had absolutely nothing to do, and yet there was a kind of strength in her as she approached Wulff, a strength that he could see. "You killed him," she said, looking at him as he bent over the car. "You killed my husband."

The sirens were all around them now. He should be going, Wulff knew, if he were going to get out of here, and yet what she had said demanded some kind of answer. Fair was fair. You did not come calling without saying the proper words of departure; you did not deal rudely with your host unless you made yourself well understood. "He deserved to be killed," Wulff said. "He was a bad man."

"Nobody deserves to be killed."

"That never occurred to your husband. He was killing people."

"He never wanted to. He was only doing what he must."

"What your husband felt he must do was something that was killing people," Wulff said.

"You're a murderer."

"So was he."

"I'll remember you. I'll remember who you are and give a full description. They'll get you for this." She looked frantically up and down the street, grabbed his wrist. "All those bodies," she said. "What are you? What kind of man are you?"

Revulsion filled him; he broke from the slippery and glassine aspect of her touch. "Your husband *made* me necessary," he said. "Can't you understand that? Anything that I am, he created."

"Kill me," she said. "I'll identify you otherwise. You don't want that, do you? Go on. You've killed everybody else."

"I don't want to kill you."

"Yes you do. You want to kill everyone. I can see it in your face, your eyes. You're a killer."

The sirens were much closer. Wulff knew that his time for escape could not be within a margin that exceeded thirty seconds. Farther behind there was dim clanging; they were sending the fire trucks too. They would send everyone to this, and they would spend the next hours pouring, sifting, photographing, arguing. "No I'm not," he said, "not by choice, anyway. It just turned out that way. I'm made. I'm a made killer."

"Killer!"

"All right," he said then, "all right, if I'm a killer, then have it your way, say it, the hell with it," and dived within the car, leaped for the steering wheel, and turned on the ignition. The car started reluctantly, moved.

"You're a killer!" the woman screamed as he backed quickly off the street, bumping prone bodies, and as he looked at her ravaged face, her thin outstretched arms, the keening and penitential thrust of her body, it occurred to him that somewhere there was a profound irony here, one of the greatest so far, because what she was trying to convey to him and what he deeply and sincerely was beginning to believe was that in a dark but yet innocent way she had really loved her husband.

XVII

After the cops quit questioning and went away, after the newspaper stories had appeared about the massacre on the Alley, but somewhat before the moment of last confrontation, Maury put the pieces together painfully in his mind. Obviously the man who had robbed them was the same man who had then gone up to the Alley and killed a lot of people, and in both cases the man was the one called the Wolf, who had been running around the country for some months now knocking off all kinds of the criminal element. It had been quite an honor for Maury, in a way, to be held up by him, but it also—and the cops made this clear during the interrogation—in a certain way implicated him in everything that had happened. They hadn't quite connected the grenades to Maury yet, but sooner or later if they did there was a chance that Maury would be netted as some kind of accessory after or during the fact, and if there was one thing that he did not need, it was shit like that. He could wind up going to prison because of something that some lunatic had done. The grenades were strictly private stock; he had had no intention of giving them to anyone who could not pay a stiff price and guarantee that Maury would not be connected with them, and now look at what had happened. Well, it meant that he had very strong, very personal reasons to want that bastard out of the way.

Sure. Wulff was the only one who could tie him, after all, to the grenades, and if he were out of the picture, that would seal Maury's safety. Of course, there were a lot of people who had tried to put Wulff out of the picture for even stronger reasons and had had no success . . . but Maury had a feeling. He just had a feeling that he might be able to do it for exactly that reason: who the hell would suspect him of having any interest in Wulff? What would Wulff himself care? Maury was just some insignificant clown, already forgotten, whom he had knocked off somewhere down the line.

And there was something else, too. An awful lot of people wanted to see Wulff dead. An awful lot of people had tried and failed, but that only made his death more valuable. There might, Maury thought, there might be a hell of a lot in it for him if he could do it. Risky, a long shot, but the rewards were real. It certainly looked better than looking forward to running in the sporting-goods business for the next thirty years or so. The hell with it.

Of course, there was the little problem of finding out where Wulff was and tracking him and doing the job, but he had one great advantage.

No one else really knew that either, and Wulff for sure wouldn't be looking for him. He was completely forgotten to Wulff, minor history. He could come up and have a clear shot.

It was worth it. It was worth investigating, anyway. Wulff would leave a spoor, and Maury would track it. Wulff would leave a trail, and Maury would be there. Close call at the shop; now Wulff's turn.

"Don't bother me," he said to his wife, who had said something irritably to him from the kitchen. "Don't bother me now, Liz, for Christ's sake. Can't you see that I'm trying to think something through?"

He shut off the light and for a while just sat in the living room smoking a cigarette and thinking about his main chance. That idiot Fred could tie him to the grenades too, come to think of it. He might have to do something about Fred as well. Later. Later on. All of the pieces would interlock like machinery winching its way toward the completion of something very complicated and deadly.

XVIII

Sperber, blinking in the sudden light, took the receiver off the shrieking pedestal. Four a.m. He couldn't talk in the dark, though, never could. "Hello," he said, "what the hell is it?"

"Leon?"

"What?"

"This you, Leon?"

"It's me," he said. He looked for his cigarettes. They were somewhere, had to be somewhere here. He found them, got one out, looked for a match. "What the hell is it? Who is this? It's four o'clock in the morning."

"I'm coming to kill you, Leon."

"What?"

"I've left my calling card in Mobile, and now I think I'll give Raleigh a try. Just moving north, Leon. Are you ready to die?"

"Who is this?" he said.

"This is your destiny," the voice said, "this is your destiny, Leon. This is retribution." It laughed in an easy and offhand way. "Four-o'clock retribution, my friend. It is four up there, isn't it? You don't have different time zones."

"Who is this?" he said again. Looking desperately for matches. "What do you want?" The body in the bed behind him moved and said, "Leon, stop talking in your sleep," and began to snore again.

"Destiny and retribution. You know, Leon," the voice said conversationally, "I thought one thing, and then I thought the other.

Should I call you and give you warning that I was coming, with the chance that you'd sneak away, or should I just come and nail you? It was kind of a hard decision to make. But I wound up making the same decision that I always do. I'm calling to tell you because I want you to sweat and know that it's coming and just wonder when and how. You don't have the guts even to run, Leon, so you'll just stay there and wait. And I'll get you. You know I'll get you."

"You're crazy. You're a crank."

"So hang up, Leon. That's what you do with crank calls, right? Just hang up. Go ahead."

He did nothing. He held the phone tightly, looking at the receiver. The receiver seemed to be sweating, of all things, but more likely it was moisture dripping from his forehead into his eyes. He lit a match one-handed finally, got the cigarette going, brought it away from his lips.

"You haven't hung up, Leon. You're still holding."

"You bastard," he said.

"That's it. Start swearing at me. That's what I like; it's a lot of fun when they start to curse, because that means that I'm really getting through. You can even start shooting if you want. Get your crack troops in and prepare a welcome for me. But I don't care. I've gotten through everybody's crack troops. Read about Jim Nolk, Leon?"

He felt the uneven palpitation beginning to move across his chest, the trembling that was the sign, his doctor had said, of nervousness, nothing to worry about, he didn't have a heart condition, shouldn't be concerned, but then again, he should do everything within his power to avoid situations of tension so that he didn't get himself into trouble; that was so easy to say. "You got the wrong man," Sperber said. "If you're who I think you are, you are talking to the wrong party." Palpitation and all, he began to feel slightly better, more in control. At least he knew with whom he was talking now, with whom he was dealing. That was better than the strange call in the night, the absolutely unknown assailant, which he had dreamed of now for thirty years. "I have nothing to do with Nolk," he said.

"Of course you don't."

"Really."

"Really. Of course really. You and Nolk were in competition, fighting for position. Getting him out of the way must have made you feel good, eh, Leon? Less to worry about. You must have felt really on top for a while then. Well, you had a short ride. You're next."

"You're crazy."

"True," the voice said, "I'm crazy. But that's not going to do you any good when you see your heart and lungs pouring out of you," and then the phone clicked.

Sperber held it for a while, smoking the cigarette and closing his eyes against the light. He could shut off the light, of course, and lie on the bed; that would have been the easier way around it, but he needed the light. He needed it in his room; he did not want to sit in the dark with this just now. The woman beside him murmured in her sleep and groaned, then yanked at the covers on which he was sitting, unseating him, and pulled them over her head. She was an attractive woman and a good fuck, but hell to sleep with. Where did that expression "sleep with" come from, anyway? You didn't want to sleep with a woman, you wanted to have sex with her, that was all. But most of the time you wound up sleeping together too, and that was the least part of it. If you could only truly compartmentalize your life so that you could use the parts of women you needed and otherwise not have to mess with them, not have all the goddamned bullshit, you would be a hell of a lot better off, that was for damned sure.

Well, too late for that now.

Nolk, Sperber thought meditatively, Nolk had been an asshole. The caller, though, was absolutely correct in one detail: he *had* been glad to get the news. Getting Nolk out of the way had been one less problem with which he would have to deal. But the caller was right too; he should have suspected that this Wulff had information and that somewhere Sperber was on the list.

That fucking Díaz talked too much.

Oh, well, Sperber thought, and put out the cigarette with one savage thrust against the wall, letting the spray of ashes come out like fireworks and momentarily consume the light, a pretty picture, something he had always liked to do. Sooner or later it had to happen; Wulff was absolutely correct, and it might as well happen now. The advance warning had been a mistake. There was a slight chance that he might have been taken by surprise, but Wulff, crazy Wulff, did not have the patience to simply do a job. He had gotten emotionally involved in it somewhere along the way. And now it was going to kill him.

Sperber stood, shut off the light, lay down in bed, drew up his knees, and thought about his plans. With the first light he would be on the phone and calling. Everything would be tight, all set. He would give Wulff a nice welcome all right.

Make the calls and arrangements by first light. And for God's sake, get this bitch out of the house first.

XIX

When Wulff walked into the bar to get some change for another phone call, the two men standing there attacked him, while the bartender, as if by prearrangement, dived for cover.

The attack was so savage, so little anticipated, that Wulff felt in real physical danger for the first time since Carlin had abducted him. It was just a quiet suburban roadhouse, too, on U.S. 1, just south of the city; that was the hell of it: you were all set for something like this in the inner city, but on the road, at noon . . . well, the hell with it. No time to think of that now.

The first man ran at Wulff, coming in low at shin level and knocking him down, and then the second, swinging a set of brass knuckles, came down on him hard, and Wulff felt the blows coming in around his kidneys, radiating pain. The first man was jammed underneath him, kicking, and Wulff could do nothing but reach out, grab what he could, and squeeze, his hands on the man's stomach, digging in; the man began to gasp. But even as he felt the strength begin to go from him, the one on top, swinging down, had hurt him with blows to the back of the neck, stunning blows that radiated pain up and down, and Wulff found his hold on consciousness beginning to weaken, as if his fingers were slipping from some bar of attention. Squealing, the man underneath him heaved, tried to unseat him, and reciprocally, Wulff's fingers came in, he felt the skin beginning to yield all the way. "No!" the man bellowed. "No, don't do it," and Wulff kept up the pressure, moving in desperately now, almost ignorant of the pain from above. Something cracked beneath, him and then he was lying on loose pulp, something horrid and slack underneath him, what had been a struggling form; and he rolled, rolled hard on the polished but splintered surfaces of the floor, not thinking of the second man now, only trying to establish some kind of distance, and reached inside his jacket to seize the gun, the pistol like a claw coming up against his hand, and then he had it, but the other man was charging, low to the floor, bent in upon himself, his body in an arc of concentration, and there was no time to level and fire. Glasses smashed on the bar, and then one went by Wulff's head, coming close, breaking on the wall just behind him. So the bartender was in that too, he thought, and then the diving man was around his knees, and Wulff was to the floor again.

It came up hard; he felt his face rebounding from the horrid impact, much faster and more painful than he would have thought, and, half-stunned, feeling that his features had grown to enormous size, he rolled on his back. The first kick came in, catching him low in the ribs, and then the second, aimed directly for his groin. But the assailant had kicked too fast, gotten eager, misjudged, and the kick went wide; as the leg came back slowly, Wulff grasped it, digging his fingers into the ankle. He squeezed, and the man gave a high, despairing shriek, not from pain but from a different hopelessness, knowing then that he was falling. Wulff yanked it back, and the man came tumbling, spattering onto the floor, landed with a groan.

Wulff tried to separate himself, stand to give the killing shot, but he could not disentangle. The man was squealing like an animal, a mixture of anticipation and fright, trying to grab Wulff, hold him in, and he went prone, seeing the slick and drenched surfaces of the bald head underneath him, finding himself forced in parody of embrace further down, and the second glass went by him, even closer. The bartender had poor aim, but everything was a matter of percentages; sooner or later he would get one of those glasses in, and then what? Then what? Fury vaulted Wulff above the man; he was on his feet, above him, and he began to kick, the first one driving through the man's ribs, caving them in with an audible splintering, which the man responded to in an almost incidental fashion, one absent scream as he shook on the floor and attempted to bring the brass knuckles up into Wulff's groin. Wulff barely got out of the way, tried a tentative second kick, which missed the man's neck and then on the follow-through got everything that he wanted, the kick, light and tentative, made while he was skittering away, catching the man in the temple. He could feel the man's skull give, thin and tentative at this point, and then the sigh he made as his brains exploded from within. Wulff recovered his balance and got his pistol fully in his hand, looked at the bartender, who was frantically digging below counter level. Something to throw, obviously, something stronger than glasses; if the man had had a gun, Wulff would have been dead by now. The bartender made a squealing noise as he saw Wulff bring the gun in on him, and then dived frantically to the boards; below there was a dim crash. Wulff came up to the bar, poised on the railing in a parody of a man about to order a drink, bent forward, peered over the bar, and aimed the pistol in.

The bartender came up fast, like a long-distance swimmer breaking to surface, using his head as a butting tool, eyes squeezed shut, panting, and the blow caught lucky, smashed the pistol from Wulff's hand and sent it skittering away. The bartender screamed and came up with a hand, swung blindly, and got Wulff on the forehead; Wulff, stunned, back-pedaled, and the bartender, reaching his hand across frantically, got a bit of Wulff's jacket and pulled him in again, got off another punch, which bounced off a cheekbone. He was fighting underwater, the bartender was, mumbling high prayers under his breath, but his luck was phenomenal; Wulff could appreciate it, even through the dull mask of pain that the blows brought, and then he could think no more, because the bartender, getting underneath the counter again, had found something really deadly, a small blackjack, which he threw with force and accuracy directly toward Wulff. Wulff could not dodge it, saw that instantly, could only bring up a hand to block the blow to some degree, and the hand up against the bridge of his nose took a stunning blow from the blackjack; he could tell from the way that it hit and the instant numbing that if it was not broken, it was close to, there was at least severe damage . . . but then again, the blackjack went skittering off his hand, banged against a wall, and the bartender, as if unmanned now by the failure of his one great gamble, had put up his hands, was staggering backward, reeling, crashing into the mirror.

He said nothing at all as Wulff came upon him with the pistol. At least you had to give him credit for that; the bartender was a professional, and how many men in this trade were? Practically none; only the old man in Miami had shown as much class as the bartender did now. Having played the game by the rules that he devised, he now seemed willing to die by them. He did not plead, he did not whine or beg, he did not even make a last, hopeless attempt to somehow cancel out Wulff's advantage. Instead he backed against the mirror, his back tight to it, and put his hands behind him, his head slightly bowed, and closed his eyes.

Waiting then. His apron, incongruously, dropped suddenly, held by only one of the strings, and then fell to the floor. He was wearing cheap corduroy pants. He was about fifty, but because of the bald head and blunt figure, looked considerably older than that. Nevertheless, he was very strong.

Wulff held the gun, looked at him. "Why?" he said.

The bartender said nothing at all.

"I just came off the highway to make a phone call here. What the hell? Were you waiting for me? How did you know that I'd come in here?"

The bartender was still shaking his head, biting his lips. His hands grasped one another, and then he wrung them slowly, despairingly, the way a woman might at hearing bad news. He was very quiet. The two men on the floor were both bleeding from the ears.

"It's stupid," Wulff said, "it's fucking stupid not to talk. You're going to die anyway. Why don't you do some good for once in your life and answer a few questions before I go?"

The bartender licked his lips. "Why should I?" he said in a very low voice.

"You want to live?"

The bartender said nothing. This was dangerous, Wulff thought. The bar was open, it was a roadhouse, it was noon; sooner or later, probably much sooner, someone was going to come in for a drink. Even in a place like this there was the possibility of trade. You just couldn't make a hell of a living beating up the people who dropped in; the word would get around, and business would fall off. You had to serve them a drink, at least occasionally.

"Jesus Christ," Wulff said, and wiped the back of the hand he thought was broken against his mouth. There were little flickers of pain, which was good; if it were broken, it would have been a screaming arc of anguish. "This isn't your affair, you know. This has nothing to do with any of you at all. Why do you let yourself get hired into it? You know what it's going to lead to?"

"Kill me," the bartender said. "Just kill me and get it over with, Eddie."

"Eddie?"

"Yeah, Eddie, you son-of-a-bitch."

"I think you missed something," Wulff said. "I'm not Eddie."

"I don't care what you say. Just shoot me."

"I think you guys have made an awful mistake," Wulff said. "You got the wrong guy. *I'm not Eddie.*"

The bartender opened his eyes fully, looked at him, blinked. "Of course you'd say that," he said. "It don't mean a thing. You're fucking Eddie."

"I wish I were."

"You can't be some other guy. Eddie was the only one we expected in. It was all set up."

"Well," Wulff said, "it wasn't set up too good. Or you got your scheduling screwed up. You got some other guy."

"Oh, shit," the bartender said.

"I'm sorry that you had to go through all that for the wrong guy."

"Oh, shit," the bartender said again. "I don't believe you, that's all. I can't believe you. Why would they do a thing like this to us? It was all set up."

"Wrong time," Wulff said, and looked at the pistol in his hand. "Now what?" he said with disgust. "What the hell am I supposed to do now? Go ahead and kill you anyway? You got screwed up."

"Nobody got screwed up," the bartender said desperately, "you're lying to me. You got to be Eddie."

"I wish I were," Wulff said, "oh, I wish I were now," and the door banged and a man came into the bar and looked at the two of them and then at the bodies on the floor and said, "Oh, my God," and turned quickly. He was a man in his early thirties with blond hair and an earring in his right earlobe.

"Eddie?" Wulff said.

The man turned and looked at him. "Oh, Jesus," he said, and then bolted through the door. There was the sound of glass tinkling somewhere, and then an engine screaming.

Wulff looked at the bartender. "I think that was your man," he said.

The bartender looked even sicker than he had before the man had come in. "Christ," he said, his hands coming down, shaking on the polished surface of the bar. "Oh, Christ." He looked much older, translucent and weak. "I'll be damned," he said.

"See what I mean?" Wulff said, and looked at the pistol in his hand. "That's clumsy work. Amateur work. Didn't you have a picture at least, or some kind of description?"

"They said he had to be in here at this time. They said that they were sending him right on. It's impossible . . ."

"Now what?" Wulff said with disgust, and looked at the bartender. "I have to kill you, I think," he said. "I can't leave any witnesses."

"It isn't fair," the man said weakly. "The whole damned thing doesn't make any sense."

"You telling me?" Wulff said. "You telling me?" He shot the man in the face and turned and went directly to his car and drove away, deciding that he would leave the business of giving Sperber a second call until he got a little closer in to his section.

XX

Sperber's first thought was to make a good line of defense and nail the son-of-a-bitch once and for all. His second, though, after much consideration, seemed to be better. He decided to pitch it in and run.

It just wasn't worth it, that was all. All of the reports were too rough, and besides that, he had six months' worth of newspapers and communiqués to study and sift through his mind. The guy was good, that was all. He was just too goddamned good and too angry for Sperber to want to deal with. If some of the best people in the business had been blown up by him, if no one from Vegas to Mexico City had been able to bring him down, one man, since this had begun, then Sperber had to be sensible about this. You had to admit your limitations; that was as important as self-confidence, and Sperber had not gotten as far as he had by being self-deluded. No, this Wulff was a one-man army. He was a shrewd, cold, cunning, and utterly efficient killer who could do the damage of a hundred men, and Sperber could not stand up against him. It was better to get the hell out, lie low for a while.

Sperber made this decision without fear. Fear was not part of the equation; after the first shock of the phone call he found that he could deal with the situation, emotionally, pretty well. He had plenty of time to think things over, and unlike Wulff's prediction, he had not used that time merely to sweat; he had instead worked things through gradually, carefully. But the more he looked at it, the clearer it seemed. He had to get out.

For one thing, nobody he called really wanted to stand with him. The contract men simply weren't having any. There was not a free-lancer around who wanted any part of the account anymore, for whatever bonus. There were a couple who owed Sperber personal loyalty and whom he certainly could have recruited, but they were all junkies. Every last one of them. You did not want a group of dopers out there trying to fend off a machine.

So it made sense to skip for a while, let Wulff blow himself down and out, let someone else take care of him. He couldn't go on this way anyway; half of the FBI was probably looking for him, in addition to what was left of the network. A couple days, weeks at the outside, and it would all be over. In the meantime, there seemed no sense to Sperber in adding his name to the kill list. It wasn't going to gain him anything. And he faced right up to it, he was an intelligent man. Wulff *could* kill Sperber. He was just too goddamned good.

Like everything else in his life, Sperber planned the skip carefully. The thing was to travel light and unencumbered and give an idea of his whereabouts to no one. That meant getting some kind of false cover story out to the few people with whom he was in daily contact, and it meant cutting Doris off very hard. The latter, at least, was a pleasure. He had had quite enough of the bitch; it had been a month with her, which was much longer than average, but she had been tenacious, had gotten hooks into him that the others hadn't. Also, he was getting older, and women were harder to shake. Still, he could deal with her now, and he did so quite cruelly, waking her up at nine in the morning and telling her that she was finished. That pleased him. Oh my, did she love to sleep; did she hate being awakened. But what he said to her would ruin her sleep for a few nights to come, he bet.

That taken care of, Sperber blew a little pot and considered his next move. He enjoyed pot; it was the only drug, soft or hard, that he would touch, but it improved his disposition and made everything always look just a little better than it had before he had a joint. He kept a small private stash in the bathroom hamper rolled up in a bag underneath dirty underwear; it was the only thing he would permit in the house. The other cache was elsewhere in a safe-deposit box. He was no fool; they were never going to get him on some cheap charge of possession. But the pot was different. Strange for a thirty-eight-year-old man to take up marijuana as he had two years ago after a lifetime of avoiding all opportunities for drugs, but what the hell. He enjoyed it. He enjoyed it now, holding the joint lightly in his fingers while he considered his next move. He would enjoy it wherever it was; the kids were right, it was fun, it was as relaxing as Scotch, without the hard, sick edge that alcohol could give you, and it was a hell of a lot cheaper and safer, at least if you were supplied with decent stuff, and if one thing was sure, it was that Sperber could find his sources of supply. Standing in his living room, he carefully tapped the butt out in an ashtray, took a small piece of silk out of his suit pocket, and pressed it reverently within, then put it all back. Waste not, want not.

Then he made his last preparations to leave. He had decided to go underground somewhere around Washington, find himself a motel off the main road, and under an assumed name just sit there for a week or two. He knew plenty of people, of course, any man in his position would, but this would be a strictly incognito job, and he would keep his cover for as long as necessary. Fortunately, no one here would miss him; that was one of the benefits of working wholly free-lance. And for himself. A lot of others kept their jobs as cover or simply used the drugs as a sideline, which meant that they were involved with a number of people on different levels, but none of this was true for Sperber. No one gave a damn about his comings and goings, when you came right down to it, except himself and the very few connections that he had. Not even the woman. It was the best way to live. At this stage of the game, when you were starting off, you had to be entirely dedicated to your business, make all the sacrifices that it entailed. Later on, when he was established, when he had less pressure of all sorts, he would put down roots, make a life for himself. But not now. The call in the middle of the night proved it, if any proof of that sort was needed. He simply could not expose a wife or a family to that kind of shit.

Sperber was not surprised when the phone rang. It didn't have to be Wulff; it could have been anyone. There were a lot of calls of a business nature coming in, particularly with the subtle arrangements he had made in order to make leaving town possible for a while. But then again, when he heard the voice, he was not surprised. It would figure that he would call again. Wulff was a thorough man. In certain ways he was almost as thorough as Sperber himself.

"Still there?" Wulff said.

"Yes. I'm still here."

"Scared?"

"I'll manage," Sperber said. The only thing he had to worry about was that the man was calling from very close quarters, that he was literally up the block, ready to strike. But Sperber did not think so. He would stake his judgment on that, if nothing else; he knew how this man operated. Wulff really wanted him to sweat. He liked the idea of coming in closer and closer, and as far as keeping Sperber alert, well, he would just take his chances. You had to admire it, in a way. "I'll get through this."

"Not much longer now."

"Can't we reach an agreement?"

"What kind of agreement would you wish?"

"There's no need to go on with this. It doesn't help anyone, and I'm not the one you want anyway. I don't have much to do with this at all."

"You'll let me be the judge of that," Wulff said.

"No. It's true. If you're so goddamned passionate about this quest of yours, then you should at least be willing to listen to reason, to hear what someone has to tell you. I'm no kingpin. I'm no operator at all, really."

"We'll see."

"I don't care what Díaz might have told you, where you got that information from. Díaz was a liar and a cheat. The only thing that I'm moving is a little pot. What the hell is pot?"

"And what the hell are you?"

"Why don't you wise up, Wulff?" Sperber said. He felt the phone begin to grow in his hand, a feeling of enlargement, pressing against the surface of his palm. Rage began to distort his line of sight, and that was dangerous; he had to remain calm, and yet, in an almost luxuriant way he felt himself descending into it. "You're not doing yourself any good, even if you think that this makes sense. You don't even know who you want anymore; you just want to kill."

"Bullshit, Sperber. Bullshit, Leon."

"It's the truth! You're coming through the South killing people, but it doesn't even make any sense! At least when you were blowing up people on the coast or in Boston you were getting at guys that I happen to know were in the racket. But here—"

"How did you know they were in the rackets?"

"I read the fucking newspapers, Wulff."

"I want you to sweat, Leon. I want you to think of me every moment, and what's going to happen to you. I want you to run."

"Oh, the hell with it," he said, "this is ridiculous," and slammed down the phone and picked up his one traveling valise, which was at the door, tugging it up with a series of grunts, and went out. He could not listen to it anymore. It simply was not worth it. Fear and anger would get him nowhere in a flight that he knew would have to be absolutely cold if he were to succeed, and beyond everything else, he was beginning to have the conviction that Wulff was crazy. Wasn't he? He certainly was not acting like a sane man, that was for sure. Picking on Sperber when Sperber really was so much on the fringes of soft-drug supply and demand that he hardly counted in terms of impact, then making unreasoning threats which simply made no sense if he were interested in catching up with him. What the hell did the man want really? That was the issue, but Sperber had no stomach to explore it. All that mattered was to get away. Somewhere in the vicinity of the capital he would find the quiet and anonymity he needed, and in just a little while, in a matter of weeks, or less than that, it would be over. Wulff could not go on. He could not go on this way; he was out of control; that fine edge of reason that he had had at the beginning was now a razor that was knifing against him, splitting him open, causing the blood of function to run away. It could not continue. You could not go up against the mass in this way. Sperber went quickly to his car and drove away from there thinking that it would not be long, it could not possibly be long now, and if his luck held out, it might even be finished, Wulff was so rudderless, by the time that he had crossed the Virginia line.

XXI

Wulff had thought now and then in his early months on the squad, while he still had a sense of humor or at least was still recovering from combat fatigue, that he might want to write a book someday called *Great Moments in Narco*. It wouldn't be as good or as colorful a seller as *Great Moments in Vice*, of course, which is the book that would be guaranteed to put the NYPD well up there on the talk shows where it belonged, but what the hell, a position on the vice squad in those days was practically hereditary anyway, and none of those guys could write. Or would have been able to find time to; the only thing that they were interested in was fucking and money, and they had plenty of both.

But *Great Moments in Narco* might have been nice if he could have persuaded some newspaper reporter to do the ghost job for a fifty-fifty split. It would mean taking the reporter around to the joints, of course, and showing him what was really going on, and you knew that you couldn't trust reporters, which was probably the reason that he had given up on the idea, that and the fact that after just a couple of months none of it was funny anymore.

None of it. It was deadly. But still there were those moments: the time when a dude on his way out of a One Hundred and Twenty-fifth Street joint with about three narcs in there arranging a small planned switch with an informant had about three bricks of heroin fall out of his pants on his waltz to the door and just stood there astonished as the white stuff broke into little pellets and began to scatter on the floor. Shades and all, you could see the dude's staring eyes, getting as white as the shit itself as the realization of what he had done began to seep through him.

But the narcs had their own problems, if there was one thing they didn't want or need, it was a heavy bust at this time. It would have opened up all kinds of areas for questioning, and furthermore, beyond that, headquarters would have been very upset with all the kilos of stuff; it would have been questions for *them* as well, and all in all it would have been a lot of paperwork either to cover it up from above or to deal with higher levels, should it become unavoidable.

So what the narcs did was merely to stand around at the bar afflicted with a sudden mutual case of blindness while the dude scrambled the bricks up and stuffed them into the side pockets of his suit and kicked around the stuff that he couldn't pick up into dust and then very hurriedly left. All the time that this had been going on the narcs had taken a great interest in the surfaces of the bar or in an inspection of the bottoms of their glasses. It was so neatly done that even the bartender had to laugh, although he did not laugh very long or hard, knowing what was good for him.

Wulff had been one of the glass-starers, of course. He had also been around when there had been a shootout in front of a tenement on a Hundred and Fifteenth Street and St. Nicholas Avenue, a shootout which later turned out to be the climax of a long drug war in the section between two rival interests, which were never really to resolve it, which continued to fight intermittently for four years, until a third group, which had been honing their weapons in Bedford-Stuyvesant, moved in and took care of both factions. But that had come later; at this time, in 1971, the war had been at its peak, and there had been bodies all over the street, some of them dead.

Wulff had been in the vicinity because he was arranging for the transfer of an insignificant amount of drugs from an informant to a student at Columbia a few blocks south. Busting college students was always fun and easy—they never resisted arrest—and they made bail quickly, so there were no long-range consequences there, either. No one got hurt when college students were busted, and for Wulff it had been an easy detail, taking up stake on the opposite side of the street five minutes before the anticipated transfer, smoking a cigarette, and enjoying the midday aspect of Harlem. Everyone knew who he was, of course, and had long since cleared the streets for him.

But then the shooting had begun, spilling out of a nearby tenement, and in a few seconds Wulff and his partner, who had been on the other side of the street, found themselves in the midst of a difficult and embarrassing situation. For one thing, the trouble with a shootout was that you were apt to get shot yourself, and for another, they could hardly claim not to have seen it. But when the street began to fill with bodies and blood, when one of the victims dropped a bag near the curb, out of which powder began to spill, Wulff and his partner were faced with a tough decision: they certainly did not want to get involved in this, they had no instructions, but then again, it was not exactly something you could walk away from. What they had done—put this down for more *Great Moments in Narco*—was to walk away from the scene very carefully, quite deliberately, and put the call in at a near callbox, then they had stood in their lounging garb about a block away looking useless until the squad cars had begun to pour in; and then Wulff's partner had reported to the sergeant on the scene that they could not reveal their identities because they had been on very important confidential business, but it was they who had arranged the misunderstandings that led to the shootout. They pulled their identification and showed it, impressing the sergeant a great deal— narco had a good reputation still in those days—and then they had strolled away from all of it, taking the subway downtown and checking in just a little more than fifteen minutes early.

No one had even questioned them about what had happened.

Oh, those had been the days, all right. It had been a marvelous opportunity; the department had been trying to do Wulff a good turn when he came back from Vietnam, and certainly the job was as represented. The hours were easy, the involvement was nil, the informants were cooperative, and the graft could add a hundred and fifty a week to the paycheck of the dumbest cop. The graft was the only thing Wulff had not touched. It was not as if at that time he had had any moral compunctions against it; he simply did not need the money, and he suspected that there might come a time when he would have to render services for which money had been so freely given in advance. He wanted to keep his options in that regard open; it was not that he hated narco at that time or felt about it the way he got to feel later on, it was just that he sensed that he *might* hate it, and in that case it would be worthwhile to keep his independence.

That had been a very wise decision, as things had turned out. Of course, narco was in the process of going downhill severely even before Wulff had separated himself from the squad so dramatically. The millions of dollars of stashed drugs that had mysteriously been found absent from the police property room had at least something to do with the loss of the squad's prestige, but the basic facts, which could not be ignored—and even the assistant commissioners, after a while, could not ignore them—was that during the great period of the squad in the 1960s the drug trade in New York City had multiplied more than twenty times in quantity, cash, and violence under the ministrations of the elite agents designated to eliminate it.

XXII

Once checked into the motel under another name, Sperber felt renewed, changed, confident, and happy in a way that he had not been for many years. It was remarkable what a little change of scene could do for you; just to get the pressure off was wonderful. Philadelphia was a wide, wonderful, beckoning jewel bobbing in his consciousness as he sat in the bar, having cocktail after cocktail and thinking of what it would be like when they all got together in the veritable shadow of Independence Hall in a few months to divide up the country, strongest first. It was going to be a wonderful party, one that would set up the divisions and lines of influence in America for the next two hundred years, and he would be at the center of it. Indeed, as the man whom Wulff had *not* gotten, as one of the few men who had had the good sense to see handwriting on the wall and flee, he would have a central role at the convention, would play one of the most important parts. Everyone would respect him, and respect as well what he had done for them. He might even come out of the meeting on top. This thought gave him a little delicious shudder of tension, like the contractions of the body just before orgasm, and he giggled. There was just no way in hell that he could fail to come out of this much the better than going in. And it was all, he thought, all because of a little sensible cowardice. That was the new American ideal for the bicentennial. "Mark that down," he said to the young bartender, who gave him a bored look and wandered away before Sperber could finish the sentence. "Cowardice is where it's going to be for the next two hundred years. Making adjustments, hanging loose, having the sense to run. This country wasn't built on heroes, it was built on cowards, and it's time that we came to terms with it." Well, fuck the bartender. He upended the glass and sucked the manhattan dry and meditatively bit on the cherry stem, feeling very pleased with himself.

A woman in her forties wearing a tight black dress came into the bar alone, sat several chairs away from Sperber, and he found in his present state that she looked attractive, certainly a reasonable fuck. Sober she might not look so good; the next morning she would certainly not look good at all, but with Sperber all women looked good at the beginning; it was only after you got their clothes off, probed them, worked them over, to discover only the same old orifices and disengagements, that the disappointments began. Still, at the beginning there was always hope. You never knew: this might be the one to change his life. He gave her a long look, and she gave it back to him in a cool, disinterested way, flicking her eyes between his and the surface of the bar, and after a time he picked up his drink and went over to her, moving slowly, delicately, in what seemed to be an enclosure of perilous space, the way things always looked when he got drunk. She ordered another drink even before he had positioned himself next to her, and the bartender contemptuously made it a double and asked Sperber if it should be taken out of his money. Sperber said all right, even though he had the vague feeling that woman and bartender in this negligible place were working together. Scheming was everywhere. Corruption moved through all the levels of existence. Still, he did not care: the time would come, he would get her back to his room, get her clothes off, and when he had her stretched and vulnerable on the bed, well, then he would see precisely how much scheming she would be capable of.

Sperber leaned toward her and began to tell her the story of his life, slanted for popular consumption: he was a businessman getting away from it all for a little while due to the pressures of his occupation, heading, however, toward an important part in his career.

She said that she had had the same career for many years and doubted if anything important would ever occur to it again, which was not to say, of course, and she licked her lips with a tongue as gray as the inside of Sperber's eyelids, that she did not enjoy her work.

Sperber said that he always appreciated someone who enjoyed their work, so few people really doing so in these difficult times, and she finished her drink, a double martini, and said that in that case they would get along very well together, because believe it or not, she loved her work. She asked the bartender for another, and Sperber, suspended somewhere midway between rage and hope, sat there quietly while the bartender without asking him whether it was all right or not made the drink and gave it to her and took some more of Sperber's money off the bar, and then, as she took a delicate swallow, Sperber suggested that she finish it off quickly so that they could go to his room. He had a bottle in his room.

"I'm not that easy," she said.

"I didn't say you were."

"Perhaps you have the wrong idea about me. I just don't go off to rooms with strangers."

"I didn't say you did."

"I'm not a whore."

"I didn't say you were a whore either," Sperber said.

"Maybe we misunderstood each other. Maybe you thought that you were going to get something that you're not going to."

"It didn't occur to me," Sperber said. "I wouldn't misjudge anyone like that, and I could tell right off that you were not that kind of woman," and very carefully laid a shaking hand on the bar and licked his lips, and she finished her drink and gestured toward the bartender, was just about, he knew, to order another one, and he was going to tell her something then, was going to lay it on this bitch as he had not done to anyone in years, because no one, least of all a woman, could get away with this kind of thing with him; he simply would not permit himself to be fucked around with this way, but before any of this could happen, someone behind him said, "Hello, Leon," and he turned, and standing right behind the chair was Wulff. He looked just as Sperber had always imagined he would, to say nothing of the voice. "Been quite a while, but better late than never, eh?" Wulff said, and hit him in the mouth shockingly hard, and the woman screamed, but in a curiously placid way, as Sperber went off the stool and onto his stomach, fumbling then for his gun.

XXIII

It figured that he would have a gun, Wulff thought. That was only common sense; a man in flight was a coward, and a coward was even more likely to have a gun than a courageous man. Still, it was stunning in those first moments to see Sperber struggling within himself to pull something out of his jacket; time stopped flowing for Wulff, poised in a wheeling frieze, and then oddly backtracked so that over and over again there was the one refracted moment in which Sperber, stumbling from the blow, fell over himself on the floor, scrambling, reaching, but if the moment was slowed for Wulff, it did him no good anyway, because his own time was stopped as well; and thus there was only an enormous, yawing chunk of time in which Sperber went for the gun and Wulff himself was unable to move.

But then the scene broke open, began to move again. The woman was screaming in a high, anguished wail; her hand to her mouth, she was backing away from the bar desperately, trying to move out of the scene, but the bartender would not let her. He had vaulted over the bar, had his arms around her, and was shielding himself from Wulff's presumptive line of fire with her body, while Sperber, still rolling on the floor, was trying to come up with the gun.

Wulff felt disgust. That was an odd emotion; rage would have been more like it, would have made more sense, but this man was vermin. Almost all of those with whom he had dealt so far, even Carlin, even Díaz, had tried up until the end to behave with fair courage, had been informed by a sense of personal courage, which, whatever else they were, had to be given to their credit; they had been wounded men, dreadful people, but there was some code with which they had conformed, even if that code was obscure or self-serving. They had attempted to meet with honor the very death that they had championed and manipulated, and this was to their credit.

But this one was something else; this one had had nothing to do at the moment of proposed confrontation other than to run. He would not face the consequences of the life he had selected for himself, and that meant that as much as any of the others, regardless of his importance to the network, regardless of his real contributions or lack of them, this man had to die.

Wulff charged him on the floor there bellowing, kicked out hard, and caught the man's free hand, which had held him in position on the floor. The man skittered back, groaning, and Wulff closed on him, leaped, fell, the heavy, sweating weight of the man's body against his, poisonous and revolting. But there was fullness in that embrace as he clasped him; a fullness which was horrid, because pressing against the man's body was like pressing against some aspect of his own in a parody of love; he felt that he knew this man's body in a way that he might have known his own, and this drove him thrashing against him, and something struck him hard on the back of the ear, a stunning blow; the ashtray, for an ashtray it had been, bouncing off the wall opposite. The bartender was throwing things at him from his perch.

Well, at least that was something: the man did not have a gun. If the bartender had had one, it would have been fired by now and all over for sure. But ashtrays he could deal with, Wulff thought, that and a poor aim, and he came up high over Sperber, rearing in continued parody of sexual embrace, and then drove his fist deep into the man's throat, and the man screamed in a voice which sounded fractured, and his one hand at his side, like the wizened limb of a very old man, came up once feebly and then fell back. Wulff brought down the heel of his left hand and broke Sperber's wrist with a single driving blow. The gun came out of it like a pellet of expectoration. His hand was close to it, and then it was over. He had it. He had the gun. He drew up his knees and came off the man, and the bartender threw another ashtray, which he ducked just in time, coming down to a knee as the heavy glass passed over him and then hit the wall with a dull smash and fell beside the other. "No," the bartender said, raising his hands as he saw Wulff coming into position with the gun. "No, don't do it."

But he had to do it, of course. He had to put the man down; there was no choice, even though the bartender had shown fair courage and had done only what he thought he must to protect himself. He had just gotten himself jammed into the middle, that was all, he had just suffered from a form of bad luck, gotten caught in struggles that went on around him and with which he had little to do. Well, it was too bad, but that was the way in which all of life itself could be conceived to function, huge centers of power and influence which became poles; in between those poles, small helpless objects like the bartender. Of course, he wasn't so damned small and helpless; you had to keep that in mind at all times. He could have killed him with either of those two ashtrays if they had struck him in the temple or throat just right, and it was not from lack of trying that the bartender had failed. Remember that. Keep that most firmly in mind. Do not suffer from compassion.

Wulff shot the bartender in the heart. The man squealed and fell across the counter, then, dying in stages, fell, one arm at a time, then torso and head underneath, flopping like a big fish on the bottom of a boat. After a moment there was silence.

On the floor Sperber moaned something thickly and tried to move, felt his broken wrist, and screamed.

The woman said, "Don't kill me." Her hands were up as if in some parody of a television serial she might have watched in which this was the approved procedure for dealing with attackers. "See, I'm not making a bad move of any sort. I'm just standing here. I don't have anything to do with this."

"Yes she does," the man on the floor said thinly, "she's a whore."

"I'm not a whore."

"She's a dirty, stinking, festering hole. Shoot her. Do something good in your miserable life, at least kill her."

"You won't kill me," she said. "I'll walk right out of here and go away. I'm not involved. I'm not involved at all; I don't have anything to do with this."

"Shoot the whore."

"Just stay there," Wulff said to the woman. "Put your hands on the bar and don't move." She must have been almost fifty, but still holding onto some mask of sensuality, the way that Sperber must, in better times, have held onto the illusion of danger. You had to give her credit, he guessed. "Don't move and don't say anything."

"I won't," she said. "Oh my God, I won't." Something broke in her cheekbones, which must have been only the layers of mascara, and then she was crying. But her hands as she brought them down on the bar were very steady, and when she brought her head up slowly, it was caught in the light like stone.

Wulff walked away from her, turned his gun on Sperber. "Get up," he said.

"Don't kill me. I didn't do anything to you. You know that's the truth; in my whole life I never did anything to you. You've got a persecution complex, Wulff."

"Up."

Sperber put his unbroken wrist on the floor, put slight pressure on it, moved his body waveringly upward. "She's a whore," he said. He rubbed the back of his hand across his eyes. "Why don't you kill the ones who really need killing?"

"That's what I'm going to do."

"How did you find me?"

"I looked for you."

"No, that isn't it. I took every precaution. I took every precaution that I could have. I left no trail, I didn't tell anyone where I was going. I'm in here under a false name. I know that I wasn't followed."

"I looked for you," Wulff said. "You aren't a hard man to find, Leon."

"Don't call me Leon."

Someone came into the bar from one of the side doors, a short man with glasses. He looked at what seemed to be happening in the dim light and obviously thought he knew what he was, because he screamed and then ran out. "All right," Sperber said, "I think we've got about thirty seconds."

"Please don't shoot," the woman said. "I just came in here for a drink. I don't know what's going on, and I don't want to know. It has nothing to do with me."

"How did you find me?" Sperber said. "That's all I want to know. No one could have found me. I'm no goddamned fool. I know how to run."

"I bet you do, Leon."

"Please don't call me Leon."

"That's all you're worth," Wulff said. "Where do you keep the stuff? Tell me now. We don't have much time."

"What stuff?"

"The stash, Leon."

"I don't have any stash."

"No time, Leon," he said, and waved the gun.

"You think I'm dealing? I'm not dealing. I don't mess with it at all."

"Yes you do."

"Maybe a little soft stuff, that's all. Maybe a little pot, but that's not even a drug anymore. You can't call that dealing. Maybe some cocaine now and then, but how the hell can you say that that counts? Cocaine isn't a drug either."

"Where is it? Did you take it with you? That would figure; you'd probably keep it in the car. You'd play a lone hand; you're too goddamned *selfish* to let it out of your hands. The lone game—"

"For Christ's sake, Wulff, there are going to be cops all over this place in just a second."

"I'll handle that. Tell me."

"No cache. Nothing."

"You're lying."

"No I'm not. It's the truth. You have this wrong. Would I lie now? Shit! Would I lie now?"

"Yes. Tell me."

"Nothing, nothing, nothing, nothing," Sperber said, and Wulff shot him in the left eye.

The man staggered back, expressing blood. The woman at the bar screamed again, but in a hopeless way, no energy in it. Wulff turned toward her, focused the gun, and then at the last minute decided the hell with it. He could not shoot. It would have been easy to, it involved no additional penalties, and it would have eliminated an important witness, but there were witnesses to other things all the hell the way over the country. It simply did not matter. It would serve no purpose sufficient in killing her to make him feel like anything other than a casual murderer. He put the gun away, looking at the dead man on the floor, thinking of the dead man behind the bar. "You keep the wrong company," he said to the woman.

Her eyes were quite wide and round. She looked childlike, credulous, too staggered even to faint. Wulff knew the feeling well.

"You ought to try to move in better circles," he pointed out, and ran from the bar.

XXIV

Looking back on it, Wulff decided that in tracking down Sperber and killing him he had for the first time in his quest become truly intuitive, had begun to operate on a visceral level of extrasensory perception.

How else could he have found the man so easily? There was simply no way in which his finding the man's trail, in picking him up, could be explained in terms of other than the mystic. It was as if Sperber had been inside him, as if some aspect of the man, reconstituted within himself, had drawn him levelly, easily to the motel outside of Washington in which he was staying. Rationality could not explain it. What it had to do with, Wulff decided, was that he had been utterly transformed by his Odyssey; now, as he moved north through the last jungles of purpose and toward the conclusion in Philadelphia, he had become something other than merely the avenger; he was the agent of all the mysterious corrective forces in the universe in whose service he had put himself.

Getting away from the bar was easy. The guest who had stumbled in there had put through a call to the police, of course, but these suburban cops just were not like those closer in to the city; for whatever reason, they functioned on a different level of priorities. If word got around that there was a murderous lunatic shooting up people in a bar, they might decide that little purpose could be served by fighting to be on the scene early. Why screw up matters by offering more targets? That was one way of looking at it; in any event, Wulff was back in the Fairlane and barreling north on the Shirley Highway within five minutes of the motel, and no one seemed to be on his trail, either.

The Fairlane had served him well. It was not a bad car, considering its heredity and the purposes it had served; he would have been a fool not to have used it. But it was obviously approaching the end of its usefulness now, wobbling badly in the tie rods, shaking ominously as he gunned the car over sixty. The tie rods were shot, that was all; if he did not get rid of the car soon, he was going to have one hell of an accident all right, and that would not be the way in which he would want his career to be ended. Let it happen at least on the field of open fire, not skittering off the road trapped like an insect in a loose suspension. No. Not that way.

No one seemed to be on his trail; the highway was broad and empty. Most American highways were empty; they were the least utilized of all transportation facilities. The highway fund was a boondoggle, lavishing more and more funds on redundant roads for a population that could not use the roads it already had. Unless it came near the inner cities, of course, in which case there was no money at all, because expensive interstate highways convenient to the inner cities would have allowed the inhabitants there to get out easily, and that was not the object of America; America was born to keep them *in*. The trouble was that he had just about run out of leads from Díaz's last confidence now.

He had no more names, not really. Sperber was the last of them. Maybe he should have pumped Sperber a little, tried to get the next chain of connection out of him, but he had been impatient to kill at the end, and it hardly would have made sense to stay in the bar interrogating the man. But now Sperber was gone, and Wulff found that he had, at least for the time being, exhausted his leads. He had nowhere to go. He had a small cache, but it wasn't going to do him much good at all, and it would hardly function as bait to lead anybody else into it.

From the beginning he had functioned on leads and bait, using what he had on hand as a means of sucking increasing levels of the hierarchy into making an attempt on him. It had been a good system, and the fish had been taking the bait eagerly, too; there had been damned little reluctance on the part of almost any of them to take their best shot, but now it had reached the end of the line, and the easy circumstantial path was no longer there. From now on there would be no leads presented him.

He would have to go into Philadelphia.

And he would have to do it blind too, months before the time that had been established for the formal meeting. He would have to do it before the alignment had even been worked out, which meant that essentially he would be at rest waiting for them to make their move rather than the reverse. It was not a comfortable situation—for one thing, he had no idea who had even called this meeting or under whose auspices it was being run—but it was the only situation that he had to work with. Unless, of course, he wanted to pack it in himself. Follow Sperber's line of reasoning, check into a motel or run out somewhere to the countryside and literally bury himself for a couple of months.

"No," Wulff said aloud, checking the rear-view mirror. Still a clear road. Whirring in the tie rod, dangerous shaking at the base of the steering column now; he cut the Fairlane back to forty-five and let it slide into the truck lane, listening to the brakes squeal as he hit them in short, burning jabs. "No, I can't do that. If I do that, if I pull off and get out of the game, I'll never get back in again."

And that, he thought, that at least was the absolute fucking truth. Once you got out of the game you could never get back in again. You had to stay in until the very end, take your chances, do the best that you could, and when you got out finally (if you got out alive, which was an unlikely possibility anyway), it was to be with the acceptance that you never would be able to get back in again. You had one shot and no more. Calabrese, the old bastard, at least he had understood that. No false retirements for him, no changes of life style, no slowing down. At sixty-three he had gone down to Miami in the biggest contest of his life because he had been willing to play the game all the way.

You had to admire that. You admired the old bastard if you had any sense at all. He was old and losing his grip, and at the end he had been defeated by sheer bad luck; who would have imagined that the plane carrying his defeated old body back to Chicago would have gone down and denied Wulff the pleasure of killing him? But he had stayed in all the way, fighting, and that was what he was going to have to do also. You could not sidetrack; how could you do so without giving up? And to give up would be to have negated everything that he had done so far.

He guessed that he would head into Philadelphia and see what was going on there.

First, though—he cautiously cleared his rear vision again, everything looked fine but he had better go at least fifty more miles before he ditched the car—he would get clear of this situation and then make a little phone call.

XXV

"Last chance," Wulff said. "I won't ask you again."

"Philadelphia is a tough town," he said. "Philadelphia is a bastard of a town. All those Phillie and Eagle jokes, they're just public relations to give it a loser's image, make people laugh. It's probably the roughest town in the country, parts of it. The south side."

"You want to or not? I told you, this is the last phone call. I won't ask you again."

Williams said, "Excuse me please," and put the phone down and looked at his wife, who was standing in the aperture of the hallway, smoking a cigarette and staring at him. There was a fixity of gaze, a level of attention that he had not seen in many months. From this aspect it was hard to believe that they had been barely talking to each other, had been sleeping separately. "I'm on the phone," he said to her.

"I know you're on the phone."

"So I'd appreciate your not listening."

"Is that so? And what would I appreciate? Am I supposed to appreciate what you're talking about now?"

"Please go away," Williams said.

"I know who you're talking to."

"Not now," he said, "we can talk about it later."

"It's starting again," she said. "Everything you went through, the whole thing. Once wasn't enough for you. You want to do it again? You want to get killed, you damned fool?"

"Please go away."

"You get killed, then. But you remember that, you're a goddamned fool," his wife said, and turned and walked away, went into the kitchen. The door banged. Williams looked after her for a moment and then picked up the phone again. A cigarette, hanging from his lips, had almost gone dead; he pulled on it frantically.

"Hey," he said, "I can't talk now. There's a kind of situation here."

"There's always a situation there."

"I think I want to meet you," he said. "But I'm not sure. I won't be sure for a little while. There are some other things I got to work out here."

"Yeah? Things? Like what things?"

"I think if I meet you I'm never going to come home again," Williams said, "or if I do, I'll come home in a box. Now, that's okay, but I got to kind of pave the way, you understand?"

"You don't have to meet me," Wulff said. "I just called to give you one last chance. I can make this alone."

"I know you can make it alone."

"I made everything alone up to this moment."

"I know you made everything alone up to this point, Wulff. I know that you were able to do everything your own way; that all I did was to screw up matters. I don't need to hear that, don't you see?" The cigarette was going again, although burned more than three-quarters down; he blew out an enormous spray of smoke, feeling the heat of it flare against his lip like an incendiary device. "No one's arguing with you on that, man. It's just that I got to work out some things here myself before I can join you."

"You don't have to."

"I think I want to."

"I'll be at Independence Hall on Thursday," Wulff said. "You show up there sometime around midnight, I'll find you."

"And how will I find you?"

"I'll do the finding."

"You always wanted control, you know that?" Williams said, not angrily. "No matter what you did, how it worked out, you were the one who wanted to be handling things."

"It's the only way."

"I agree with you. I absolutely agree with you there. But sometimes I got to have control too."

"So don't come."

"But I think I may," Williams said, "I think that I really may," and Wulff said, "Okay, then," and hung up. Williams put the receiver down carefully, cradling it, and went into the living room to lie down on the couch again, but before he could get comfortable his wife came in, ready for him. Her hands were clasped, her expression was tight, as if layers of her face had collapsed within themselves to a harsh brightness. She had never looked that way to the child.

"You're starting again," she said.

"No," he said, "I'm ending this."

"Why?" she said. "That's all I want to know. Why can't you bring an end to this? Why can't it finish?"

"Because they won't let it," he said.

"I don't understand you."

"You never understood me," Williams said, "but that's all right. I never understood myself. Not until the last week or so. Then it all came into focus. I hope it's not too late."

"When you came back from Los Angeles, you said that it was all over. You promised me—"

"And what did I get?" he said. "What did I get from you? You've treated me like shit in my own house."

"That's the way you wanted it. You wanted it yourself, David, you know you did."

"It's no good," he said. Painfully he brought up his knees, the slash in his stomach aching reminiscently, as it did when he was tired, changed position suddenly. "None of it is any good. This is not the time for this. It should have happened a long time ago, this talk, or never, but not now. I'm done."

"What are you talking about?"

"It's shit," he said, "it's all shit. The system stinks; you can't work within it because all it does is make sure that the criminality pays off. It's not there to make an end to criminal behavior, just to keep it in channels so that dues are paid. That's easy to see. But you can't go outside the system either, because everybody's out after you, and there's something even worse than that."

"What is it? What are you saying now?"

"I'm saying that if you go outside the system you are probably crazy, because a man outside of the institutions is going to be insane. We are social creatures, we are creatures of circumstance. But it doesn't matter now, because if you get whipsawed one way or the other you might as well do what you want to, and that's what I want to do."

She stood there, looked at him. "I can't take this anymore," she said. "I simply cannot."

"What are you taking? I was almost killed in Los Angeles. You've done nothing except keep the home fires burning and treat me like shit, of course."

"I'm through," she said. "This is the end, David. If you go out of here this time, there's never going to be another. I promise you."

"Listen to me," he said. He brought up his knees, touched his chin, groaning, turned to his left, and then lurched out of the couch, palms first, coming to an uncomfortable standing position. "Listen to me and try to understand this one time."

"Understand what?"

"That it's all a plot."

"What? What are you saying to me now?"

"Junk," he said, "shit. Smack. Heroin. It's been a plot from the start. Not for money. I mean, money was a part of it, the men who did the actual operation did it for the money, of course, but they were only put in business by the government. It was the government that gave them the license, and they weren't doing it for the money at all. They had something else in mind, and they didn't care if money was made out of it or not, as long as it could be done."

She was standing at the door now. "I'm not going to be your audience," she said. "I'm not going to listen to you while more insanity comes out. You're not the man I married."

"Who is? First it was the slave trade, and then the plantation, and then, after Lincoln, it got a little tough, so it had to be the industrial revolution, keeping our people at the machinery, having them do all of the work so they couldn't think, but then the wars came along and the pressure started to build again, because they were dying just as good as the white folks for about the same reason, and it didn't seem fair. A lot of people got very angry, and then you had the NAACP and the civil-rights revolution and the Supreme Court integration decision and there was a time in the middle fifties that it seemed that we were pushing right along, that we wouldn't be able to take much more of it without breaking through. That's when they got serious and pulled the plug on us. That's when the stuff really started to flow."

"You're crazy."

"They gave us the drug trade," Williams said, "they gave it to us so that we would stay where we always were. The smack was the new slavery, that was all. The whole thing was worked out at the highest levels. They didn't give a shit, not a damn, who ran it or what they pulled out of it, as long as the stuff went through. Then they could do a rigmarole of control just so it didn't look as if government was licensing it out. But that did not fool anyone. At least," he said, "it hasn't fooled me. Now I see it. Now I see what they were doing to us."

"David—"

"You have no use for me," he said passionately, "you haven't had any use for me for a long time. Ever since I came back from Los Angeles you figured I went over the deep end, that there wasn't too much that was left. But you did what you could, squeezing a little here and there, taking what was possible, holding out a little promise here, a little hope there, when all the time I was being milked. But we weren't going nowhere, and I should have seen it right away, just as I see it now. And the government's going nowhere too. It's all a charade. The only guy going anywhere at all is Wulff, and I don't know how far *he's* going, but I'm going to lend him a hand."

"You have it all wrong. You didn't see—"

"I saw everything. Everything. I got a good insurance plan. I got life insurance up the ass; any cop does. You'll get yourself a couple hundred thousand I get knocked off in Philly. You won't have to worry about anything for the rest of your life; you'll be doing better than you are on a cop's salary."

She stood at the door and said nothing. Her mouth opened, she seemed on the point of making some statement, then it closed, and she sealed up from the inside, tight. Standing now, leaning a calf against the couch, he was ready for her, ready to hear anything that she had to say, ready to take it and deal with it as he could, but she said nothing.

After a time she turned and left the room.

Williams stood there for a little while and then went to the downstairs closet where his valise had been for a long time and tugged it down. This time he thought he might need a little more than just overnight gear. Los Angeles, in any case, had been training for this.

When he left, standing by the door for a moment of indecision, he thought that he should perhaps go upstairs and say something to her, but he had the feeling that if he did she would be crying there, and he could not deal with that. He had managed well up to this point; he could continue, but he could not handle her tears. Nor was there any reason for him to.

So he went out the door with the valise and just started walking. The subway was eight blocks away and would take him right to the Port Authority. She could have the car. The place where he was going, he didn't imagine that he'd be having much use for it at all, now or ever.

XXVI

Maury's first lead to Wulff came from the reports of the bar shootout in Elktown. It just seemed to be Wulff's kind of work, that was all, and after reading down in the story to find out the identity and possible occupation of Leon Sperber, the second victim, Maury thought that it all came pretty clear. The bastard was on his way north, just as Maury had suspected, killing his way into some kind of climax, which would probably be—he would make a bet on this—New York, his home town.

But that news was promising. What it meant to Maury was that if Wulff was up in Elktown and under heavy pressure of the sort that would explain the killings, then he probably would have gone to cover somewhere in the area for a little while anyway, until some of the heat came off. He would have never done something like this, Maury figured, unless he was under pressure to start with, and the pressure would have doubled now. Wulff would have gone underground, and the best bet to Maury seemed that it would be in the very vicinity of the murders. That was the way the bastard operated, in a kind of superficial cunning out of a contempt for the law. He would hide so near the scene of the crime that they would never think to check it out; that was the way his mind would work. Maury was ecstatic, or at least happier than he had been since the bastard had come into his sporting-goods store and humiliated him. He threw the big map that he had just gotten on his kitchen table and marked a big circle around a ten-mile radius of Elktown in red, then put a black mark in the center. "There," he said, "he's got to be somewhere in there. We'll get him."

Fred, his hands on his hips, smiled. Fred was along for the ride now, because Maury had asked him and because Fred said that he felt as humiliated by what Wulff had done as Maury did. No one was going to pull that kind of shit on Fred and get away with it, no matter who he was. Fred said that he would be glad to go along with Maury, full partners on the quest, not even a share in the reward if Maury was able to find something; all that Fred wanted as his payment, aside from all expenses, was to be in a room alone with an unarmed Wulff for ten minutes. With Fred holding a gun, of course. That was sufficient for Fred, and it was fine with Maury; he promised Fred one of the finest pistols from his own private stock, a .23 special little handgun which was rumored to have once been in the possession of Eva Braun. Very hard to kill with a gun like that even at closest range, but it was painful; a wound from that .23 might be worse for the victim than simply dying.

"Sure," Fred said, "we'll get him good."

"I think we should just hit the road," Maury said.

Fred said, "That suits me." Fred was married but made it clear that it was in no serious way, and after six months of it was more than willing to try free-lancing again. Thank God she was sterile anyway, Fred had said; that was the only thing that had saved him, because this bitch had tried everything to get pregnant, and now that she wasn't, was talking about adoption. Anything to hook him in, seal him off for life. But Fred did not think that any marriage was a permanent arrangement, particularly when you realized that you had been married under false pretenses. The woman was as frigid as the barrel of an antique rifle. "I'm ready to go anytime that you are."

"There are no guarantees, of course."

"Who needs guarantees? We'll find him. If he's still alive; if he's there to be found."

"He's still alive."

"I don't have to put up with that kind of shit," Fred said seriously. "He didn't even take us seriously. We were just something to knock off on his way to somewhere else. He didn't even look at us as human."

"I know that," Maury said.

"I can't take something like that. He's going to pay."

"He'll pay," Maury said. Fred was just bullshitting, he knew, but for him it was serious. Getting this guy would change his life, would change the lives of everyone with whom the guy had been dealing. That could be worth something in hard cash, to say nothing of future prestige. Who the hell wanted to run sporting goods all his life? "He'll pay, and we'll pay. But he'll pay first."

"That's right," Fred said seriously.

Maury folded up the map into quarters and tucked it into the valise that he was using to carry special supplies like the two extra .45's and identification that marked him as a member of the Minutemen and the National Rifle Association, just in case anywhere along the way he ran into some blustering cop. He figured that that would cool him right down. He patted the valise and put it aside and then looked at Fred as the man hoisted his own suitcase, ready to go to the car. Ready to assist him, ready to participate, that was Fred; he was not very bright, but he was loyal. He was exactly the kind of man that you would want to have along on a mission like this, because he would do everything that he was supposed to, and he would never ask questions. Just getting to Wulff would be enough, just having the satisfaction of working with Maury toward the kill. No war would last twenty-four hours if it were not for people like him. "You know," Maury said, "I could have forgiven him an awful lot of things. I really could."

"How's that?"

"I mean, he's fighting against drugs, and that's pretty awful stuff. What they do to kids, what happened to the younger generation with all the radical stuff and the antiwar demonstrations and everything, all because of heroin. So he's got a point fighting against the hard drugs; I can understand a guy like that."

"Yeah," Fred said, "I know what you mean."

"You can give him points. And killing lots of people, well, you can't make cider without crushing apples. It wasn't going to be easy to get anywhere unless you started to kill a lot of people."

"Fucking A."

"But he shouldn't have taken my grenades," Maury said. "That was private stock. They weren't any plain old shit; they were stuff that I was planning to hold onto for a long time. I had plans for those grenades. They meant something to me."

"Right," Fred said. "They were beautiful. I knew those grenades, Maury. They were the best I ever seen."

"Killers," Maury said, "the little buggers were deadly. Give the right guy a hundred of them and he could have blown up the fucking city. And he stole them."

"No good. No good, Maury, no shit. That's really rotten. I'm not just saying that. It is, it's the truth."

"I'll get him for that," Maury said sullenly, "and I'll get them all back, too."

"Right."

"And I'll use one and shove it up his ass," Maury said bitterly.

XXVII

Wulff now had the feeling that he was moving into the last act. Finally. He had had it in New York the second time around, that same sensation that everything was coming to climax, that things were winding up and down simultaneously to a point of completion, but never so strong as now when he pushed the Cadillac Coupe de Ville along old U.S. 1, heading north toward Philly. All of the pieces were coming together; the call to Williams had been one of the last. He was pretty sure that Williams would join him, would be outside of Independence Hall in two days. Sometimes you had a feeling whose force outweighed reason; this was one of them. The black man would be there, and he would fight this last round with Wulff, because he too saw the truth now.

There was nowhere else to go.

It was good to be behind a Cadillac again. He had ditched the Fairlane in a shopping mall and picked this one up instead. Another housewife who had left the keys dangling in the ignition while she ran into a supermarket, probably to complain about wilted celery. Another housewife who would get hell from her husband for the next month. At that, he had done them a favor; the transmission on this yellow 1971 was slipping badly, the brakes needed relining and were subject to fade, had the characteristic high scratching noise in the drums which threatened serious failure, the engine had a highly defined miss. Book value on this baby might be about seventeen hundred wholesale, and considering that there was five hundred dollars of work in it right now, the happy couple would be coming out ahead. The body wasn't too hot, either.

Still, a Cadillac was a Cadillac. If Wulff had indulged any personal obsession during his Odyssey, it was this car. He had driven cross-country in a 1964 Coupe de Ville, he had wrecked numerous 1962's and 1963's at various times; he had driven a magnificent Fleetwood at one point in his pursuit of Calabrese. His actual tastes were for a Cadillac either much older or newer than this medium-grade vintage; he preferred all of that elegance varnished or instead turned, like America itself, to pure rotting corruption; a 1971 was neither here nor there, like a nervous college girl, who had had a little sex-on-the-run here and there and neither understood nor totally misunderstood the nature of the act, had to be retuned from the ground up. Still, he would take it.

And the highway patrol, he saw, giving another due-thirty-second sweep of his rear-view mirror, the state cops looked about ready to take *him*. There was a black cruiser coming up low and hard behind him, the signal light already turning, and as Wulff looked down to check his speedometer, the siren began to go. He was going sixty-three miles an hour in the right lane, a little bit over the speed limit, to be sure, but nothing drastic on the dry, empty highway; it was more likely that the cruiser had picked up the stolen-car report and was tracking him.

That was bad. It was very bad, and the easy, aimless drift of his thoughts stopped; he felt himself slowly coming into focus, and at the same time he drove the accelerator down to the floorboards, moving the car in a series of lurches at over eighty-five miles an hour.

The planetary gearset in the turbohydromatic whirred and screamed, chattered loose as the transmission wavered frantically between second and third, then it seized on a downshift—to first—which was really not there at all, and in a catastrophic explosion of gears, the flywheel went. The transmission gave out; Wulff could feel the unmistakable *clank* of a GM transmission that had given up the ghost, and then the car decelerated with a violence surprising in something so padded and insulated, the doomed transmission grabbing the gears, clasping them. The transmission screamed like that of a clutch car whose clutch had not been depressed in shift, and then he was burning oil at twenty miles an hour, the cruiser hot on his tail, going into the emergency lane.

The siren was on high now. The trooper must have been very excited in there; it was not often that a stolen car was grabbed on the fly like this. It was not so much honor in the department but the thrill of the capture itself that was energizing the man; Wulff remembered the feeling. He drove one-handed, arcing the wheel, putting the car through its paces as it staggered to a halt on the pebbles, and he already had his pistol cocked when the Cadillac stopped in a spray of sediment. The cruiser came in hard behind him, banging his bumper, shoving him forward a little, and then they both chattered to a stop, and for a moment, inside the Cadillac, the power windows sealed tight, the motor idling perfectly at fifteen hundred rpm neutral, Wulff felt himself insulated behind glass, locked off from the world. Would that it would continue that way. He kept both feet on the floor, hand on his pistol, pistol inside his pocket, and waited, looking into his rear-view mirror. After a time the door of the cruiser opened, and the state trooper came out slowly. He was about twenty-four years old, wearing a wide hat and dark glasses, an uneven set to his mouth that might have been determination briefly taking over from uncertainty.

He had his gun out, Wulff saw. The trooper walked forward and passed out of the line of sight of the rear-view mirror and was then beside Wulff on the driver's side, looking at him. The open muzzle of the gun flared like a snout in the window, separated only by glass. The trooper gestured with his hand, indicated that Wulff should roll down the window.

Very carefully Wulff reached his right hand across his lap and hit the power gear. The window unfurled slowly. His left hand was still tight on the .38. The window came into the door, the gearing whisking quietly, and then the cool, strange air of Route 1 was blowing on both of them. The gun could not have been more than an inch now from Wulff's cheek.

"License and registration," the trooper said.

Wulff said, "I'm going to have to reach for them. They're in my inner coat pocket."

"All right. Reach for them."

"Couldn't you put the gun away?"

"License and registration," the cop said. His voice was high but flat on the syllables. Young he might be, but he knew what he was doing. He would not have lasted a month on narco, of course.

"All right," Wulff said, "they're coming out right now."

He brought out his gun and in one sweeping motion aimed and fired and knocked the pistol out of the trooper's hand. The trooper's .45 special arced upward and fell about forty yards downrange on the grass. "Put both hands up," Wulff said very pleasantly.

The trooper's face had a look of utter astonishment. If Wulff had been a woman and had bared breasts to him he could have had no more stunned an aspect. He simply stood there, dropping both hands then to brace himself on the doorsill. His eyes were brooding, however, and intensely fixed. He seemed to be reproving himself.

"Come on," Wulff said gently. "Please get your hands up."

The trooper slowly drew his palms into the air after inspecting them to see whether or not they were still there. There were little circles of damp underneath his arms: the excitement of the chase, of course. Right now neither of them was sweating.

A truck went highballing the other way across the divider, one muffler out, eighty miles an hour in top gear. The noise for a full thirty seconds was overbearing. Wulff let it go. An old Ford sighed by on their side of the road, children's heads dangling from every window, looking at them incuriously.

"Come on," Wulff said. "It's not that bad."

"You're in trouble," the trooper said weakly. "You're in real trouble."

"Not if you act right."

"A stolen car, and now this. Resisting arrest, using a firearm. You're in real trouble, friend."

"Come on," Wulff said. "Stop being such a cop. There's no reason for anybody to be hurt now. You lost, and you lost honestly. Now we just have to work a way out of this."

"Give me your gun," the trooper said. "Turn your gun over to me and place yourself under arrest."

"Don't be ridiculous."

"If you do that now, you won't be in half as much trouble as you're going to be."

"I'm trying to work this out," Wulff said. "Why don't you walk back to your cruiser and get inside now? I'll go with you, and we can put the radio out of commission together. Then you can go across the divider and drive the opposite way, and I'll be getting along."

"I won't do it," the trooper said. He bit his lip. "Give me your gun."

"I'm trying to work this out sensibly," Wulff said. "I don't see any need for anyone to be hurt here. It's just a matter of letting you go in a way that will give me a fair chance to get out of this."

The trooper took a deep gasping breath, then another. His eyes blinked. He wore a wedding band. "I'm going to take that pistol away from you," he said. "Unless you hand it to me, I'm going to grab for it."

"Then you're going to get shot."

"You wouldn't shoot me. You wouldn't shoot a state trooper in the process of making an arrest. You'll go to the chair for sure then. They got the death penalty in this state."

"They won't get me. I'll be in another state."

"Give me the pistol," the trooper said.

"Don't be a fool. I don't shoot cops. I don't think I've ever deliberately hurt law enforcement; there might have been a few caught in some of the mass scenes, but that was their fault. Face to face I'd never hurt a cop."

"Now," the trooper said, and dropping his hands surprisingly deftly, went for the gun. He had it in clasp before Wulff wrenched it away, and then with a twisting motion the trooper had forced it all the way around so that Wulff would have to drop it or have a broken wrist. It was clever, courageous work. This was a cop, all right. There was a time when Wulff would have admired him very much. Now he was only a dangerous fool.

The pistol fell to the ground. The trooper clumsily bent over, scrambling in the dirt for retrieval, and that was a mistake. Wulff threw the switch for the power door locks, flicked them up, put his hand on the lever, pulled, and came out of the coupe hard and fast, throwing his weight against the door. It hit the trooper hard across the shoulders, sent him staggering away, and Wulff was on his feet, using the door as cover before the trooper had regained his balance. Wulff pushed the door hard, and it hit the trooper on the rebound, knocking him all the way over and coming off the hinge partway, to lie at a crazy angle on the ground. Wulff pushed it out of the way, went to where the trooper lay, and kicked the man hard once in the ribs. The trooper screamed. Wulff turned and got his pistol, which was six feet away, and checked it, then pointed it at the man, who was feebly trying to get up. Another truck went by fast on the opposite side of the divider. No one else seemed to be on the highway at all.

"That was stupid," Wulff said. "Damn it, that was as stupid as hell."

The trooper was erect, holding onto his ribs with one hand, groaning, tears coming out of his eyes, gasping as he faced Wulff. "You dirty bastard," he said.

"I warned you. I warned you not to try anything."

"You hurt me."

"You fool," Wulff said, "you goddamned fool, I could have *killed* you," and the trooper put his crew-cut head down, showing Wulff a fine, developing bald spot, and charged.

He butted Wulff hard in the solar plexus, and the shock of the blow drove the air from his lungs and sent Wulff sprawling, this time with the gun in his hands. The trooper immediately was on top of him, beating him behind the neck and around the ears, using his weight skillfully to pin Wulff and keep him from getting in a blow. Wulff could feel the pistol dangerously close against him, and the danger of the attack was that the pistol was more dangerous to Wulff than to the man on top of him. He could not use it without risking blowing a hole in himself, he could not even attempt a shot. He did then what a less experienced man would probably never have managed to do; he forgot about the pistol. Wulff let it fall from his hands after putting on the safety, just let it roll under him and forgot about it, and then he tensed, heaved, rolled the trooper off him.

The man went off to one side, rolling, and Wulff closed on him. The trooper, gaining his feet at the same time that Wulff did, threw a looping right hand that, had it connected, would have been very dangerous, but Wulff was able to duck it, and the trooper's follow-up was very poor, a little twitch of a left hook. He was courageous, and he knew a little about hand-to-hand combat, but he had also had a gun shot from his hand, had been pummeled to the ground, and was functioning out of a good deal of terror. He was a remarkable man, though.

Wulff came in on him and leveled a right hand to the chin that carried everything that he could deliver. The trooper took it silently, his eyeballs seeming to explode with color, and then he fell forward and lay there. After a little while it was evident that he was unconscious. Only that would have explained his not trying to get up, because as long as consciousness remained, he would have struggled.

Wulff stood there looking at the man and then up and down the highway. Not another car had passed during the fight, nor if one had, would it have stopped. Anything could happen on the road; people traveled on it the way that they sealed their hotel rooms at night and went to sleep or fucked. What did screams in the corridors have to do with them? Nothing. Still, it was pushing his luck to stand here, and there was also something about his posture over the trooper, like a man staring through a bedroom window, watching a woman perform some intimate but unglamorous action, like douching. He had no right. He had no right to partake of the man's vulnerability.

Wulff walked away, picked up his pistol, shoved it in his pocket, went back to the trooper. The man was breathing peacefully, quietly in the murky air; his face now seemed placid, as cleansed of expression or torment as might be one of the dead. He had not been badly hurt, and he would awaken and come away from this, and when he looked back upon it in weeks or years, he might remember it as one of the high points of his life. He would remember himself as having had courage, and that was no small thing. It might be the most important of all the possessions that he would carry as baggage with him as he passed along the shrouded line called life.

Wulff sighed and shrugged and went to the Cadillac and cleared out his gear, lumbered with it in two trips to the cruiser, hurled it into the back, threw the Cadillac keys next to the unconscious trooper, and then went into the cruiser. The keys were in it, the engine still idling, the radio crackling along. Someone was asking the trooper to report. Someone was saying that he had not reported for a hell of a long time: what was going on there?

Wulff knew how to operate the machinery. He took the microphone and checked in, saying that he had flagged a speeder and written the ticket. The dispatcher said that that was all right but please keep responding to calls from now on. All voices sounded the same through the transistors, Wulff knew. Wulff apologized and said something about his inexperience, and the dispatcher laughed and said that there were no complaints that he knew of, and went along the band, checking. That would take care of things for fifteen minutes anyway.

Wulff shut off the blinker and disconnected the siren and drove away at a good clip. Thirty seconds down the road he could see nothing in the rear-view mirror at all, not the yellow bulge of the Cadillac, certainly not the small form of the trooper. It was astonishing how insignificant many things were when you had just a little distance. All your life you enacted scenes within an area of maybe a couple of cubic feet: love, pain, courage, death. Move away from those little circles of space, and they meant nothing. Only the darkness mattered. Darkness and the quest.

He moved toward Philadelphia and the rites of the bicentennial.

THE END

THE LONE WOLF #14: PHILADELPHIA BLOWUP

by Barry N. Malzberg

Writing as Mike Barry

This Liddy, he's some kind of a nut, isn't he? … but he is strong. He is a strong man.

—Richard M. Nixon

Where am I going? I think I'll go to the moon.

—John D. Mitchell

Kill the beasts, the pushers and the poisoners. Kill them all.

—Burton Wulff

PROLOGUE

Well, he hadn't killed the cop. That was something, anyway, Wulff thought, driving north—and driving fast—through the darkness. That *was* something in his behalf. Even though he might have to pay for it in some intricate fashion; even though the young state patrolman had only been stunned, and might at this moment have staggered back to his car, radioed in an alert ... Still, Wulff had not killed him. He had stayed within the line of scruples which had been his from the very beginning. He was out to kill the pushers and the dealers and the users, not enforcement personnel. However corrupt or incompetent, they were, at least, on one side of the line while the vermin stalked the other. He had spared the cop. Even if they roadblocked him somewhere before the Delaware Memorial Bridge, cut him off and put him into custody without even a phone call, he would have that on his side. He had done nothing to the cop. Of course there was the matter of some five hundred other murders. One way or the other they would get him. They would get him good.

But that would be later, and was not something to think about now while he was still inside the Fairlane, sliding perilously on the turnpike with a hint of loss of control at seventy. But the wheel was in his hands; hands tight with the confidence that he would make it. He would make it. He would get through. He was going to Philadelphia with a sack full of weaponry in the trunk of the Fairlane that would lead him inexorably through the maze of connection and to the end of his quest. There was going to be a big meeting in Philadelphia. There was going to be one hell of a meeting in the first month of the bicentennial year, in the bicentennial city, and he was going to break it up. All of the drug dealers, of those who were left, that is to say, were going to be coming into Philadelphia, clustering in the virtual shadow of Independence Hall to celebrate the beginning of the third century of the country by cutting up the territory and getting a good start on the year two thousand.

That much he had learned from Diaz in Mexico, who had yielded more specific details about identities, plans, and places of residence. But what they did not know—or maybe the dealers knew it by this time, but Wulff simply did not care—was that he would be there, too. And his explicit purpose was to make the end of the second century the end of their business in America. A far hope, perhaps even a crazed dream ... But there were almost a thousand dead men who if once again given speech, could testify to the fact that Wulff had gone further with a crazed dream than any other man in the history of the law enforcement trade. By himself, he had almost destroyed the top echelons of the drug trade in America. Now he would move to the survivors. And then he would quit.

There had to be an end sometime. Wulff was willing to be reasonable about it. You could clean them down to the ground and there would still be other vermin pouring from the crevices to take their place. You had to face that fact, face as it were the impermanence of all human effort … But, at this moment, he would settle. He would settle for one last terrible conflagration in Philadelphia which would eliminate the cunning survivors and then he would quit. It was enough. At first murder had been a business, then it had numbed him, but now it was becoming a pleasure. And the moment that it became sensual was the time to quit. One final confrontation and enough. He did not want to enjoy murder; murder was only a necessity. Oh, there was a thrill in it now and then. You could not deny the passion and delight in dealing with a Cicchini face-to-face, or dispatching a Carlin in a basement in Mexico City with a single shot. But it led nowhere. Breaking the borders of business did horrid things to the soul. Wulff was getting out.

He drove the Fairlane north, blanking his mind as he had so many times before, turning out sensation, damping down the information filters so that little more than the knowledge of the road seeped through: the long, dank corridor of purpose through which he eased the stricken old car. In only a little while he would be in Philadelphia. He would meet Williams, they would confer together. Williams with the promised weaponry. They would decide what they were going to do, would figure out a plan of action. And then they would put it into practice. Just like in Los Angeles, the two of them: a tight team. It was something to look forward to. Everything at last was coming full circle. He pushed the Fairlane north. He hadn't killed the cop. Whatever else they had against him they did not have that: he had refrained. He had spared the man. Although at the moment of levelling down on him the need to murder had clawed within him, and he had pushed it down with a kind of terror which would have burst to blood if he had only brained the man.

I

Williams made a quick pass at picking up some weaponry in Harlem, but it came to very little, and he finally decided to go to Philadelphia for the Independence Hall meet with Wulff empty-handed except for his service revolver and a rifle he had tucked away a long time ago for special use. The thing was that none of the sources that he had cultivated wanted to do business with him—of any kind. They all seemed to know that he was dealing with Wulff, even though he denied it, and they did not want to get involved with Wulff on any level at all. Father Justice had long since closed up his rectory and Brotherhood of the Soul Church with the altar in the storefront and the huge ordnance room in the back. But someone who knew Williams said that Father Justice had a friend named Rodney who worked in a pet shop near the George Washington Bridge, and it was from Rodney, among the singing parakeets and shivering dogs defecating in the cramped cold space of their cages, that Williams had gotten the final word. "Your man is crazy," Rodney had said implacably, holding his cigar tightly while bending to swab some feces from a cage in which sat a cramped and unhappy dachshund. "I'm not going to get involved with that guy at all. I don't know nothing about no weapons."

"It has nothing to do with my friend," Williams said, and then caught himself and added, "I don't even know who you mean by my friend, I have no friends. This is just business."

"No," Rodney said, and nodding soothingly at the dachshund, withdrew the rag, using his other hand to scratch the animal's ears and setting off a small halo of dirt that sparkled in the deep fluorescence overhead, "I can give you no help at all." He had a curiously ponderous speech which might have come from his position as contact man for some free-lance ordnance specialists. But then again, it might have come simply from working in the pet shop servicing tormented animals for too long.

"I'm not coming as a cop, Rodney."

"That makes it even less promising. If you were coming that way I might listen to reason. We want to help the police all we can," Rodney said. "We know that a lot of you boys are arming up with heavier stuff than service revolvers. But I wouldn't believe you even if you said that you just wanted it private issue. I know who you're working for. That man is crazy." Rodney said, squeezing the rag in his left hand. "He is bad news."

"I have nothing to do with him."

"You had something to do with him. You had plenty—"

"That was a long time ago."

"No," Rodney said. He walked away from the cage toward the stockroom at the rear of the store, Williams following. The clerk far in the front was trying to interest two stout old ladies in a singing finch. "Stay away from him," Rodney said. "That's my advice to you."

"I don't know what you're talking about."

The man turned toward him with sudden earnestness, and put his hands on Williams's shoulders. "It was all right at the beginning," he said. "Someone *had* to do some shaking, had to get the job started. There had to be a cold, desperate killer. But he's reached the end of the line now. He's just out of line. He's going to do more damage than good, going to bring the whole fucking business down around him and then what? Instead of supply channels there will be ten thousand freelancers; every guy in Harlem will be hustling, looking to score. This way at least it's restricted. Not everyone can think of moving in and making a mint. He's gone too far now."

There was nothing to say. Sooner or later in this life you had to learn when a situation had broken for you; when it was no longer worth exploration. Williams had finally learned that somewhere along the line, probably in Los Angeles. "All right," he said.

"You know where he is?" Rodney said. "Turn him in."

"What?"

"You trying to get stuff to him, and you got a location of some sort. Shit man, everyone knows you were working together. You can do Harlem the biggest favor anyone has done it in years; you can phone in his location and get him picked up. Because if he goes on any further he is going to blast Harlem wide open. He is going to be the *end* of Harlem. Do you think he's doing us any favors? The hell he is! He's just leading to a complete opening of the shit markets."

"I don't follow that."

"Of course you do," Rodney said. "Any fool can follow that line of reasoning and so can you, patrolman. At least the system that we've had all these years—as lousy as it's been—has managed to *control* supply, limit it for its own profit. So if it was difficult getting hold of shit, if a habit was expensive, it made the thing a little less tempting. But you know what your man wants to do?" As Rodney pivoted in the back room and turned toward him, Williams became aware of a clinging, stinking odor of musk and animal droppings coming at him in slow waves, mixed sickeningly with what might have been odor from the man himself. But then it might have been only some interior corruption coming high and dense through his nostrils, intimations of his own body's doom mixed with the yelping of hounds from the back. "I'll tell you what he wants to do," Rodney said. "He wants to give every man his own Jones, make every man's monkey his pet," and the man moved back into the stockroom with Williams pursuing, and then stopping when Rodney reached inside his shirt and took out a small pistol. Williams made it a small French model, a point fifteen caliber or something like that, but none the less deadly for all of it. "No," Rodney said, "I won't help you."

"You don't have to pull a gun on me, do you?"

"Some people don't listen to words," Rodney said. "Some people have to be demonstrated." His face in the small light looked clotted, distract. "Some people have to see."

"I'm a police officer."

"You're not coming here as a police officer."

"Put the gun away."

"You go," Rodney said. He held the pistol tightly, his palm drooping over it, concealing it as it might the small breast of a woman. "I mean that now. I'm not here to help you." A cocker spaniel behind him threw itself at the bars, screaming. Rodney turned, gave the cage a kick, and wheeled back on Williams. "It's all over," he said. "Your friend has no support here. Your friend has no support here at all. Harlem is no friend of the Lone Wolf."

"Put the gun away."

"Go on," Rodney said, "you just go. Go and you don't have to worry about the gun. I'm not here to draw on you, only to get you out of my place."

There was nothing to do. Williams knew it on every level. There was a time to make a stand and there was another when you had to accept the essential hopelessness of what you were up against, turn, cut your losses, and try to get out with some kind of self worth. It was the same feeling that he had had on 137th Street near the methadone center just before he had gotten knifed. There was nothing to be done. He should have left. But he had not left. Instead, he had continued his way down the block, looking for the sources who were peddling the methadone in the streets, and in the same way, he could not leave the pet shop now. It was stupid; at night there was a dull fire around his heart to remind him of that kind of stupidity, and there would be every night of his life. But he could not get away from it. "A fool," he said to Rodney, "you're a goddamned fool."

"Get out of here."

"This is the only guy in thirty years who has ever tried to help Harlem, who has taken on the job. Who the hell else did anything? The shit has been moving in for decades. Since nineteen sixty it's been mainlined right in through 125th Street and who changed things? Who tried to bring it to its knees, until this one man came along?"

"I won't help him," Rodney said. "I swab shit out of cages, I walk the dogs, I pop seeds in parakeets' mouths. Get out of here," he said, and with a convulsion in his hand showed Williams the revolver in a terrible silent rage. "Get out of here now or I'll shoot you, you motherfucker. Had enough of people coming in, telling us how to live, telling us what's right. Had enough of this white fucker deciding *he's* going to clean out shit.

Ever thought that the people here *need* shit, maybe? At least they could count on it regular if they scrambled for it. Now where are they? Out motherfucker," Rodney said. "Get out of here."

Williams said, "All right. All right then." There finally was a time to cut your losses; he saw that now. Even on 137th Street he had learned that only when the wickering knife had cut fast into his ribs, and he had felt with a gliding sensation that his life was beginning to run out. He could not stand up against Rodney. Then too there was the parallel feeling underneath this that the man might be right. He just might be right. Who was Wulff to decide how Harlem should live, what a man's Jones should be? Who was Williams to decide on his own that Wulff should be armed up again so that he could destroy Philadelphia? Where did the judgments finally cease? When did you decide, at last, that people should simply be allowed to live their lives; that the processes which were the accumulation of those many lives should be allowed to go on at whatever seeming cost because the system, at least, paid?

"Fuck it," he said and turned quickly and walked down the corridor of the pet store toward the front. "Fuck it, I don't give a damn." And that was almost the truth, was as close to the truth as he was likely to get on this cold morning. The old ladies looked at him with blank eyes, then moved closer to the clerk. The clerk was balancing the parakeet on his finger now, his hand a hook inside the cage, talking to the bird in a slow, patient voice. "Come on little baby," the clerk was saying, "sing you mother you, *hop*," and the old ladies giggled. Williams walked straight out and into the blank dazzling well of the street and hailed a cab to take him to the Port Authority terminal and straight toward Philadelphia. Weaponless. The hell with it. He would deliver unto Wulff his body and his blood; the steel would have to come from somewhere else. Of course there was his service revolver, but how far would that go at Armageddon time?

II

Wulff had been a narcotics patrolman for several years in New York City until he had gotten sick of the whole swindle, the false arrests, the manipulation, the winking at the real purveyors, and had tried to bust an informant for flagrant possession. The lieutenant at the booking precinct had not taken too kindly to that and the evidence had mysteriously disappeared. The informant had gone back on the street after a two hour hold and Wulff had been busted back to patrol car duty while they tried to figure out what the hell to do with him. However he had taken a call about an unidentified young woman OD'd out in a single room occupancy tenement on West Ninety-third Street, and as a result of that call Wulff had solved the problem for the NYPD; he had quit and turned into a one-man army against the international drug trade. The unidentified girl had been his fiancée. She had been murdered, deliberately jacked in with heroin and abandoned. The fact that Wulff's car had received the call appeared to have been pure, disastrous coincidence, but then you never knew.

You never knew about anything in this business. Wulff was bound to try, however. He had been pretty damned fed up with the drug dealers even before he had found Marie dead; far before he had busted the informant, and, in fact, far before he had been on narco. But Marie's death sealed it for him. It was one-way now and to the end—whatever the cost. They had killed the feeling part of him on West Ninety-third Street, but the functioning part had been left alone. He had been a combat infantryman in Vietnam for two years in the mid nineteen sixties when it was just starting to get difficult there; he had a pretty good sense of how to fight a war. He went out to fight it.

Wulff killed three top men in New York City and several smaller ones, went to San Francisco and blew up a docked freighter with a couple of hundred who had been involved in a big delivery, had gone to Boston to blow up a few more of the higher echelon, and then to Las Vegas, heading south toward Havana and Peru before coming back to finish up matters—or so he thought—in New York. Along the way he had picked up a lot of enemies, a huge bounty, and a little help from David Williams, the young black patrolman who had been the driver of the car on the night that they had gotten the dead girl squeal. Williams had a neat little house in St. Albans, a pregnant wife and a devotion to the system, but through the course of the months he had turned around, first working on getting heavy ordnance to Wulff and then joining him in Los Angeles for an abortive campaign that had still resulted in slaughter. Williams had thrown in the towel then and had gone back to the system, but Wulff had gone on to Miami and to beachfront massacre. He returned to New York then and even solved the mystery … found out that the man who had murdered Marie had been none other than the lieutenant at the booking precinct.

But by that time it was too late. It was too late to make the solution of a mystery the end of a quest. They had had Wulff in detention in Manhattan for a while, but he had gotten out, carried the fight to Detroit, Phoenix, and down to Mexico City and a resort south of there where he had met a man named Diaz who had a notebook full of names of second echelon people. The second echelon, Diaz had said, was now, thanks to Wulff, the first echelon and would be assembling in Philadelphia around the time of the bicentennial to make the decisions for the American drug trade for the *next* two hundred years, or at least a fraction of them. Wulff had killed Diaz, taken the names, moved north and then east, slaughtering, working his way patiently toward Philadelphia where, hopefully, he would make his own impression on the meeting. Meanwhile, Williams had, for a variety of reasons, re-enlisted. Maybe Wulff's way was the right one after all. They arranged to meet at Independence Hall in Philadelphia.

Wulff had not wanted it to work out this way. Sometimes there was the realization that he had gone far beyond his original intention which was to get even, knock off the top echelons, and be done with it. It was just that the top echelons were so *fluid*, and the network was so complex. Open it up as he had and there was virtually no way out of it clear to the bottom.

He had seen, in Vietnam, what drugs had done to an entire country. Vietnam was not an ideological war at all. It was a drug war, pure and simple, with levels of influence contesting in that arena for control of the international markets. There in Saigon all of it had flowed free, and coming back to New York Wulff could see that the issues being fought out in Vietnam were going to be carried to all the capitals of the world. And from those capitals would flow the decisions determining how drugs would be funneled and by whom for the rest of the century. The American Legion and Westmoreland—to say nothing of Johnson—could have their patriotic bullshit to ram down the minds and hearts of fools because Wulff had the truth: Vietnam was a drug war, pure and simple. All of the ideologies were constructed to hide that simple fact.

Wulff was not the kind of man who the NYPD should have put on its narcotics squad, but the NYPD, in its ignorance, thought that it was doing Wulff a favor. It thought it was doing something nice for perhaps the only patrolman on the entire force who had given up his automatic deferment and enlisted for combat. They couldn't figure Wulff out, and thought that he would have to be crazy, and he was crazy—in a guilt-provoking way. Narco was a payoff for him; easy duty, regular hours, almost everything on the arm and a fair amount of graft. Vice would have been even nicer, but vice was practically a hereditary assignment. There was no way short of direct intervention of the commissioner that you could maneuver an outsider onto vice.

So Wulff had wound up on narco. The idea was to keep your traffic with the informants who would now and then turn over a small, convenient bust to you, and in hard times—that is, when the press energized the mayor's office which in turn began to make unpleasant sounds to the commissioner—the informants themselves would be busted and moved around the courts on bond procedures for just the amount of time that the squad itself felt was necessary to give the impression of action and keep the commissioner happy. The commissioner was made happy easily in those days. There was always something new coming along. A badly decomposed body would be found in a woodland of Richmond or a couple of student nurses would be pretty badly mangled in the east eighties, and the focus would shift. Now and then U.S. Customs would even cop a little smack at Kennedy, thus easing things.

III

Wulff didn't exactly know what the key was to the Philadelphia situation, but he had ideas. Diaz had let a couple of useful names drop and he had picked up some valuable leads in the southland. The important thing, he knew, was to *get* to Philadelphia to make contact with Williams and establish some kind of means of operation. Once they had done that the rest of the thing would fall into line. They would look someone up who had a connection with the international drug trade and they would start killing. The first kill would inevitably lead to the second and so on. That was the way the method had worked in twelve cities for eight months up until now, and Wulff saw no reason to change.

There was vague news about some big assemblage of the new echelon, each of them bringing along a little bit of their business, to decide how the territory would be cut up in the future. But if Wulff had his way, there would be no meeting at all. He would cut them down before they ever had a chance to get together and make their plans for the continued poisoning of the nation. He would not give them the time, that was all. He was on top of the situation now, and as long as the Lone Wolf remained in business they would never be able to destroy the country. When you considered the whole thing objectively, he was practically the only force in the country that was working against these people. If it were not for him they would have had everything by now; and they might do it yet. But he was shrewd. Shrewd and cunning. And as long as he was able to function they would not find things easy.

Now he was in Philadelphia. His meeting with Williams in front of Independence Hall was still eight hours away. In the meantime he had checked into a cheap hotel in the business district, ditched the Fairlane, and was carrying his small ordnance in a valise, his jacket packed with handguns. Small hotels in the business district were just about Wulff's speed; he felt comfortable in them, they gave him the anonymity he needed and he liked the grubbiness, the bleakness of their character. Here was something which, in any city, seemed to match his own mental state, his purposiveness. The furniture of the rooms and the look of the streets through the dirty windows complemented the decor of his own interior. You could travel light into one of these hotels, live there on the margins, disappear, murder, be found dead or perform unspeakable acts, and do all of it with the assurance that it wouldn't make any difference to the other tenants, who were all inhabiting similar margins. There was no other place for a dedicated assassin to live.

In the early part of the century, before the automobile had come to break the cities open, these hotels had been places of light and laughter in which people who had real business to transact in the cities would stay with one another, but now the people who had business in the cities all lived outside of them or stayed in the great hotels which had been made over, just as the city itself, for the absence of life, for convenience. But in a Colony Arms or Heritage Hermitage you could come as close as it was possible in 1975 to making some sense of how the country had turned out, what America had truly become at the end of all of this, and Wulff liked it. He was happy to be there, the hotel made him comfortable; this was where he ought to be.

He checked in at the desk, the old clerk nodding in front of him as he signed the register, paid twelve dollars in cash, and adjusted his ordnance inside his clothing. Fumes of whiskey roiled from the clerk's breath to Wulff, but the aspect of the clerk was not merry, and he did not seem particularly conscious of the fact that he was drunk. Wulff capped the pen, handed it to him and bent to pick up his valise. There was, of course, no bellhop. The mailboxes behind the clerk were dark and empty except for stray sheets of single papers; the ones folded once, probably rent due notices.

"You like Philly?" the clerk said.

"What? What's that?"

"You like this town?"

The clerk had an unusually piercing expression, but then again it might only have seemed so because of Wulff's alertness. He was carrying a hell of a lot of metal. "It's all right," he said.

"Just all right?"

"It's great."

"No," the old man said, "no seriously. I really want to know what you think of the town? You come from New York, right?"

"East of there."

"East of New York? Where's that?"

"The goddamned Atlantic Ocean," Wulff said, stooping to heft his bag. "I think it's an okay town."

"Gets bum rapped," the clerk said. "People come in from New York, think that Philly's a dump, a town for losers. But not since the Flyers."

"Flyers?"

"The hockey team. They beat the shit out of people."

"I don't follow hockey."

"Beat them to pulp," the old man said contentedly, rattling a magazine beneath counter level. "Pounded some respect into them. Got a world champion team now. That's the only way to be champions. Got to pound the shit out of people. You like to pound the shit out of people?"

"What's that?"

The old man swallowed several times, the small joints in his neck popping and bulging like little grapes, and wiped a hand across his forehead. "We don't go for that here. Run a nice quiet place. In the Spectrum, that's where you beat the shit out of people. Here you just go about your business."

"Sure," Wulff said. "I'll just do that."

"If we get any trouble I'll have to run you out. You understand that of course. We have good contacts with the police; we can get them here in a jiffy."

"All right," Wulff said, "all right," and went away from the desk, struggling with the valise. As he walked into the small, self-service elevator whose door was ajar, he looked at the key to his room and pressed number three. The clerk looked at him intently, poignantly. The shelf of door cut off the clerk's line of sight, and Wulff could see him looking at him with curious intensity; certainly far more interest than he might have generated considering what Wulff took to be relatively limited social contact.

The elevator moved up in trembling, slow jerks, and hesitated at the second floor with the door closed for so long that Wulff thought that it might be stuck. He had long since figured out what he would do if he were trapped in an elevator: he would shoot his way out. He had a fear of self-service elevators which was almost irrational. It was not as strong a feeling as his hatred of drugs or dealers or his love for Marie Calvante, but it was on that level, and he was perfectly willing to pull a gun on a stalled self-service elevator if that seemed to be the only way to get out of one. First he would put a shot through the door to crack open the locking mechanism, then another one overhead through the skylight, carefully placed so that he would be able to pull down a beam and wriggle through. And if neither of those two shots did it … well, then he would go mad, putting a fusillade down until someone in the corridors got the message. But the car moved shakily upward after a while and clung to the third floor for only a short time before reluctantly opening its door like a stubborn child might release a fist sticky with hidden candy.

Wulff went out into the corridor and down to the third room on the left, struggled with the latch, and let himself into a room as bare and clean as he knew the interior of his soul to be. He put his valise down with a sigh, and turned then to inspect the spaces of the room which were the spaces that he had inhabited in a hundred others like it. His life had turned full circle; he was tracking through it all again and knew nothing would ever change. Wulff sighed once, very deeply, feeling a revulsion shiver through him; revulsion which was circuited more than anything else around impatience. Impatience for it all to be done with, and impatience for the moments to crawl forward toward confrontation so that in action again it could all be over. He kicked the door closed, went to the valise, opened it to see that the armaments were still there—lined up in their gleaming little rows like surgeon's materials— and then went to the bed, sat on it, and lay on it, bringing his knees up to his chest. Six hours until he met Williams. He could have killed the time just as well with a woman as in any other fashion, but since the girl Tamara had been killed in Miami there had been little of that for him, and even Tamara had been merely a short-circuit in what had become the dead wiring of his sexuality since Marie had been found killed.

No, whatever he needed, it was not a woman. It was only a twitch; it had nothing to do with sex at all. On the bed he closed his eyes, drifted absently through dreams which themselves seemed to contain circuitry and wiring; dreams which had little flickers in them which seemed to come off the vast, dense machinery of purpose which hummed within him. And in the pit of that sleep he twitched a few times, reaching once reflexively toward the point forty-five which was in his side pocket. In the dream someone had come into the room and was staring at him, looking down at him on the bed with a gun in his hand. He was an enormous man with eyes that were only surface, and as the color and motion of the dream became more penetrating, like a knife within him, Wulff twitched again and opened his eyes … and the dream merged with the aspect of what he saw.

There was a man standing near the border of the bed, a tall man whose features were invisible in the little trapped light filtering through the first dusk, but Wulff could see that the gun, enormous in his hand, was levelled on him. It was strange how you could see certain things and not others coming out of sleep that might have to do with the light, or then again might only be some freak of attention. Wulff lay very quietly waiting for the man to do what he would. His own gun was not within hand's reach. If the man was going to kill him there was nothing to be done. He had had a good run, all things considered, Wulff thought. If it was truly all over now he would have to take it with the assurance that it could have happened a long time ago and he might not even have gotten this far. He had gone a good distance. "Get up," the man said.

Wulff lay there looking at him. The man said again, "I know you're awake. Now get off the bed very slowly and don't put your hands anywhere but where I can see them. If you reach for a gun, if you do anything peculiar at all, I'll kill you."

Wulff brought his knees down slowly, arched his feet toward the floor, and moved off the bed. The man, wearing a heavy coat in the mild November, was six feet tall or a little more, and handled the gun with absolute professionalism. He might have been about forty years old. "Now," the man said, "Stand."

Wulff stood. The man reached out his free hand, patted Wulff's pockets very carefully, and came in and then out with the gun. He held it delicately, the way one might balance a puppy, and then put it in his pocket. "All right," he said, "what do you want? What are you doing here?"

Wulff said nothing. There was really nothing to say. He measured the man carefully. It was barely possible that he might be able to close the distance and knock the gun from his hand. Not yet, however. It was an ultimate risk maneuver, the kind of thing you would do only if there was no apparent alternative. Right up until that time, however, you tried to negotiate, look for any other possible move. Behind the façade of the man in the overcoat Wulff saw or thought he saw a hint of uncertainty, which could only come from being in a place where there had not, perhaps, been sufficient preparation. The man looked vaguely unhappy, as if he had been cajoled or ordered from bed to take care of this. "I'm not kidding," the man said. "I want to know who you are. You'd better talk to me. You want to get shot?"

"No," Wulff said, "I don't want to get shot."

"Who are you?"

"The clerk tipped you," Wulff said. "The question is why? Who did he think I was? What do you want from me?"

"I'm asking the questions here."

"I'm entitled to know."

"Look," said the man in the overcoat, the uncertainty in his voice exaggerated through volume, and filtered through the hoarseness sounding as if the man were not demanding information but somehow pleading for it, "I want to know who you are and why you're staying here. You see this?" he said, lifting the gun slightly. "I can use it. I'm not just waving this goddamned thing around. I know what it is and what it can do and how to handle it."

"Do you?"

"Damned right I do," the man said as Wulff put out his leg, hooked it behind the man's ankles and tripped him.

The man came forward, sprawling, gasping, the gun hand splaying out at an awkward, painful angle. He was too much of a professional to fire it on such a precarious hold, but his attempts to regain control, silent and intense as he dragged his arms back, made him scream with pain. Something in a shoulder had been dislocated. Wulff kicked him in the small of the back and sent him lurching forward, then dove for the gun, coming in low and hard behind him. The gun came into his hand, small and hard like a fist, slapping against his splayed fingers with that sense of absolute conviction which was always an indication that you were moving well, doing the right thing, and as the man feebly tried to hold onto it Wulff wrenched it around and through his fingers, and then pushed up hard. Something snapped inside the man's wrist, and he screamed once, lightly. Wulff brought up his knees, rode the man all the way down, dug his fingers into the back of his neck and yanked hard, and the man screamed again, this time with greater solemnity. Wulff stood upright then, dragged the man up with him, and pushing him into the wall, caught him on the rebound and threw him back again. The man shielded himself from head impact by coming against the wall with his shoulder blades, and this seemingly woke him up, took him out of the unconsciousness to which he had descended. Wulff pointed the gun at him. Little streams of sweat were running off the face now in cracked rivulets and the man looked much older, not forty at all but rather a wasted fifty-five, an athlete gone toward disaster. His hands reached for the lapels of his overcoat, and he drew it around him with a hunched, protective gesture, swaddling himself within it like a child.

"Don't," he said, "no more. Don't hit me."

"Who sent you here?" Wulff said. "What do you want?"

"He called me," the man said weakly.

"Who? The clerk?"

"Yeah. Yeah, Jerry downstairs. He called me. He thought you might be somebody they were looking for. He thought that you were—"

"Who?"

"You know," the man said sullenly. "You know who he thought you were. Everybody knows what you look like. There's no goddamned big secret about it."

Wulff hit him backhanded across the left cheekbone. The man's eyes went wide and empty and his head rolled into the wall. He did not, however, collapse. A little bit of blood, showing first in his eye, rolled out of a corner of the mouth. "Bastard," he said.

"Who sent you?"

"I won't—"

Wulff hit him again. One could get into a simple rhythm of connection where he did not have to think about what he was doing at all; everything was reflexive, simple. Not only the captive but the torturer responded to the simple imperatives of the situation: who then was the captive? "Come on," he said.

"He'll kill me."

"Be killed," Wulff said and hit the man. The blood had come down to the left shoulder of the overcoat now and oddly had not sunk in, but rather it was travelling, sliding down with gravity to the sleeve and pooling in one distended drop near the cuff. "I'm quite willing to kill you," Wulff said. "It doesn't make any difference to me whether I do or not. You'd be one of a thousand."

The man looked at him and something in his face changed; it was as if at that moment some absolute perception of Wulff which had not been there before came to him, and his eyes were suddenly dull and pained like those of a suffering dog. "You're Burton Wulff, aren't you?"

Wulff sighed and used another backhand. This one caught the man, slamming him into the wall even harder, and the man rebounded. He looked weary, as if he had long since expended energies worthy of an employee and was now beginning to think about the long-range fringe benefits of his job—of which there seemed to be very few. "Martin," he said, "Martin sent me."

"Who's Martin?"

"It won't do you any good to know," the man said. "It won't make any difference whether you know or not." He seemed to be reasonable now, pleading, settling upon a vein of desperate earnestness which, if he could only properly track it through, might carry him all the way home. "There's no need for this," he said. "Nobody really wants to get involved; nobody wants to hurt you. I was just sent to do a job. But what the hell, if I can't do it that doesn't mean there's any hard feelings; it doesn't mean that the situation has to go on this way at all."

"Who is Martin?"

"Just a guy in business," the man in the overcoat said. "Just a guy who I work for—"

"Just a guy who wants me killed."

"All business," the man said sullenly, "just business."

"So is death."

"You go out to do a job, that's all. You do the best you can. It's like war, isn't it? So I couldn't do it, so I fucked it up. You're a better man than I am. So it should just end like that, shouldn't it?"

"Let you walk back to your own lines."

"Something like that."

"That's an interesting attitude," Wulff said. "I've never really met anyone with your attitude about the business up until now."

"Well," the man said ponderously, rubbing his chin as a hopeful little light came into his eyes; light that filtered down from his eyes and through all the cracks of his face. "Maybe that's because there aren't enough guys who have thought this out the way that I have, who don't have my attitude on the business. It should just be a job, that's all. If I fail why should I be killed?"

"That's true," Wulff said, "I see your point. Completely business."

"Right. That's right."

"Who is Martin?"

"Now I can't tell you that. Now that wouldn't do you any good at all even if you knew who he was. He's just a guy—"

Wulff shot the man in the shoulder.

He squawked once and hammered into the wall, grasping himself, looking at Wulff with disbelief. "You can't do this," he said, "you can't do it," and then the pain caught him fully and his features seemed to cleave, break open in little glistening jewels of sweat. He pounded an elbow into the wall, his shoulder heaving within his grasp. "No," he said again, "oh no."

"Who is Martin?"

"I don't want—"

Wulff pointed the gun again. "The other shoulder," he said. "and then I'll start to work on the knees. Four points. I'll have you crawling around like a frog."

"Oh Jesus," the man in the overcoat said. "Oh Jesus Christ," and then he began to talk. Little pieces of information, words, and phrases came out, painfully moving at cross-angles to the movement of his mouth so that they seemed not to be so much impelled as squeezed out like a long-delayed and hopeless ejaculation after too much self-stimulation. He told him more about Martin than Wulff could conceivably have wanted to know. Not only the man's full name, address and business and why he had sent the man in the overcoat to assassinate Wulff simply on information phoned in by the clerk, not only all of that, but also Wulff was told certain things about Martin's personal life and obsessions and interests which had nothing to do with the situation. And yet, in a different and more obvious way, of course, they had everything to do with it because what controlled a man's actions were not only the mechanics of necessity but also what the man had constructed the necessities *from* … and the shit dealers were into it because in one basic sense or another they had always wanted shit.

When the man in the overcoat had finished he ran down with little sighs and groans, as if turning off his speech was as difficult as getting started; as if a man who had lived all of his adult life in the belief that to talk at all was to risk danger could not, when forced to speak at last, see any limitations to what should be said. He stood there then, leaning against the wall, head lolling, grasping his shoulder. His eyes were bleak and ruined; on some vague level he did not so much seem to be destroyed as he did beyond any sense of himself. He might have needed a new self-image, as the speaker. "I'm hurt," he said, "I'm really hurt."

"Of course. You're shot."

"I'm bleeding. It's really bleeding in there. If I don't get this attended to I'm going to be in trouble."

"You shouldn't mess around with guns," Wulff said. "You see, you have no idea what kind of people you're going to run into if you go around with a gun."

"Will you let me go?"

"What?"

"I said will you let me go?"

"I don't think so," Wulff said and paused. "No, I don't think that I will. I don't think that it's going to do any good at all to let you go because then you're just going to be one more complication and I've got too many. Too goddamned many complications, too much already. I've got to simplify," Wulff said, pointed the gun, and shot the man over the left eye. He pumped another shot, and then backed away like an artist considering the final draft of a canvas to which he had, at the last moment, slashed on a final explosion of color, and watched the man fall. The man pitched onto his face heavily, dead meat from bottom to top; dead meat moving heavy and useless within the sack of his clothing. Wulff put the gun away. There was simply nothing else to do.

He thought for a while about staying in the room for a few more hours because the corpse didn't bother him and it would have been even kind of comforting to doze on the bed with the presence of the dead man an assurance that he had not lost his touch. But he finally decided that was pretty silly, because sooner or later the man named Martin who had sent this man would begin to worry about the absence of a report and would send someone else to check on him. People like Martin always worked that way. They sent their assassins in waves and shifts but they never did the work themselves. No need. There was no need for Wulff to stay either.

So he left. Might as well go to deal with Martin directly. Or, then again, maybe pass a few hours in a movie house, meet Williams with, hopefully, some new ordnance and go into Martin's quarters fully armed. No point staying though. The lobby was empty and the clerk, huddled over his newspaper, looked up and gave one startled peep when he saw Wulff, and then dove expertly beneath counter level.

Before he could come up with whatever he was going to come up with Wulff went over, leaned over the counter with the gun drawn and shot the gleaming mass of the clerk between the shoulder blades.

Then he went out. Nobody had paid any attention at all. It was a not very successful hotel that was in a very poor section of a town and now in as bad trouble as anything else on the east coast.

IV

Martin lived in a big house just east of Harrisburg and preferred to work by telephone. Now and then—particularly when he was dealing with those above him in the hierarchy—it was necessary to present himself, to deal face-to-face, but for the most part he could handle everything he needed over the phone and this was better. It imparted a sense of mystery to his directives; he could really intimidate people more if they did not know what he looked like. And also there was a good deal more protection in handling things in that way.

He had gotten the word from the clerk in the hotel in Philadelphia about Wulff's checking in on the phone, and had dispatched the assassin in the same way. The clerk was paid a small retainer to pass onto Martin little pieces of information that he might inherit on the south side, and also to now and then run a packet of live goods to some prearranged contact. He had not really come up with much in the past, but that did not mean that there would not be something in the future. The purpose of keeping an informer around was precisely that he was unpredictable, and you never knew what he might come up with. The best informers were not predictable. Certainly the word on Wulff had been worth all of the hundred dollar bills that Martin had been feeding the ruined old man month by month for a long time.

He had known that Wulff was coming north, but the luck of his actually coming into a place which Martin had under this kind of surveillance was just too good. It was outstanding luck, that was all. It confirmed for Martin what had long been an instinctive feeling that he occupied a plane of possibilities higher and finer than most other men. He had sent the best man available to the hotel with the feeling that he was getting rid of a particularly urgent problem before it had even had a chance to hurt him; long before it would force itself into his life. It was like a free finesse in bridge—that was all—to learn that Wulff had checked into a near-flophouse in the south section and that he was apparently alone. He had tried a couple of people before getting Vines to agree to take it, but Vines had been all right. Well past his prime, of course, and a little slow and on the cautious side, but certainly as good with a gun as anyone around, and, after all, how much skill did an assassin really need? Wulff was alone; it was simply a matter of going into the room and shooting him.

So, he had been happy. Everything had been moving along in the proper way; and now that Wulff was out of the way it was all going to fall into place. He would be able to make the meeting and establish control, no two ways about it. He was going to come out of this one on top. No one would stop him: he would have the whole goddamned northeast and he could thank Wulff for that. Had to give the bastard his due. If anyone had cleared the decks for Martin it had been this guy killing off all of the prospective competition. In the long run everything worked out for the best, that was all. It even served well to be a second-rater, the way things were going nowadays.

So the phone call had been a shock. It had been an extremely bad shock; one of the worst that he had had in a while. And Martin was getting to an age now—easing near forty—where he was beginning to worry about his heart, to worry about the cancer that was back there in his family tree, the rheumatism, the glaucoma, the strokes, and all of the things that lurked to destroy a man just when he had managed, on his own, to beat the game cold. Life was a bitch that way. The phone call had been a shock all right; it had generated what he knew the medical texts called a *sympathetic storm*, or a sudden escalation of the pulse rate accompanied by shortness of breath and flushing which indicated severe stress upon the heart itself and which had to be guarded against if one wanted to survive to a good age without a heart attack. Most of the aerobic exercises were designed to build up the body against the sympathetic storm, which was the reason why Martin had done them for a time before losing interest a few years ago.

"Hello," the voice on the phone said, "this is Wulff." Martin had known right away that it was. Sometimes he got a crank call even with his unlisted number, but there was no way of looking at this as a crank. He knew, and from the moment that he knew Martin felt his metabolism start to slide out of control. One had to watch that kind of thing if he wanted to live a long or at least a longer life, and so what Martin did right then and there with the man on the other end of the phone and with, as far as he knew, his virtual life at stake, was merely to stand there drawing the even breaths down, stroking his epiglottis with little strobes and wires of intake, trying to bring his heartbeat down in a deliberate and calculated fashion from the unreasonable 130 that it had hit.

On the other end of the phone the caller waited him out with uncanny patience, almost as if he knew what Martin was doing, as if he had made enough calls of this sort in the past to be able to judge, without need of explanation, exactly what was happening to the man that he had reached. That was pretty frightening when you came to think about it. All of this was pretty frightening; but then, Martin had long since decided it was a lousy business. If you were going to be in it, though, it meant that you had to deal with all of the penalties, one of which very definitely was calls of this sort. There was no way around it, and it was hardly the first time that he had had to deal with a man whom he loathed and feared. But even within that context of reassurance he was trying to find, this was bad. It was very bad. Finally he said, with his pulse storming down to an uneven ninety-six, bobbling and jerking in his chest like vagrant cells that had been torn loose from the heart muscle to be overtaken in the ruin of the blood, "All right. It's you. I accept the fact that it's you."

"You'd just better do that."

"What happened to Vines?"

"Vines?" the man said. "You mean the guy in the overcoat? He's no longer with us."

"You killed him?"

"I dealt with him," Wulff said. "And now I'm going to deal with you."

"That wouldn't be very bright," Martin said. "That would be ill advised."

"How so?"

"Don't do it," Martin said. "Whatever you have in mind don't come near me. Get out of Philadelphia, Wulff."

The man seemed to laugh at him. Well, all of the reports that Martin had received indicated that Wulff was a lunatic; but that meant nothing. "Is that an order?"

"It is for you."

"I'm going to get you," Wulff said. "I know where you live and how you seal yourself up and what kind of security system you have. I even know about your basement entrance. Vines got quite talkative before he died. Even chatty. It just goes to show you what a little fear will do for a man. Or maybe a good companion."

"You son-of-a-bitch."

"That won't do you any good either."

"Why are you calling me, Wulff? What do you want?"

"I want you to sweat. I want you to know that I'm coming and to think about it all the time, that's all."

"You've got to be crazy."

"No," the man said, "I'm not crazy. I'm absolutely sane. I want you to suffer like the junkies suffer. Like the busted out kids in Harlem, like the bodies stretched out in the shooting gallery, like all the hip kids in Berkeley who got strung out in 1969 and went crazy. That's what I want you to feel like Martin."

"You're crazy," Martin said again. "You think I mess with that shit? I don't have anything to do with that; I'm a businessman. I wouldn't run drugs; that's a black business."

"Black business," Wulff said, "black heart," and laughed into the phone, one short, terrible bark and then put it down. Martin could hear the emptiness moving in little waves of pain into his ear, and he yanked the phone away and in fury threw it at the pedestal. Missing, and instead striking the wall on the bounce, the phone and receiver then skittered somewhere underneath the bed. Martin turned from his bedroom and went into the living room, headed for the liquor cabinet, reached for the shelf of gin, thinking that he would pour a short one to try and calm down, beat off the ravages of respiration, and try to figure out what he was going to do with this lunatic who was hard and heavy on him. But even as his fingers had closed on the bottle Martin knew that it was no good, no good at all. He could not escape that way. There was only time for one thing. He would have to take what protective action he could. He had been lucky so far; up until this point he had been safe from Wulff because he was well insulated and because he was at too low an echelon for Wulff to even pay much attention to him … But that was going to change now. All of that had obviously changed. What he had always feared at some level was going to happen had happened at last: the man's line of sight had zeroed in on Martin and now … well now he had to do something. Obviously this was intolerable. He had to do something fast because this madman had him marked down as a major drug dealer and unless this was quickly come to terms with Martin was going to be added to the list, already in the hundreds, of victims.

Son-of-a-bitch, Martin thought, and son-of-a-bitching Vines, too, for that matter. He was no damned good, that fucker, no good at all. You gave a man a job because you thought that he could do it, because you showed some faith in a person who really did not justify it at all … and what did you get? What did you get for that?

Better off dead, Martin thought. Better off dead than this. But, oh no, this will not go for me. It is not going to happen. I will not be another neuron in the synapse of a kill-crazy madman … and he lurched toward the phone, his first and final line of defense.

V

Williams was at least able to retail a couple of point forty-fives from a source in Queens who had once been a patrolman and now in his retirement was selling off a little of his private, stolen stock to stay away from the inflationary spiral. And he was able to pick up a shotgun from a contact of the retired cop's from a depot in the distant Bronx. The shotgun had been a particular coup; he hoped that Wulff would be proud of him. Of course, in the state that Wulff had reached now it was not likely that he was still in a position where he could understand or appreciate anything going on outside of him, but even though praise was strictly not to the point, Williams hoped that Wulff would acknowledge what had been done. It had been remarkable—particularly after all lines of conventional supply had been closed off to him—that he had been able to get what he had. The shotgun alone could probably hold off a crowd of forty, and the pistols would come in handy. Wulff would have every reason to be pleased. But then again the way that the man was behaving now, after all that had happened to him, Williams thought that he would be lucky if Wulff even acknowledged the efforts. Probably he would not. He was just too deep into his situation now to comprehend, let alone appreciate anything that was outside of himself.

That was all right though, Williams guessed. That was the way it had to be and it would be foolish to become emotionally involved with Wulff's moods at this stage of the game. Wulff was hardly significant to Williams in the emotional sense. It was only that he was going his way and Williams another, and there was a point of intersection. That was all. You had to keep that in mind at all times. You did not want to make any more of this thing than existed.

Williams rode a Greyhound bus to Philadelphia, sitting over the rear wheels, smelling the exhaust and enjoying the relative isolation of this unfavorable spot in a bus that was less than half full. No one near him, no one to smoke in his face, no one with whom he had to fake conversation or turn from in disgust. The ordnance was in a valise over his head, tucked into a tight space between the railing and the top of the bus, undetectable as far as he knew. Also undetectable was the resolve within him which had come stealing upon him slowly from the time that he had left the second retired cop's house with the shotgun. The resolve had come upon him almost absently like the little forgotten images of a dream from which you would awake with an erection and no clear inkling of what had inspired it, and at first he had ignored it, but as it continued growing upon the screen of his consciousness, it was now unavoidable and he allowed himself to inspect it like a collector appraising a rare and hidden jewel. Turning it in mental fingers, he toyed with it, letting it revolve as it caught all of the twinkling aspects of his life: *In Philadelphia it all has got to end. This is the last.* Then: *In Philadelphia I'm going to have to kill Wulff.*

In Philadelphia I'm going to have to kill Wulff. Where had this come from? What area of the consciousness had disgorged it? It did not matter, of course. No one cared about origins in this business or in any other. It was only the results which counted … and as Williams allowed the thought to overtake him, as he allowed it for the first time to escape from whatever crowded corner of the consciousness it had occupied to breathe the open if musty air of attention, he saw that it was right. It was going to have to be done. Unbidden the thought had come to him, vomited out by some shrewder and more knowing part of the brain which must have been making its careful evaluations a long time ago, pending this moment. *That may have been why I agreed to go to Philadelphia.* Williams twitched on the seat and began to shake with excitement.

That might have been it. He had been on something called the "Wulff squad" back in New York after he had come back from Los Angeles and before Wulff had been intercepted in Harlem. It had been a seedy group of losers and drunks, most of them refugees from the bow-and-arrow squad put together by the commissioner in a hopeless attempt to deflect possible adverse publicity and give the appearance that the department was making serious attempts to collar one of its own renegades. The Wulff squad had not come to much, although it had given Williams interesting material and further resolve to take nothing about the system seriously except its twice-a-month paychecks. But from the beginning he had not quarreled with the purposes for which the squad had been put together. Wulff *should* have been apprehended. The department could *not* countenance his activities, whether he was hitting the dealers or not. He *should* be in custody. And now, months later, after having traversed more ground in and out of his head than he would ever want to trace again, Williams had reached the same set of assumptions. All along he had been kidding himself to think that he was going to go to Philadelphia to bring Wulff ordnance, to lend him a hand. He had wanted out of the system, that part was clear. He had come to see that Wulff was right about the essential corruption and hopelessness of any bureaucracy that would inevitably *collaborate* with those it was created to destroy … but seeing that Wulff was right about the system did not mean that the alternative Wulff represented made any more sense.

Wulff was crazy. That much was clear. Maybe if you pitted yourself absolutely against the system you would *have* to be a crazy man; that was not to be discarded, but it was not right. Just as he had in Harlem at the end, Wulff had embarked again upon a career which would result mostly in a great many innocent people getting themselves killed. It seemed that Wulff could no longer discriminate, and he had also become as deadly as any of those whom he was fighting. So what was the point of it? It was all getting out of hand, that was clear. It would continue to get out of hand unless he stopped it.

"I have to stop it," Williams said aloud staring ahead into the tunnel of night, his hands clasped before him. "Damn it, I have to stop it or a lot of people are going to get hurt."

"Excuse me?" said a man in front of him, half turning. Williams could not see his face, only an aspect of color, of white pasted against black. "What was that?"

"Nothing," Williams said, "absolutely nothing."

"Who's going to get hurt? What are you going to have to stop? The bus?"

"Has nothing to do with you at all," Williams said heavily and the man turned away, and quietly said something which Williams could just pick up; something which had the word *fuck* in it. Williams thought yes, it is true, that if I were Wulff and this man had said that about me I might kill that man, might shoot him dead in his seat with the silenced point thirty-eight I have in my pocket. I might shoot him for cursing me and no one the wiser, and if I were Wulff this very well might have happened. But I am not. I have learned to draw a line and I do not think that he has any more. I believe that he has lost the line. That is what has happened here, and he no longer perceives the discrimination between what is unacceptable and what, although dangerous, must be tolerated for the sake of humanity. He does not understand; he does not understand at all. He understands nothing whatsoever, Williams thought, and as the bus prowled on to Philadelphia he thought three hours or a little less up until Independence Hall. I wonder what I'll do. I wonder what I'll do when I see him. Whether I'll shoot him at once and the hell with it or whether I'll try to work him around to some quiet place and time where I might be able to do it and come out of it clean. They would always think that it was some member of the organization. They would give credit where credit never would be due … but where, to be sure, it would be taken.

VI

Maury, on the other hand, was doing nothing so contemplative or essentially passive as sitting on a Greyhound bus working out the philosophic delicacies of Wulff's living ethic. Maury was barrel-assing it north on Route One, the radio screaming, whipping the Pontiac through the turns at something close to eighty-and-a-half, whistling against the sound of the radio and making his plans in the pauses between whistles, at the top of his lungs. He was pretty sure where Wulff was now. The conviction had grown in him that he would nail the son-of-a-bitch to the ground in Philadelphia, and he knew a couple of people up there who could give him a good lead onto him. Philadelphia would be no problem at all as a place where he could level this Wulff character to an ultimate justice. The only problem was getting the fucking Pontiac *to* Philly. The transmission was shot and there were at least two-and-a-half cylinders under that hood that weren't putting out, to say nothing of a brake pedal that went through the fucking floorboard. Still, you did the best you could. That was all that could be asked of a man; that he did the best he could. And at the end—the very end of it for him and his time—they had a soft bed for him and a girl with breasts like headlights glowing, glowing for him to find his way home. All right. All right. He patted the rifle beside him on the seat.

Maury had an M-15 lying next to him on the vinyl. The M-15 was just in case any fuckers gave him a hard time. State troopers too. He would take the thing and blow their fucking heads off. No one was messing with him on this great mission of revenge. But beyond that, beyond all of the good reasons for having a rifle beside him, there was the simple satisfaction of having it *there*, tight behind him on the seat so that at any time he could put out his hand, fondle it, and feel its power. There were a lot of people around—and he knew them—who would say that this kind of conduct was that of a nut; that there must be something wrong with a guy who had to reach out and fondle a rifle for kicks. Maybe the guy really wanted to fondle his nuts or something like that. Reassure himself that he had a big prick. But Maury was there to say that it was all a bunch of crap. He wasn't feeling the rifle because it had anything to do with sex at all. The rifle was a pleasure to fondle on its *own*, and there was enough significance in the stock and barrel, trigger and hammer edge of its own. As long as this bugger was next to him nothing bad would happen. He had that faith.

You had to have faith. He had faith in his ability to trap the wolf. Maury was a sporting goods store proprietor in a shopping mall in Atlanta. A week ago the wolf had knocked over his store to load up on some of Maury's ordnance. That had been bad enough. Bad enough to have your store knocked over in daylight and made an example of to every cheap thug in the business, but the wolf had done worse than that. He had gotten into Maury's best private stock of grenades, some smuggled beauties which were private stock and which had planned to save for his own use some day when they got the country back, he and his, and claimed their inheritance. If there was no revolution, he would have sold them to the highest bidder, and surely would gotten up in the high hundreds apiece and would have had enough to get out of the business. Those goddamned grenades were, in sum, his retirement fund. Beauties of German manufacture at least thirty years old, the weakest of them would have blown up a square block of Atlanta. No saying what it would do in a more cluttered place like New York City where the wolf appeared to come from.

But the son-of-a-bitch had come in and taken them. Taken all of Maury's grenades away and then headed north. Toward Philadelphia, Maury knew. He had humiliated him in his own shop, made a fool of him in front of one of his own customers and injured his reputation, possibly seriously, and Maury simply was not going to put up with any of that. If you let them take even an inch off you, if the word got around that you could be knocked over and your most prized possessions taken away from you, well, then there would be no end to the succession of punks who one-by-one would be shaping up at the door of his place or his home, aching to take him on. So Maury had gone after the wolf. It was as simple as that.

He knew he would get him. Sometimes you had a feeling, that was all. A conviction which moved in all of the panels of the guts and then stirred itself through the Philadelphia head and the arms. A conviction or certainty, they called it, and he had it; the knowledge that he would run this man down to earth and get his goods back. And after that was taken care of, he was going to shoot Wulff, kill him because he had taken a public oath that he was going to destroy the man and he was never going to be in the position of being set back on something to which he had committed himself like that. No, it was a vow that he was going to honor. Singing, patting the rifle, the feeling of the rifle was like flesh underneath his

palm. The hard, grainy feel of it was sensual and promising to him like
the skin of a big-breasted woman that you would, after a while, strip to
find the terrible and reaching softness within. Patting and pressing and
fondling the rifle, Maury drove madly north, feeling himself drawn along
the line of roadway toward destination like a big fish being hooked in
by the reel of purpose, soon to surface and mesh with his destiny.

VII

Strolling through the south side, killing a little time before meeting
with Williams at Independence Hall and beginning his mission of
revenge upon Martin, letting the man sweat for the time being, Wulff
came upon two addicts nodding out in a hallway. They were hunched
against one another mumbling in the abcess beyond light, as if in the
deep collaboration of the sex act. But when Wulff stopped, turned,
went back to where he had seen them and pulled them out, he could see
that it was nothing like that at all. They merely had been exchanging
confidences, that was all. Getting high together in a way which made
them the more likely to cling. One was white and one was black. But
aside from this appealingly inter-racial aspect they looked quite similar;
the color was merely a texture laid over faces that could have been those
of twins, with clothing and postures that were images of one another.
They might have been twenty-five years old apiece, although with
addicts it was hard to tell. The aging aspect. Most likely they were in
their late teens. Their flesh clung to him like cellophane as Wulff
dragged them away from one another, giving up the connection with a
vague and disgusting sucking sensation, and he just looked at them for
a while in the waste of the afternoon.

There was no one else on the street; they had picked a side alley which
was behind the enormous grey walls of housing projects vaulting
upwards, on the block opposite, all of which on their side was dull glass,
puddles and wire. The block itself had been stripped, presumably for the
next housing project which had been held up after original demolition
because of lack of funds. It was a block in Philadelphia, but it could as
well have been one in New York or the back streets of old Spanish Los
Angeles which Wulff had seen. Junkie territory was its own terrain; it
was one vast linked city of blood, and the passage from one part of that
darkness to another was accomplished just as the furious passage of the
blood might occur between the cells of a destroyed organ. The kids in
his grasp looked at him with terror, but the terror was merely
momentary, convulsive, a quick gathering of attention which could as

easily dissipate, were they to be released. If he were to release them they would pass back into the alley and begin the exchange again.

"What is it?" the white said. His hand deep in his pocket jiggled something. "What you want?" Wulff reached forward, grabbed his wrist, bringing his hand out of the pocket. The hand tightened around something, then released. Gleaming things fell into the gutter: an eyedropper, spoon, a little packet. "Son-of-a-bitch," the white said. "Dirty bastard."

"None of it," the black said pointlessly and turned to run. Hands twitching, arms pumping, knees moving erratically, he must have imagined himself to be in full gallop, speeding away from Wulff and the alley with great and increasing speed. But in truth he merely lurched, stumbling over himself. Barely six feet away, imagining himself to be at distance, he tossed something onto the ground. Glint: a needle. Shuffling faster, the black moved away.

"No," Wulff said, "stop!"

The black did not stop. In the dream to which he was locked Wulff must have been backed away several blocks now, receding in interior vision, tiny, pointless. Wulff took his gun out quickly and fired a shot over the black's head.

The white screamed something and went to the pavement muttering, his hands helpless tentacles clawing idly at Wulff's ankles, but the black did not stop running. Magnified in his consciousness, the shot must have stunned him, raised him to a new level where fleeing, dreamily, he believed that he was dead and was only surprised at how easy, how very much like life death itself could be. "Stop!" Wulff shouted again and the white muttered and clawed underneath him. The black was now a hundred yards down range, slowing with the effort of flight but still in motion, nearing a corner. Soon he would turn the corner and then he would be on a main street in Philadelphia.

Wulff did not want to shoot him. Just as the black was now running in a dream, so this had been a dream for Wulff, a means of making passage before the meeting with Williams. He had gone out into the slums of the south side to look for addicts simply so that he could remember what his quest was, so he could keep a tight perspective on where, despite all of the manipulations and murder, it originated. Who he was killing for. When he had seen the two in the alley the impulse to go over to them had been clear. So had been what he thought he was going to do: he was going to seize the works from them, grind them down under his heel, and settle for giving them a lecture and scaring the living shit out of them. In the state that they were in it would have been enough. All right, he might have busted their heads or threatened to in order to find out the name of their dealer, but that wouldn't have amounted to much. They would have disgorged the name easily in their terror, taking him for once to be an honest, angered narc. And all right again. Okay, if their connection had been near. If he had been able to get there conveniently and deal with him in the time that he had before he was due to meet Williams, he might have done that as well. He wasn't to deny that either. He had looked for a little spot action on these trails, and if he had gotten anything to follow through he would have. If the dealer were anywhere in the neighborhood. He didn't want to risk screwing up the meet with Williams. Williams was going to give him some real heavy ordnance so that he could get into Martin's house and really blow the shit out of it in the old way, the way that it had been in San Francisco at the boat.

But now he was in a different situation. He hadn't stage managed this one too well; he had to admit that part of it. It had been really lousy work letting the black run away. Put it down to overconfidence then or overplaying his hand when he really had no hand to play. But now it was obviously serious. He couldn't afford to have the black get away; couldn't afford to get involved with police authorities at this time. And although the crazed junkie might run straight into a hole somewhere, he might go to the cops, too. You simply couldn't tell with junkies. They were unpredictable; they were apt to do anything whatsoever.

All of this calculation went through one part of Wulff's brain very low-key, very carefully. But it was, really, as if he was behind it rather than letting thoughts drive him. He was merely a witness to his stream of consciousness rather than the subject, and while he was thinking a gun was in his hand, was extended, and fire was leaping from the deep end as he lay down shots into the man at target practice range, cross-stitching him with the bullets. Each of them was placed in a perfect shot pattern, and it was classic shooting in every sense. The dummy was levelled precisely in sight, except that the dummy was down, the black man at the edge of the corridor suddenly obliterated, and the white behind him was moaning. He had killed the man. Wulff turned and looked at the white who was not a man at all, only a boy. All of the twenty-five-year old scraped from his eyes, the age that had been laid in by dope, and now an eighteen-year-old face stricken and hopeless looked up at him. It was the face of a child who in different circumstances might not have been there at all, could have only dreamed what he had become, as the boy said, "You didn't have to do that."

Wulff looked at him. There was nothing to say.

"You didn't have to do it. We didn't do anything to you; what the hell did you do that for? Why would you want to off a guy? You a narco man or are you just trying to rip us off? What is this shit?" the white said, his fingers scrambling at the earth, little puffs of dust coming up. "What the hell is this?"

"You don't understand."

"Don't understand?"

"You don't understand anything," Wulff said. His voice sounded dry, meaningless, off the point. He was not sure that he himself knew what the hell he was driving at. Maybe nothing. That, as likely as not, was the explanation. Why did everything have to mean something? "Get out of here," Wulff said.

The boy was on the ground, shaking. He seemed to want to stand, drew up his knees to shoulder level to try and force accommodation, but he did not quite have the strength and instead flattened out against the ground, like dough. "Murderer," he said. "You off people and then you tell them they don't understand."

"If you don't get out of here I'm going to off you too. I don't need any witnesses."

"Oh Jesus," the boy said. His body convulsed, then he was on his feet. "Why?" he said. "That's all I want to know. Why?"

"You don't understand," Wulff said again and raised the gun and pointed it, and then in a dream which must have been like the boy's or like the running man's, a dream which intercepted with theirs, diving in and out of the same murky patterns, the net of the dream grabbing and holding them together, he shot him in the head once with a brutal shot that went in behind the left ear and spattered blood. Even before the shot hit, the boy was down, as if he had apprehended death; as if, in fact, he had needed it. And death was only the last confirmation of all circumstance.

"I told you," Wulff said weakly. "I told you, there can't be any witnesses to this. I gave you a chance but you wouldn't take it," he added and then he put the gun away and went from there quickly, heading toward the hotel, toward Independence Hall, and toward Martin. It did not matter, nothing mattered, because at that place of grave intersection, wherever it would be, there would ultimately be only one judgment, and whatever that judgment would be he would take it, he would take it.

VIII

When he had made all the arrangements, as far as he could anyway, Martin blew a little pot alone in the house which had been staked out by competent men fore and aft, and thought about fucking. He could definitely use a little fucking, there was no question about it. The life force and all that. And besides, it was both a drag waiting for some lunatic to appear at your house for a heavy attack and impossible to leave the barricades and wait him out in a less shielded position … So what you had to do was to kill the time as conveniently as possible. Pot helped a little, and Martin had an airy, disconnected feeling working it over. The joint went down so easily that it seemed to make him a different person, and that different person was definitely interested in a little screwing. He went through the numbers and called the most pliable and expensive of all the prostitutes with whom he had been dealing recently, and then waited in a pleasant haze of pot and increased disconnection while she made her way over in her own Corvette, through the checkpoints that he had set up and all the way to the vestibule where he found that the anticipation and necessity were so great that he had her practically out of her clothes and indeed was on top of her before she had come into the living room, fucking and groaning and pinning her on the couch within four minutes of the time that she had pushed the door closed behind her. When the orgasm came it came off-center in a sudden torrent of depression which surprised him, and he fell on top of her, his head sunk between her breasts, breathing through clenched teeth and feeling the slow weakness begin again.

"What's wrong?" she said. She was a very nice girl; any expensive prostitute working in the area of Harrisburg, Pennsylvania would have to be a nice girl or she would have found the territory utterly impossible. As it was, she had managed to adjust herself to Harrisburg rather than the reverse, and although her clientele was restricted, she assured Martin that she had never once lowered her price or her standards, even though that would have been the easy way. "You look depressed," she said, and expertly eased him out of her, twisted to the side, pivoted to an elbow and looked at him with a serious, committed expression that was nicely framed by her breasts, which were slightly pendulous at this angle—but none the worse for wear. "Did it have to do with all those men outside? Are they waiting for someone?"

"Something like that."

"Problems," she said understandingly. She had an inkling of his business, although she had never pressed it. Still, it was his assumption that she knew what kind of man he was; what he was dealing with in the underlay of the relationship which he had with her. He had never felt so close to a prostitute in his life. Often he found it hard to think of her as a prostitute at all, but rather simply *Jeanine*, an attractive girl, an easy lay whose affection he rewarded with gifts. "Everybody's got problems. You have another joint?"

He said, "I might."

"Why don't you get up and get me one?"

"Not now," he said.

"You just don't want me smoking," she said. "You're very conservative. You don't want someone you know blowing pot in your house even though you do it yourself."

"That's not fair, Jeanine."

"Who's looking to be fair? What does the truth have to do with being fair? You're like a guy who sleeps out four nights a week but doesn't like anyone looking at his wife and gets homicidal if he thinks that his daughter is behind the bushes."

"Come on, Jeanine."

"Come on yourself," she said. "You know it's the truth."

"I just don't want to hear it now."

"Give me a stick."

"They aren't in here," he said.

"So go where they are and get me one?"

"Listen," he said, shifting his position. He came off her slowly, rolling to one side, and began to sit painfully on the couch feeling that his body had been partitioned into various sections, none of which were collaborating vigorously with any other. "Maybe you just ought to go now."

"What? How's that?"

"Maybe this isn't a good time to talk," he said.

"Who's talking? I want to blow a little pot."

Something in her aspect, lying there on the couch naked but with a knowledge in her face which gave her more poise than if she had had clothing on and been uncertain, twisted within him and Martin began to feel the situation moving away from him, a lapse of control. He had had that feeling before, although not quite in such a situation, and certainly not with this woman. "I don't want to talk," he said. "I have things on my mind."

"You just wanted to get laid."

"So what the hell's wrong with that?"

"Nothing's wrong with that," she said, "except that you fall on top of me before I'm even through the door and now you won't even give me a joint when I want one. You won't take me seriously."

"Oh come on," Martin said. It was too much. It was simply ridiculous that she should be engaging him in this now, that all of this should be happening at such a point of complex difficulty in his life. There was a madman who had declared his intention of killing him, and there were men pacing outside who were paid one hundred and fifty dollars an hour because they were quite capable of killing people like Wulff … or like Martin. Meanwhile there was a prostitute on his couch who was angry because he would not give her a joint and somehow took his fucking her too fast as a reflection upon her personality. Somewhere if you dug deep enough within this there was a moral or at least a proper irony, but Martin did not have the time. "All right," he said. "All right, Jeanine, now that's enough now. I think you'd better go."

"I'd better what?"

"There's nothing more to talk about. You'd better leave."

"You just called me over here to get laid and now you want to throw me out," she said. "Now what the hell does that mean?"

"It means I want you out."

"You're treating me like a whore."

What the hell do you think you are? He almost said it, but he did not. He did not say that. Certain factors in any relationship were understood without statement; if they were indeed spoken the relationship was forever changed and not at all for the better. That was another one of those ironies about human relations. Everything was its opposite. "Not at all, Jeanine," he said. Patience was a virtue. You had to cultivate patience in or out of this world. With what else could you compose yourself against eternity? He had always believed in it, even though factors in his life like Wulff tended to make him fall apart. "It's just that I have some things to do—"

"After you got laid."

"Come on," he said. He looked at her. She was an attractive woman. Not bad for Harrisburg; not even bad for New York. She could have made two hundred dollars a night easily in Manhattan, no strain. Just an answering service and a valise would have been sufficient equipment. Instead she was working in Harrisburg and its suburbs, settling for gifts and considerations which when averaged down could not even be half of that. Still, maybe she was happier this way. She would last longer, and she was away from the more immediate pressures of the terrifying situation of New York. She would be able to pace herself; might be making the same modest living at thirty-three without having left three-quarters of herself poured out over a thousand beds.

Then, too, maybe she merely wanted to build up a set amount of money and get out of the game. Maybe she liked what was being done and enjoyed Harrisburg. Martin did not know. He really had no relationship with her.

"All right," she said, "I'm coming on. You're throwing me out; you could at least give me a stick."

"No," he said.

"I'll take it with me. I won't have it here."

"No," he said again.

"You're flagrantly opposed to pot."

"I didn't say that."

"You're against it on moral grounds. You think that people are destroying their minds, polluting their consciousness. Actually you think that it's the enemy of youth, a scheme by the pushers and criminals and dope dealers to ruin people."

"That's ridiculous, Jeanine," Martin said. "We're not getting anywhere," he said. "This just isn't moving us anywhere at all. I want you to go now."

"I'll go. Permanently I'll go."

"Just get out," he said. "Please."

She stood, went over to her dress which lay crumpled to one side of the room, stooped, picked it up, and unfurled it with disgust. "You ruin everything," she said. "Look at the mess you've made of this. I'll have to take it to the cleaners."

"Do that."

"I can't even find my goddamned brassiere."

"It's behind the couch," Martin said.

"Oh," she said and looked that way. "That's right. You kind of threw it there. You tore it off with your teeth and spat it out over there, didn't you?"

"Shit."

"Nice restrained behavior."

"I've had all of this I can take," Martin said. "I don't know why you're doing this but I can't take it any more. I want you to get out and get out now."

"All right," she said, stopping. "Pot," she said. "Blowing a joint but anti-pot, and won't even pass on a joint to a friend. You're really something," she said. "You know that? All of you are the same."

"What?"

"All of you are the same," she said. "You'll deal in it and you'll even use a little bit of it on your own, just for the kicks, of course. Never anything serious like doctors taking a little hypo of shit just to relax. But when it comes right down to actually passing the stuff onto somebody you *know*, when it becomes a matter of having to face the person and see them doing it, then you can't take it. You just don't want to face the truth of what you are," she said angrily and bent down and picked up her brassiere, started to put it on, and then, apparently thinking better of that, dropped it over the couch and instead began to struggle with her dress, pulling it down over her shoulders with strange little grunts. "None of you want to face the truth, that's your goddamned trouble."

Martin stood, walked away from her, adjusted his clothing. Always, at moments of great crisis or when under pressure, he wanted to feel that he was well dressed and that everything was in order. Call it crazy if you wanted but that was just the way it had to be if he was going to function. He smoothed his shirt, tucked it away underneath his belt, adjusted his tie, and then reached down to jerk his fly closed, and feeling his hand literally shake as it fumbled on one of the striations, momentarily jammed, he finally forced the zipper all the way up. "What are you calling me?" he said.

She had the dress over her head, peeking out angrily like an animal between bars. "Oh come on," she said. "Come on, don't be an asshole."

"I'm not being an asshole. I want to know what you were trying to say."

"You know what I was trying to say."

"You calling me a dealer?"

"Oh," she said, "oh come on and be reasonable, Horst." This was the first time that she had ever used his name. He had no idea that she even knew it. *Where had she learned his name?* Had he cried it out in sleep?

Unconsciously, not even sure of what he was doing, Horst had walked over one, two, three steps toward her and hit her hard across the face, backhanded with his right hand, centering the blow so that it did not send her sprawling so much as it rooted her further into place, brought her to bear with a surprised and terrible attention. Her eyes were rolling as he said, "Don't you ever call me a dealer and don't you ever use my name," and hit her again. She crumbled this time, making little sounds within her. Seeing her broken like this was not enough for him; indeed, it fed the rage. It was not fair that this kind of pain should come from one who was, really, so vulnerable, and he was ready to hit her again and might have lost all control except that at that moment there was a dim whistling unlike anything he had heard in the thirty years he had been back from the European theatre. The sound was like metal colliding against itself, and then with a shocking and yet somehow satisfying sense of implosion, the house, the carefully built house, the house that he had made his protection and his life, blew.

IX

Wulff had stolen another car and headed directly toward Harrisburg after the business with the junkies. Standing Williams up, then. Well, that was just tough shit. He couldn't be everywhere, could he? He wasn't expected to be every damned place, and he was busy, goddamned busy now. The thing that had happened on the south side had given him the feeling, no longer vague, that matters were closing in on him rapidly and that if he had any real business to do he had better transact it quickly. Do it damned quickly while he still had the options to work with because after what had happened with the kids there was no saying how long he would remain free. They were closing in on him from all angles, and two new bodies would register further clues. But then again it was his fault in a way. He had to admit that. He really had no business offing the two of them if what he wanted to do was to wait out Williams and take care of Martin. Scratch one for him on that; he had overreacted. Still, how could he have resisted? Once matters were started, once he had come up against them, he knew his duty. It was a cop's duty. You could not look upon a junkie and let him go on that way unless you were an accessory to murder. You had to help them. And these kids were beyond help; death surely was the only answer.

But in the restlessness—and yes he would admit it—in the stabbing panic after the double murder Wulff had realized that his time was running out. He was working short term now; he would have to do what was necessary without reference to others and particularly without waiting for Williams. What did Williams matter anyway? He was not to be trusted. None of them were to be trusted, and Williams had betrayed him in Los Angeles. If he did it there he would be all the more likely to do it in Philadelphia, which was closer to home, closer to the little lawn in Saint Albans which he treasured. Wulff had Maury's grenades tucked fore and aft into his coat. Six of them, beauties capable, he was sure, of the greatest destruction. He had two pistols, a point forty-five bore and a point thirty-eight. In the jungles in the night skirmishes he had gone up against a hundred invisible guerrillas with far less and had managed, one way or the other, to come out of it. America had to be looked at in the same way, then. America was a night jungle; the guerrillas were the swine like Martin and they were pinned to their positions. If you were a true soldier you went in and fought them on their own terms. You did not look for outside help, nor did you depend upon those who had already proven that they would betray you.

Obviously he would have to go into Harrisburg and take care of Martin himself and the hell with Williams. People like Williams would always manage one way or the other. What the hell had they ever done for him? What had Williams ever done for Wulff?

He stole the first car he laid eyes on, a ninety-eight Oldsmobile, 1966, idling at a light with a heavy black man alone inside wrapped sullenly in his overcoat as he peered at the light and then at Wulff's exposed gun as if they were equally menacing. "Get the fuck out," Wulff said at the driver's side, talking through the open window and showing the point thirty-eight as the driver got out. He opened the door and stepped out quickly, rubbing his hands in the sudden cold and trying not to look at Wulff, who had already forced his way past him.

"I don't care," the driver said, "it's all right with me. You can take the fucker. I can't get nowhere with it, and at least I'll get book value." Two blocks after he had slammed the car into gear and rolled into the first stretch of open highway Wulff saw what he meant. The transmission chattered and banged like a group of talkative whores, the body had a severe rattle, and the car seemed to have no power at all, losing speed over thirty-five. The wheel seemingly disconnected in his hands. Driving the car was like being in isolation above a small factory which was falling into a deteriorated state, hearing the ominous noises coming from the machinery, and the cries from the operators as they tried to contend with levers that no longer worked. The car contained both machinery and complaint; it was a mobile disaster area—and yet it could run. That was all that mattered. It was still functional, although just barely, and it would get him to Harrisburg.

Wulff settled himself for the requisite period of misery, and probed the car west. The route was not familiar to him, and there were many slowings to look at signs on the highways; much frantic checking of what he thought might have been the proper exits after he had passed them. At every stop the transmission clanked and the car vomited out clouds of yellow exhaust which blocked his rear vision for thirty seconds at a time. He knew that the mission was perilous. There was never any doubt in his mind but that going to Martin on his own was a risky and dangerous process … But he had never felt before that he was in actual danger in the process of driving a car. The Oldsmobile gave him moments of panic that, in their special way, Wulff had never known before.

At one point he braked too hard, getting back into lane behind a Corvette that had cut in spasmodically, and, with a terrifying wrench, the brakes had gone all the way to the floor, forcing him to barrel the car left in a straight dive toward the divider to clear the other car and to try and take off some speed. He had managed to save himself, although without much margin, and the Olds had taken a terrific jolt on the left front that had gone all the way through him. Then, regaining control and with the insolent Corvette far ahead of him, he had to contend with the fact that he would have to use those brakes again. Was there any reserve at all? Cautiously playing with them, he had been able to establish that vacuum reserves could be boosted through several applications that brought them up to half-pedal and gave him some fraction of original braking force. But undoubtedly the car would be no good in a panic stop. It would override its brakes in a moment and pitch him and his load of grenades through the windshield leading to a particularly ominous risk ... he might not only kill himself, but in the process by impact blow up half the countryside as well.

He seriously considered rolling the car to the side and trying to get another. The driver had not been kidding, all right; book value for this ninety-eight would be a steal. The insurance company would never know how badly hurt it had been. But stopping the car and trying to get another on a big state highway in the middle of the night was not going to be easy. He would have to flag down cars which would, of course, not stop. He might have to start shooting in order to bring them down, but the drivers would be fleeing in terror and the only way that he would be able to bring a passing car to a halt would be via bullet holes in the tires ... and he did not think that the car would be any more use to him at that point than it would be to the driver.

No, he was pretty well stuck. He would have to do what he could with the Oldsmobile. The next time around—if there ever was a next time— he would learn from this and make sure never to steal a car that was more than two years old. The trouble was that he had been betrayed by his attraction for rotting luxury cars for several years. He had gone crosscountry in rotting Cadillacs. But the Cadillac appeared to be a car of more intrinsic quality than the Olds ninety-eight. Same body frame and components, but maybe the Cadillac assembly line took just a shade more pride in fitting the panels together, or maybe there was some spirit in the Cadillac which could not inhabit the essentially ersatz ninety-eight.

Nothing to worry about. All these speculations managed to do was to keep him preoccupied, kept his mind buzzing and mumbling about matters other than what he wanted to do to Martin and how really frightened, at base, he was by what he had done. No question about it: stealing a car like this and going after the man directly had been an impulsive gesture. It did not jibe with the calculation that had marked many of his moves up until this point. His quest may have been insane, but it had been approached in a businesslike and professional fashion. If you did not approach something as wild as this from that aspect you could not last in it for more than a day or so. But now there was nothing systematic about it. Not when he was off to Harrisburg to murder a man whom he had never met but still hated; when he had ignored an appointment with a man who might help him but who he did not wait to see. Trying to pick up another car on the highway would have been a compounding of the madness. He would not do it. At a certain point you had to haul back in, had to take things as they came and try to shape yourself to situations.

So he kept on driving, locked into a bitter tight place, twirling the knob of the radio which was surprisingly functional until he got some music in the background that he found complemented his mood. Something which must have come out of one of the Philadelphia soul stations, it was bitter and bleak music with drums and dull sucking noises underneath it like alien mouths planting themselves in brief, horrid explosions upon flesh which Wulff would never see, of which he could never conceive. He began to sing idly along with the music, mingling obscenities and empty little breaths of sound against the rhythms. Not concentrating too much upon the lyrics, which did not matter—neither theirs nor his—but only trying to establish a certain rhythmic basis against which he could work, all of the time he thought of Martin.

Martin was the key. According to the sources that he had spoken to in the south, and more importantly according to his own instincts, Martin would definitely be the most significant kill. He was the entire purpose of the Philadelphia breakdown. This was what Wulff thought. He was the head of the second echelon, and as a result of the meetings which would occur in Philadelphia preceding the bicentennial, he would be promoted to a position of maximum influence. In line with that, eliminating him now might save the nation from two hundred years of slaughter, two hundred years of dead children, tangled hair in hallways and od's, twisted bodies and broken mouths pouring fluids in the explosion of pain from the planted needle. He could save an unborn generation from all of this if he could only kill Martin. Dope would always be there, you had to face that. Dope was part of a republic that flowed upon one or another kind of junk throughout all of its history, and it would need that sustaining fire. But he could set back the process, could hurt the trade badly, and make a real difference. That, perhaps, was all that one could hope for: to set up a kill, to set back the course of history. Nothing, ultimately, would really change.

The radio kept on, shifting to a different, more urgent beat. Pulling in to the rim of the signal, the sounds of an easy-listening station to the east and the coiling of the strings around the sound of drums was, to Wullf, like the feeling of shit coiling around the nation. America was easy-listening. At the heart it was an easy-listening country with smooth tunes and forgettable melodies trickling out of all the empty places of intersection and passage into America in the early 1950's that accelerated as the nation turned inward. And as the profit began to flow, the coil of drugs had been tightened around it. Soul smacked around easy-listening America, tightening and tightening until finally, from the inside, the country began to explode; first the assassinations and then the riots and then Vietnam, which was the biggest drug war of them all. The issues for the next fifty years were being fought over hard on the farmlands where the power was rooted, and after Vietnam the country had been driven explicitly insane, and the easy listening became an easy, precipitous slide toward universal smack, easy shit for everyone … Only Wulff had stopped that. Wulff had been the only variable in the entire equation which the country had become. He had done well; he might have altered the course of history. But it would all go down the drain unless he killed Martin.

He had to kill Martin. And he would do it, that was all. He was going to do it because the man needed killing. He represented the total force of evil in the universe as far as Wulff was concerned, and Wulff did not want to hear any of Martin's excuses or defenses, but only information that would lead to his murder. He began to track signs toward Harrisburg then and felt himself funneled down from the brief high of the radio and his stream of consciousness. Now that he was close upon it, he was all business again, and with that came a real sense of the risks of his position. He was in a very difficult, exposed way here and he had a lousy car as well, to say nothing of damned little maneuverability. Martin would probably have his house as thoroughly staked out as possible. But then, too, Wulff had one advantage: Martin could not possibly believe, after all of the preparations he had made, that Wulff would be audacious enough to actually strike at him immediately. He would have to be unprepared for this immediate, surprise attack. That would be the key to this, too, just as it was to almost every proper guerrilla action in the history of twentieth century warfare: total surprise.

He drifted off the turnpike, found his way. He didn't know shit about Harrisburg except that it was the state capitol and had had some pretty serious floods a couple of years ago which had put about a fifth of the city underwater and had the city declared a national disaster area. That was nothing exceptional, of course. Only the declaration made it unusual. Every city in the country was a national disaster area, declared or not; every city in the country was drowning, if not by water then from shit, poison, corruption and from the garbage left by those who came in every day to take what they could out of it and to flee at night. Near Harrisburg was Hershey, of course, the famous chocolate factory which had been started up by a crazy millionaire who never smoked or drank or advertised. But the crazy millionaire had long since passed on to whatever place there was that gave dead millionaires a fresh start, and now Hershey chocolate bars were advertised everywhere, even in all of the better markets, and had reduced their weight and quality by at least a half while doubling in price. Progress.

He was also making progress toward the place in his mind where he felt he had located Martin's home. All of his pursuits had been mapped out in some area of the mind which more often than not were in accordance with the reality that was then presented. It was not so much as if he were pursuing these bastards through the real Boston or San Francisco, but rather as if they were occupying terrain which he had created and which absorbed them. The same thing with Martin. The same thing with all of them. He was omnipotent, he was driven by righteousness, he was utterly in control of himself, and this righteousness would inevitably lead him toward a righteous outcome. He had to believe that. He had to accept the fact that his cause was correct and that it would lead to victory.

So he drove through the streets of Harrisburg, working on instinct, working on little more than his knowledge of urban geography to take him to where Martin would live. He would be far from the inner city and probably to the east, but he would not be so far that he could not conveniently reach the runners who would have to work that inner city. He would have to be near the turnpikes, too, because he would be dealing with people who would be coming in from New York, Philadelphia and Chicago, and they would want to come right in, conduct their business, and get out again. So the house would be in a fairly nice residential area about three miles east of downtown, and Wulff, now that he was here, drove with splendid patience, resting easy on the wheel, all the time in the world.

No need for the radio now. The car made its own music from chirping fan belts and little pulleys tearing at one another in the bowels of the engine. It actually seemed to be running a little better, now that it had been on the highway for a while. Maybe if the owner had treated it with respect, had blown out the carburetor now and then, he would not have had so much reason to complain. These big bombers desperately needed to be taken out on the road and run at speed. Of course, that really did nothing to solve the brake problem. The brakes were really bad. Once he came into the residential area, he settled for driving on the transmission, dropping it into low at the stop signs, slowing up a block before traffic lights, using the brake only at the early stages and then in a series of light taps rather than jolts to coax a little vacuum out of it. The brakes were not encouraging. One thing that Wulff distinctly did not need right then was to hurtle through a stop sign and be stopped by a cop or a car.

He knew exactly when he had reached the street where Martin lived. It had the patrolled look that he had seen on so many streets that he had approached in the past. There was a car, its headlights doused, sitting in the middle of the street to his right, idling slowly. Forms appeared to be inside it, but it was impossible to really tell. Behind a tree, half concealed, stood a man with a hand in his pocket. Wulff let the Olds drop right by the block, moving with maximum caution and playing for inconspicuousness, then rolled down three blocks and angled right into a sidestreet out of their line of sight. He cut his own lights, brought the car to a stop and shut the engine. Very carefully, he removed the grenades from his coat and stacked them in a little pile beside him. Then he took out the two pistols and checked them carefully, both barrels and stocks, making sure that all was in order. As he did all of this he hummed to himself the same way that he had done on the highway with the radio, to a merry, tuneless little snatch of song repeated over and over again with vowels rather than words in perfect rhythmic constancy to the sounds that the pistols made when snapped into order, and to the gentle rolling of the grenades on the seat as he carefully counted and restacked them.

They were curiously warm to the touch, and felt almost gelatinous. If he closed his eyes, he felt that he would see them glowing in the tight spaces of the seat. But there was no time to look upon the grenades with a sensual air. That would get him nowhere, and besides, it would be a hell of a sad comment on him if he were to admit that the grenades had more of an effect upon him that way than anything had in a long time … since the girl, Tamara, had been killed in front of him on that beach in Miami. He had not thought of sex since, and knew that sex no longer existed for him in any form. Strange then that the grenades attracted them in this way. He shook his head, spat on the floorboards, started the car again. Tamara had died on that beach so that Wulff would have a second chance, so that the dealers and poisoners and scum of the world would not be able to destroy him and go on in their evil work. If he were to quit, even at this stage, it would be as if her sacrifice had been meaningless, as if he had never been there at all. You had to stay on top of the situation. The vermin were everywhere. They were absolutely everywhere. Look at Martin. You turned away for one moment and there was another rooting to the fore, ready to take over. The basic issue was poison.

With delicacy and precision, Wulff turned the ninety-eight around in the street in a broken U-turn without clashing the transmission at all and without having to pump the brake, and keeping the carat the lowest possible rpm's without stalling out, manipulated the transmission lever between neutral and reverse with the greatest of delicacy. Facing the right way, he idled up to the corner, cut left, and with infinite patience hung to the curb, creeping up on the third block down at no more than two or three miles an hour. It was two in the morning. They could not be at a high state of alertness. It was three hours until the faintest touch of dawn in this late fall, and if he did not accomplish what he had to within those three hours, he did not know his business at all. He would be truly worthless to have any worry at all about the time element now, he thought. He had his lights off, the radio playing softly. It would take fifteen minutes to creep down on that block at this pace, and at the rate he was going the Olds would be almost on top of them before they knew what had happened. Human metabolism was at its lowest at this hour; alertness might come from the brain but it could never come from the blood in the deep night. The ape that man had been slept in trees and trembled in the darkness.

He kept on moving, coaxing the car down the line. He was half-a-block away now, and still the guards had not looked up. The man against the tree seemed to be slumped there, rooted in place, possibly dozing, and there was no movement within the car. They were sleeping there, too, beyond attention, beyond interest, sure that nothing was going to happen on this quiet street in the darkness. Soldiering on the job. Hired help rather than those personally involved. If Martin had used people who were really, directly concerned with him, this would not have happened. But that was the way it worked out. Almost all of these people had to hire help, and almost none of the help really cared. Ultimately they had only the friends which money could buy.

It was very easy.

He stopped the car at the corner, cut the engine, and in the same motion took the point forty-five, balanced it, pivoted, opened the door and shot the man who was standing behind the tree. The shot went in quickly, efficiently, and the man fell as if he were not and never had been a living thing, but was merely an ornament, an appendage to the landscape which had now been cut down. The lights of the parked car flicked on and Wulff heard the grinding of the starter, but the people within had already squandered whatever edge they might have had.

They should have been prepared before, not after, the shot, because Wulff put a blast of gunfire into the car that stopped it in mid-scream. The driver had put the accelerator to the floor, revving it up for some misguided plunge in the darkness toward Wulff, but that was not going to work. Flooring the car in neutral had only managed to waste five seconds that might have been better used in trying to run Wulff down … But there was no time at all, would not have been, anyway.

He put the shot right between the driver's eyes.

From within the car there was screaming; the bubbling, terrified cry of what was either an infant or a man who had been hurt very badly, and then the door on the driver's side opened and something fell out. At the same time, the door on the passenger side came open less abruptly, there emerged a hand, and the first shot followed by a matter of seconds. The passenger, unhurt or not as badly hurt, was trying to gun down Wulff. But he could not see. Visibility was almost nil, and he had been dozing in that car and was in a state of diminished alertness, so the shot went nowhere in particular, and missed Wulff by a good margin. He returned the fire, diving to the ground, heard an immediate scream, and fired into the scream and heard nothing whatsoever.

The car engine idled unevenly for a while in the darkness and little plumes of discolored exhaust drifted up into the streetlight behind. Otherwise there was no sound whatsoever.

After a little while Wulff went over to the car to check it out. The man on the passenger side had been killed instantly with a clean shot through the heart. A man in his fifties, he lay on his back coldly and peacefully looking up at the stars. The one who had been the driver, however, was not quite as fortunate. Wulff's shot had split his skull, and his brains were running out in a seminal ooze. But he was not quite dead nor alive, for that matter, and was an animal lying crumpled there in the roadway with only little whimpers contained in the expectoration of breath to contain his humanity; his humanity destroyed and spread through the thousand bone splinters and droplets of blood which lay like a shot pattern around him. Wulff knelt over the man transfixed, staring into the eyes that were no longer alive, looking with fascination at the aspect of something that hovered between life and death, humanity and bestiality, without partaking any more of either. Time was short now. Surely Martin would have heard the shots; surely there would be investigation within a very few moments, and he could not waste seconds in looking at the man. And yet Wulff could not force himself from that aspect.

He had never quite seen so clearly the line between life and death as it was defined in the thing that lay before him. Suspended between the two, brains imploded but the organs still convulsing in the ritual and march of life, the thing seemed to partake of the best—or then again it might have been the worst—of both conditions. The timelessness and anonymity of death had closed upon the thing and yet it still knew the squalor of existence. Trapped within a corpse that would not fall from it yet would not sustain life either, the thing seemed to waver on some level of horrid intelligence. The eyes blinked as a further little grey stream of brains came from the open cavity in the crushed skull. Light moved in the eyes. It groaned and then it whimpered, birdlike.

Wulff could look no longer. Even to this, even to suffering and vengeance there had to be an end. Even to the anguish of those who deserved it there had to be some point of termination, he thought, because this was the only thing, perhaps, that defined humanity. Men were willing to bring one another both in and out of this world, administering life to one another in careful and often secretive ways, infusing one another with the artifacts of life that often came in darkness and under the guise of sex or necessity. But they also gave one another death, death through murder or in kind administration, and this was really the only thing which tied humanity together, justified everything Wulff knew of its existence … that it could maintain in a universe which drove every single living thing to death in its time that set of options which would at least make death possible on its own terms. To administer death, then, was to at least exercise a little control over it, and looking at the man, Wulff felt himself overcome for a few horrible moments by some realization of what he would be, what he was already well on the way to becoming, and what he would become more thoroughly if he did not kill this man. He could not allow what had happened to continue, could not sentence him to this middle ground between the living and the dead without giving him the expiration which he deserved. And perhaps that was all; all that humanity itself could be. Expiration. That administration of grace which marked passage between the living and the dead, and at the very end of time might be all that would stand to make the difference.

"I'm sorry," Wulff said to the thing that lay drowning underneath him. "I'm sorry, I'm sorry," and pointed the gun and shot the thing in the skull, killing it instantly, and ran from it weeping and already fumbling for the first grenade that he would throw into Martin's house so that Martin, too, and in damned quick time, could join that vast legion of the living-given-grace that went under a different name, the dead.

X

Williams changed his mind when he came into Philadelphia, and decided to rent a car after all. It was foolish to put himself in an exposed position considering who he was going to meet and the mission he was going on, and if he was going to drop out of the system all the way as appeared likely if he killed Wulff, he might as well grant himself the little amenities that the system could bring. One thing that being in the NYPD could do for you—and he still had all of the identification—was to cut the red tape and make it easy for you to get your hands on things like a rental car. Of course, while you were drowning in all of the amenities they were taking it out of your hide with a bigger and more terrible stick, but that would be something to worry about only after the fact. So when he got out of the terminal, the first thing that he did was to get to a rental counter and take a cheap Falcon on a dropoff deal, arranging to drop it off in Manhattan at no penalty, paying for gas himself, of course. He imagined that after he killed Wulff he would go back to New York and turn himself in. Of course, they would have to slap his wrist or something. They would never let him get out of it clean, but if he was lucky it wouldn't involve a jail sentence. After all, Wulff was an escaped felon. They would settle for throwing him out of the PD, which they virtually had already done anyway, and the rest he would play by ear. In any event, it was very doubtful if the bills would ever catch up with him.

He drove to the old hall, listening to the radio. He was twenty minutes early for the meeting and the only car in the district that he could see. No one moved in the central city after sundown any more. There were a few forms sleeping in doorways and a derelict was staggering around the entrance to one of our oldest and most famous landmarks, but on his next sweep around the block the derelict had vanished and Williams did not imagine that he would be back. It was an ideal place to meet; he could appreciate Wulff's sense of irony and the rightness of things, although, if you understood Wulff well enough, you would have to realize that there was probably no irony at all. Wulff just did what had to be done; he was not too concerned with looking below the level of things.

Williams put on the radio, listened to it as he began to circle the hall at a steady pace. The news about the two murdered men found shot to death in the south side sounded to him like something that Wulff might have done. It had exactly the man's imprint on it, even down to the fact that the two appeared to be junkies and derelicts. Random murder had always been Wulff's kind of thing; now instead of doing it by the numbers he might have settled for the impersonal but more satisfying device of anonymous face-to-face violence. It would figure. The entire pattern wheeled into place. Williams would not be in the least surprised now if Wulff had needed to murder those two men, if he did not, in fact, now need to murder just as badly and in almost the same way that the junkies themselves had needed the intake of the needle. It was coming to the same thing. The signs had always been there.

The signs were also there that Wulff was not going to show up after all. On the first circuit Wulff was not there. On the second he was five minutes past due, and on the third of his patient, extended sweeps, Williams found him not there again, and knew with that feeling of cold certainty which came over every cop at some stage of an investigation (and that was exactly what Wulff had become to him now: he was an investigation) that the man was not going to be there. He had gotten diverted and into something else. The murders sounded like his work and might have led him into a different trail. Even if the murders were not his—and there was no reason to assume that random, violent murders like these necessarily had to do with Wulff at all—he had to be reasonable about this. The man could not be everywhere, and there was no accounting for the trail that the man might be taking at this time. And then, too, with that cunning which he had had from the beginning, a cunning which was often connected to events only in the most peripheral fashion, Wulff might have scented what Williams's intention was and had circumvented it by simply staying away. Wulff was no fool. Throughout his quest there had been one line of consistency: he knew precisely what he was doing and he did it with forethought and with that cold kind of precision which showed that there was an apparatus of intelligence controlling his activities. Staying away from Williams then would fit into that. He had suspected something over the phone or later, and thinking all of this through on his own, had come to that conclusion.

Third sweep.

No Wulff.

Williams went around again. If Wulff were not to show this would make matters vastly more complicated in one fashion, but in another it would be simpler. The complicated part of course would be that he would have to find Wulff, and in a city like Philadelphia that was not going to be easy at all. Nor were there any guarantees that Wulff would even be in the city. He might have already gone on his way, or he might never have come here at all. Or, if he had murdered the two addicts, that act might have induced him into flight.

That was the complicated part. But there was a simple part to it also, and Williams could see the advantages.

There was now no doubt at all of the rightness of his intentions, the truth of his instincts. Now there need be no ambivalence at all, no doubt that he might on balance be doing the wrong thing.

He was doing the right thing. If he found Wulff it was going to be easy now. He would shoot him on sight.

And if Wulff had indeed committed the south side murders—and there was not much reason to doubt this—he would kill him with the full gratitude of the Philadelphia police force. He would have acted in the cause of immediate justice. He would have killed a dangerous felon.

He would solve all of his problems then. Not only the feeling that he had to kill Wulff, that he was compelled to do so, that he was acting in the interest of society by eliminating the man, but also that he might even restore his career to the NYPD in that one shot. Whatever they thought of him there, the Philadelphia PD could only appreciate his services. Furthermore, if he maintained that he indeed was detailed from a secret squad of the NYPD to track Wulff and capture him—

Well, it would all fall into place. Even the assistant commissioner would see that. The worst of which they could accuse Williams would be having taken his assignment to the Wulff squad and Wulff himself too seriously. But what could be held against him for that? Wasn't Wulff dangerous enough, an escaped criminal, the proven murderer of hundreds of people not all of whom had broken the law?

No. It would all come into place. All he had to do was to kill the man and all manner of his problems would be solved.

Williams, excited now, hands sweating a little against the shiny wheel of the compact, made a fifth circuit.

XI

Wulff had gone into Vietnam with no illusions whatsoever. He did not think that he was defending democracy, did not think it was a matter of getting them in Saigon before they beached in San Francisco. He was unable to equate the survival of the free world with the obliteration of the North Vietnamese, who seemed more or less indistinguishable in all respects from the South Vietnamese. Both groups seemed mostly interested in getting Americans out of the country, alive or dead. None of that had ever entranced him for a moment; even in his earlier years Wulff could not have been induced to think of himself as a patriot.

Rather, he had gone to Vietnam simply to see what was going on.

Something was going on, that was for sure, and eventually half a million military would have the opportunity to see it and do a little search and destroy themselves, but due to certain vagaries of the civil service law, all members of the NYPD were exempt from military service. Perhaps under the theory that they were already doing their frontline work in that most Saigonized part of America, New York City. Wulff would have found it easy to sit out the war and, indeed, when he had enlisted all of his superiors and most of the men with whom he was serving had thought that he was crazy. What man, given any kind of a choice, would place himself into that hellhole? Surely Wulff did not take seriously all of that patriotic political shit that was necessary to whip the country up into a state of war preparedness and make it unnecessary to drag eighteen-year-olds off to their draft boards to register and be sworn in. Any man who had been around, who had accumulated a few points and a little maturity could not possibly believe that crap. Could he? Unless, of course, he was a member of the regular army cadre which lived off this stuff and of which Wulff was definitely no part. No one could make any sense out of it at all.

They had been respectful, however. There had to be a divine kind of craziness to a man of twenty-four who would throw over a patrolman's shield, three years seniority and a fairly easy beat in Bedford-Stuyvesant to go into the slime of Vietnam. Even if Wulff were bucking for an officership or for easy duty, even if he was trying to turn his enlistment to his advantage, or was looking for points to be accumulated later on in the department, there still had to be some kind of respect for a man crazy enough to do this. So when Wulff had come back from Vietnam three years later as a master sergeant skilled in ordnance and guerrilla technique, they had done the nicest thing possible for him, which was to take a man of his experience and put him in the narcotics squad where if he was lucky he would never have to draw a gun again.

Well, they *were* trying to be nice. You could be cynical about almost everything concerning the NYPD, but only up to a point. They had carried over the full three years of service toward pension and seniority credits, and they had made it quite clear to him when he came back that duty had been chosen for him in an attempt to show respect for services rendered, even if they had their doubts as to why he had actually rendered them. But Wulff could not be unduly bitter toward the PD for putting him in on narco; they had done it for the best of motives and for what they thought were the highest of reasons. Whatever happened from there on in, utterly destructive as it was, could hardly be the blame of a group of people who had only been trying to show consideration.

All things considered, however, he and everyone else would have been a hell of a lot better off if he had been put on foot duty back in Bedford-Stuyvesant or had been detailed to stand guard outside one of the foreign missions, which was also a nice detail if you could get it, although extremely boring. Then again, the way that things worked out everybody might have been better off if he had re-enlisted in the army, which was something that they were very anxious to have him do anyway. There weren't many ordnance experts of his caliber. They had been willing to give him a direct commission to first lieutenant with indications that captaincy in some easy state post could be his after a time. Or, then again, he could be detailed for special intelligence training at Fort Holabird and head into the Pentagon if he wanted. It was up to him. Wulff, however, had never thought seriously of re-upping. One hitch was definitely enough, and one hitch in Vietnam was like several lifetimes.

Wulff never spoke about his experience in Vietnam. He tried as well not to think about it. Now and then for a while in sleep he had found himself on patrol again, struggling through the swamps with a bag full of ordnance which could have blown a square mile of jungle to flatland, sweating and scrambling in the terrible mud to keep control of the explosives on which, in turn, the platoon depended. Vietnam came back to him at these times. Even to this day he could sometimes see the wasted land and the burnt sky in his dreams, and at other times he could see the faces of Saigon, the people of a country which had been so ravaged that it existed only in the reference of a thousand years of war, while the efficient Americans, skidding and sinking all the time, reconciled themselves to years, and finally decades, realizing too late or not at all that their concepts of life and time were entirely different from the terrain which they were trying to occupy.

Vietnam was little more than a drug war; the shit would be flowing points east and west through Saigon for the next hundred years, and what the war was really about was which element of capitalist would control the important access doorway and direct the fruit of the Far East. But there was no way to tell anyone that. There was not even any fashion in which this truth could be accepted by the army itself because if it had been it would have blown up the war … So Wulff kept it to himself, and kept the memories of Vietnam as well tightly bound in, harnessed against himself. Anyway, after he had gone on the road he had had too much current with which to concern himself, and his nightmares when they came in the little sleep he was able to get as often had to do with the girl who had OD'd out on West Ninety-third Street as with Vietnam itself. Every experience, no matter how awful, could at least be contained and modified by time; that was why America itself had been able to go beyond the sixties and the more terrible convulsions of the seventies, still lying.

But every now and then on the rare occasions when he thought about an experience which he never talked about, Wulff wondered if it would have been better for everyone if he had not been so damned interested in paying his dues, if he had been a little less goddamned curious and a little more certain earlier rather than later as to what that damned war was really about.

He might have still been a beat cop in Bedford Stuyvesant, calling in on the hour, or long since moved up to sergeant and comfortable work in a patrol car. Probably the latter, for he was certainly a capable cop, always had been. He might well have been captain by now, sitting in a station house in Fort Greene issuing attack signals through a transistor while the city blew up, which every so often it did, and which it certainly would do again for good within the next few years.

But then again what the hell. You could not look back; the past could not be recovered. There were five hundred, six hundred people he had dealt with, minimum, who could give testimony to, at least, that point.

XII

Maury took the waitress that he had picked up at the diner off the Interstate, back to her dismal two-room furnished apartment, and fucked her there, while still in her uniform at four in the morning. Waitresses were the easiest fucks in the world, it was true. They dealt all day with people who did not see them at all, saw only the uniform and the food they brought, and the few who paid attention to them were foul-mouthed men trying to score their own points. All you had to do was to pay a little attention to them at a time when they could talk and you had them, Maury knew. It was an old and useful trick that he had picked up going off post in the Army many years ago, and it had yet to fail him. If you absolutely had to get laid and only had a few hours to spare, you could always find yourself a waitress. Of course, most of them were not particularly good-looking, and this one was no exception, but a fuck was a fuck. She was about thirty-eight and had good legs anyway, strong and tireless, even though the rest of her could have been stuffed in a bag somewhere and put over in a corner. Still, she was the best example he could offer of an old decision: all things being equal, it was always better to get laid than not to get laid at all. Life was too short for you to make calculations. Shit, you might die tomorrow and have passed up the last fuck of your life.

When he was finished he rolled off her and looked at the ceiling. In just a minute, of course, he would leave. No reason to push this. He had gotten what he had needed, and now he had to get back to the wagon which was parked right outside and find the Lone Wolf. He was closing in tight on him, he knew that now. "Where are you going?" she said to him when he began to shift on the bed.

He took his hand off her breast, which was quite insubstantial anyway. "Got to go," he said.

"Go where?"

"North. I'm headed north."

"Right now?"

"Afraid so."

"Stay a little while."

"No," he said after a pause which he hoped would show that he had seriously considered what she said. "No, I couldn't do that. I'm in kind of a hurry."

"That much of a hurry?"

"Afraid so. No time to waste."

"Just fuck and run, huh?"

He patted her wrist. "Now don't feel that way," he said. "There's no reason at all for you to feel that way. You're a *fine* person, but it's just that—"

"Why you heading north?"

"I've got business there."

"I'm entitled to *ask*," she said, with a catch in her voice. "Why don't people *tell* me anything. I have a right—"

"Of course you have a right," Maury said soothingly. He sat up on the bed, his eyes quite adjusted to the frail light of her room by now, the clutter of furniture a pattern in the darkness through which he could see himself in just a moment, weaving toward the door. He reached heavily over his stomach to the end of the bed, took his underpants, began to meditatively dress. "I'm looking for a man."

"What kind of a man?"

"A guy I know."

"Oh," she said. "A guy you know. Why do you have to go now?"

"It's just one of those things. I don't have too much time to waste; I have to get there."

"It sounds like you want him very badly."

"In a way," Maury said. He turned toward her. She had her knees drawn up, one forearm against her eyes, her tiny breasts settled to her sides, floating on her rib cage, distinguishable as breasts only by the nipples. She was not an attractive woman. He began to regret his impulse. Always in the aftermath of getting laid, even from some damned attractive women, he had had this feeling: the vague suspicion that it was all useless, time-wasting, that he might have spent the time better doing something else that would have at least been productive. This way, what the hell did he have to show for it? It probably was the most convincing reason he could think of why he had never gotten married. He could keep his need to get laid down to three or four times a week and compress it into minutes, whereas being married he never would have been free of it. That is, he would have been free of it most of the time, but he would have been trapped into a life situation where he never would have been away from its consequences. Ah, what the hell. He looked past her, looked at the chipped walls of the room in which she lay alone, at the street lamp which cut through the shade in a glare that made his eyeballs hurt. Atlantic City, New Jersey, for Christ's sake. Living here alone at her age, working in a diner. It was a raw deal, any way you looked at it. There were a certain amount of people in the world who made you feel fortunate just in being themselves and in not being you or vice-versa. As bad as things had been for him at times, even with all the humiliations and difficulties, he had more than this to look forward to. He had a hell of a lot to look forward to if he became the man to kill Wulff. Just to make her feel better, to put something into her life that would cheer her up and give her something other than her own miserable existence to consider, Maury said, "Actually, this man I'm looking for. I'm going to kill him."

"What?"

"He's a bad man," Maury said. "A very bad man, a criminal, a murderer, an escaped convict. He's killed hundreds. I happen to be a law enforcement officer and it's my detail to find him. I've been on his trail for a long time and now I'm closing in."

"That's incredible."

"You don't believe me?"

"I didn't say I didn't believe you. I just said that was incredible."

"It's not easy," Maury said, putting his shirt on. "Not easy chasing a bastard like this, let me tell you. I'll be glad when it's all over. You don't think that I'd rather leave here do you? I'd like to stay. But duty calls."

"You're so full of bullshit," she said, and drew her other forearm up against her eyes. "So full of bullshit."

That hurt Maury. He really did not have to take stuff like that. Not under the circumstances, anyway, when he had been nice enough to take her home from the diner in his own car and fuck her without a thought while he was doing it of how ugly she was. "You think I'm full of bullshit?" he said.

"It doesn't matter what I think."

"I'm from Atlanta. I'm a sheriff."

"That's great. That's really great."

"No, It's true. I'm a sheriff from Atlanta. You think I'm not telling you the truth now?"

"I don't care," she said. She moved slightly on the bed. "Why don't you just take your badge and get out of here?"

Rage moved within him. He was surprised at its force; he really had not expected anything like this. He almost never reacted to the women he fucked except in a mechanical way. He had just told her what he had because he felt sorry for her, to give her something interesting to think about. "You'd better cut it out," he said.

"Why? I'd be in big trouble, sheriff."

"Never mind," he said, putting on his sweater slowly, carefully. "Just never mind."

"You're going to kill a man. You shouldn't care what I say. You chasing after a man so important to catch you think you should be fucking around?"

"I do what I want," Maury said. "I always do what I want."

"They always do what they want in Atlanta, is that right? That's the spirit of the new south."

"Don't piss me off," he said and paused. "Don't piss me off."

"I'm not doing anything. Just go."

"I'll go when I'm ready to go."

Her body shook a little on the bed, not pleasantly. "You're crazy," she said. "You know that? You're really crazy."

"You're getting to me now."

"That's the only explanation I can think of," she said. "That's the only thing that would explain all of this, the business about chasing a man who's a murderer. This business about being a sheriff. From Atlanta. Oh Jesus," she said. "Oh Jesus, I knew I was scraping bottom. I've been heading down for a long, long time, but this part, this is really too much. Winding up in bed with someone who thinks that he's the sheriff of Atlanta county—"

Too much. It was too much to take; anyone could see that. Anyone could see that he had taken far more than there was any reason to take from this bitch who should have been merely grateful that he had taken the time and energy to throw her a fuck she would probably otherwise not get in months; a fuck which, whatever its limitations, showed care and attention. He stood, sucked in his belly and said, "You'd better just cut that out now. You'd better shut the shit up if you know what's good for you."

"Shut the shit," she said and giggled. "Is that the way they all talk in the new south?"

Suddenly, furiously, the gun was in his hand. He always travelled with the point forty-five, of course. Kept the heavier stuff locked in the trunk of the car downstairs. But the small, handy pistol was within reach at all times, even when he was fucking. Now he was pointing it at her. And the damned thing was, how quickly her entire mood changed. Even in the darkness he could see her features collapse and dive toward one another, her poor, naked, wasted body caving in against the sheets. Her fingers dug into the sides of the bed, and she began to breathe in uneven, terrible, terrible gasps. "Oh my Lord," she said. "Oh my Lord now, you're not going to—"

"You shouldn't have done that," he said. "There was no reason to talk in that way," and he felt the gun in his hand. The transfer from pocket to hand must have been accomplished in a way almost unconscious; he had no memory of taking it. Still, there it was. The trigger was against his finger. Killing was easy. That was one thing you learned if you hung around guns a bit; killing was awfully easy. The body was just dead meat when you took the life from it, and the taking was automatic. With a pistol here was no confrontation at all. Just machinery. "Why did you say that?" Maury said, and he shot her in the heart.

She died instantly. She must have died instantly; she made no sound at all. Nothing, merely fell back onto the bed, and when he came upon her, the pistol tangled in his fingers like a tool, and bent over her, he could see that her face had not gone slack at the moment of death the way that faces were supposed to, but instead in that passage had convulsed and come to a fine and deadly point of attention. All of her features seemed informed by alertness; her eyes, open, seemed to be fixed upon something of particular interest. Her mouth was pursed to an *"O"* that might have been in appreciation of a point of information she had just been given, often overlooked, but highly valuable. He had seen a lot of dead people, Maury thought, but he had never seen one like this. One who seemed to have gathered in death a dignity and a perception which she had never had in life. She seemed, indeed, to have welcomed it. Fucking and dying within fifteen minutes of one another. Two profundities gathered together to take her from life as gainfully as she had participated within it.

Maury felt cold, cold with emotional reaction, cold with the force of what he thought he might understand. He had killed her and he knew the realization of this had still not moved to a level of true acceptance. He still had not, on an emotional level, come to grips with the fact of murder, and he would not—he simply would not—for a while. But until then he had to go through the motions as best he could. The motions now had to do with those of evasion; obviously he had to get out. He had to leave at once and make sure that to the best of his knowledge he had left nothing which would tie him to the murder. *Murder*. That was a strange word, all right. He said it once, deep in his throat. *Murder*. He had killed someone She was not much, but she had lived just as he had, looked at the same sunrise and sunset, moved through the slow motion of her days like a living thing, just as had he. Now she was gone by his hand and he was still here, breathing. Moving on. Moving outward. It was as much of a miracle, the act of murder, as sex, Maury thought. The same strange transaction between people in the face of a mortality that could not care less. And then he thought, oh my, that is a strange thought. Strange, yes, indeed, and checked the room as best as he could in the colorless illumination and saw that there was nothing at all that could tie him to this. He had been an anonymous fuck for an anonymous woman; he could have been any one of a hundred men. It did not matter. Nothing mattered at all.

Wulff had infected him. Wulff had to be blamed for this. He had never been a murderer, would never have considered an act of this sort if he had not, somehow, gotten his psyche intertwined with Wulff's. It was all that maniac's fault, for it was he and not Maury who had brought blood and pain to the world. He either killed everything that he touched, or turned that thing into a killer. Maury could not be blamed. He was merely Wulff's agent. Wulff's agent, the commissioning force of the destruction within the man. Of course. That was the true and final explanation. He was not responsible for this at all.

He retched deeply in his throat and then began to shake with dry heaves, but that passed very quickly and he was already moving out of the room. He opened the door carefully through his pocket to leave no stains, and containing the heaves within him, went downstairs and to his car. By the time he got there he was fine. By the time he got back into the car and got rolling the nausea had passed and he was himself again and had but one thought: to find Wulff and to bring him to an end before, by contagion, the man had made not only Maury his agent but also the entire world, and had brought all of them to murder. All his fault. All of it. Maury and the rest of them merely machines, enacting that terrible will which whispered irresistibly to them in messages understood only by the mysterious and hammering blood.

XIII

Martin knew that the woman was killed in the explosion. That was all that he knew, and then only subliminally. He came out of the house with the image of her down beside him, buried under sudden rubble, her eyes open and anguished, and he had known at once that she was dead, without being quite sure what had happened or what all of this had to do with him. Memory and situation had been blown from him, and like an animal with a bare hold on consciousness, some incoherent beast, he had fought his way out of the ruins of what had been his house, working his way through levels of smoke and fire in the density to where he imagined the door had been. It was falling in upon him, what had been his house, and not only he but the world seemed to be trapped in that destruction. And yet he was able to hold onto enough of his sensibility to know that he must get out of there. After a long, imprisoned time spent stumbling through the debris of what had been his sanctuary, he found himself in an open space, and then after another time he was out on the street itself, flames leaping around him, the sound of many wings in his ears. He lay down on a little space of grass like a dying animal feeling reality close in around him tight like a blanket, feeling history itself recede and everything coming down to the dry wrenching sound of his breath moving unevenly in and out of his lungs, with only his heaving body to lend him awareness. He had neither any idea of where he was nor was he quite sure what had happened. Something had blown up and reality had shifted, memory was gone, and he was an animal. He lay on the grass waiting for everything to go away from him.

It was comfortable this way. He should have known it a long time ago. Whatever he had been he had not been as happy as he was now. Everything was explained by the absence of thought. The only thought he had was that he was not thinking. That was interesting, and he would come to terms with it somehow. Sometime. Not now, however. Martin closed his eyes and felt consciousness roll away from him, and then it abruptly returned. Someone was yanking at him. He felt a hand clawing on him and something digging into his eyes. He opened his eyes to pain and knowledge. A man was looking down at him. He could not distinguish the features, but it was definitely a man. "All right," the figure said, "where do you keep it?"

Martin said nothing.

"Where do you keep it?" the figure said again, and Martin felt something, probably the hand, shaking him again. There was pain moving below his neck. He began to feel sensibility return. He did not want it to return. "Go away," he said.

"Where is it? Where do you have it?"

"Have what?" he said. The words were painful. Each syllable was a grunt, each grunt a jab of pain. Something was seriously wrong inside him; something had been terribly altered. But he could not even focus his consciousness on the point of pain.

"The shit," the figure said. "The smack." It leaned closer. Martin could see the face now; hard, crude features defined by shadows, and in the hand a gun. Suddenly he understood who the man was and what had happened to him. A sense of connection came to him, the loop of circumstance which tied this to all the other things which had happened, and he was himself again, hurt and dying on a lawn. There was the sound of thunder in the distance. "Tell me," the figure said.

This was Wulff. This was the man who had blown up his home. The man who had called to threaten him, who Martin thought he had outmaneuvered by having the house guarded, by taking every reasonable precaution. How had he gotten through? This was the man who had killed Jeanine, who had destroyed his property, killed his guards, had brought him to the edge of death. He opened his eyes wide and considered the man. He wanted to look on him. "You're crazy," he said.

"I have no time."

"You have to be crazy," Martin said weakly. "I have no shit."

"Where is it? Back in the house or do you carry it on you?"

"You have to be out of your mind," Martin said. Of course he was. It had never occurred to him with this simplicity and clarity up until now. Wulff was crazy. Everything that he had been, everything that he was doing was the action of a crazy man. "Leave me alone," he said. "Let me die." Oddly he felt a little stronger. Accepting his weakness, the imminence of his death, his total destruction energized him slightly. He had always anticipated this in small corners of the night. He had known that he was heading for an ending like this. At least I don't have to face old age, Martin thought. At least I don't have to face being wheeled to a corner in a nursing home, faced away from a window and left to die. At least I won't see all of me turn to dust and gelatin. I have that. Say what you will for quick, terrible and violent death. It may outdo the hell out of old age. In any event, which of us can see our passage?

The figure slapped him. The blow was not unpleasant; it resolved further connections inside Martin's mind, fused him more closely to circumstance so that he could smell smoke, the odors of the lawn, and taste the grass and fire in his mouth. Assimilating it was like assimilating all knowledge itself. "No time," Wulff said.

"No smack."

The man slapped him again. It still did not hurt. He felt his hold upon the situation beginning to go, however. Voyage in, voyage out. Drift together, drift apart. He spat out blood. "Fuck you," he said.

"You'd better tell me."

"You're crazy," Martin said. "I don't deal."

"Yes you do."

"No I don't. I never did. You have this all wrong. I blew a little pot, I had a little cache of the stuff upstairs for myself and friends. That was all."

"You're lying."

"It's true," he said. He did not have to convince this man. He owed him nothing, and it made no difference, Yet he had a sudden lurching need to convince Wulff that he was telling the truth. It would take the heart out of Wulff if he were to accept the fact that he had done all of this— that he had killed—in error. "You're crazy, Wulff," he said. "You've killed an innocent man."

"I don't believe you."

"I don't care," Martin said. "I don't care whether you believe me or not, you see. It doesn't matter any more because I'm going to die no matter what I say or do. You're crazy, Wulff," he said. "I don't deal. You got it all wrong."

The man looked at him, jerked his head up, looked right and left. There was a vague sound of sirens, rolling in, still far away. It was impossible for Martin to tell from this angle how much of the entire block had gone up, but surely someone would have put the call in. Sooner or later the disaster equipment always arrived, but there was no equipment for that ultimate disaster of life. "No time," Wulff said. "I don't have any time for this."

"You'd better get the hell out of here, Wullf. You still have a chance. Run."

Wulff looked at him. He seemed confused. Martin would have laughed, but he had sense of his body. If he laughed he knew that he would hemorrhage on the spot and he did not want to do that. No, he wanted to keep on looking up at Wulff. That was all he wanted. He wanted to see the way the new apprehension was sinking into the various planes and levels of the man's face. Leaching through the grey skin, every place where the knowledge rested it burned. "You mean there's no smack?" Wulff said.

"That's right." You had to be very slow and patient with the insane. You had to repeat a truth over and over again until, in their own fashion, on whatever level where their frightened birdsouls fluttered, they were able to accept it. Here he was lying on his back dying amidst smoke and sirens, and yet he was administering to Wulff. That figured, however. Everything figured if you considered it deeply enough. "There's nothing," Martin said.

"Nothing at all?"

"Nothing."

"Oh my God," Wulff said. "Oh my God, I think I believe you. I think this time I believe you."

"That's great."

"You don't deal?"

"No. I never dealt."

"Then who does in the neighborhood?" Wulff said. "I know that it must be someone. It's got to be someone around here; otherwise Diaz would never have sent me here."

"Sent you here?"

"His notebook. His notebook had you down."

"I don't know Diaz," Martin said. Pain flooded his throat, he tasted blood, felt the liquid begin to move within him, his body breaking in the sudden pressure. "I don't know anything."

"They couldn't have lied to me," Wulff said. "They wouldn't do that."

"I don't deal," Martin said again. "I'm dying," he said, with sudden conviction. "You've killed me. You've killed everyone."

"Then you deserve to die," Wulff said. He ran a hand across his forehead, shook his head. "If you deal, you deserve to die. All pushers are murderers."

"But I'm not a pusher."

"Then you deserve to die," Wulff said uncertainly. The sirens were building, but slowly; too slowly Martin suspected, for him to ever see another man again. Let alone a woman. He would die here on the grass of his lawn looking at Wulff. This is the image which would transport him from life, that of the man who had killed him. "You must die," Wulff said, "all the dealers must die."

"I'm not a dealer."

"You have to be a dealer," Wulff said. He looked over his shoulder, as if checking for the approach of the sirens. He was not nearly as big a man as Martin had imagined him to be, but then again Martin had judged him to be something in excess of seven feet tall when what he was looking at was a trembling, preoccupied man under six-and-a-half feet. Wulff turned back toward him, and brushed the hair out of his forehead. "Last chance," he said.

"Last chance to what?"

"To tell me where the stuff is."

"There is no stuff," Martin said. "There is no stuff. I am not a dealer. You're crazy. You're just crazy if you think that I'm what you're looking for. I'm not a dealer," he said and something within him wrenched and he vomited thickly, the dry heave full in his stomach, but reduced, when it made passage to his mouth, to a thin, dense trickle of burning material which came from a corner. "Oh shit," he said, "oh shit on this."

"Shit on you," Wulff said and pointed the gun. Martin looked at the gun, the gun closing in on him, and as he saw the finger tighten, it occurred to him with absolute clarity that he was seeing the truth now, and not only seeing but *being*. He was participating in an absolute reality which arced between his head and the gun, nothing else, and as he saw that, as he saw the reality toward which his life—all of it—had been moving from the very first, he stared absolutely transfixed. It was not given to every man to see in the moment of his passage the sum and destiny of his life, and that made him fortunate, he thought. That made him more fortunate than most because such knowledge was not often granted … But this was the last or the next to last thought that he ever had, because something came out of the gun with terrifying force to make a hollow impact within his consciousness, and he moved toward obliteration. But there was a clear moment then, a moment in which he saw the man's face, and Wulff was saying *you've got to, you've got to*. All of it was quite distinct to him, and as he saw that, Martin had a sudden vision of the torturer as trapped, the assassin as victim of his own dreams of murder. But before he could quite follow it all the way through to the interesting and complicated insights which he no doubt would have derived, the shroud of death came over him and was tightened, and he saw and heard no more, at least on that brief if complicated cycle.

XIV

The assistant commissioner was summoned by the commissioner for a conference. This was something which made the aycee automatically nervous, since he had not seen the commissioner more than three times in the last four years. Two of them were at public functions and another was at a New Year's Eve party. Being called in was automatically bad news, but the aycee had no choice in the matter and was relieved to find that the commissioner was even more nervous, it would seem, than the aycee himself. The commissioner had files spread out all over his desk and was clawing at his cheeks, reading them, when the aycee came in. The commissioner said without looking up, "We've got to get this Burton Wulff now. We've simply got to get him."

The aycee sighed and sat down in a straight chair facing the desk. He was covered on the Wulff issue, at least. There were a hundred issues on which the commissioner could have called him and the aycee would not have been sure what to say, but Wulff was clear cut. "I've done a lot of work on that," he said.

"He's in Philadelphia now. There's been a bombing which is obviously his work. At least *they* say it's his work. How the hell would I know? How the hell would I know what's going on? Rizzo himself called me on this. They're pretty goddamned mad in Philadelphia. They seem to think that it's our fault."

"I know all about that," the aycee said.

"Then tell me," the commissioner said, "Tell me what the hell is going on with this guy? He used to be one of us, right? But I don't see where that goddamned makes us responsible if he's turned into a maniac. There are fifty thousand ex-cops in the country. What am I supposed to do? Keep a personal file and attendant on every one of them who gets drunk someplace or knocks over a supermarket?"

"It isn't quite that simple," the aycee said, and laid out the facts of the Wulff case to the commissioner. The presentation, if he said so himself— and he was sure that he would many times in the future, if only to his wife—was notably concise and explicit, and managed to wrap up the circumstances in less than ten minutes. The commissioner listened with great interest. His predecessor had known all of this, of course, but there had been a change of administrations and a reshuffling at the top, and the Wulff case was one of the responsibilities which the new commissioner's secretary had delegated from the start. Then, too, because the old commissioner was not exactly a great admirer of his successor, certain facts that might have otherwise been given at the routine series of briefings preceding a change of administration had never been turned over. You started from scratch all the time, the aycee thought. That was the key to any understanding of the processes which ran the government. There was no history, and turnover took care of all knowledge. And if there was no turnover, stagnation took care of the rest. Either way there seemed little reason for hope.

"That's incredible," the commissioner said when the aycee was finished. He did look genuinely astonished. He put his feet up on the desk and leaned back, shuffling the files. "I've never heard of anything like that. He's done all of that himself?"

"Apparently."

"Twelve cities, six hundred murders? All because he has a grudge against the narcotics squad?"

"Not quite that simple but something like that. You have to remember that he lost his fiancée, and it turned out that one of our own was behind that."

"So what the hell!" the commissioner said angrily. "We can't be responsible for every damned man who works here! Of course there's going to be corruption, there are going to be some rotten ones at every level. But it has nothing to do with the department, and there certainly has been a considerable elevation of standards—"

"I know," the aycee said. "But he doesn't think that way." The commissioner, under pressure, always politicized, and since he constantly felt himself under pressure, it was almost impossible to catch him without defenses at ready, mired in semi-speech. Still, this did not mean that the aycee had to accept the implied responsibility. He had to keep himself covered, too, and he knew a hell of a lot more about the devices of the NYPD than did the commissioner, who had originally been in sanitation and public works before being moved over, an object of departmental resentment but good for the press and the mayor's office, who liked the idea of a new man not beholden to any of the apparent power groups in the department. "He seems to pin it on us," the aycee said. "And since he's pretty goddamned mad—and out of control in the bargain—a lot of people blame us also."

"Our men aren't like that. He is no longer one of us. He left the department."

"That man escaped from custody," the aycee pointed out. "It really wasn't our fault. It was, in fact, one of those things that couldn't be anticipated, but nevertheless, it was. He *is* an escaped criminal now."

"Rizzo is mad as hell," the commissioner said. "Miserable bastard. He can't control his *own* department and couldn't when he was commissioner, but when something comes in that they can pin on New York—"

"They're damned grateful," the aycee agreed. "New York can always take the heat off. Next to it they think they can look good in comparison. I've had several talks with his ex-partner, you know, the patrolman who was in the car with him the night this whole thing started. I think that this man, Williams, may have some information as to his whereabouts, or at least may have had it."

"And you let him get away?"

"Well," the aycee said. "He's had problems of his own, Williams. He was hurt pretty badly near a methadone center a few months ago. Knifed up and almost died, and he's pretty lucky to be here. Under those circumstances we wouldn't look too damned grateful pushing him. But

I have a hunch that Williams has a lead into him."

"That doesn't do us much good."

"It might," the aycee said thoughtfully, "because I have a feeling that Williams has come around to feeling just as we do; that Wulff is intensely dangerous. And if he ever catches up with him he might take a more direct kind of action."

"Like kill him?"

"I don't know."

The commissioner took his feet off the desk and leaned forward. "That doesn't do us much good," he said. "That doesn't say much for us at all, in fact. That Philadelphia business was very bad. Have you heard the reports?"

"I read the papers, that was all. There wasn't a hell of a lot."

"He blew up damned near a whole block in Harrisburg."

"I know it was Harrisburg. So how did Philadelphia get involved anyway? What is Rizzo calling about?"

"There were some pretty important people on that block. Also, they had him definitely tied to Philadelphia just a few hours before the blast. They had him in a hotel downtown there and the Harrisburg police know it. They don't know exactly who he is yet. They're still doing investigation, but they're going to make the tie pretty soon and then we're going to be in it," the commissioner said. "I've been checking around, and we're going to be in it pretty damned deep."

"We are already."

"So I think we're going to have to get him," the commissioner said. "We're bound to this case anyway. We're going to have to get in and take part because we're going to get dragged in within a matter of days or less. We might as well take what credit we can by plunging in now."

"All right," the aycee said.

"They're scared in Philadelphia. They're damned scared. They don't like the picture and they say that we're to blame. They say they're going to approach Harrisburg themselves unless we do."

"And do what?"

The commissioner said, "Who the hell knows? Tie the tin can, that's all. Make sure that we don't get away without being held responsible for every goddamned thing this guy has done since he ever took a civil service examination. Is he crazy? He is crazy, isn't he?" The commissioner put a hand to his tie, straightened it absently, then stood and went over to the window. "Any man who wants to eliminate the international drug trade, well, now—"

"I guess he's crazy," the aycee said. "He's pretty damned angry too, though. The anger came first."

"One way or the other. I want you to get him."

"What's that?"

"I'm putting you in charge of this. I'm giving you a detail. You can pick the men you want, do it the way you want. I want this man picked up now. He's around Philadelphia again, they seem pretty sure of that. You can send them down there, send them to Harrisburg, split the squad, fan out …"

"Why me?" the assistant commissioner said.

"Because you've been on it already. You've been in touch with Williams. You've done some investigation, and you were in charge of this damned silly squad they had here—"

"All right," the aycee said. It was hopeless. And part of surviving in any situation like this was to know exactly that point where you had passed no return, where you had to do their will, where yours no longer mattered and you could then only impose your will by sliding around rather than going head on. The earlier you saw it the smarter you were, and the longer your career was bound to last. "I'll do what I can."

"Maybe you can put Williams in command," the commissioner said, "if he knows so damned much about this guy."

"I don't think he'd want any part of it."

"You can try. He was on that squad before himself, wasn't he?"

The commissioner had done more background than he had admitted. It was, the aycee admitted, a good trait. Little bits of knowledge piece-by-piece were being broken off the block of his intent now. "It wasn't much of a squad," the aycee said.

"They got him, didn't they?"

"In kind of a coincidental way, yes."

"Well, coincidence is as good as anything else. What the hell is wrong with coincidence as long as you can break the case? Something like that is probably the only way something crazy like this is going to be ended, anyway."

"No doubt," the aycee said. He stood and went to the door, turned there, and saw that the commissioner had turned from the window and was looking at him intently. "Sam," the commissioner said. "Sam, he *is* crazy, isn't he?" His voice seemed near pleading. "He's got to be insane; a man who would do something like this, kill people, bomb buildings, blow up neighborhoods, ships. Damned fool, endangering life—" His voice faded and he looked much older and confused. "It's madness," the commissioner said quietly. "Madness."

"Yes it is."

"He *is* crazy."

"Yes," the aycee said, "of course he's crazy. How could he do something like this and not be that way."

"I've got to believe that."

"I know what you mean," the aycee said, standing at the door. "You see I know exactly what you mean." And he did. It was interesting how his thoughts seemed to track with those of the commissioner. Usually they did not, but every now and then there was that kind of hollow apprehension of what the man was thinking that depressed the aycee, because it meant that he had the same mentality. "Because if he isn't crazy," he said to the commissioner, "if by any chance that man is sane and he's going about this in the right way, then it means that we, that all of *our* methods are mad." And then he went out of there quickly before he could see the commissioner nodding back at him. He simply did not want to see agreement at this moment. He could not stand the sense of collaboration. He could not bear the thought that there was a chance that all of the devices of the PD and law enforcement itself as they bore down now on Wulff were not in the pursuit of justice … but merely to replace the system that Wulff had torn down with its gleaming and awful homonym: reconstructed.

XV

Wulff returned to Philadelphia. Harrisburg had been a disaster. It did not seem possible that Martin was not the man he had been seeking, but even dying the man had denied his involvement. It had been Wulff's observation that at the end all men told the truth. He had certainly been with enough of them, and he had never known one yet who at the very end would not confess what he was and what he had wanted, trying to make pact before passage. So the fact that Martin had refused to admit it was very disturbing. It raised the possibility that Wulff had been pursuing an innocent man, that the material in Diaz's notebook had not been as dependable as he had thought. But, then again, had he gotten it out of Diaz's notebook? Was he really sure that he had been given reliable information that Martin was dealing? It was hard to be sure. His recollection was not quite what it had been in the past. It came in odd white flashes, off-center, grey on grey. His memory was not all what it should have been, but then he had had so much to deal with. It was not easy keeping all the strands together. If he had made an error on Martin, he was sorry. But it was just one of those things. It was difficult enough to have to carry his responsibilities and be letter perfect in all of the identifications in the bargain. If he had fucked up it had been for the first time, and that was all. Probably he hadn't fucked up. Some men were just liars anyway. Martin was not willing to give him the satisfaction. That was all.

What the fuck did they want of him anyway, Wulff thought. He was doing a difficult job all alone and under very difficult circumstances. They could not expect him to be perfect. Anyway, it was over. It was all over now. He would not think of it any more.

He was back in Philadelphia. He had just gotten out of the burn site before the police and disaster crews had arrived, and he had been well clear by the time they had come. Everything was a matter of timing. If you had a little confidence in yourself, in your ability to slide around the edges of a situation, then you could come to grips with it and nothing, nothing could ever trap you. Entrapment was a state of mind. Martin was dead and Wulff was off the street before the first of the cars had closed in. And then in the confusion and the flames, with four dead men with which to deal and the secondary explosion of the grenades which were still flaring and popping on the lawns … the police had their hands full. Particularly the Harrisburg police. They did not even know who to look for.

Wulff had gotten out of there. He had gotten out in the original ninety-eight in which he had come. He did not want to deal with that car anymore. He was, more or less, done with it, had explored all of its advantages, but under the circumstances he had very little option. He could not take the car in which the two assassins had been because that was pretty damaged, and under the pressure of sudden flight he did not have the time to find another car or flag one down. So it had been back to Philadelphia in the Olds.

The Olds had at least settled down. The transmission was tighter and the engine quieter than it had ever been before. All that it had apparently needed was a little road work. Even the radio functioned, and driving back Wulff was able to listen to the reports from Harrisburg which were pretty muddy, confused and unclear. No one could quite sort out what had happened, let alone what it all meant. There was an all-news station in the area, and for a while it was delivering five minute reports from the disaster scene on the quarter hour, but the reporter had no more idea of what was going on than did any of the dead men. They were having a hell of a time identifying the bodies. For a while they were not even sure who Martin was, and then they called him a businessman dealing in imports. Wulff had to laugh at that. *Imports* was right, all right, but they weren't quite willing to come out and say what the goods were. Sons-of-bitches. They understood nothing at all. By that time Wulff had gone back to believing, of course, that Martin had lied even as he was dying. Of course he was in the drug business. Of course he was one of the major figures in the international drug trade. How or why else would Wulff have declared vengeance upon the man if he were not exactly what he had been taken to be?

So he went back to Philadelphia, getting bored with the all-news reports after a while and putting the radio back to some music instead. Music was fine, it enlivened and invigorated him. The mission to Harrisburg could hardly, he decided, have been a failure. Not if he had been able to accomplish the murder of the international drug dealer, Martin. Of course it left him a little at loose ends, for the first time without a trail to follow, but that would work out. He would pick up something. He always had, after all. He would find a way.

Wulff went to another cheap hotel, once again in the inner city. It was the kind of place in which he was most comfortable and where he was positive that he would not be identified. Anonymity was what made the inner city run; nobody there wanted to know anything or anyone else, and there were no channels of communication. It was possible to stay in the inner city for years and years: no one would ever find you there unless you foolishly exposed yourself. On the third floor of the Stafford Arms Reasonable Rates and Suites, Wulff filed away his ordnance and pondered what his next move would be. He would come to it sooner or later. In the meantime, he had at least gotten rid of the ninety-eight safely. He had ditched it seven blocks away with the keys in it and walked his way into the Stafford Arms. The owner would be right pleased when the recovery was made. His car would be a revelation to him; it would be almost—if not quite—like having a new one.

Wulff tried to figure out what his next moves would be. Up until this point, he had always been able to trace one thread of possibility through circumstance and move from one event to the next, from one part of the chain to the next link. It had never failed him. Not from the time in New York when he had opened the door of the idling Eldorado, almost at random, and met the small-time pusher and user Ric Davis who had led him inexorably up and up the line and finally to the lieutenant who had killed his girl. Then again, breaking out of custody and heading toward Detroit he had found the leads easy to follow.... and Diaz's notebook containing definite information on the personalities which would be attending a meeting in Philadelphia to cut up the territory for the next two hundred years had seemed to clinch the task, and hand him his last mission cold.

But now at last it had trickled out. He had slaughtered his way through the southern rim, he had come north to Philadelphia and finally, in Harrisburg, he had reached the end. Martin was the major dealer in the emerging echelon; Martin was the man who was going to bid for power at the bicentennial get-together. With Martin dead and with the contents of Diaz's notebook all eliminated, there was, for the first time since this had all begun eight months ago, nowhere to go. The chain had run its way through. It had come from Ricker Davis straight through to Martin, and now he was finished.

He could have started again, of course. The man he had been in August would have done exactly that. The man he had been in August would have gone back to step one and started to pull people out of ghetto Eldorados once again. He could, in fact, do exactly that. South Philadelphia had more than its quota of Cadillacs whose quota had more than its share of men in dark glasses sitting behind the idling engines, tapping the accelerator and smoking while they stared out at nothing in particular. If the top levels had been slaughtered, at the bottom things remained pretty much the same. Business as usual while the corridors of supply were realigned, that was all. And he could have gone around tearing them from their automobiles, slaughtering.

But where would it lead him? That was the question to consider. He had already been to the top, and all that further investigations could take him to would be a damaged and quivering middle. And he did not have the energy for it either; he had lost his taste for investigation. He had to admit that. The killing was fun, was more fun than it had ever been. The killing, in fact, was great, but it had nothing to do with the investigations, which were pretty dull. Also they took too long. It took too long if you were investigating to find someone who was really worth killing. You plodded on and on for days that way before you had a lead, and more often than not it turned out to end up nowhere or take you into a blind alley where you understood that the killing would make no difference at all.

No, that was no good at all. That part of the mission, the stalking, the careful threading of the line of connection … that meant nothing. He would not go back to it. If he were going to stay in the game now he was going to go directly into the meaty, rich part; the only part that had ever appealed to him, that had any justification at all … the killing. Like hitting New York the second time, throwing a bomb into the bar on 125th Street, the fifty-at-a-time hit that was so much more satisfying and direct than the careful piecing out. That kind of thing. If he stayed in the game at all that was how it was going to be, now.

But. You had to work this thing out quietly. You had to decide—or at least Wulff thought *he* had to decide—if this was the way you wanted to deal with matters. Maybe it was time to get out of the game entirely. Maybe it was time to concede that he had gone as far as he could, that he had made his contribution. Live quietly, decently, in obscurity and retirement. There was time to leave the country, to go to some place like Peru, perhaps, which he knew quite well by now. Live out the rest of his days in exile like all of the Nazis there. Yes, he could do that. It would be easy. In fact, it was quite tempting to feel that his mission was done, that although he had not accomplished his final goal he had done as much and as honorably as any man could be expected to do. How long could you go on? How much could you take upon yourself single-handedly? Surely it was not completely his responsibility.

But Wulff realized something else too: that he had been shaped by his quest, and that his mission had defined him. He *was* his mission. It would be impossible to get back to the man he had been before this had started. Nor would he ever be happy again being that man. Even if he could go back before West Ninety-third Street, before all of this had ever happened, be back in the bar with the informant … well, even then it would not be the same. He was not sure that he would have taken that recovery even if offered.

He knew too much. That was all. Knowledge was compelling and if he had known those burdens he had at least taken some of the power also. Once you knew what was truly going on, once you had that understanding of who you were dealing with, and of the simple and terrible equations that the world had become, you could not go back to being the man who did not see, because the man who did not see was a fool. Wulff did not want to be a fool. He had struggled too hard, worked too long, killed too many to go back to being in that class …

She would not have wanted him to be a fool, Wulff thought. If Marie had been here, if she had seen all of it, if she had been witness to what he had become, she might have been happy. Or then again merely terrified, but one thing surely was clear: she would have wanted him to go all the way. Not to deny what he had become but rather to move on, to be even more of it, no matter what the price … Because only that would define and give continuing life to her own sacrifice, her own death.

Wulff paced the room at the Stafford Arms Reasonable Rates and Suites. He paced it back and forth for many hours, through all the shades of the day and evening, and as he did so he sometimes thought one way and he sometimes thought another. But through all of this one terrible constancy glowed: he knew he would go on for as long as he could. He knew that he would pick up the trail again even if it was blind and indiscriminate because the creature that he had become through all the months of this was one which could exist only as it had before. And in the splinter of bodies, the shatter of bone, and the explosion of blood, that self would be framed over and over again, cleaving the fine high arc of purpose toward the necessary but often delayed demolition.

XVI

Back in New York, summoned by the aycee, Williams went. There was nothing else to do. He was still carrying a gun and a place on the payroll of the PD, and until that was taken from him he had to conform to their orders. He did not want to see the aycee at all, but as his wife had pointed out in what was probably to be their last and most terrible argument, unless he kept the appointment he was as likely as not to be in more trouble than he could handle. His interest became mildly aroused however when the aycee told him that they were putting the Wulff squad together again. With Williams heading it up this time. An honor which the aycee made clear he did not expect Williams to decline.

"He's gone too far," the aycee said, "and the commissioner himself has gotten into this. Now he's demanding that we bring this to a resolution. This Harrisburg business—"

"I know about that," Williams said.

"Everybody knows about it," the aycee said. "But the way things are going now Harrisburg is going to stick us with it. They may bring in a federal strike force on this damned thing now and unless we can bring it to a resolution we'll have feds crawling all over the place. You know what that means, don't you?"

Williams knew what it meant all right. Once this fell under federal jurisdiction not only Wulff but the PD itself would be fair game. Lines of authority would be severed, files would be open, federal hands would be into information about Wulff, and by implication the PD—which could not be exposed. Then too the attitude of the federals toward New York could not be characterized as helpful or patient. Quite to the contrary. Since January 20, 1969, there had been one policy toward the big cities in Washington and it had not changed. No, Williams could see the aycee's point. Wulff, like it or not, was the responsibility of the PD. He was their product, he was their felon, and it was their custody which he had escaped. If they did not take him in, things were apt to get much worse, and they had not been good for the PD in a long time. "You want me to head this up," Williams said.

"I think so."

"So I get stuck with all of this."

"All of the glory."

"And if I can't get him, if it falls through you've got someone to blame."

"You'll get all the cooperation you need. You can set it up your way. We'll give you whoever you want." The aycee was sweating, but it did not seem to be from nervousness. Rather it seemed that he was concentrating so fixedly on Williams, on giving him the assignment, that all of his organs were throbbing, every sensory device was at full attention. He took a handkerchief from his pocket, shook it out, wiped his forehead with broad, savage strokes as if it were a windowpane, and then balled it up and put it on the desk. "We're pretty sure he's back in Philadelphia," the aycee said, "so you can focus on that. But you can handle it any way you want. You'll get full cooperation."

"Why me?" Williams said.

"Because you're the man for it. You were on the first squad. You were his partner. You've been closer to this from the beginning than any one of us. And you had some contact with him at the very beginning. Don't deny that; we're not holding it against you. We're not implicating you at all. We're just saying that when this started you were hearing from him."

"I don't hear from him anymore."

The aycee shook his head, and fingered the handkerchief absently. "We're not talking about that now," he said. "That isn't the issue. Nobody's trying to stick you with this. We're not saying that you were aiding and abetting, just—"

"Just that I might have been and that this would be a hell of a way to clear myself. By producing him for you. So then you'd close the books on this. That's what you're saying, isn't it commissioner? Whatever involvement I might have had you'll ignore if I can pay you off now by bringing him in."

"I'll ignore that. I'll just ignore that. I'm afraid you're under orders now patrolman. This is not a take-it or leave-it proposition you've been offered."

"I figured that."

"You're to begin putting together a group right now."

"From what? The bow and arrow squad?"

The assistant commissioner looked at Williams for a long time in what Williams supposed was meant to be a withering glance of appraisal, but it went through and around him, and it had no effect whatsoever. He simply could not respond the way that situational ethics might have dictated. A lot of feeling had been purged out. Perhaps most of it had gone on the long, meditative ride back from Philadelphia, when he had had a chance to look over his relationship with Wulff and what these last eight months had really meant to him with a kind of care that he had not had previously. Wulff was important, but only in relation to what he had done to Williams. Which meant that in a sense he was not important at all because Williams had to put all this behind him. Go on in a world where Wulff's ethics, Wulff's considerations would no longer play a role. That was the essence of what he had pieced out to himself carefully in the back of the bus, and now the PD wanted to put him back in a position where Wulff once again was paramount. Unless he took control of this situation, unless he truly saw it for what it was, he would never be free of Wulff, Williams thought. He would go right down into the pit with the man and he would not have a sheaf of grenades to bid him out. "That was uncalled for," the assistant commissioner had been saying sometime throughout all of this. "There was no reason for any of that."

"Sure."

"What the hell do you think you are, patrolman? You're lucky to still be on the payroll after all you've been through."

"Damned right," Williams said, "damned right I'm lucky to be on the payroll. I was almost knifed to death, remember?"

"All right," the assistant commissioner said after a pause. "All right. I don't want to get into that. We have a permanent detachment of men who can be called into headquarters for special projects. That's your pool. You pick them."

"And what if I refuse this honor?" Williams said. "what if I unequivocally refuse the honor of going out to Philadelphia and killing Wulff or bringing him back trussed up so that the department can save its ass? What happens then?"

"You won't refuse."

"No?"

"No," the assistant commissioner said. "I think I understand you pretty well by this time, patrolman. I may be wrong, but in my business there's one thing which you can cultivate. You can make judgments which are pretty accurate most of the time. You want this assignment. You want it bad."

"You think so."

"I *know* so," the assistant commissioner said. "I have a feeling that you want this man even more than any of us do because with you it's somehow personal. It's not just that he's fucking up a lot of people in a way which is maybe good, maybe bad. You could argue it either way, but because personally you don't believe in what he's doing and you've gone so far along that line, you take what he's doing as a reflection on you because you were there at the start. You could have stopped it all at the beginning."

"Never," Williams said. "Never."

"Are you absolutely sure of that? You were with him the night that that girl was found." The commissioner paused, cleared his throat, opened a desk drawer and handed Williams a file folder. "Here," he said. "Here are some personnel. You go through it in an office out there, and pick the men you want."

In an abstracted way Williams took the folder, hefted it, put it on his lap. "So I was with him that night," he said. "So what? What did being with him have to do with anything? I couldn't have stopped him. Once it started no one could."

"Nonsense. You know it's nonsense."

"Then tell me," Williams said. "Tell me what I was supposed to do, how I'm responsible for this?"

"I didn't say you were responsible for it. I said that you *felt* responsibility, which is a different matter. And you feel responsibility because you didn't do something that might have been wrong, but which you could have done. Anyone in your position could have. But how would you have known?"

"You don't mean—" Williams said.

The commissioner nodded. "That's exactly what I mean," he said. "And of course the penalty would have been pretty high because we would never have known what we know now. You would have gotten life imprisonment and been a severely misunderstood man. But you *could*," the commissioner said, "you *could have* shot him dead, you know." He added mildly after a while, "I don't know if you would have made the organization or us happier."

XVII

That thing in Harrisburg sounded like Wulff's work. You got a feeling for techniques after a while, and Maury knew his customers. All right then, Wulff had done it, Wulff had bombed out that block in Harrisburg. But what did that mean? Did it mean that Maury should also go to Harrisburg and try to pick up the trail from there? No it did not. You had to follow through on a single course of action no matter how wrongheaded, and carry it on to the end; otherwise, you got screwed up. There had to be a certain singlemindedness to what you were doing because you had to have faith in yourself. If you abandoned faith in yourself, then what you were doing was something that became meaningless. So he would go onto Philadelphia. And ignore Harrisburg, which might not have been Wulff's work anyway. There were lunatics all over. Perhaps some lunatics imitating Wulff's modus operandi had carried out the Harrisburg job, only because they had a chance to get away with it, and because the authorities would blame it on Wulff.

Maybe not. You did not know.

In any event, Maury went on. Once he got to Philadelphia he would spread some money around to find out where the man was. He couldn't be too hard to find. Maybe this didn't sound too logical, but then again it was the best method that he could think of, and the important thing was to keep on moving, not to despair. No man could humiliate him the way that Wulff had and get away with it. It was a matter of his pride, self sufficiency, literal manhood. If something like this could happen, then the next thing would be that they would be knocking over his store *and* home daily, and Maury would not tolerate it. You had to have faith. If you were meant to discover something, if your cause was right, then somewhere along the line God would provide. He would be provided with Wulff's whereabouts. In the meantime, he had to place himself in as close proximity to the man as possible.

Maury kept on driving north, the radio on, playing for him. The business about the woman was in the back of his mind, but he did not even think about it too much. At the beginning he had felt guilty, but the guilt had passed. And in any case, how long could you go on brooding about something like this? She had brought it on herself by taunting him, by saying and doing things which were absolutely intolerable. Once again, it was a matter of his pride being at stake. If you let people get away with things like that, if you really let word get around that you could be fucked with this way ... then where the hell were you? It would be absolutely destructive.

Actually, Maury kind of agreed with Wulff as far as he could follow, whatever line of reasoning had started the lunatic. The drug dealers *were* vermin, and they did deserve to be killed, all of them. What kind of a world was this? What kind of future could you have if kids were being peddled dope before they were even out of high school, if millions of dollars was being made by turning on poor people and blacks to heroin when they could be out earning a living and staying off the welfare rolls. All of that welfare money was being spent on heroin, and Maury knew that. So Wulff was right. The trade had to come to an end. These vermin could stand elimination ... but what the hell did that have to do with him? You just did not go around shooting up or threatening innocent people because you had taken it into your mind to get rid of the international drug trade. That was all fine and dandy, thinking stuff like that, but when you came down to practicalities—

Maury tried not to think about the waitress. Every now and then, driving, his thoughts would veer a little bit in that direction, go lurching toward a recollection in which he could see her lying open on the bed, the look in her eyes as they must have been when she had received the shot, the sound of the impact, the fact that he had become a murderer … Those thoughts were all there, but he had dropped his protection around the part of his mind which contained them, had shut them off. He would not think about it. Wulff had opened him up to a world of madness and pain in which these things happened; in which you might have to do them yourself to survive. But that was still no excuse to dwell on it. Maybe he had done the wrong thing, then. At worst it was a momentary lapse. He, Maury, was not really a murderer. He was not capable of committing acts like that. Anyone could make a mistake. He had made one with the waitress, he guessed, but he would not be pinned on to it for the rest of his life. He would just find Wulff, kill Wulff, put all of this madness behind him and go home. He would resume his life as if none of this had ever happened. If there was a reward in the works for killing Wulff, if there was a certain amount of notoriety or cash which might become his by virtue of the fact that he had killed the Lone Wolf … well, fuck it. That was all: fuck it. He wanted no part of it whatsoever. All that he wanted, really, was his life back.

On to Philadelphia then. He would track him down. He would get this over with. He would be out of it yet.

XVIII

Wulff decided that he would phone Williams. He would go out on the streets, do some more tracking, and start from the beginning. Find a couple of petty dealers and start work from the bottom up. Good enough! Just like old times. But first he would put a call through to his old friend, his ex-partner. Standing him up in front of Independence Hall had certainly not been nice, Wulff had decided, although on balance he really had had no alternative. After all, he had had to go and kill Martin. A job always took precedence, even if it was a meeting with an old and valued friend. Williams would understand if the point could only be made to him, but he was, perhaps, owed an explanation.

So Wulff went out of the hotel and called him from a bar about two blocks down, empty except for the old bartender, some dust and an exhausted female drunk sitting at the far end. Williams himself picked up the phone, which was a good thing, because Wulff did not think that he could bear to talk to the man's wife. Whatever relationship they had had was very complicated and delicate, and it had certainly been blown up good by the Los Angeles partnership. She would not have liked that at all.

"It's you," Williams said. Oddly he did not sound at all surprised. He was a matter of fact kid, this one. Of course, blacks did not show as much emotion in their day-to-day relationships as did whites. They had learned to bottle it all up for self-protection, and you had to understand that. "Where are you calling from?"

"Oh, I'm around," Wulff said. He patted his jacket where one of Maury's grenades nestled comfortably, and braced himself in the booth. The bartender, an old man, was slumped down at the end of the bar. The female drunk was barely conscious, but you couldn't be too careful. You just couldn't be careful enough in a place like this, particularly after the reputation Wulff had established for himself. They could be coming after him at any moment. Desperate men, terrified of their lives, could have formed bands, have had him trailed. At any time they could burst into the bar from the street and there he would be, in the fight of his life. But he would take a few of them with him, he thought with satisfaction, and patted the grenade. Oh yes, indeed, he would take more than a few with him. They would remember the Lone Wolf. It could not be said that his passage through the territory had been quiet.

"You there?" Williams was saying. "Where did you go? What the hell is this Wulff, are you here or not?" His voice was high, urgent.

That was a little better, Wulff thought with satisfaction. Williams was hardly so cool now. "I'm here," he said. "I thought I'd call you. I wanted to check in."

"Well, tell me where you are."

"In the same general area."

"So was I," Williams said. "Where were you?"

"I had some business to attend to," Wulff said. "It couldn't be put off. I'm really sorry about that though. That's the reason I called you now. I wanted to apologize for not being there like I said I would. It was just that something came up—"

"Well, tell me where you are now and we can get together after all."

"I don't think so," Wulff said.

"What do you mean, you don't think so?"

"I mean just what I said." His leg was beginning to go to sleep in its difficult propped position. Wulff shifted it down slowly, rubbed circulation back, and felt the little pinpoints of pain diminish, shifting throughout his system. "It's just better if we don't. Get together I mean."

"Why not?"

"Because I've got to play this one by ear. Do it all myself."

"Do what yourself?"

Wulff paused, leaned back, and rubbed his shoulders against the dull wood. "Well, I'm not sure yet. That's what I'm trying to figure out."

"Well, whatever it is, you'll need some help, right?"

"You that eager to help me?"

"I was all ready. You stood me up. I was in front of the hall for hours. Driving around, I should say. I brought down a lot of heavy stuff and I had a good car."

"You still have it? The heavy stuff?"

"You bet," Williams said and cleared his throat. "Got it all downstairs. You want it?"

"Why should I believe you?"

"Why not? You think that I'm lying to you about something like that? After all we've been through?"

"I don't know," Wulff said. "I simply don't know."

"You arrange for a place to meet, and I'll come down again with all of this stuff. Only this time you have to promise that you'll be there, Wulff. You put me through a lot of inconvenience."

"I'll have to think about it," he said. He looked out through the window of the booth. The bartender had shifted his position, was stooping now, apparently looking for something underneath the bar. That could be bad. It might mean that the bartender had spotted him for what he was and was now at this very moment reaching beneath the panels for a weapon. The bartender was a freelancer working for the network, and he would bring enormous credit upon himself by killing Wulff. It might change his entire life. Even an old man could be ambitious. He watched every move with great care, his perceptions acute. "I can't talk much longer," he said. "Something's going on. I'm a little nervous here."

"Where are you?"

"I think that bartender knows who I am. I wouldn't swear to it but it's a real possibility. If he does, I'm in trouble."

"Bartender? You're in a bar?"

"Yeah," Wulff said. "I'm in a bar."

"Where?"

"I don't know," Wulff said. He paused, watched with fascination as the bartender seemed to stoop lower, his hands fluttering bird-like over the concealed panels. The female drunk suddenly collapsed over the bar, all elbows and neck muscles, lolling there like some enormous plant. "She might very well be in it," Wulff said. "The two of them are probably working together."

"Two of who? Working together at what?"

"You just want to find out where I am," Wulff said. "You have no interest in what's happening to me. All that you care about is that I might be able to give you a leg up in the PD. Maybe the PD has sent you on a detail to find me and bring me in."

"That's wrong, Wulff. I'm on your side."

"You sure about that? I'm not."

"All right," Williams said. His voice seemed distracted, as if he were no longer concerned with Wulff but was concentrating on other issues far removed. Perhaps he was contemplating running a phone tap, doing a trace on the number from which Wulff was calling. That could not be passed by, that possibility. Not with modern technology being what it was, and also the record of betrayal which Williams had established in his relationship with Wulff. "If you don't believe I'm on your side, Wulff," Williams said, "I can't convince you."

Any moment the bartender was going to seize the gun, straighten up, and start firing at him. Wulff was quite sure of that now. The time for doubt had passed. He knew exactly what was going on and what they intended to try with him next. The organization never gave up. The organization was always working, always closing in on you. It numbered in the hundreds of thousands, and could recruit millions more. And as many of their number as you thought you could eliminate, ten times that number would appear to replace them. The organization was both immortal and very efficient. It reached down to the lowest bartender in the sleaziest bar in the worst section of town. He should have known that a long time ago, Wulff thought. He should have judged the resources of the enemy, and then it would not have come to this.

"There's nothing more to say," he said to Williams quickly. "The hell with you. The hell with them all. You'll never get me. From the beginning all you sons-of-bitches ever wanted to do was to use me." He slammed the phone down. The idea that he could have ever wanted to call Williams to apologize was repulsive to him. There was no reason for apology. He owed them nothing. He owed no one anything. How could he? They were all out to kill him. He stood up in the booth, pulled the door open, and stepped angrily out into the space of the bar. The bartender, caught in mid-dive toward the gun, saw Wulff's eyes, his aspect, and stood up rapidly, his face congested with terror. Wulff's point forty-five was in his hand now, solid, comforting. This was the only thing that they would ever understand. The only message. They sold death and lived by it and so, at last, it was only death which they could understand as the medium of exchange. "Put your hands up," Wulff said.

The bartender backed against the mirror, his old frame shaking. He must have been in his mid-seventies; a senior man in the organization. Fifty years behind a counter, freelancing for them. "Put them up!" Wulff screamed, and the bartender's hands came up. He backed as far as he could, his old, shrunken mouth opening and closing. The female drunk sighed heavily, threw out an arm, and knocked over the stale glass of beer in front of her. This woke her up. "Another one," she said, her head moving off her forearms. "Pour another one, Jim."

The bartender looked at Wulff in a pleading way. "Don't," Wulff said. "Don't think of it."

"I need another beer—"

"Shut up," Wulff said. The woman looked up at him. She might have been as old as the bartender; or then again it might only have been the clotted dense lines of slow hemorrhage in her drunk's face which gave her the appearance of age. She was probably working with him. All of them were working together. They were one unit; the organization, and the lines of interconnection, which soldered them all. "Put your head down," he said. The woman dropped her head immediately to her forearms, her eyes on the gun all the time. "Don't move," he said.

"Listen," the bartender said. "Listen, there isn't much money. What do you think a place like this can take in? You can see, nobody's come in except you in the last fifteen minutes. Nobody comes in until five, six o'clock, and then it's one beer, two beers and gone. There might be twenty in the register but—"

"Shut up," Wulff said. "Stay away from the gun."

"Gun? What gun?"

"Don't go for the gun," Wulff said. You had to stay calm. You had to keep a lid on your feelings and not panic them even if at a moment like this it was all you could do to stop yourself from pumping three or four shots into them to show them once and for all that they couldn't get away with what they thought they could do to you. "Just point," he said slowly. "Point to where it is."

"There's no gun."

"Show me where it is."

"You think there's a gun here? What the hell is this? Is that what you thought I was trying to do?" The bartender's face, oddly, was slack with gladness. "Oh hell, no, if that's what you're worried about. I don't keep no stuff below the bar. I don't want to mess with shootouts. Anything you want you're entitled to have. That's my policy, to turn it right over. What little there is, I'm not going to kill myself to hold on to."

"Show me the gun," Wulff said again. "I don't think you're listening. I don't think that you're listening to me. Give me the gun now. Show me where it is."

The woman raised her head again and said distinctly, "I think he thinks you've got a gun down there, Harry. I think that he thinks that you were trying to shoot him. That's how this whole thing started."

"That's ridiculous," the bartender said, not to Wulff but to the woman. "I wouldn't have no gun. What's there to protect for Christ's sake?

Anyone knows there's nothing here."

"Sons-of-bitches," Wulff said. "I know that you're lying to me. I know that you've got a gun down there; that you were going to shoot me when I was in that booth." The bartender shook his head, and looked at him helplessly. "Admit it," Wulff said. "You know it's the truth."

"Harry," the woman said, "I figured the thing out. It took me a little while but now I got it. The guy is crazy. He's out of his head. He comes in here looking to shoot. Let me out of here," she said, standing abruptly, weaving by her bar stool. "I just came in here for a little conversation and to pass a sunny afternoon. I don't want no part of this."

"Stay," Wulff said. "Both of you stay."

"You wouldn't shoot an old lady, would you?"

"Don't move."

"You can fuck if you want," the woman said. "Maybe he's that kind of nut," she said to the bartender hopefully. "If he's crazy enough to shoot, maybe he's crazy enough to want to fuck. You want to screw me?" she said. She opened her arms. She was wearing a black coat, many-holed, which hung in a single straight line to her feet. Her old cheekbones, however, were dazzled with light. "Look at that," she said. "That's not such bad stuff after all, is it? You give an old woman a chance, she'll show you she's learned a few things." Her mouth quivered then opened. "Please don't shoot," she said. "There's no reason to kill people."

The bartender screamed suddenly and dived below the level of the counter, but his knee hit something and he screeched with pain, then up-ended and sprawled full-length behind the counter. The woman screamed too, in a voice even more hoarse and desperate than the bartender's, and then began a desperate side wise waddle, trying to get to the door. She would get away then. She would get away and get to the police and tell them everything. Either that or she would go right back to the network captain, the head for the district, and tell him everything about Wulff, including his appearance and his whereabouts. Either way he could not let her out of the bar. That was obvious. They were closing in now to the degree that everything was covered by their operatives. Even a sleazy, ruined neighborhood place like this. The next thing would come when they picked up his trail, started to track him on the streets. But at least he could forestall that a little. "Don't," he shouted to her as she came near the door. "Don't do it."

She did not react. Moving within her own conception of time, her own dream of event, just as the kid on the south side had been, the woman continued to hobble to the door, her palms thrashing, knees scuttling. Obviously, nothing would stop her now. She was moving within a conception of event which was entirely different from his own or from that of anyone who might have tried to stop her. And there was nothing that he could do, nothing at all, because in order to stop her by persuasion he would have had to have entered into her scheme of time, and that was as private as her own death would be.

"Please," Wulff said nevertheless, pointlessly, "please stop."

She did not. Her body crashed against the door and then she was struggling with it and the door was open. She lifted a foot and started to move outside.

And Wulff shot her in the head.

She gave one squeak, like a bird, and collapsed in the doorway, half-in, half-out, totally immobile. Her legs kicked once, uselessly, and then he could tell by the way that they flexed and froze that she was dead. He had seen enough dead people. For sure, he had studied death from enough angles to know its presence.

He went over to the bar and craned over the counter like a customer looking for a bill that had drifted behind, standing on toes, peering. The bartender was down there on his stomach lying on the slats, his hands drawn in little fists against his cheeks. He was apparently unconscious, or at least skillfully playing possum, respiration fast and shallow, face slack, eyes closed.

Wulff shook his head. Somewhere there was a sense of overwhelming choice, but as he stood on the rim of that circle, he could not seem to penetrate. Whether or not he shot the bartender would key into his sense of destiny, determine what he had become. But he could not, somehow, take it seriously. "Look at me," he said to the man. "Look up at me."

The bartender lay there rigidly, made no effort to come to terms with what Wulff had said. Perhaps he really was unconscious. This was a possibility that had to be considered. Still, someone was going to see that woman pretty soon. Even in this section of the city the sight of a dead woman wedged half in and half out of a bar would attract some attention. "Look up," Wulff said, "or I'll kill you now."

Slowly, hesitantly, the bartender's head, and nothing else, came off the floor. It was just as he had known. The man was not really unconscious at all; he had merely been manipulating Wulff, trying to make him think that he had passed out. You could not trust people. That was the final lesson of all of this. You could no longer trust their actions, expect them to behave honestly. Given the chance, all of them would lie, look for an edge. You found the same dishonesty here as you did at the highest levels of the organization. Of course, that had to be kept in mind too. In all fairness to humanity you had to admit that the bartender was part of an organization which did not subscribe to the highest rules of ethical conduct. The man's eyes were dull, yet seemed to give back to Wulff a reflection or two reflections of his own face peering down at him. The eyes were frozen, perfectly fixed, like those of an animal by night. "You should not have done that," Wulff said.

"Done nothing," the bartender said. His voice was buried deep inside of him; he had one hand wedged protectively now against the back of his skull. "Not a thing."

"You shouldn't have done it," Wulff said. "You knew that I was going to catch up with you, didn't you? That freighter in San Francisco. Those men on the beach in Miami. They didn't think I was there but I made it."

"I don't know what you're talking about."

"You've got to understand that it catches up," Wulff said. "This is fate. This is your death. You thought you could avoid it but you were wrong. You never could. You never had a chance. Not from the moment that you got into this. Look at me," he said. "Look at me."

The bartender tried to twitch his head in Wulff's direction, but he could not make the full circuit. It fell, lolling to the boards. *"Look at me,"* Wulff said sharply, and the head came up slowly, reluctantly, the eyes longing, deep in the face, solemnly looking at Wulff now like a child in an amusement park being granted one last wonder before it was time to leave. He was no longer an old man, but a credulous, vulnerable eight-year-old. Why could we not stay that way, Wulff thought. Everything would have been so much easier, always, if we could only have stayed that way instead of fragmenting into the corrupt and pained adults that we are. "You know you're going to die," he said.

The bartender ran his tongue across his lips. "I don't want to," he said. "I don't want to die."

"But you know you must now don't you? Nod your head. Show me that you accept it."

The bartender nodded his head slowly, but the eyes, lustrous and dismal seemed to stay locked to Wulff's, unmoving.

"Say it," Wulff said.

"I'm going to die," the bartender said.

"Why?"

"Why what?"

"Why are you going to die?"

"I don't want to."

"Bullshitter," Wulff said, thinking of the onlookers that were surely going to see the body lying in the doorway, that were surely going to phone the police. Which meant that his margin was diminishing all the time; had severely diminished it. He could not now have more than two minutes, after all. But he could not leave until all was sealed. "Bullshitter, thief, bastard, pusher, dealer. I don't care whether you want to or not. Tell me why you're going to die."

"I have a bad heart. I'm going to have a heart attack."

"Then you don't have to worry about the gun, do you? Then that shouldn't worry you at all."

"I'm going to die because you're going to kill me."

"And why am I going to kill you?"

"Because you're crazy."

Wulff shook his head. It was too much, that was all. Sometimes you would run up against someone stubborn who would not make the concession, who simply would not under any circumstances admit what he was and what he had done. That was psychopathology for you. He had dealt with his share in the PD. There were perpetrators who literally did not believe that they *were*, and you could do nothing with people like this except to protect society from them, lock them up some place, keep them there until they rotted. The bartender obviously fit into that category. He was not going to give Wulff the satisfaction of a confession, no matter what happened.

All right. All right, you had to deal with these disappointments. You had to realize that you could not bring the whole world into line. Some would confess, and others would not. Some would admit what they would become and others would never separate that truth from themselves. The important thing, of course, was that you did your job, that you got the work done. That one way or the other you removed them from the earth. The matter of admission could be left to other judgment.

"All right," he said, "all right," and shot the bartender in the head in just the fashion that he had killed the woman, with the same short, quick burst of fire. A terrible bark belched from the man, followed by the collapse of that body toward the well-known waxy flexibility, the melding with death, the absorption of death by what had once been alive. Wulff was already out the door. He leapt over the body of the woman as he had leapt through the fields of the enemy, and was on the deserted streets then and moving. Moving high, moving high and free, leaping toward the gauzy surfaces of the day as the bartender had leapt at death at that moment where it seized him by the throat and thunderously took him beyond all pain.

XIX

With a free hand, with a promise of all the co-operation he asked for from the PD, Williams, after studying the situation for a day, decided to settle for taking just one man with him to Philadelphia. The Wulff squad had been a joke; he did not want to deal with that group of clowns again. He had asked for a competent weapons expert who also knew a little about demolition technique, and the aycee had delivered Evers, a grim sergeant from the bomb squad who said that after ten years on that job his nerves were shot and that he would appreciate the opportunity to set some explosions rather than to try to defuse them. Evers had brought along some heavy ordnance from the most heavily guarded cache the department had, an installation in Bedford-Stuyvesant's outskirts that only the high officials and important gangsters knew about. He had also brought his own speculations about Wulff which were based on a great deal of what Evers remarked to be honest, heavy thought, and with which he regaled Williams all the way to Philadelphia. They were definitely going to go to Philadelphia, Williams had decided. There was no point in waiting around in New York for news about Wulff's next strike. Surely Wulff would stay in the area. That was his method, always had been; to clean a place right down to the ground before going onto the next one. And in Wulff's obvious present state of mind, he probably would not consider Philadelphia to be cleaned down to the ground while there was still a body moving within it.

At least Williams had not had any trouble with his wife, in clearing out on the next assignment. They simply did not speak to each other any more except about casual or necessary matters, and Williams knew that whatever else came from Wulff, when this assignment was finished his marriage would be finished also. That break was permanent. He simply was not the man his wife had married, and he found himself incapable of taking anything to do with St. Albans or the middle class seriously any more. If this assignment was ever finished, he would have to devote his attention to the situation for a few days, decide what would be the least painful and most friendly means of clearing out so that she could have the house, but he would not worry about that now.

He would not worry about anything now. All that mattered was catching up with Wulff. The last conversation had been definite, if he had needed to be convinced any further. The man had gone absolutely crazy now. He was a menace to everyone, and that did not limit itself to the network. He would probably be committing random murders, if he was not already, and this kind of thing was obviously intolerable. The aycee had been right after all. Anything had to be done to bring the man to heel, and if that involved Williams, if Williams had to make a large-order sacrifice to head up a patrol, then it would have to be. It simply would have to be that way. Anything was worth it. The long shot gamble of putting Williams in control of a pursuit might not have made much sense in an objective way, but when you were in over your head—and all of them, PD and Wulff alike were certainly in over their heads—you simply had no alternative.

So Williams, with Evers this time, headed toward Philadelphia again. Evers, for a change, was an interesting PD man, and the conversation at least was stimulating. Also, they had been given the use of a big fast 450 SEL, which was a special commissioner's car, and which was beyond a doubt the best that Williams had ever driven, even though the steering was so devastatingly quick and the suspension so tight that the slightest error would pitch the automobile off the road. The SEL, like Wulff himself, was not a forgiving institution, and for a driver like Williams, accustomed to the slow, wallowing performance of the American cars which transmitted right down the line, the SEL was an almost devastating experience. It demanded his total attention to driving and made conversation very difficult. For that reason, he spent the hours on the New Jersey Turnpike listening to Evers almost non-stop, and contributed little, but that was not too bad, because Evers had a lot to say. Some of it dove-tailed with Williams's own thinking about the situation, other parts extended his insights, so to speak, so he was able to look at Wulff in an entirely new way.

Evers was a big, solemn, once-divorced detonation expert from Massapequa who had been around, seen a great deal, and looked at Wulff in a slightly different perspective. He had made a hobby of studying the man's activities, and he felt that the clearest thing indicated was that Wulff was out of control. He had, in fact, become the very person that he was chasing, his outlook and methods indistinguishable from that of the network heads themselves. According to Evers it was inevitable.

"There's no shade of moral difference after awhile," Evers said. "Killing is killing."

"There are all kinds of kills."

"Granted," Evers says, "absolutely. But when killing becomes the major activity—the modus operandi—and is repeated over and over again, you begin to phase out the moral distinctions. Or, I should say, Wulff does."

"I don't follow that."

"Sure you can," Evers said, "and watch that goddamned steering. You're getting me nervous as hell. One inch of arc and they'll be scraping us off the retaining wall." He lit a cigarette from the car lighter, sighed, leaned back. "Great cars though," he said. "Now our friend, Wulff, he may be performing good kills, necessary kills, or at least that is the way that he rationalized it in his mind when this started. For all we know they *are* good kills; we may feel that way ourselves. No question about one thing. He's made enforcement a little easier since he got on the road."

"That's for sure. But I don't follow you."

"Just a little bit of psychological training," Evers said. "You start to mess around with twenty-ton devices that have been rigged by idiots, some of whom occasionally get blown to kingdom come by their own experiments, and you get interested in psychology. You do a lot of reading if only for self-protection. This job," he said and inhaled at length, tapped the cigarette in the ashtray, and jammed his elbow comfortably in the enormous armrest, "makes you a thoughtful man. Now inside everybody there's a subconscious mind which is about five years old. If you're lucky it's five years old. Some very bright people have a subconscious which might make seven or eight. Now it's that subconscious sitting under every thing which makes the final decisions on your behavior and decides how you react, and no matter how smart you get and how well you learn to rationalize your acts, you're still dealing with something which is essentially very stupid. Also which doesn't do much talking. You can't make it *listen* you see. You can't control the data you're feeding into it. It just takes everything and messes it all around and comes up with its own answers. And that's the end of it. Wulff's carrying around one of those just like everybody else, except for a few psychopaths who have no feelings at all and are capable of anything. But Wulff is definitely not one of those."

"How so?"

"Because he was emotionally triggered by the death of his fiancée," Evers said. "Wasn't he?"

"I guess so," Williams said, and saw West Ninety-third Street before him again. One flash, one trickle of light and he was back in the patrol car watching Wulff's face; he was up in that stinking SRO again seeing Wulff as he stood over the OD'd girl…. "Yes," he said, "yes, you're right about that part."

"No psychopath," Evers said, "but a feeling man, reasonable emotional equipment, all of that. Well, he's got reasons to kill and he's killing a lot of the right-type people. No question about it. But as he goes on, as this goes on for months and months, as he starts to slaughter from coast to coast hundreds that we know about and other stuff that we can only suspect—"

"Go on. Get to it."

"I'm getting there. As he starts to kill them by the hundreds, what do you think his subconscious is saying? Remember, you can't get to that subconscious. You can't have a sensible dialogue with it, prove that you've got to kill all the drug dealers because they deserve to die and you're doing enforcement a favor. It takes in everything but says nothing, and you can't reason. So what do you think that underneath it's saying?"

Williams could see it. He really could see it. Still, it was better to take it Evers's way, track it in slow and easy like being back in a classroom, having it laid out for you by a competent instructor. He ran his hands over the wheel, cut left very gently to pass a truck, sat at rigid attention feeling a flick of mild terror for exactly seventeen seconds as the Mercedes cleared the lumbering van by four carlengths, and then dropped it back in. He sighed then, and heard Evers sigh as well. Wulff's was not the only subconscious that was at issue here. "Tell me," he said, "what is it saying?"

"You tell me. Think about it."

"Bomb expert," Williams said and smiled. "Of course. It's telling him that he's a murderer."

"Exactly," Evers said, and stubbed the cigarette into the armrest, said excuse me to it, carefully killed all the little embers, and then scuttled the butt into the ashtray. "It's not making any discriminations, remember. It's just bearing witness to a brutal and continuing series of murders. Mostly of strangers. It *knows* that it's a murderer, then, that it's doing something awful. It's only about five years old, remember. It's afraid of mommy."

"Yeah."

"So what does that mean? Never mind," Evers said, "I'll tell you, not tease you along. It means one hell of a load of guilt. How do you discharge guilt? Remember you're hounded by the thought that you're a bad person, you've done evil things. The subconscious is whispering that to you all the time now, absolutely convinced of it, and it has a pretty persuasive voice for a five-year-old. What do you do with this load of guilt? And anxiety, I might as well point out, because guilty people get punished. Mommy finds out or daddy comes after them with a strap and beats the shit out of them. That's a hell of a load to carry around. But what do you do. I mean, you can't go around listening to that stuff from the subconscious all the time without making *some* effort to deal with it."

"I guess," Williams said, paused and thought it through, and it seemed pretty right. "I guess that you just increase your killing. You step up the pace. You can't walk around with that kind of guilt unless you let it out somehow. And you wouldn't kill yourself, would you?"

"Some people might."

"But not Wulff," Williams said thoughtfully, "not Wulff. *He* wouldn't."

"Not directly, anyway," Evers said. "You're dealing with a pretty angry guy who can still see the dealers and the organization as being to blame for his basic problem, and he would just step up the pace to prove to his subconscious that it was full of shit. But then in another way, stepping up the pace the way he has *might* be a form of suicide anyway, might it not?"

"You mean he's trying to get caught," Williams said.

"Or killed," said Evers. "As far as I can judge, he's just going in for indiscriminate slaughter now. He's lost any of that sense of pace or detection or motive which he had at the beginning when he was making a serious effort to make sure that he was killing the right people. You go out of control like this and you're going to go too far. I think he wants to," Evers said. "I think that he really wants to come up against a situation which he can't control; a situation where someone is going to turn on him. But he wouldn't put himself directly into suicide. The ego is still too strong by far for that. The subconscious hasn't gotten through to break it all the way down, so what the guy would do would be to *arrange* a situation where he'd be out of control, and yet not let himself know that he's done it."

"In other words—"

"In other words," Evers said and he smiled, "in other words he thinks that *everyone's* a dealer now."

Philadelphia breakdown, Williams thought, and he began to drive very fast. He had been doing seventy, but it was not near enough. The SEL went to ninety-five on one stroke of the accelerator.

Neither of them said anything for a while.

XX

Maury knew he was going to get the son-of-a-bitch now. The feeling was hotter and sharper now, moving through him in pulsing little flashes of knowledge which alternately excited and then depressed him. Excited him because he was moving in for a kill which would give him as much pleasure as anything in his life, and depressed him because when he committed the kill it would be over and he had the feeling that nothing in his life, no matter how long he lived or what became of him, would delight him as much as killing that big son-of-a-bitch would.

But he was picking up on the trail all the time. Now in Philadelphia itself he felt as if the actual emanations of the man's physical presence were moving in on him, even though he was doing nothing more than standing in a downtown bar drinking. There was nothing intrinsically exciting about that, but the fact that he was actually in the same town that the man was known to be in, that he had gone this far in pursuit and now needed to close only a little more ground … this excited him to the point where he could hardly hold the glass steady, hardly keep himself contained. It was all he could do not to throw the glass into the mirror and scream: *hot damn son-of-a-bitch I said I'd come to get him and look at me now!* But that would have brought improper, useless attention upon him, and if by any chance the son-of-a-bitch had been around would have tipped him off. Better to stand quietly and just relish the drink and consider his further plans now. Philadelphia! He would have to find a hotel, of course; maybe one of those big motels on the pike just beyond. Impossible to go directly at him. He would need to rest for a while just to get himself in shape. He had been on the road almost continuously for forty hours now; he desperately had to break.

But he was close. Oh shit he was close now! He could breathe it, literally could smell the son-of-a-bitch. Or had the feeling, anyway, that he could. After a while he began to tune in to the conversation in the bar, and as he did, Maury began to shake with excitement. He could not quite believe what he was hearing, but nevertheless, it was there. Finally, he could not stand by any more. He leaned over, motioned to the bartender, brought him over. There were ten or fifteen around the bar, a few in the booths back there, and everybody anxious as hell for drinks, so the bartender was nervous and anxious to get back on duty. Nevertheless, Maury held him in place.

"You mean there was a murder here yesterday?" Maury said. "In this goddamned place?"

The bartender shrugged, reached for his apron. "I'm just a relief man, Jack," he said. "I don't know anything about it."

"But they were all talking about it!" Maury said. He realized that his accent was all out of place in this bar, and felt suddenly exposed and ridiculous, and this only made him angry. "Come on," he said, "you'd better tell me."

The man on his right said, "You heard it right, Jack. There was a double murder."

"I've got to know about this," Maury said.

"So do the cops."

"I mean it. Who did it?"

"Nobody knows," the man on his right said. "They were both dead. The bartender and some woman. What the hell you so excited about? You did it?"

"No," Maury said, "I didn't do it."

"Some son-of-a-bitch," the bartender said. "Some son-of-a-bitch did it, all right. I sure as hell would like to know who it was. First it's one thing and then the next," he said vaguely. "Before you know it he'll come in again. You think I like this? But in relief work, you got to go where you're sent. If I had known when I called in that they were sending me to this place I would have taken the job in Trenton instead. I ain't crazy."

"They'll get him," Maury said confidently. "They'll get the son-of-a-bitch who did it."

"How come you're so sure?"

"I just know," Maury said. He finished the shot glass, slammed it on the bar. "Give me another. There's only one crazy son-of-a-bitch would start walking into bars in Philly and kill people with no reason at all. It's a sign. I swear it's a sign that sent me here. Out of all the places I might have stopped for a drink it would have to be this one. I'm close to him now. Jesus, I'm close to him."

"What are you talking about?" the man on his right said. "Are you a cop or something?"

"Not exactly," Maury said, and waited for the bartender to refill the glass. "Just a guy with an idea, that's all." The bar was filled, and he suddenly understood he was not with his kind of people but with northerners who would never understand him. Whatever happened, whatever he said, they could not be brought to understanding. He had already talked too much. "Forget it," he said, and when the bartender filled his glass Maury choked it down neat and turned to leave the bar. The man on his right, however, put out a hand, took him by the lapel and hauled him back.

"I don't like the way you're talking," he said. "You're trying to communicate something but it's not coming out straight. You know who killed those people?"

"Probably," Maury said before he could stop himself. "Most likely not," he said. "Just let me go now."

"If you know who killed them I think there would be a lot of people who would be interested. Don't you Frank?"

The bartender said, "I don't want anything to do with this. I'm just the relief man. I could have gone down to Trenton and worked, but I didn't know what I was getting into so I came here. I don't know who this guy is and I don't know who you are either. I would appreciate your not calling me Frank."

"Just hold on, friend," the man said. He was in his late thirties or early forties and for the first time Maury became aware of him, began to see him in physical terms. He was a tough customer. At his best Maury could deal with him, but he was not at his best, he had been on the road for a long time and he had had too much to drink on top of it. "I think I want to ask you some questions."

"Let go of me," Maury said. "Let go of me now."

"You seem to know a good deal about what's going on here and I think I'd like to get a few details."

"I don't want any part of it," the bartender named Frank said. "Originally I didn't even want to do shift today. So when the call came in and I had a choice of Trenton or here I figured what the hell. I'd save the mileage and come here. But I could have gone to Trenton just as easily. You got anything to do you take it outside."

"Screw it, Frank," the man said. "Just get out of here."

The bartender threw up his hands in an absent, dismissive way and backed off. No one else at the bar was looking at them at all. Possibly two men checking gambling slips in a corner booth might have looked up to see what was going on, but at the bar itself everyone was absorbed in their drinks or in sudden trips to the bathrooms. Maury felt an enormous sense of quiet descending around him; the kind of quiet which you were supposed to experience at the beginning of a heart attack. He had never had a heart attack, not yet anyway, but he was well prepared for that feeling of being sealed off into a private and absolute sense of doom where no one could penetrate. No one except the man next to him. A hand was suddenly on his shirt. "Who killed them?" the man said.

"Get away from me."

"You're shooting off your mouth a hell of a lot for a guy with a southern accent who just happened to be in the territory. Those people were friends of mine. I did a lot of drinking in this bar, spent a lot of hours. You tell me what you know."

"I don't know anything," Maury said. He thought of the pistol in his right pocket. He could go for it, but it was a risky maneuver, and if he was blocked, what would he do then? It could lead to a very unpleasant situation. Even worse than this, if the man next to him could find Maury in the act of going for a gun that he could not reach. The feeling of doom intensified, but it must have only been the fatigue, the unfamiliarity, the sense that he was drifting beyond his depth here and should have kept his mouth shut. What, after all, could be done to him? It was just a neighborhood bar. "Take your hand off me," he said.

The man slapped him across the mouth once, hard. The impact was shocking to Maury; he would not have believed that a blow with that little arc, delivered only with the wrist, could hurt that much. It seemed to rebound within his consciousness, and slowly the blood began to roll again in the place that had been struck and he felt little slivers of awareness and pain. "Stop it," he said.

The man said, "I don't like southern bastards coming into my bars and telling me that they know who killed my friends. I don't like that at all."

"You're crazy," Maury said and he thought, he's not the only one who's crazy though. There's a lot of craziness around. The man who tied me up in my own shop, who stole my grenades, he's crazy too, and in about the same way. "I'm getting out of here," he said.

The man grabbed him by the arm. "No you're not," he said. "You're going to stay here and let me beat the shit out of you because of what you did to my friends."

"I didn't do anything to your goddamned friends. I don't know what you're talking about."

"Take it outside," the bartender said, coming back to them. "Nothing doing in here; there's not going to be any of that stuff in here at all. You got to settle something take your business on the street."

"Get away," the man said to the bartender. "Just get away," and turned toward Maury full face so that Maury could see the little dead spaces and unhealthy hollows of his features, so that he could see the broken but purposeful light in his eyes, as he lifted his hand and slapped Maury again in the same place but even harder.

"You son-of-a-bitch," Maury said, and something broke within him. Yet, he was not sure what it was, could not locate it, would not know for a long time what, if ever, had come over him. Only that he was diving into his pocket, going for his gun, oblivious of the reaction of the man, not caring whether he saw it or not. Not giving a damn what happened as long as he got the gun, the pistol leapt into his hand, warm and familiar, an old friend. *I should never have let you go*, he thought and brought it out in one motion, cocking it and pointing it into the astonished face of the man, who was already winding up for another swing, not conscious of what had happened. Maury shot the man in the face.

The impact literally tore the features apart, and the face exploded like fruit that had been thrown at a wall. Little fragments of brain paste and bone burst in a sudden halo that showed on Maury's hands, and then the truncated form of the man, head lolling, was spinning and kicking beneath him, the disconnected legs, the dead appendages still rolling in neurological response to shock and pain. Maury looked at what lay beneath him in astonishment, and yet underneath that, underneath the fear which started to work through him as if a wound long sealed had burst open, along with this there was—and he admitted it—a little bit of pride, too, because he had shown that people could not get away with this. People could not do this to him. One man once—Wulff in Atlanta— had humiliated him, but he would pay for it and even if he did not, that would be the only time. *The only time*. He would not be tampered with.

He looked down at the man who was bleeding copiously, almost decapitated by the force of the shot and then up at the bartender, and at the faces around the bar. He was drawing attention now, he noticed. No one was making an effort to avoid his eyes now. "Drop the gun," the bartender was saying. "Drop the gun. Drop it now. Nobody has to see this, nobody has to try to stop you. Just drop it and leave. Drop it and leave." His eyes bulged, his face itself seemed squat and protuberant, like an overripe melon. "Please," he whispered. "Get out."

Maury looked at him, at the gun, at the panorama of the faces, and then he looked once again at the corpse. He was, he supposed, in the worst trouble that he had ever been in his life; worse even than at that moment in Atlanta when he was sure that the man was going to kill him, but it was hard to come to terms with that understanding, hard to deal with anything really except that he had killed a man who had much deserved killing. He turned the gun toward the bartender. "Get down," he said. "Get down behind there."

The bartender dived immediately below counter level, vanished. Maury looked at the others. They said nothing whatsoever. Someone had pulled the cord on the jukebox. He had never heard it quieter in a public place in his life, not even in the diner he had been in when the word came through that Kennedy had been killed. "You sons-of-bitches," he said to them, "you-sons-of-bitches, you don't understand anything. You don't understand why I did it."

And that was true, he thought. That was absolutely true. *He* could barely understand why he had done it. It had something to do with Wulff. Wulff had fucked up his mind, fucked up everything within him, made him not a murderer once but a murderer twice now, and the end not yet in sight. Wulff had plunged him into a world where killing was as routine as on a coon hunt and the victims meant no more than coons either. That was what Wulff had passed onto him, and yet it should have been different. At the very least, he should have been allowed to have killed the man instead of misdirecting fire in a bar. "You don't understand," he said again, rather wildly. He knew that he was not making too much sense, but then again what in this world made sense? What in the whole fucking panorama of events would even reproduce in true color? "No way," he said. "There's just no way that you can do this to me you sons-of-bitches."

They all looked at him, but none with understanding. They just did not understand, that was all. They were not aware of the pressures that could come upon you just from doing your job, and then, too, there was always some son-of-a-bitch, some dirty son-of-a-bitch who would try to stop you, manage to keep you from carrying out what you had been ordered to carry out. That was just the way of the universe. For every doughnut a hole, for every birth a death, for every action a reaction, and you could not carry something through straight forward and simple. No, they would get you coming or going, in or out, because the whole fucking thing was rigged. Like Wulff, himself, who had arranged a universe for himself only so that he could kill within Maury's life. It had been stage managed in the same way. He did not know what he was saying. He did not know what he was thinking, but it seemed to make sense. Everything made sense if you could only get to the end of it and look at it within perspective. All of them were out to get him. He had never had a chance.

"I never had a chance," Maury said almost conversationally. "Damn it, I never had a chance. But that doesn't mean that you can't try," and with enormous casualness, offhandedly really, the way that you might slap dirt off your shoes in the vestibule of a house, the way that you might slam the door of your car at a roadside stop heading toward the men's room, Maury raised the pistol to his head, gave the bartender a shrug and a wink, nodded without rancor at the patrons of the bar who were watching him with great attention, and blew his brains out.

XXI

Wulff dreamed that he was back in New York again doing routine work for narco, hanging around a joint with a couple of informants and pretending to be in deep conversation, while really watching the door for the score that the informants had promised him. He dreamed that he sat at the bar at easy attention, listening to the informants mumble, while the lights changed and he worked out the slow hours of the afternoon toward the meaningless bust. He dreamed that he was twenty-nine again in Red Hook and did not care, but when he awoke he was back in the hotel room in Philadelphia and everything was as it had been before he had passed into the thick and trapped doze. He tried to burrow back into the sleep again, telling himself that now he was with Marie in Queens somewhere; they were looking at houses and evaluating how many bedrooms they would need for how many children how soon. Marie was close to him in the empty spaces of the houses they were seeking, and her hand was against his. He took it and kissed it, and as she came against him they began to grind against one another until in the cold and in front of the real-estate agent they began to sink into the flat boards of the living room seeking one another …

But when he came from this second sleep it was with a feeling of doomed alertness, still Philadelphia, still the hotel room, and this time he had been torn from the sleep in a way that told him that he would not be able to get back there. He could not put himself in New York even on narco; he could not bring himself back to Marie …

Finally and incontrovertibly he was in Philadelphia, back in the reeking hotel room and eight months beyond even the conviction that things could have been different. They never could have been different. Everything had led him always to this, and he should have recognized that a long time ago. You might think that you had a series of alternatives, that your life was a reckoning composed of thousands of smaller reckonings at all of the corridors of choice, but that was bullshit. That was bullshit, indeed … Los Angeles and Chicago and Lima and Detroit and Philadelphia itself were as fixed in destiny from the moment that he had stepped into that room on West Ninety-third Street as his face in the mirror might have been fixed by the tilt of his head as he sought the reflection. You had to believe that. You had to believe that your life could never have changed, that you always became the sum of what you were meant to be because if you believed anything else, if you believed that it *could* be different, if you believed, for instance, that the girl could have been alive and that you might have been with her at just this moment—

Wulff got out of bed and turned the lights on. He had had trouble sleeping for a long time, and now he no longer could sleep at all. In that first onrush of true sleep would come the dreams of narco, dreams of Marie, dreams of Vietnam, and he would come torn from within them the instant, gasping and unable for the moment to accept the fact that his waking life was not a dream. And dropping back into sleep it would really be the same again, those moments relived over and over … It was better to stay awake; it was better to avoid sleep altogether than to go through this. He put his face in some water and checked the room, just to make sure that everything was still safe, and then he opened the valise in which he had stored the little ordnance that he had and took out a bottle of rye and began to drink it neat in straight, sullen gulps.

He had never really been drinking before, had avoided it throughout his quest. Goddamn it, if he was going to fight the drug trade it would be ridiculous to need a drug himself. But now there seemed little enough harm in it. It had been a long time. He had picked up the bottle in a local store after coming back from the bar, and it was surprising how quickly it went down, how good the rye felt. He needed it. Seagram's Seven. It was all right. It beat all hell out of the way he had felt when he came back, after the way the dreams had assaulted him. A quick image of what had happened in the bar lurched at him suddenly. He saw the way the woman had looked when he had shot her, heard the whimpers of the bartender lying on the slats, and his stomach convulsed a little, the fumes of Seagram's coming back at him sourly from the interior. He lifted the bottle again, drank in a series of choking gulps, much as if it were beer rather than hard whisky that he was downing. His stomach heaved once more, then took the alcohol gratefully, and he began to feel the old sensation of drunkenness, something he had not known since Vietnam, when in the fields there was nothing to do night after night. Little fibers and strands of knowledge seemed to extrude from within him, and he felt as if his system was pouring perception richly into him. Time itself seemed to adjust itself around him like a shawl, drawing in comfortably to a proportion that was right for him. He might have sat there for several hours, or only for minutes, continuing to drink the rye, it did not matter. All that concerned him was perception, and perception worked with the liquor. Hand in hand. Beat the band. He felt good.

He ought to feel good, he had beaten the game. He had come in with all the odds against him and had had more of an effect upon his enemies than had all the enforcement agencies in a decade. One angry man had managed to prove what everyone had known for a long time, anyway: that the system was bullshit, and acted only to preserve itself, and in order to preserve itself it *needed* what it was supposed to oppose. That was what the hell it proved. Of course it was more difficult than he would have thought, and his enemies were still around in good measure. As a matter of fact, he had more enemies than ever before because everyone was now out to get him, but still. Still. He had made some progress. That was all that counted in the long run anyway, that you were able to make some progress. You could not be depressed, you could not give up, you could not succumb to the illusion that you were a failure simply because your enemies were always increasing while you were simply trying to carry on a job. Evil would always demand that one's enemies increased. Anyone who ever tried to do some good in the world found that. Kennedy had tried to do some good and look what had happened to him. To his brother. And Martin Luther King. Malcolm X, who had tried to drive the pushers from Harlem, who had started to put together a vast movement at the core of which was the religious opposition to drugs. They had taken good care of Malcolm. They had, come to think of it, taken care of just about everyone who had tried to make some progress in the fight against drugs, but that was no excuse. That was no reason to give up. Was it now? Was it really.

He felt, with the onrush of rye coming over him now, the rye deep in his system, moving through all the coils of his consciousness, the urge to go out on the streets again and kill. The two in the alley in the south side. Martin. The bar. It was not enough. All the time that he was in here resting up and brooding, his enemies were waxing stronger and stronger. Working together. Working out their plans. Their plans to kill him and to increase the international drug trade. They were all over. There was not a portion of the world which did not contain his enemies, and all of them were plotting at just this moment how to overcome him. I cannot let this go, he thought. I cannot give them this chance. I must go out onto the streets again. Start outside. Start anywhere. Before they destroy me.

Are you sure that this is the way to do it, some other voice said within him, a quiet, rational voice which strangely enough sounded very much like his own, although much less excitable. Are you sure that your enemies are out there.

Of course I'm sure, he said. They're all over. Can't you see what it's come to? I have to kill everywhere now. Everyone's turned against me. Everyone is in this together.

Are you positive about that? Don't you think that this is maybe a little extreme? I mean, the voice said, what you've been doing recently looks a little bit like indiscriminate killing to me.

Well of course, he said, a little angry now, taking another pull on the bottle. Of course it's indiscriminate. Just like they are. *They're* indiscriminate. They don't care who gets the drugs or where the drugs wind up. They just keep on tunneling them into the cities. They put the poison in the system and they couldn't care less, they couldn't care less— any of them—where it winds up or who it kills. They kill at random; they did it in Vietnam too. So the only way to fight them is to be just as indiscriminate as they are. That keeps them off balance.

That's one way to look at it, the voice said, but there's another way too. Is there? What's that?

It's possible that you've gone crazy, the voice said. It's possible that all of the pressure has driven you off the edge and that you're killing people now who have absolutely nothing to do with the international drug trade. That's just a theory now, so don't jump up and down and get excited, but have you ever considered that, Wulff?

It's possible, Wulff said. Anything is possible. Maybe you have to be indiscriminate to get anywhere.

But how indiscriminate? How indiscriminate, Wulff?

I don't know, he said. This is beginning to bother me, he said and put down the bottle. Leave me alone, he said.

I'd leave you alone but you don't want that. Not really.

No?

You summoned me. I wouldn't be here if you didn't want to listen to me in some way. I'm only telling you what you want to hear.

Well, I've heard it. I don't want to hear it any more.

You can't kill the world, Wulff. You can't kill everyone. You started to do the same thing in New York the second time, remember? When you blew up that bar in Harlem. You weren't sure that they were dealing in there at all, Wulff. You just did it because you felt like blowing up a bar.

It had to be done.

They took you away then and put you in jail. Maybe they ought to take you away now, have you ever thought of that? Maybe that would be the best thing.

Leave me alone, he said. He stood and went over to his valise, opened it, pulled up the leather tray and looked at the grenades lined up inside. Five of them still left. He had seen at Martin's house the detonative power of the instruments. They were everything that the southerner had promised, they were sheer death. Five of them carefully placed could probably take out a square mile. He looked at them and then bent and gathered them up. All right, he said, not quite sure of what he was talking about but responding to some unasked question. All right.

That's what I mean, Wulff, the voice said. You're going to take those damned things out now and start throwing them at people.

You let me decide what I'm going to do.

Some innocent people are going to get hurt.

How the hell do you know that they're innocent?

Not everybody can be in the international drug trade, Wulff. A hell of a lot more people than you would think have never even heard of it. Besides, you can't kill the world.

He hoisted the grenades, began to stuff them into his coat. He felt good, a little bit uncoordinated with the rye within him, but that would pass in time, and as he hit the air essentially he felt cold, composed, utterly in command of himself. Liquor only accentuated what you were already, anyway. It was a lie that it reduced your reflexes. Actually, if you knew how to use it and how to compensate for its presence in your system, it made you stronger. Fuck off, he said.

I'll do that. It isn't my responsibility.

Good. Get lost. Leave me alone.

It's your life, Wulff. But at the rate it's going now it's not going to be a long or a happy one.

It was never going to be long or happy. I knew from the start that it wouldn't last. I didn't think I'd get this far.

You got this far by being sensible. Now you're not being so sensible any more and now you know it.

I think I told you to fuck off.

It's my pleasure, the voice said. I have nothing to do with this, it added. It doesn't affect me either way. I just thought that you would like the benefit of some advice.

I've had it and thanks he said. He patted down his pockets, the grenades smooth within like little walnuts secreted in the pouches of his jacket. Smooth and tight and a walking land mine. He selected the point thirty-eight and added it to the point forty-five he already had, and then slammed the lid and walked toward the door. You're making a mistake, the voice said. You know you'll regret this.

Get lost.

I'll get lost. You can lose me any time you want you know. I have no existence unless you summon me. You know who I am, Wulff.

He opened the door, stood there in the vagrant breezes that seemed to stir through the dank hallway of the hotel. All right, he said. I do know who you are. But that doesn't make any difference. It doesn't make any difference at all.

If you think so.

It has to be done. I can't stop now. I've got to carry it all the way through to the end.

Only if you think that way. No one else does.

It's just me, he said. It's always been just me, I know that. So even at the end why can't it be my decision?

You're protesting too much, Wulff, the voice said. You're protesting just a shade too much.

Fuck you, Wulff said. Fuck you, he said again, and went through the door and into the hallway and out, remembering only when he was near the steps that he had forgotten to close the door. That was pretty stupid, all things considered. That indicated a real loss of control. Angrily he went back and pulled the door closed and started walking again. He thought that he could hear the shrieking and stirring of the voice, now trapped within the room, but as he got onto the stairs he understood that once again he had called the shots wrong. It was neither shrieking nor stirring which he heard from within. Not that at all.

It was laughter.

But too late for any of that; too late to consider, too late to turn back. You went on course and you followed it through to its logical end because … because, well, there was no other way to do it and to still be a man. To turn back would be to raise the possibility that your cause had not been right in the first place. Absolute goals, absolute means.

Wulff went out into the streets of Philadelphia to blow them all up.

XXII

Sometimes you got lucky. You could stumble around for years and years just trying to get a break, watching better men than you fall apart inside and outside because nothing would happen to them, and then when you had reached your own diminishing returns, when the miserable, wrenching taste of your failure was turning over in your gut, making everything you touched seem rotten, you could hit a door somewhere by accident which you had not even intended and blunder into the discovery of what had evaded you for so long. Serendipity they called it: the theory that almost all human progress could be viewed in terms of accidents caused by those who were looking for something else. On the fifth day of the eight month of his involvement with Wulff, Williams suddenly got very lucky, and in a way which had never happened to him before. It happened *deus ex machina*, which is to say that his luck was not of his own causing, nor was he even involved in it.

It came as a matter of fact over the radio of the Mercedes which Evers, tired of talking, had snapped on as they rolled the last twenty miles toward Philadelphia. There was an all-news station on the FM band, and after the sports segment which involved a rumor that the Eagles had been sold to a syndicate headed by Arab officials and Joe Kuharich was going to come back to coach, the station put on a bulletin from South Fifteenth Street that an explosion of indeterminate origin had caused an evacuation of two buildings and had still not been brought under control. Fire crews were at the scene. So was the reporter who hopefully would have further news shortly. Back to the main desk now. Williams said, "That's the lone wolf man. I know that's him."

Evers turned toward him and said, "I could argue with you but you're probably right. We ought to head that way."

"I know his method," Williams said. "This is the way he's working now. That was what he was doing in Harlem just before they caught up with him. He had blown out a place next to the Apollo just on the suspicion they were doing trade in there."

"All right," Evers said. "That connects with what I was saying. The only thing is whether or not we'll find him anywhere near the scene. Is there any point in going there at all if he's already gone?"

"He won't be gone," Williams said. His foot was to the floor, the SEL was doing a tight seventy-three now in difficult traffic. His concentration was absolute, and yet within the compass of that and the absolute respect the car demanded, he found that he was quite able to talk. "He'll be there. He'll want to see it."

"Probably," Evers said after a pause. "He probably would, come to think of it. That would be the only pleasure that he would get now." He paused for a while and said then, "The poor bastard."

"Not by me," Williams said. "My fund of pity has just about run out for good now. The aycee was right. Everyone was right, you see. This is intolerable; it can't go on. You think that you can find South Fifteenth Street?"

"I've been around here," Evers said. "I can fake it. I can fake the city. You just keep on driving and I'll tell you what to do."

So Williams kept on driving, turning up the all-news station loud so that he would not miss anything new that came through. Not that there was much. The reporter was inexperienced, and even though the desk kept on switching back to him at five minute intervals he reported little more than a competent dispatch man could have in one or two sentences. Firemen were on the scene. A crowd had gathered. Two buildings were on fire but the firemen were apparently bringing the blaze under control. Police were on the scene. A large crowd was on the scene. It was not yet known whether anyone had been injured in the blast or for that matter if there were any dead. Police were investigating. Firemen were in the premises and investigating. The crowd was quiet and orderly but angry. Everyone was angry. Everyone thought that the fire was a disgrace and probably caused by arson. This could not be deduced at the present time. The fire lieutenant on the scene would have no comment.

"I bet he has a comment," Evers said. "But they can't put it on the air. Left at the end of this ramp."

"The son-of-a-bitch is on the scene," Williams said. "I just feel it. He's probably right there taking it all in. Listening to the commentary."

"Don't be too sure," Evers said. "Don't count on long-distance psychoanalysis. It was just a theory."

"No," Williams said, "you're right. When a man's right, he's right. I give you that credit. I don't resist truth. He's everything you say he is."

"You learn a little working with explosives," Evers said. "Now just highball straight down about two-and-a-half miles and stay within the speed limit. I think we'd lose more time being pulled over and explaining to cops than we would just moving along at forty. It's an amazing car," he said, "but if the newspapers ever learned that we had this kind of stuff in the garage we'd be in worse trouble than we are now."

The all-news reporter came on again. He sounded about twenty-four years old and scared, as if he had never been on a disaster before and at last the sense of it was getting through to him. He announced that he had someone to interview, a patrolman something-or-other. Patrolman something-or-other who did not sound happy said that there were apparently no victims from the explosion. There had been at the time of the incident only three people in the building, all of them old, and all of them had managed to get out on their own. Everyone else either worked or was in school or had been evicted. Patrolman-something attributed the explosion to devices of some sort, but he could be no more explicit than that. The bomb squad was on the way and might have further details.

"Barn door," Evers said. "barn doors and horses."

Patrolman something-or-other could venture no explanation as to what might have been the reason for the blast or as to whether it had been deliberately set. Yes, it might have been a revolutionary group, it might have been anyone, but it was hard to know exactly what a revolutionary group would hope to gain by blowing up a couple of buildings in this section of Philadelphia. "You mean a slum section," the reporter asked.

"No, I did not say that at all," the patrolman said. "I would not even refer to it as a disadvantaged section."

There was an unhappy pause for a while and then patrolman-something said that he would have to excuse himself, he would have to return to the site. The reporter said certainly and thank you very much and then said that that was about the way it was on South Fifteenth Street at three o'clock p.m., and that of course he would remain on the scene for further bulletins should further bulletins break. However, since there was apparently no loss of life and since police did not think that it was a revolutionary group, he doubted that it would be necessary for him to go back on the air, although, of course, he would remain available for on-the-air duty should the situation change. He signed off uncomfortably, tentatively and there was a hanging dead space on the air. Then the desk man came on and said there definitely would be further bulletins from the site, to stay tuned, that every breaking news story was covered exactly as it broke and until conclusion, and that listeners should be aware that they would be kept closely informed as to all incidents on the site, including the possibility that the bomb had been set by active political revolutionaries demonstrating against injustice. Williams shook his head and turned off the radio. Up ahead they could see two patrol cars, flashers turning, at an intersection which would have to be South Fifteenth.

"I don't think that man is long for the slot," Evers said.

"He's doing the best he can."

"He said it *wasn't* revolutionaries," Evers said, "and you just don't do that kind of thing in the all-news business. You don't turn off any possibility of a story until it's impossible to run with it any more. How you going to hold an audience otherwise, ripping off the AP wire? I think we should walk from here. They're going to have the site pretty well sealed off."

"Just walk in there?"

"We can't drive in," Evers said, "be reasonable."

"We'd better take some heavy armament then."

"You really think we're going to come up against him?" Evers said. "You're sure of that?"

"I'm not sure of anything. I think there's a goddamned good possibility that we might, yes. I'd feel a hell of a lot better in a car, let me tell you that."

"You want to tell the police?"

Williams let the car coast to a stop, double-parked, then shook his head and began to crawl front first into a small parking space just ahead. "No," he said. "I think we should go into this alone. I may be wrong," he said, "there's a chance it isn't him. We'll look like goddamned fools. Shit, we'll be likely to get busted on suspicion ourselves."

"All right," Evers said. "I'm nothing if not accommodating. I'm just along for the ride and the walk. Anyway, it beats all hell out of disassembling dynamite caps. We can go in there with our guns; what else can we take?"

Williams bumpered the car ahead, tracked it into reverse, let it roll back an inch, and then cut the engine. Thick fumes began to roll into the car carried by the wind and the now dead air-conditioner. He thought that he could see little particles of soot move, dazzling in the grey air outside. "Nothing," he said. "Just ourselves."

"All right," Evers said, reaching for the door handle. "Let's go in and see what's there."

"Wait," Williams said.

Evers paused, his hand hanging on the handle, looking at him intently. "You don't have to go," Williams said.

"What's that? I don't understand."

"I don't know how to put this. This doesn't concern you. You're not in it at all. You don't have to put your life on the line going up against this guy. I do. But you don't have to be involved. You stay here."

"That's ridiculous," Evers said. "I'm not letting you go in there alone. We're going together or not at all."

"I appreciate that," Williams said, "but you don't have to. It could be very bad, this thing. I see now just how dangerous he could be. I don't want you to get hurt."

Evers hit him in the shoulder lightly and said, "Fuck off. I'm going in with you," and went to the handle, then came back toward Williams and said, "of course I'm in it. We're all in it. We're all in it, don't you see that, me just as you."

"No I don't."

"He's ours," Evers said. "He comes from the PD. We created him. We made him possible, we created the circumstances that sent him on his way, we screwed him into this. In a way every man in the PD is responsible and has to do the same thing. We started him, we've got to remove him. Don't you see that?"

Williams said, "Maybe I do. Maybe I do then. That's one way to look at it," and hit Evers back just as lightly, and then they clambered out of the SEL into the stinking air to fight the good fight, to fight it all the way to the end, to see the wolf, to guard and cage him, and if this did not work—because a wild animal could not be caged—to deal with him in the only way that they could.

Their identification worked fine at the hasty checkpoint which the Philadelphia cops had set up. They moved down the block through the haze and right to the center of the action. When Evers saw the bright orange helmets of the demolition squad pouring from their special truck, his face twitched with gladness.

XXIII

He had done the best that he could. He had moved right in to one of their nerve centers and had bombed it out with two cleverly flung grenades. No one could have asked any more of him than what he had done, and he should derive satisfaction from it.

But he could not. He simply could not. Why were they all still alive? Why after two dead hits on the buildings that were the absolute nerve center of the international drug trade, two hits which should have cleaned them out for good and for all … why were they spilling from the building still alive, still alive-o, with police on the scene to help them, no less, to escape. Didn't the police understand what was going on, what Wulff had done? Didn't the police realize which side of the law they were working for? It was so frustrating that Wulff could have gone off the deep end right then and there if he were not so careful and controlled; if he did not have such a clear sense of mission.

He had come to Philadelphia, the bicentennial city to finish off the job, to strike a killing blow at the center of the great twitching nerve which came to surface here, and the stupid goddamned cops did not even know that he had been doing it all for *them*. From the start he had been working for these sons-of-bitches, and who appreciated it? Not only that, but they had called in the goddamned demolition squad to guard against further damage. Where did that come off? What did they think that they were doing?

Wulff knew that he should get the hell away from the scene. There were other battles to fight, bitter, better battles to fight in the light and in the night. He should not stay around this dismal street to be frustrated at the stupidity of officials who did not know the good he had tried to do them. Also, it was quite dangerous to stay around. He knew that his features were recognizable, and there were assassins; all over there were assassins eager to kill him for the bounty. He should get back under cover, return to the hotel, check out his remaining grenades, plot further action. One swallow was not a summer, two bombs were not a campaign. He should return to fight another day. But he could not, somehow, bring himself to leave.

Instead, he stood in an alley not more than a hundred yards from the point where the radio and television crews had come in with their trucks, and watched it all. No one watched him, they were busy enough attending to the wounded and conferring with one another and checking out the scene of impact where the outer surfaces of one of the buildings had burst open, scattering concrete like sawdust. Also the street was packed with residents who had every reason to want to see what the hell was going on, and the haze and stink were so thick at times that it was difficult to see exactly what was going on. Any one of them would have the same difficulty spotting him. So he was safe, he guessed, for a while, just standing quietly and taking it in.

But he could not do it much longer. He knew that. He knew that he was pushing the rim of discovery; he ought to get the hell away. It was just that it was so goddamned frustrating after all he had been through to see this and to know that the bastards had gotten away again. Shit, they had to have been in that building. He had been sure that they would all be there. All of his enemies, all twenty or thirty of them, plotting to reorganize the international drug trade from the base of

Philadelphia until he had come along and bombed them out. What a surprise for them! To die knowing that the lone wolf, implacable, had struck again. But they had gotten away. They were not there after all. It was goddamned frustrating, that was what it was. You knew you were up against a cunning and dangerous enemy, but until you saw that enemy operate it was hard to believe that he was so resourceful.

It was pretty interesting all right, though. He had to admit that. What was going on was pretty interesting. What with the disaster trucks and the bomb squad and police all over the place, and fire equipment and newspaper reporters and a couple of people huddled around a mobile television unit being interviewed just a hundred yards away. They were no doubt describing their narrow escape from holocaust. What they didn't tell the television crew, of course, was that they were major pushers and dealers who had wriggled away from final judgment. Television reporters were pretty stupid as a group and certainly they would not think to ask those questions on their own. For that matter, the television crews themselves might have been in on the conspiracy. Everyone in the entertainment business was a drug freak of one sort or another and if television news wasn't entertainment, what the hell was it?

Wulff knew that he should get out of there. He still had four grenades jammed into his pockets. That was plenty for another strike; plenty to create a little chaos elsewhere. Waste not, want not. There were still the four grenades carefully hoarded for further action, and if he could place his fire carefully he should be able to hit four more residences. Two anyway, if he wanted to do a really thorough job. He was creating a risk situation by hanging around here, there was no question about it. Sooner or later someone might pick him up, come in to ask him some questions. What the hell could he say? He had nothing to say. He would have to start shooting, that was all. But that would lead to more complications than it was worth. You really did not kill law enforcement personnel or civilians. Unless they were crooked, of course. Most of them were.

Wulff moved slowly from the alley. He looked like anyone else on the street. His face was a little streaked now, his jacket a little lumpy with the grenades. His pockets holding the pistols were a little distended as well, like a fat man's stomach, but no one was going to look at him that closely. Of course, his face was familiar, and everyone in the world was gunning to get him. But there was a chance they wouldn't look too closely. Who would really want to look at him when they had the disaster site itself to contemplate? He stood there on the sidewalk for a little while, his breathing irregular, his hands clenching and unclenching, looking at all of it. Two cops standing near the foot of the building were in deep conversation with a disheveled man, another cop with a sergeant's stripe was leaning against the wall of an adjoining building smoking, which was a hell of a thing to do with all of this stink around; dragging that stuff directly into your lungs. Still, what the hell, it was his funeral.

Then Wulff looked in the other direction and saw a man he had never expected to see again.

XXIV

"That's him," Williams said. He was astonished. It was one thing to calculate a bizarre possibility, even decide that it might be true, but it was another to actually see it develop. Nixon must have reacted that way when the pressures began to build. "He's just standing over there," Williams said, trying to restrain his excitement, pulling Evers back against a building wall out of Wulff's line of sight. "I'll be damned."

Williams looked at Wulff and said, "He looks pretty much out of it to me. What the hell is he doing there?"

"I don't know," Williams said, "I don't know," and staring at Wulff, he thought *that much* was the truth anyway. The man was just not in relation to the circumstances. Something in the way he was standing, the abstracted way in which he was looking at the ground, at his hands, at the television crew which had set up about fifty yards down range, gave him the impression that indeed his attention had turned inward, and that he was simply not paying attention to what was going on around him. He had never expected it of Wulff. If nothing else, Williams had expected to find him at the catastrophic alertness which had always characterized him, but then again you never knew, did you? It was hard to say what a man might be until you came up against him, and much had happened to Wulff, as well as Williams, since he had last seen the man in Los Angeles. "All right," Williams said. "I'm going to take him."

"Take him?" Evers said. "Isn't that a little premature? Are you sure that you shouldn't—"

"I'm going to take him," Williams said. He felt slow waves of purpose building. Or, it might have only been dread, he did not know. That was the cop's curse anyway, to move into situations which had no definition, which could either end harmlessly or with you dead on the pavement within thirty seconds, your life oozing away, and unless you disguised the terror that you were moving into and cloaked it with a different name like curiosity or eagerness or a businesslike sense of method, you would be unable to function at all. He had his service revolver with him. Nobody seemed to notice what was going on. There was a small cluster of police around the television crews, and the crowd had drifted that way. Otherwise, the block had already become sealed off, just as it might have under quarantine. The television cameras covered everything anyway. People could only define or justify their existence through the media. If the crews had not come here there might have been no one on the street at all.

Wulff leaned against the wall of the tight little alley, one leg crossed against another, his eyes half-closed, seemingly a picture of the most enormous casualness. He appeared to see nothing, to be locked wholly into himself, but that could only have been cover. And then again, he might have been stuporous. You did not know. You did not know what lurked behind any apartment door.

"All right," Evers said. "I'll cover you; I'll be right behind all the way. Let's go."

"No."

"You want to shoot him right down here? That's risky," Evers said, quietly. "That could lead to a lot of explanations we don't want to get into. But then again, maybe that's best when you're dealing with someone like this."

"You don't understand," Williams said. "It's all right. You couldn't understand. I'm going to take him face-to-face. I want you to stay back."

"Stay back?"

"This is between us," Williams said. "It had to be this way from the beginning. Just me and him."

"This isn't a gunfight," Evers said. "This isn't the OK Corral or High Noon."

"In a way it is," Williams said. His pistol was in his hand. He checked it, checked the cartridges, put it back, holding his hand in his pocket, and began to move slowly toward Wulff. "Don't interfere," he said.

"I'm here to help."

"The only way you can help is not to interfere."

"All right," Evers said. His face seemed to flood with understanding. Or, then again, it might have only been submission. Williams was nominal head, and any experienced cop understood chain of command. "Whatever you say, then."

"It has to be that way," Williams said, and began to move slowly down range toward Wulff. The man was still not looking at him, seemed sealed off within himself, but in that posture you just could not be sure. You could not be sure of anything. The high acrid smoke was in the air, little clumps of rubble lay on the ground, but it had been an implosive charge. Most of the damage was inside. Williams wondered what would happen if Wulff looked up and saw him. You never could tell. He could hold back he supposed, and do as Evers had suggested: he could shoot him. The man was open for a clean shot now; no one would ever know the difference. He would be acclaimed by the NYPD; they would not give a damn. Philly might, but they would have the whole story straightened out for them by PD and then they wouldn't give a damn either. Easy. It would be so easy. It was not the way it was going to be. He closed the ground easily.

Wulff lifted his head and saw him. His eyes showed recognition. He clawed for his gun.

XXV

Wulff had never expected to see Williams here. How had Williams gotten here? How could he have possibly known? There was a moment of panic, but then the gun was in his hand and he knew that it was going to be all right. Everything, eternally, would be all right as long as you had the gun. Had it in your hand.

"Stop," he said to Williams. He said it loudly and distinctly. No way that the man could possibly misunderstand him, could have missed the meaning. Drugs. Williams must have been drawn to the site by the drugs which were in the apartments he had bombed out. He was probably looking for the cache before the apartments were sealed off. *Which meant that Williams was in it too.* How, otherwise, would he have known to come here, would he have picked up the trail, unless he knew unerringly where the drugs were and that Wulff was in their pursuit. He should have known. He should have known it from the beginning.

Williams was one of them. All the time that he was working with the man, depending upon Williams, listening to his advice, Williams had actually been in the employ of the dealers. Had been funneling information to them, had been laughing—and laughing at Wulff—as he collaborated with the enemy to abort everything that Wulff had tried. That was why his mission had been so difficult. How could it have been otherwise? "Stop you son-of-a-bitch," he said and motioned with the revolver. "Stop or I'll shoot you." He would have long since won by now. His quest would have ended in Chicago, in Peru, in Los Angeles. If it had not been for Williams, laughing, taunting, teasing, observing and turning over everything he had received to the enemy. "You dirty bastard," Wulff said. He thought he had Williams levelled in his sight. The distance was a little tricky to estimate and the light peculiar: it seemed to dazzle his eyes. But, then again, he was very tired, and tricks of light would never disturb a real marksman. He aimed the gun and shot.

XXVI

The bullet went by his left ear and Williams hit the ground at once, bringing his pistol forward. He had known from the start that it must end this way. In some subterranity of feeling, surely, he must have known that he and Wulff would wind up in this stinking street and that one would have to put the other down. In the night he must have dreamed it below the threshold of recall, but it had been one of those dreams which had informed his days. He lay on the ground, prone, his pistol extended in front of him.

Behind him there were sounds, but he could not distinguish them: shouts, cries, warnings, running, they were no longer differentiated. All had become a tunnel, and at one end of the tunnel was Wulff and at another was Williams. He aimed his own pistol. In a way he had very little time for the shot before Wulff would get off one of his own, but in another, he had sufficient time, all of the time that he needed. All of the hasty, discolored instants of his life which had rushed by seemed to have been in anticipation of this one moment when he could extend confrontation slowly toward sufficiency. There was almost a leisurely sense to the way that he pointed the pistol at Wulff, a time during which he felt he was able to consider what he was doing and how, on balance, it would work out. He could kill Wulff. Then again he could pull or wait on the shot and let Wulff kill him. Either way it did not seem to make a hell of a lot of difference. They were both dead. One way or the other they had been killed a long time ago, and the fact of respiration or attention did not seem likely to change that.

Too abstract. Too metaphysical. Bullshit. Life was life; you could not value it so cheaply. It did make a difference. Everything made a difference. To go on, to deal with one instant after the next was in itself its own solution, its own justification. It was easy to say you were dead, that you were better off dead, that death made no difference, but that decision could itself only be made in life. Death was a kind of life then. Well. You did not know.

You simply did not know. Williams pulled the trigger.

XXVII

Raising the gun he could see that the other man was going to get the shot off first and there was nothing to do. Sometimes you could see your death even as it happened to you: he had had that sensation in Chicago when Calabrese could have killed him. He had known exactly what it was like and here it was again. Hello death. Pleased to meet you death. Been with you for a long time death, waiting in these rooms for your call, and now here you are old friend, old bastard, and absolutely nothing to do. Have a chair, death. Warm your hands by the fire, pal, rest easy. We'll be together for a long time so don't feel in any hurry at all to start talking. We have a thousand years. Ten thousand years. All of the millennia to get acquainted, so just take it easy, don't rush, don't stammer the way you often do, death, when you get excited. Just take it easy. Slow and easy and everything will come into place.

He pointed his pistol to shoot the man because that was the kind of thing you had to do. You had to go through the motions right up to the end, even when you knew the solution, because that was also the way the game was rigged. But he knew that the shot would go wild and he knew that it was meaningless. Everything was meaningless. The shot went wild. Williams' fire hit him right in the temple.

Wulff felt it. He vaulted to meet it. It was much easier even than he thought it would be. Death seized him in an embrace and he fell through West Ninety-third Street and down the crevices of later circumstance.

Wulff died.

EPILOGUE

Williams said to the aycee two days later, "I had no choice at all, you know."

"We know that."

"Not the way you think, I mean. I didn't have to kill him. I could have put him down with a shot anywhere. He didn't have to die. But I knew that I was going to shoot to kill. I knew I would go for the killing shot."

"No one's blaming you," the aycee said. He stacked some papers on his desk, looked at his watch. It had been a long summary interview and it had come after a day of dealing with the commissioner, with the Philadelphia commissioner, with the FBI, even with the U.S. Attorney's office and the federal strike forces. He was obviously tired and wanted to go home. "It's over," the aycee said, "and under the circumstances this was the cleanest and the best way. He was a dangerous man and of course he had gone completely out of control at the end."

"He was always completely out of control."

The aycee shrugged. "This could be."

"It was only when he stopped shooting mobsters and dealers and started to kill at random that he had to be put down," Williams said. "Isn't that the truth? Until then, whatever we said, every man in the department was secretly cheering him on. Every cop in the country felt there was a little less weight because the wolf was in action. But he was just as crazy then as he was at the end."

"Maybe," the aycee said. He picked up a paperweight, fondled it, put it down. "Everything you say has a good point to it, but there really seems no reason to go on with this. You're in the clear, we're all in the clear. It's been a long day and I think we should all go home and just try to forget this now."

"I'll never forget it."

"Put it behind us then."

"You knew I was going to kill him," Williams said. "That's why you put me on this. You couldn't be as sure of any other man as you could of me. You wanted him killed."

"We wanted it ended."

"You wanted it ended and then in order to end it you had to have him killed," Williams said. "That shut him up for good. That sealed him off. Otherwise he might have talked," Williams said again, "and then a lot of people might have seen how completely he was our creation."

"That's ridiculous."

"The creation of every one of us," Williams said. "The PD and the Army and the pushers and the users and the whole country. They all created what he became. He was only them after a time. And he might have tied it all up if he had talked."

The aycee stood. "That's enough," he said. "It's very interesting, and you can take it to the newspapers if you want. No one will stop you from expressing your theories."

Williams stood too. "It's all right, commissioner," he said, "I'm not going to take it anywhere. No one outside of these offices will ever hear about it because, you see, he's my creation, too. I made him what he is just as thoroughly as the bastard who killed his girl. We were all cops, we were all system and the system creates everything, even its own poisons. Even the poisons are system-created, just to flush the other poisons down the drain."

He turned then and went to the door, and when he got to the door he reached into his pocket, took out his shield and very neatly, very deliberately laid it at his feet. "Here," he said.

"What does that mean?"

"It's quite obvious what it means, isn't it?" Williams said.

"I'm not quite sure I follow."

"You follow," Williams said. He stood in the doorway, looked at the aycee. What an old, foolish man he was, for all of his position. How little he understood. How little any of them understood. They simply did not know what was going on. And never had.

"I quit," Williams said, and walked out the door and out of headquarters and into the mindless, tumultuous day.

THE END

"HOME IS THE HUNTER, HOME FROM THE HILL AND THE SAILOR HOME FROM THE SEA"

By Barry N. Malzberg

Too abstract. Too metaphysical. Bullshit. Life was life; you could not value it so cheaply. It did make a difference. Everything made a difference. To go on, to deal with one instant after the next was in itself its own solution, its own justification. It was easier to say you were dead, that you were better off dead, that death made no difference, but if that decision could itself only be made in life. Death was a kind of life then. Well. You did not know.

—*Philadelphia Blowup*

And so the banal, the ever predictable conclusion; one adumbrated from the opening yet suppressed for the purposes of commerce and perversity for the span of the fourteen novels. George Ernsberger was neutral: quit or don't quit, take it as you will, the door is open, the door can be closed; objects in the rear view mirror may appear smaller than in the actuality. He conceived of the series as a kind of Fellowship; I had written three novels for him (the middle, *Underlay* I consider over half a century later still to be my best), they showed reasonable promise, he wanted to keep the kid working and sufficiently compensated that he could do his "real" work and the Lone Wolf was the fly in the ointment, to be made useful as flies could occasionally be. ("They kill us for their spite.")

But I felt that it was time to close the show. Pendleton was my doppelganger or perhaps my own fly in the Lone Wolf's ointment; he had pushed the series already into the twenties or thirties (I did not follow it at all) and there was already the specter of ghost writers who would take a portion of the now huge advances and do all of the work. What had been intended by Pinnacle to be a one-off novel, then with a few sequels, had become an industry and the publisher, now California dreaming of the California sun, certainly had no intention of walking (much less running) away from it. But the series problem manifest even in the best such work, Le Carré's Smiley for instance, or Robert Sheckley's Gregor and Arnold science fiction stories, was one which few publishers and certainly no Don Pendletons could solve. The books, revenge porn by the numbers, would reach their logical or illogical conclusions, they would do so again and again, the iron boots of predictability would stomp them into the ground, Orwell's boot on a human face unto eternity but I had taken my mad protagonist beyond a limit where even a small raise in the advance did not tease ambition. I had deliberately failed to tie off the series in the New York City where it had begun and driven the final four novels through that aperture but enough ultimately (and to quote Ambrose Bierce) was too much. "You should never kill an active series" said Dale Copps, Ernsberger's young assistant, "Remember Doyle, Holmes and Moriarty," and I took that seriously but not seriously enough. (I remain the only adult I have ever known who has never read a word of Sherlock Holmes.)

This was a series whose premise reposed wholly upon Wulff's demolition and I took care of that, showing ambivalence only in the fact that it was Wulff's former partner, assigned to the chase, who did away with him. If this was startlingly predictable, if the death had a suggestion of banality, neither was less predictable or more banal than the revelation, finally, of the events which sent Wulff out of narcotics, out of the PD and onto his mission; yes, Marie had been murdered but not by drug traffickers enacting vengeance.

No, Marie had been murdered—I should put up the *Spoiler Warning* sign here but the triumph of Trump, the teetering of Constitutional democracy did not have a spoiler warning in October of 2016 and that was a somewhat larger issue than a paperback series built upon the poisoned artichoke buried in the heart of the heart of the country. Marie had been killed because Wulff, that silly man, had been perhaps the one incorruptible narco in the Division and he was screwing up the trade for the inside boys in the back room. He had to go. They had to get rid of him. So they did. The entire construct was a Robert Sheckley short story or a Phil Dick novel: the universe was put to destruction because its Maker had severe indigestion causing an even more severe tantrum. Trump apparently had been miserably treated by his father. On such conditions consequence will range.

We tremble now at the precipice, looking into the abyss and past it to the deepest of nights for the beloved land. We staggered toward the light and inherited only that consequence. "Wulff needed to kill, he needed to be free. Perhaps they were the same." I wrote that a long time ago. Everything is a long time ago.

But still, in the absence of hope, still Forward the Foundation.

January 2022: New Jersey

L'ENVOI: "DON'T TREAD ON ME," CRIED THE WORLD-SNAKE

By Barry N. Malzberg

It was my intention to make apparent from the beginning that *Lone Wolf* was not an *Executioner* knockoff, pastiche, carbon copy, exploitation. I had serious, even desperate purpose; that purpose was at the dead-center of the fourteen novels and had been set from the beginning. Vigilantism was the core to be sure and also the excuse; Burton Wulff was an instrument of vengeance driven or at least centered by madness and the series in toto was a scream yanked to high fidelity by Norman Mailer. Mailer had observed of Oswald's assassination by Jack Ruby in a *police station* of all venues that this internationally televised event, contrapuntal to intermittent solemn coverage of JFK's catafalque lying in state in the Capitol was the moment at which the nation had gone insane. This ultimately brutal act in the presence of press, police and hundreds of millions of witnesses, this act in the heart of the heart of the "law and order" government was an act which could not be explained through the most earnest valedictories which were taken on immediately and have persisted through six decades, up to and projecting well beyond the present moment. The law and the lawless fused, the circumstance itself synchronous and inseparable and so the accelerating descent through a half century to the present circumstance. Wulff of course was operating in early societal PTSD, less than a decade after the precipitating event and the shadows cast over the Grassy Knoll were entrapping the narrative itself. Law was vigilantism, order was repression, Federal response was in the form of agents and agencies which were indistinguishable from the criminal activities they were allegedly battling. All circumscribed, in fact only further defined the act.

This shaky metaphysics seemed quite obvious to Mailer who fancied himself as the rat in the church vestry, the canary in the coal mine, the ultimate observer, the ultimate assassin ... this Mailer who had stabbed his wife to the ledge of her death two years later and was to write of all the bloody secrets of the Republic. Mailer who subsumed the stabbing in his serialized novel, *An American Dream*, three years later, Mailer who ran and trained with Muhammed Ali in Zaire, Mailer who, drunk, heckled Sonny Liston at a morning-after press conference the day after Liston had knocked Floyd Patterson silly. Mailer who ran for

Mayor of New York eight years later and copped enough votes from otherwise Badillo voters to deny that worthy the primary and allowed a handsome but essentially failed John Lindsay to run against the noxious Procaccino and sneak into a second term. Exhibits X, Y and Z.

Mailer obsessed the intelligentsia and its enemies almost as thoroughly as Trump was able half a century later to take the politics of lunacy into the White House and then everywhere, but make of him what you will and I made plenty, his contrapuntal placement of madness against the long result of Oswald's murder set the stage for Pendleton's *Executioner*, for Trump's election and eventually the Schrödinger's Cathouse which the nation became: neither dead nor alive, nor dead *and* alive but some mean, tangled, self-consuming beast. A beast of a world-snake which illuminated everything implicit in the nation's origin and its Constitution, that the nation, its "democracy," its flaccid and sentimental "American Dream" had been constructed to self-consume and to die. The Constitution was a lie ("All *men* are created equal"), the lie was at the core of a 250 year disastrous devolution into self-destruction and when RFK, five years before Wulff took up his cudgel was killed (again in the romping and dedicated presence of supporters and laugh enforcement) the deal was sealed. We had been born to die. Vietnam was one means of acting this out; another was the War on Drugs which of course was a war *for* drugs in which the enforcers, the victims, the profiteers and the police were in the same slow, inexorable Titanic voyage into hell.

So what did we know and when did we know it? To respond: "Everything … but too late" is to be glib but glibness like ripeness was all in the simple equation of the anarchic Burton Wulff to the crumbling nation and then too, science fiction. Science fiction seemed to me in the earlier stages of my struggle to make a statement was also a World-Snake, a creature born and placed to consume itself … it was a narrative of collision between advancing tech and overwhelmed humanity, humanity being unprepared and fundamentally unskilled in the procedure to control, amass, employ a technology which like Hiroshima or Nagasaki seemed to carry the potential to obliterate its origin. I wrote essays about this for two science fiction publications, a continuing column over 46 installments, two markets, three or four years exploring the possibilities and then the advance of this insight. The series in *Baen's Universe* and then *Galaxy's Edge* took me to the near brink of outright statement: science fiction, manifestation and symptom of a polity and its culture was created only to explore the impossibility of controlling that technology. The inevitable outcome, the *only* outcome would be fascism and by 1973's *Night Raider* we had a hell of a good start.

I drove methodically through the lanes and pains and highways of this insight and then, at column 26 for *Galaxy's Edge* improvidently, impulsively and out of revulsion for my own insight quit, leaving the final installment to the audience imagination and incurring the anger of the publisher who felt I was quitting him. Quitter I was but having driven the rattling vehicle to the precipice I lost any desire to prove my sincerity by driving over the edge. I bolted the opposite way. The conclusion seemed quite obvious to anyone paying attention.

But I had not bolted from the Lone Wolf; circumstances were plain, the protagonist had been driven mad by the very conclusion I had not wanted to commit to *Galaxy's Edge*, the Union, an impractical concept was uncontrollably if still somewhat distantly aflame and it was time to quit before certifying the Reichstag fire which the future would become. I must have known this from the start; Wulff was born to die, Wulff was insanely committed to his death after all of those he had caused and I neither saw any other end to the series nor did I want others to meddle with it. Wulff is shot dead by his partner after having run terror through the streets of Philadelphia, David Williams throws his glittering police badge away and all is done. "It is finished." But no next day in Paradise.

I did the best I could with the series, even in one of these afterwords emerged with a theory of the true unwritten history of the Vietnam War. I slunk off into the shrubbery of rationalization: "I did it for the money, it was a dirty job but it suited my abilities such as they were and I handled a crazed protagonist with some integrity." It is the fate of humanity perhaps to shout rationalizations from the abyss. If I had not done this it would not have been done or (maybe worse yet) done with less integrity and more for the Olsen and Johnson belly laughs. The cow from the ceiling. Sprawled on the ruined stage, the inevitable fires seeping through all of the apertures of the Good Ship Titanic.

24 August 2022

Barry N. Malzberg Bibliography

FICTION (as either Barry or Barry N. Malzberg)

Oracle of the Thousand Hands (1968)
Screen (1968)
Confessions of Westchester County (1970)
The Spread (1971)
In My Parents' Bedroom (1971)
The Falling Astronauts (1971)
The Masochist (1972, reprinted as Everything Happened to Susan, 1975; as Cinema, 2020)
Horizontal Woman (1972; reprinted as The Social Worker, 1973)
Beyond Apollo (1972)
Overlay (1972)
Revelations (1972)
Herovit's World (1973)
In the Enclosure (1973)
The Men Inside (1973)
Phase IV (1973; novelization based on a story & screenplay by Mayo Simon)
The Day of the Burning (1974)
The Tactics of Conquest (1974)
Underlay (1974)
The Destruction of the Temple (1974)
Guernica Night (1974)
On a Planet Alien (1974)
Out from Ganymede (1974; stories)
The Sodom and Gomorrah Business (1974)
The Best of Barry N. Malzberg (1975; stories)
The Many Worlds of Barry Malzberg (1975; stories)
Galaxies (1975)
The Gamesman (1975)
Down Here in the Dream Quarter (1976; stories)
Scop (1976)
The Last Transaction (1977)
Chorale (1978)
Malzberg at Large (1979; stories)
The Man Who Loved the Midnight Lady (1980; stories)
The Cross of Fire (1982)
The Remaking of Sigmund Freud (1985)
In the Stone House (2000; stories)
Shiva and Other Stories (2001; stories)
The Passage of the Light: The Recursive Science Fiction of Barry N. Malzberg (2004; ed. by Tony Lewis & Mike Resnick; stories)
The Very Best of Barry N. Malzberg (2013; stories)

With Bill Pronzini

The Running of the Beasts (1976)
Acts of Mercy (1977)
Night Screams (1979)
Prose Bowl (1980)
Problems Solved (2003; stories)
On Account of Darkness and Other SF Stories (2004; stories)

As Mike Barry

Lone Wolf series:
Night Raider (1973)
Bay Prowler (1973)
Boston Avenger (1973)
Desert Stalker (1974)
Havana Hit (1974)
Chicago Slaughter (1974)
Peruvian Nightmare (1974)
Los Angeles Holocaust (1974)
Miami Marauder (1974)
Harlem Showdown (1975)
Detroit Massacre (1975)
Phoenix Inferno (1975)
The Killing Run (1975)
Philadelphia Blow-Up (1975)

As Francine di Natale

The Circle (1969)

As Claudine Dumas

The Confessions of a Parisian
   Chambermaid (1969)

As Mel Johnson/M. L. Johnson

Love Doll (1967; with The Sex Pros
   by Orrie Hitt)
I, Lesbian (1968; as M. L. Johnson)
Just Ask (1968; with Playgirl by Lou
   Craig)
Instant Sex (1968)
Chained (1968; with Master of
   Women by March Hastings & Love
   Captive by Dallas Mayo)
Kiss and Run (1968; with Sex on the
   Sand by Sheldon Lord & Odd Girl
   by March Hastings)
Nympho Nurse (1969; with Young
   and Eager by Jim Conroy &
   Quickie by Gene Evans)
The Sadist (1969)
The Box (1969)
Do It To Me (1969; with Hot Blonde
   by Jim Conroy)
Born to Give (1969; with Swap Club
   by Greg Hamilton & Wild in Bed
   by Dirk Malloy)
Campus Doll (1969; with High
   School Stud by Robert Hadley)
A Way With All Maidens (1969)

As Howard Lee

Kung Fu #1: The Way of the Tiger,
   the Sign of the Dragon (1973)

As Lee W. Mason

Lady of a Thousand Sorrows (1977)

As K. M. O'Donnell

Empty People (1969)
The Final War and Other Fantasies
   (1969; stories)
Dwellers of the Deep (1970)
Gather at the Hall of the Planets
   (1971)
In the Pocket and Other S-F Stories
   (1971; stories)
Universe Day (1971; stories)

As Eliot B. Reston

The Womanizer (1972)

As Gerrold Watkins

Southern Comfort (1969)
A Bed of Money (1970)
A Satyr's Romance (1970)
Giving It Away (1970)
Art of the Fugue (1970)

NON-FICTION/ESSAYS

The Engines of the Night: Science
   Fiction in the Eighties (1982;
   essays)
Breakfast in the Ruins (2007;
   essays: expansion of Engines of the
   Night)
The Business of Science Fiction: Two
   Insiders Discuss Writing and
   Publishing (2010; with Mike
   Resnick)
The Bend at the End of the Road
   (2018; essays)

EDITED ANTHOLOGIES

Final Stage (1974; with Edward L.
   Ferman)
Arena (1976; with Edward L.
   Ferman)
Graven Images (1977; with Edward
   L. Ferman)
Dark Sins, Dark Dreams (1978; with
   Bill Pronzini)

The End of Summer: SF in the
  Fifties (1979; with Bill Pronzini)
Shared Tomorrows: Science Fiction
  in Collaboration (1979; with Bill
  Pronzini)
Neglected Visions (1979; with
  Martin H. Greenberg & Joseph D.
  Olander)
Bug-Eyed Monsters (1980; with Bill
  Pronzini)
The Science Fiction of Mark Clifton
  (1980; with Martin H. Greenberg)

The Arbor House Treasury of Horror
  & the Supernatural (1981; with
  Bill Pronzini & Martin H.
  Greenberg)
The Science Fiction of Kris Neville
  (1984; with Martin H. Greenberg)
Mystery in the Mainstream (1986;
  with Bill Pronzini & Martin H.
  Greenberg)